Scottish
Myths

T0273694

Scottish
Myths

General Editor: Jake Jackson

Associate Editor: Catherine Taylor

**FLAME TREE
PUBLISHING**

This is a FLAME TREE Book

FLAME TREE PUBLISHING
6 Melbray Mews
Fulham, London SW6 3NS
United Kingdom
www.flametreepublishing.com

First published 2020
Copyright © 2020 Flame Tree Publishing Ltd

24 23
5 7 9 8 6

ISBN: 978-1-83964-170-1

The cover image is © copyright 2020 Flame Tree Publishing Ltd,
based on artwork courtesy of Shutterstock.com/oscarmcwhite.

All inside images courtesy of Shutterstock.com and the following:
Swetapol, Zoart Studio, ReVelStockArt, Marek Hlavac, Kristina Birukova.

Contributors, authors, editors and sources for this series include:
Loren Auerbach, Norman Bancroft-Hunt, George W. Bateman, James
S. de Benneville, E.M. Berens, Katharine Berry Judson, W.H.I. Bleek and L.
C. Lloyd, Laura Bulbeck, J. F. Campbell, Jeremiah Curtin, F. Hadland Davis,
Elphinstone Dayrell, O.B. Duane, Dr Ray Dunning, W.W. Gibbings, William
Elliot Griffis, H. A. Guerber, Lafcadio Hearn, Stephen Hodge, James A. Honey
M.D., Jake Jackson, Joseph Jacobs, Judith John, Michael Kerrigan, J.W. Mackail,
Alexander Mackenzie, Donald Mackenzie, Chris McNab, Minnie Martin, A.B.
Mitford (Lord Redesdale), Yei Theodora Ozaki, Professor James Riordan, Sara
Robson, Lewis Spence, Henry M. Stanley, Capt. C.H. Stigand, Rachel Storm, K.E.
Sullivan, François-Marie Arouet a.k.a. Voltaire, E.A. Wallis Budge, Dr Roy Willis,
Epiphanius Wilson, Alice Werner, E.T.C. Werner, Morris Meredith Williams.

A copy of the CIP data for this book is available from the British Library.

Printed and bound in China

Contents

Series Foreword 8

Introduction to Scottish Myths 11

Magic and Mystery 11

Another Country 12

Several Scotlands 12

Celtic Heroes 13

Irish Tales Told in Scotland 14

Linguistic Loyalties 14

The Magical and the Mundane 15

Spectral Spirits 16

Beauties and Beasts 16

Historical Heroics 17

Heroic Mythology 19

Conall Cra Bhuidhe 20

The Feen 28

Conall 31

The Poor Brother and the Rich 45

A Puzzle 47

The Two Shepherds 48

Thomas of the Thumb 49

The Story of the Lay of the Great Fool 50

The Hoodie and the Fox 52

The Reason Why the Dallag (Dog-Fish) is 53

Canonbie Dick and Thomas of Ercildoune 54

Gold-Tree and Silver-Tree 59

The Three Widows 67

Tales of Fairy Folk 73

The Brownie 74

The Young King of Easaidh Ruadh 75

The Tale of the Hoodie..82

The Girl and the Dead Man...85

Sanntraigh...87

Cailliach Mhor Chlibhrich..88

The Smith and the Fairies 89

Man 91

Thomas the Rhymer 92

The Page-Boy and the Silver Goblet............................ 101

The Elfin Knight 104

The Witch of Fife.. 110

Farquhar MacNeill 115

The Minister and the Fairy.. 118

Habetrot the Spinstress... 120

The Fairy Boy of Leith 128

Spirits, Monsters & Ghostly Tales 131

Peerifool... 133

The Doomed Rider 142

Michael Scott.. 144

The Battle of the Birds 148

The Sea-Maiden 157

The Draiglin' Hogney 166

The Ghosts of Craig-Aulnaic....................................... 170

The Fiddler and the Bogle of Bogandoran 174

The Bogle.. 176

The Death 'Bree'.. 177

Animals & Fables.. 181

The Well of the World's End 182

The Wedding of Robin Redbreast 185

The Fox and the Wolf 188

The Story of the White Pet 192

The Burgh... 195

The Tulman.. 195

Oisean After the Feen.. 196

The Widow and Her Daughters.....................................198
The Sharp Grey Sheep...202
The Fox and the Little Bonnach...................................204
How the Cock Took a Turn Out of the Fox.................205

Historical Legend 207

The Inheritance 208
Castle Urguhart and the Fugitive Lovers 210
Young Glengarry, the Black Raven............................... 216
A Legend of Invershin...218
Allan Donn and Annie Campbell.................................222
Coinnach Oer 229
The Dwarfie Stone..231
Saint Columba 242
The Origin of Loch Ness.. 245
Prince Charlie and Mary MacLeod.............................. 245
The Rout of Moy 251

Series Foreword

STRETCHING BACK to the oral traditions of thousands of years ago, tales of heroes and disaster, creation and conquest have been told by many different civilizations in many different ways. Their impact sits deep within our culture even though the detail in the tales themselves are a loose mix of historical record, transformed narrative and the distortions of hundreds of storytellers.

Today the language of mythology lives with us: our mood is jovial, our countenance is saturnine, we are narcissistic and our modern life is hermetically sealed from others. The nuances of myths and legends form part of our daily routines and help us navigate the world around us, with its half truths and biased reported facts.

The nature of a myth is that its story is already known by most of those who hear it, or read it. Every generation brings a new emphasis, but the fundamentals remain the same: a desire to understand and describe the events and relationships of the world. Many of the great stories are archetypes that help us find our own place, equipping us with tools for self-understanding, both individually and as part of a broader culture.

For Western societies it is Greek mythology that speaks to us most clearly. It greatly influenced the mythological heritage of the ancient Roman civilization and is the lens through which we still see the Celts, the Norse and many of the other great peoples and religions. The Greeks themselves learned much from their neighbours, the Egyptians, an older culture that became weak with age and incestuous leadership.

It is important to understand that what we perceive now as mythology had its own origins in perceptions of the divine and the rituals of the sacred. The earliest civilizations, in the crucible of the Middle East, in the Sumer of the third millennium BC, are the source to which many of the mythic archetypes can be traced. As humankind collected together in cities for the first time, developed writing and industrial scale agriculture, started to irrigate the rivers and attempted to control rather than be at the mercy of its environment, humanity began to write down its tentative explanations of natural events, of floods and plagues, of disease.

Early stories tell of Gods (or god-like animals in the case of tribal societies such as African, Native American or Aboriginal cultures) who are crafty and use their wits to survive, and it is reasonable to suggest that these were the first rulers of the gathering peoples of the earth, later elevated to god-like status with the distance of time. Such tales became more political as cities vied with each other for supremacy, creating new Gods, new hierarchies for their pantheons. The older Gods took on primordial roles and became the preserve of creation and destruction, leaving the new gods to deal with more current, everyday affairs. Empires rose and fell, with Babylon assuming the mantle from Sumeria in the 1800s BC, then in turn to be swept away by the Assyrians of the 1200s BC; then the Assyrians and the Egyptians were subjugated by the Greeks, the Greeks by the Romans and so on, leading to the spread and assimilation of common themes, ideas and stories throughout the world.

The survival of history is dependent on the telling of good tales, but each one must have the 'feeling' of truth, otherwise it will be ignored. Around the firesides, or embedded in a book or a computer, the myths and legends of the past are still the living materials of retold myth, not restricted to an exploration of origins. Now we have devices and global communications that give us unparalleled access to a diversity of traditions. We can find out about Native American, Indian, Chinese and tribal African mythology in a way that was denied to our ancestors, we can find connections, match the archaeology, religion and the mythologies of the world to build a comprehensive image of the human experience that is endlessly fascinating.

The stories in this book provide an introduction to the themes and concerns of the myths and legends of their respective cultures, with a short introduction to provide a linguistic, geographic and political context. This is where the myths have arrived today, but undoubtedly over the next millennia, they will transform again whilst retaining their essential truths and signs.

Jake Jackson
General Editor

Introduction to Scottish Myths

STORYTELLING HAS BEEN CENTRAL to the Scottish identity for a great many centuries. The tale of the Sea-Maiden (page 157), who barters with the poor fisherman for the life of his eldest son, was told among the coastal communities of Inveraray, Argyll, into modern times. That of Thomas the Rhymer (page 92), and his seven-year sojourn with the Fairies deep beneath the Eildon Hills, comes from the Border country of Berwickshire. For generations, children in Barra, in the Outer Hebrides, shuddered with delight to hear 'How the Cock Took a Turn out of the Fox' (page 205) or (when they were a little older) of the grisly machinations of 'The Three Widows' (page 67). The story of Mary MacLeod, Maid of Moidart, who saves the life of Prince Charlie, the Young Pretender (page 245), belongs to a highly-coloured history, as does that of the 'Black Raven', Young Glengarry of Lochaber (page 216).

Magic and Mystery

Mythology is by definition more exotic – stranger, more romantic; at times more entertaining but at others maybe darker – than daily life. Every culture has its legacy of legends, handed down over countless generations; weird and wonderful now, when they are retold. In certain countries, however, for what can be complex reasons, these mythologies appear more immediately present in the modern culture and seem to resonate more strongly somehow with the way things are today. Scotland is one such country, widely seen around the world as a land of special magic and mystery.

This has of course in large part been a matter of outside perception – frankly, of stereotyping: small nations like Scotland are often patronized by the larger ones which get to call the cultural tune. Scottish society has in reality been amongst the most industrialized and urbanized in the world. Over the last few decades, the failure of its heavy industries has cast a darker blight than any witch's spell. Scots today are haunted more by the need to pay their bills than by any ghost or spectre; their fears for their children revolve more around cyber-bullying or drug abuse than around their possible abduction by fairy folk. By the same token, though, the sense Scots have had over hundreds of years that, in an English-dominated Britain, they are viewed as vaguely alien and 'Other' (that little bit 'primitive,' even) has served to strengthen their defiant patriotic pride.

Another Country

That they *are* seen as different is certain – and by no means new. Win Jenkins, the faithful family maidservant in Tobias Smollett's novel *The Expedition of Humphry Clinker* (1771), is amazed to discover that England and Scotland share a land-border and that, consequently, to get to Edinburgh, the household won't have to go by sea. (Actually, many people chose to, rather than face the long and often hellish journey overland. As of 1760, there was only one coach a month from London to Edinburgh, and that took anything from fourteen to sixteen days.)

No wonder, then, that another character in Smollett's novel comments that 'the people at the other end of the island know as little of Scotland as of Japan.' This remark is generally interpreted as a criticism of English insularity and chauvinism – and fair enough: Win is surprised to be offered anything but oats to eat. But it also points up the fact that, right up until relatively recent times, Scotland really did seem extremely remote.

Several Scotlands

Not that there could even be said to be a single Scotland: the division between Highlands and Lowlands is not just geographical but cultural – and extremely longstanding. In important ways, the Western Highlands have more in common with Ireland than they do with Scotland's east and south. A millennium and a half ago, indeed, southwest Scotland was actually linked with northeast Ulster in Dal Riata – a Celtic kingdom that spanned the strait between the two. Such were the difficulties of land-travel in that period that the sea didn't seem so much a barrier as a connecting corridor.

In Roman times, of course, Caledonia began at Hadrian's Wall (now entirely in England). The whole of what is now Northumberland was 'Scottish' by that measure. Conversely, after Rome's withdrawal, the eastern Lowlands as far north as Edinburgh belonged for several centuries to the Anglo-Saxon kingdom of Northumbria. As late as the fifteenth century, the Orkney, Shetland, the Hebrides and the western extremities of Argyll were ruled by 'Lords of the Isles' whose primary allegiance was not to Scotland, but to Norway. Through medieval times and into the early-modern era, the Borders developed their own identity, forged in hundreds of years of raiding – and the odd all-out war.

Celtic Heroes

The Roman advance into Caledonia was famously resisted by the Picts (from the Latin *Picti* – 'painted' people), really a loose alliance of local tribes. It is hard to pin down who they were: to characterize them as 'Celtic' is justified, but not much help, because being a Celt was always more about cultural equipment than ethnicity as such. Whilst a small group of Iron Age warriors, originating in Central Europe, had indeed expanded across the British Isles (as they had across much of Europe and even Asia Minor), taking charge as chieftains wherever they went, they were never more than a tiny elite across these territories.

Even so, they had established their languages and culture – everything from richly decorative art to extravagantly magical myths. The association of the Celtic legacy now with an outlying western fringe (from Spain's Galicia to Brittany, Ireland, Wales and Scotland) is an accident of history. Celtic culture clung on where Roman ways didn't quite displace them.

The Celts never wrote their stories down: they seem to have had a religious taboo against script, indeed, so it fell to early Christian monks to record their mythology. Much as they evidently loved this material, they jibbed at a pagan pantheon which featured many scores of gods and goddesses so demoted these divinities to the status of mortal heroes and heroines, sorcerers and fairy folk. (They had special powers, then, without ultimately usurping the authority of God.)

Irish Tales Told in Scotland

It was from Ireland that St Columcille (Columba) came to Iona in the sixth century to set about the Christianization of Scotland. He and his followers established a network of monasteries across the Highlands and Islands. Along with the Gospel of Christ, they brought their broader learning, which now included this rich repertory of mythic lore. It is in this form, then, that these ancient Celtic stories have endured into Scottish modernity, in atmospheric cycles of epic and enchantment which overlap with those of the Irish past.

Hence the appearance of an explicitly Irish hero, Conall (page 31), nephew of the king of Erin (often spelt 'Eirinn', meaning Ireland), who travels to Alba (Scotland) and Sassun (England) to seek help from the kings of those lands in fighting for his right to the throne of Ireland. Stories about figures named Conall crop up 'all over the Highlands', according to nineteenth-century folklorist J.F. Campbell (see 'Conall Cra Bhuidhe' page 20, collected by him on the Hebridean isle of Islay). Perhaps the most famous of the Irish heroic traditions, that of Fionn MacCumhaill and his warrior-brotherhood, the Fianna, is present in 'The Feen' (page 28, also spelt as 'Fèinne' and 'Fine'). The band has here become a symbol of Celtic solidarity, Fionn's preparedness to make his peace with his love-rival Diarmid enabling them to resist the assault of the Scandinavian Danan people. Such stories were to be an inspiration to the Gaelic-speaking peoples of the Highlands and Islands striving to uphold their ancestral culture under severe pressure in modern times.

Linguistic Loyalties

The otherworldly 'wildness' of the Highlands and Islands was underlined well into modern times by language (people here spoke Gaelic) and by events like the Jacobite rebellions – most famously Bonnie Prince Charlie's of 1745. The Stewart pretenders were pursuing dynastic ambitions (and backed by European monarchs with strategic agendas of their own). Even so, the unrest undoubtedly channelled the sense the Highland clans felt of an identity under threat.

In Lowland Scotland, by contrast, so obviously alien an identity had not existed since medieval times. Though incomprehensible to the English hearer, the various versions of 'Scots' weren't actually that different to the language of their southern neighbours once written down. And, though marked from the Reformation on by a strongly Calvinistic religious tradition, Scottish culture didn't seem quite so 'foreign' either. That didn't mean that the Scots of the Northeast and South didn't feel proud and patriotic, though; nor that their folkloric traditions were in any way impoverished.

The Magical and the Mundane

They did, however, for the most part set a clearer boundary between the realms of everyday life and enchantment; between those of human mortals and fairies, ghosts and spirits. Whilst, in this as in the Celtic culture, the magical and mundane dimensions co-existed, the former was relegated firmly to the background. This only made its occasional irruptions into ordinary life more startling – like the shock reported by the writer John McNeillie, visiting rural Galloway as recently as the 1930s, on seeing a cat killed and lashed to the neck of an injured horse as a supposed 'cure'.

That was in the countryside, of course – the same southwestern countryside from which, two centuries before, Johny Williamson, the 'Boy of Borgue' (a village near Kirkcudbright), said he'd paid a succession of visits to Fairyland. But when, around the same time, the ten-year-old 'Fairy Boy of Leith' (page 128) disappeared into the earth inside Edinburgh's Calton Hill to spend time with the fairies there, he did so from the kind of early-modern urban environment that would have been readily recognizable to tens of thousands of inhabitants of England's towns and cities. It's doubtful, though, that he would have been as readily believed down there.

Nor should we be misled by the label 'folk belief' into assuming that this credulity was confined to poor or unschooled Scots. In his book *The Secret Commonwealth* (1691), Robert Kirk – a Church of Scotland Minister – seriously proposed the scientific study of 'the subterranean and (for the most part) invisible people, heretofore going under the name of elves, fauns and fairies'. His call received widespread support in educated Scottish circles.

Spectral Spirits

Ghost stories too underscore the permeability of the boundary between the 'Other Side' and this one: the spectre invades an otherwise ordinary world. As 'The Ghosts of Craig-Aulnaic' (page 170) and 'The Death Bree' (page 177) shows, the subject is as likely to be handled with irreverent humour as with anything approaching gothic horror. Even as they warn us of the claims the dead may continue to make on those they leave behind, they also comically dampen the fear of death.

The Bogle we encounter in 'The Fiddler and the Bogle of Bogandoran' (page 174) is also a ghost. More often (as in 'The Bogle', page 176), this spirit is a mischievous trickster-spirit, like Shakespeare's Robin Goodfellow or Puck.

Beauties and Beasts

A menagerie of curious creatures add colour and interest to Scotland's mythology. By no means all of these are vicious monsters. 'The Mermaid Wife' (page 132) describes the kind of water spirit more often described as a 'selkie' in Scottish myth. These beings live in the sea as seals, but shed their skins when they step ashore, appearing in human guise. Selkie women are frequently so beautiful in this form that watching men fall in love with them and steal their skins to prolong their stay on shore. Regardless, as here, of any pre-existing feelings or commitments they might have.

If the selkie is a sympathetic figure, the kelpie is anything but. We meet this malevolent water-horse in 'The Doomed Rider' (page 142). It can appear as a docile pet to lull children into a false sense of security before dragging them down into the water or become a beautiful bathing woman to lure a man to his death. 'The Battle of the Birds' (page 148) involves, not just a big black raven and a golden pigeon and other birds but a terrifying snake and a colossal giant.

Less alarming – indeed exemplary – animals feature in the kind of old-fashioned fables to be found in just about all folktale traditions. Like that of 'The Hoodie and the Fox' (page 52), for instance.

Historical Heroics

One of the other great subjects of Scotland's mythology has been Scotland itself, as represented in its history. Which is not to say that stories of this kind aren't 'true.' One of the most important things about a country's myths is that they exemplify important aspects of its culture and its image of itself – and the kind of historic destiny it aspires to. Robert Bruce's victory at Bannockburn (1314) is a recorded fact. It is mythic in representing to patriotic Scots a country that – though much put-upon by an overbearing English neighbour – stands up for itself and, by dogged courage and resolve, prevails.

The whole story of Charles Edward Stewart's Jacobite Rebellion of 1745 and its eventual crushing by the forces of the Hanoverian Crown might be seen as 'mythic' in the same way – again, despite its events undoubtedly having taken place. It derives that status from its romantic pathos; a plangent story of thwarted idealism which has somehow seemed to typify Scotland's wider historic plight. On a smaller, more anecdotal, scale, stories here like 'The Rout of Moy' (page 251) offer iconic snapshots of a heroic – if also in important ways tragic – history.

Heroic Mythology

attle joined; giants slain; perilous journeys and princesses won. Such is the stuff of heroic legend in every culture. Generally, though, the folk tradition has looked for something more than military prowess and derring-do. The Scottish tradition is certainly no exception. As the stories of Conall figures show, heroes have been valued not just for their courage but their quick-wittedness; or for the quieter foresight the hooded crow shows in 'The Hoodie and the Fox'. Heroic mythology frequently touches on the macabre ('The Poor Brother and the Rich') and the mysterious ('A Puzzle'; 'Canonbie Dick and Thomas of Ercildoune').

Ultimately, though, these stories have in common an upbeat estimation of human resourcefulness: our capacity to prevail, whatever the difficulties we face, when we summon up all our intelligence and resolve.

Conall Cra Bhuidhe

CONALL CRA BHUIDHE WAS A sturdy tenant in Eirinn: he had four
sons. There was at that time a king over every fifth of Eirinn. It
fell out for the children of the king that was near Conall, that they
themselves and the children of Conall came to blows. The children
of Conall got the upper hand, and they killed the king's big son. The
king sent a message for Conall, and he said to him – "Oh, Conall! what
made thy sons go to spring on my sons till my big son was killed by
thy children? but I see that though I follow thee revengefully, I shall
not be much the better for it, and I will now set a thing before thee,
and if thou wilt do it, I will not follow thee with revenge. If thou
thyself, and thy sons, will get for me the brown horse of the king of
Lochlann, thou shalt get the souls of thy sons." "Why," said Conall,
"should not I do the pleasure of the king, though there should be no
souls of my sons in dread at all. Hard is the matter thou requirest of
me, but I will lose my own life, and the life of my sons, or else I will
do the pleasure of the king."

After these words Conall left the king, and he went home: when he got home
he was under much trouble and perplexity. When he went to lie down he told
his wife the thing the king had set before him. His wife took much sorrow
that he was obliged to part from herself, while she knew not if she should see
him more. "Oh, Conall," said. she, "why didst not thou let the king do his own
pleasure to thy sons, rather than be going now, while I know not if ever I shall
see thee more?" When he rose on the morrow, he set himself and his four sons
in order, and they took their journey towards Lochlann, and they made no stop
but (were) tearing ocean till they reached it. When they reached Lochlann they
did not know what they should do. Said the old man to his sons – "stop ye, and
we will seek out the house of the king's miller."

When they went into the house of the king's miller, the man asked them to
stop there for the night. Conall told the miller that his own children and the
children of the king had fallen out, and that his children had killed the king's

son, and there was nothing that would please the king but that he should get the brown horse of the king of Lochlann. "If thou wilt do me a kindness, and wilt put me in a way to get him, for certain I will pay thee for it." "The thing is silly that thou art come to seek," said the miller; "for the king has laid his mind on him so greatly that thou wilt not get him in any way unless thou steal him; but if thou thyself canst make out a way, I will hide thy secret." "This, I am thinking," said Conall, "since thou art working every day for the king, that thou and thy gillies should put myself and my sons into five sacks of bran." "The plan that came into thy head is not bad," said the miller. The miller spoke to his gillies, and he said to them to do this, and they put them in five sacks. The king's gillies came to seek the bran, and they took the five sacks with them, and they emptied them before the horses. The servants locked the door, and they went away.

When they rose to lay hand on the brown horse, said Conall, "You shall not do that. It is hard to get out of this; let us make for ourselves five hiding holes, so that if they perceive us we may go in hiding." They made the holes, then they laid hands on the horse. The horse was pretty well unbroken, and he set to making a terrible noise through the stable. The king perceived him. He heard the noise. "It must be that that was my brown horse," said he to his gillies; "try what is wrong with him."

The servants went out, and when Conall and his sons perceived them coming they went into the hiding holes. The servants looked amongst the horses, and they did not find anything wrong; and they returned and they told this to the king, and the king said to them that if nothing was wrong that they should go to their places of rest. When the gillies had time to be gone, Conall and his sons laid the next hand on the horse. If the noise was great that he made before, the noise he made now was seven times greater. The king sent a message for his gillies again, and said for certain there was something troubling the brown horse. "Go and look well about him." The servants went out, and they went to their hiding holes. The servants rummaged well, and did not find a thing. They returned and they told this. "That is marvellous for me," said the king: "go you to lie down again, and if I perceive it again I will go out myself." When Conall and his sons perceived that the gillies were gone, they laid hands again on the horse, and one of them caught him, and if the noise that the horse made on the two former times was great, he made more this time.

"Be this from me," said the king; "it must be that some one is troubling my brown horse." He sounded the bell hastily, and when his waiting man came to him, he said to him to set the stable gillies on foot that something was wrong with the horse. The gillies came, and the king went with them. When Conall and his sons perceived the following coming they went to the hiding holes. The king was a wary man, and he saw where the horses were making a noise. "Be clever," said the king, "there are men within the stable, and let us get them somehow." The king followed the tracks of the men, and he found them. Every man was acquainted with Conall, for he was a valued tenant by the king of Eirinn, and when the king brought them up out of the holes he said, "Oh, Conall art thou here?" "I am, O king, without question, and necessity made me come. I am under thy pardon, and under thine honour, and under thy grace." He told how it happened to him, and that he had to get the brown horse for the king of Eirinn, or that his son was to be put to death. "I knew that I should not get him by asking, and I was going to steal him." "Yes, Conall, it is well enough, but come in," said the king. He desired his look-out men to set a watch on the sons of Conall, and to give them meat. And a double watch was set that night on the sons of Conall. "Now, O Conall," said the king, "wert thou ever in a harder place than to be seeing thy lot of sons hanged to-morrow? But thou didst set it to my goodness and to my grace, and that it was necessity brought it on thee, and I must not hang thee. Tell me any case in which thou wert as hard as this, and if thou tellest that, thou shalt get the soul of thy youngest son with thee." "I will tell a case as hard in which I was," said Conall.

"I was a young lad, and my father had much land, and he had parks of year-old cows, and one of them had just calved, and my father told me to bring her home. I took with me a laddie, and we found the cow, and we took her with us. There fell a shower of snow. We went into the herd's bothy, and we took the cow and the calf in with us, and we were letting the shower (pass) from us. What came in but one cat and ten, and one great one-eyed fox-coloured cat as head bard over them. When they came in, in very deed I myself had no liking for their company. 'Strike up with you,' said the head bard, I why should we be still? and sing a cronan to Conall Cra-Bhui.' I was amazed that my name was known to the cats themselves. When they had sung the cronan, said the head bard, 'Now, O Conall, pay the reward of the cronan that the cats have sung to thee.' 'Well then,' said I myself, 'I have no reward whatsoever for you, unless you should go down and take that calf.' No sooner said I the word than the two cats and ten went down to attack the calf, and, in very deed, he did not last them long. 'Play up with you, why should you be silent? Make a cronan to Conall Cra-Bhui,' said the head bard. Certainly I had no liking at all for the cronan, but up came the one cat and ten, and if they did not sing me a cronan then and there! 'Pay them now their reward,' said the great fox-coloured cat. 'I am tired myself of yourselves and your rewards,' said I. 'I have no reward for you unless you take that cow down there.' They betook themselves to the cow, and indeed she did not stand them out for long.

"'Why will you be silent? Go up and sing a cronan to Conall Cra-Bhui,' said the head bard. And surely, oh, king, I had no care for them or for their cronan, for I began to see that they were not good comrades. When they had sung me the cronan. they betook themselves down where the head bard was. 'Pay now their reward,' said the head bard; and for sure, oh, king, I had no reward for them; and I said to them, 'I have no reward for you, unless you will take that, laddie with you and make use of him.' When the boy heard this he took himself out, and the cats after him. And surely, oh, king, there was 'striongan' and catterwauling between them. When they took themselves out, I took out at a turf window that was at the back of the house. I took myself off as hard as I might into the wood. I was swift enough and strong at that time; and when I felt the rustling 'toirm' of the cats after me I climbed into as high a tree as I saw in the place, and (one) that was close in the top; and I hid myself as well as I might. The cats began to search for me through the wood, and they were not finding me; and when they were tired, each one said to the other that they would turn back. 'But,' said the one-eyed fox-coloured cat that was commander-in-chief over them, 'you saw him not with your two eyes, and though I have but one eye, there's the rascal up in the top of the tree.' When he had said that, one of them went up in the tree, and as he was coming where I was, I drew a weapon that I had and I killed him. 'Be this from me!' said the one-eyed one – 'I must not be losing my company thus; gather round the root of the tree and dig about it, and let down that extortioner to earth.' On this they gathered about her (the tree), and they dug about her root, and the first branching root that they cut, she gave a shiver to fall, and I myself gave a shout, and it was not to be wondered at. There was in the neighbourhood of the wood a priest, and he had ten men with him delving, and he said, 'There is a shout of extremity and I must not be without replying to it.' And the wisest of the men said, 'Let it alone till we hear it again.' The cats began, and they began wildly, and they broke the next root; and I myself gave the next shout, and in very deed it was not weak. 'Certainly,' said the priest, 'it is a man in extremity – let us move.' They were setting themselves in order for moving. And the cats arose on the tree, and they broke the third root, and the tree fell on her elbow. I gave the third shout. The stalwart men hasted, and when they saw how the cats served the tree, they began at them with the spades; and they themselves and the cats began at each other, till they were killed altogether – the men and the cats. And surely, oh king, I did not move till I saw the last one of them falling. I came home. And there's for thee the hardest case in which I ever was; and it seems to me that tearing by the cats were harder than hanging to-morrow by the king of Lochlann."

"Oh! Conall," said the king, "thou art full of words. Thou hast freed the soul of thy son with thy tale; and if thou tellest me a harder case than thy three sons to be hanged to-morrow, thou wilt get thy second youngest son with thee, and then thou wilt have two sons."

"Well then," said Conall, "on condition that thou dost that, I was in a harder case than to be in thy power in prison to-night." "Let's hear," said the king. – "I was there," said Conall, "as a young lad, and I went out hunting, and my father's land was beside the sea, and it was rough with rocks, caves, and geos. When I was going on the top of the shore, I saw as if there were a smoke coming up between two rocks, and I began to look what might be the meaning of the smoke coming up there. When I was looking, what should I do but fall; and the place was so full of manure, that neither bone nor skin was broken. I knew not how I should get out of this. I was not looking before me, but I was looking over head the way I came – and the day will never come that I could get up there. It was terrible for me to be there till I should die. I heard a great clattering 'tuarneileis' coming, and what was there but a great giant and two dozen of goats with him, and a buck at their head. And when the giant had tied the goats, he came up and he said to me, 'Hao O! Conall, it's long since my knife is rusting in my pouch waiting for thy tender flesh.' 'Och!' said I, 'it's not much thou wilt be bettered by me, though thou should'st tear me asunder; I will make but one meal for thee. But I see that thou art one-eyed. I am a good leech, and I will give thee the sight of the other eye.' The giant went and he

drew the great caldron on the site of the fire. I myself was telling him how
he should heat the water, so that I should give its sight to the other eye. I got
heather and I made a rubber of it, and I set him upright in the caldron. I began
at the eye that was well, pretending to him that I would give its sight to the
other one, till I left them as bad as each other; and surely it was easier to spoil
the one that was well than to give sight to the other.

"When he 'saw' that he could not see a glimpse, and when I myself said to
him that I would get out in spite of him, he gave that spring out of the water,
and he stood in the mouth of the cave, and he said that he would have revenge
for the sight of his eye. I had but to stay there crouched the length of the night,
holding in my breath in such a way that he might not feel where I was.

"When he felt the birds calling in the morning, and knew that the day was,
he said – 'Art thou sleeping? Awake and let out my lot of goats.' I killed the
buck. He cried, 'I will not believe that thou art not killing my buck.' 'I am not,'
said I, 'but the ropes are so tight that I take long to loose them.' I let out one of
the goats, and he was caressing her, and he said to her, 'There thou art thou
shaggy, hairy white goat, and thou seest me, but I see thee not.' I was letting
them out by the way of one and one, as I flayed the buck, and before the last
one was out I had him flayed bag wise. Then I went and I put my legs in place
of his legs, and my hands in place of his fore legs, and my head in place of his
head, and the horns on top of my head, so that the brute might think that it
was the buck. I went out. When I was going out the giant laid his hand on me,
and he said, 'There thou art thou pretty buck; thou seest me, but I see thee
not.' When I myself got out, and I saw the world about me, surely, oh, king! joy
was on me. When I was out and had shaken the skin off me, I said to the brute,
'I am out now in spite of thee.' 'Aha!' said he, 'hast thou done this to me. Since
thou were so stalwart that thou hast got out, I will give thee a ring that I have
here, and keep the ring, and it will do thee good.' 'I will not take the ring from
thee,' said I, 'but throw it, and I will take it with me.' He threw the ring on the
flat ground, I went myself and I lifted the ring, and I put it on my finger. When
he said me then. 'Is the ring fitting thee?' I said to him, 'It is.' He said, 'Where art
thou ring?' And the ring said, 'I am here.' The brute went and he betook himself
towards where the ring was speaking, and now I saw that I was in a harder case
than ever I was. I drew a dirk. I cut the finger off from me, and I threw it from
me as far as I could out on the loch, and there was a great depth in the place.

He shouted, 'Where art thou, ring?' And the ring said, 'I am here,' though it was on the ground of ocean. He gave a spring after the ring, and out he went in the sea. And I was as pleased here when I saw him drowning, as though thou shouldst let my own life and the life of my two sons with me, and not lay any more trouble on me.

"When the giant was drowned I went in, and I took with me all he had of gold and silver, and I went home, and surely great joy was on my people when I arrived. And as a sign for thee, look thou, the finger is off me."

"Yes, indeed, Conall, thou art wordy and wise," said the king. "I see thy finger is off. Thou hast freed thy two sons, but tell me a case in which thou ever wert that is harder than to be looking on thy two sons being hanged to-morrow, and thou wilt get the soul of thy second eldest son with thee."

"Then went my father," said Conall, "and he got me a wife, and I was married. I went to hunt. I was going beside the sea, and I saw an island over in the midst of the loch, and I came there where a boat was with a rope before her and a rope behind her, and many precious things within her. I looked myself on the boat to see how I might get part of them. I put in the one foot, and the other foot was on the ground, and when I raised my head what was it but the boat over in the middle of the loch, and she never stopped till she reached the island. When I went out of the boat the boat returned where she was before. I did not know now what I should do. The place was without meat or clothing, without the appearance of a house on it. I raised out on the top of a hill. I came to a glen; I saw in it, at the bottom of a chasm, a woman who had got a child, and the child was naked on her knee, and a knife in her hand. She would attempt to put the knife in the throat of the babe, and the babe would begin to laugh in her face, and she would begin to cry, and she would throw the knife behind her. I thought to myself that I was near my foe and far from my friends, and I called to the woman, 'What art thou doing here?' And she said to me, 'What brought thee here?' I told her myself word upon word how I came. 'Well then,' said she, 'it was so I came also.' She showed me to the place where I should come in where she was. I went in, and I said to her, 'What was in fault that thou wert putting the knife on the neck of the child.' 'It is that he must be cooked for the giant who is here, or else no more of my world will be before me.' I went up steps of stairs, and I saw a chamber full of stripped corpses. I took a lump out of the corpse that was whitest, and I tied a string to the child's foot, and a string to the lump, and I put the lump in his mouth, and when it went in his throat he would give a stretch to his leg, and he would take it out of his throat, but with the length of the thread he could not take it out of his mouth. I cast the child into a basket of down, and I asked her to cook the corpse for the giant in place of the child. 'How can I do that?' said she, 'when he has count of the corpses.' 'Do thou as I ask thee, and I will strip myself, and I will go amongst the corpses, and then he will have the same count,' said I. She did as I asked her. We put the corpse in the great caldron, but we could not put on the lid. When he was coming home I stripped myself, and I went amongst the corpses. He came home, and she served up the corpse on a great platter, and when he ate it he was complaining that he found it too tough for a child.

"'I did as thou asked me,' said she. 'Thou hadst count of the corpses thyself, and go up now and count them.' He counted them and he had them. 'I see one of a white body there,' said he. 'I will lie down a while and I will have him when I wake.'

When he rose he went up and gripped me, and I never was in such a case as when he was hauling me down the stair with my head after me. He threw me into the caldron, and he lifted the lid and he put the lid into the caldron. And now I was sure I would scald before I could get out of that. As fortune favoured me, the brute slept beside the caldron. There I was scalded by the bottom of the caldron. When she perceived that he was asleep, she set her mouth quietly to the hole that was in the lid, and she said to me 'was I alive.' I said I was. I put up my head, and the brute's forefinger was so large, that my head went through easily. Everything was coming easily with me till I began to bring up my hips. I left the skin of my hips about the mouth of the hole, and I came out. When I got out of the caldron I knew not what to do; and she said to me that there was no weapon that would kill him but his own weapon. I began to draw his spear, and every breath that he would draw I would think I would be down his throat, and when his breath came out I was back again just as far. But with every ill that befell me I got the spear loosed from him. Then I was as one under a bundle of straw in a great wind, for I could not manage the spear. And it was fearful to look on the brute, who had but one eye in the midst of his face; and it was not agreeable for the like of me to attack him. I drew the dart as best I could, and I set it in his eye. When he felt this he gave his head a lift, and he struck the other end of the dart on the top of the cave, and it went through to the back of his head. And he fell cold dead where he was; and thou mayest be sure, oh king, that joy was on me. I myself and the woman went out on clear ground, and we passed the night there. I went and got the boat with which I came, and she was no way lightened, and took the woman and the child over on dry land; and I returned home."

The king's mother was putting on a fire at this time, and listening to Conall telling the tale about the child. "Is it thou," said she, "that were there?" "Well then," said he, "'twas I." "Och! och!" said she, "'twas I that was there, and the king is the child whose life thou didst save; and it is to thee that life thanks might be given." Then they took great joy.

The king said, "Oh Conall, thou camest through great hardships. And now the brown horse is thine, and his sack full of the most precious things that are in my treasury."

They lay down that night, and if it was early that Conall rose, it was earlier than that that the queen was on foot making ready. He got the brown horse and his sack full of gold and silver and stones of great price, and then Conall and his four sons went away, and they returned home to the Erin realm of gladness. He left the gold and silver in his house, and he went with the horse to the king. They were good friends evermore. He returned home to his wife, and they set in order a feast; and that was the feast, oh son and brother!

The Feen

THE FEEN WERE ONCE, and their hunting failed, and they did not know what they should do. They were going about strands and shores gathering limpets, and to try if they should fall in with a pigeon or a plover. They were holding counsel together how they should go to get game. They reached a hill, and sleep came on them. What should Fionn see but a dream. That it was at yon crag of rock that he would be, the longest night that came or will come; that he would be driven backwards till he should set his back to the crag of rock. He gave a spring out of his sleep. He struck his foot

on Diarmid's mouth, and he drove out three of his teeth. Diarmid caught hold of the foot of Fionn, and he drove an ounce of blood from every nail he had. "Ud! what didst thou to me?" – "What didst thou thyself to me?" – "Be not angry, thou son of my sister. When I tell thee the reason, thou wilt not take it ill." – "What reason?" – "I saw a dream that at yonder crag I would pass the hardest night I ever passed; that I should be driven backwards till I should set my back to the crag, and there was no getting off from there." "What's our fear! Who should frighten us! Who will come!" "I fear, as we are in straits just now, that if this lasts we may become useless." They went and they cast lots who should go and who should stay.

The Feen altogether wished to go. Fionn was not willing to go, for fear the place should be taken out before they should come (back). "I will not go," said Fionn. "Whether thou goest or stayest, we will go," said they.

The rest went, but Fionn did not go. They stopped, on the night when they went, at the root of a tree; they made a booth, and they began to play at cards. Said Fionn, when the rest were gone, "I put him from amongst heroes and warriors any man that will follow me out." They followed after Fionn. They saw a light before them, and they went forward where the light was. Who were here but the others playing at cards, and some asleep; and it was a fine frosty night. Fionn hailed them so stately and bravely. When they heard the speaking of Fionn, those who were laid down tried to rise, and the hair was stuck to the ground. They were pleased to see their master. Pleasant to have a stray hunting night. They went home. Going past a place where they used to house, they saw a house. They asked what house was that. They told them there was the house of a hunter. They reached the house, and there was but a woman within, the wife of the fine green kirtle. She said to them, "Fionn, son of Cumal, thou art welcome here." They went in. There were seven doors to the house. Fionn asked his gillies to sit in the seven doors. They did that. Fionn and his company sat on the one side of the house to breathe. The woman went out. When she came in, she said, "Fionn, son of Cumal, it is long since I was wishing thy welfare, but its little I can do for thee to-night. The son of the king of the people of Danan is coming here, with his eight hundred full heroes, this night." "Yonder side of the house be theirs, and this side ours, unless there come men of Eirinn." Then they came, and they sat within. "You will not let a man on our side," said Fionn, "unless there comes one that belongs to our own company." The woman came in again, saying, "The middle son of the king of the people of Danan is coming, and his five hundred brave heroes with him." They came, and more of them staid without on a knoll. She came in again, saying, "The youngest son of the king of the people of Danan is coming, and his five hundred swift heroes with him." She came in again, saying, "That Gallaidh was coming, and five hundred full heroes." – "This side of the house be ours, and that be theirs, unless there come of the men of Eirinn." The people of Danan made seven ranks of themselves, and the fourth part of them could not cram in. They were still without a word. There came a gillie home with a boar that had found death from leanness and without a good seeming, and he throws that in front of Fionn with an insult. One of Fionn's gillies caught hold of him, and he tied his four smalls, and threw him below the board, and they spat on him. "Loose me, and let me stand up; I was not in fault, though it was I that did it, and I will bring thee to a boar as good as thou ever ate." – "I will do that," said Fionn; "but though thou shouldst travel the five-fifths of Eirinn, unless thou comest before the day comes, I will catch thee." They loosed him; he went away, and gillies with him. They were not long when they got a good boar. They came with it, and they cooked it, and they were eating it. "A bad provider of flesh art thou," said Gallaidh to Fionn. "Thou shalt not have that any longer to say;" and the jawbone was in his hand. He raised the bone, and he killed seven men from every row of the people of Danan, and this made them stop. Then a gillie came home, and the black dog of the people of Danan with him, seeking a battle of dogs. Every one of them had a pack of dogs, and a dozen in every pack. The first one of them went and slipped the first dozen. The black dog killed the dozen; he killed them by the way of dozen and dozen, till there was left but Bran in loneliness. Said Fionn to Conan, "Let slip Bran, and, unless Bran makes it out, we are done." He loosed him. The two dogs began at each other. It was not long till Bran began to take driving; they took fear when they saw that; but what was on Bran but a venomous claw. There was a golden shoe on the claw of Venom, and they had not taken off the shoe. Bran was looking at Conan, and now Conan took off the shoe; and now he went to meet the black dog again; and at the third "spoch" he struck on him; he took his throat out. Then he took the heart and the liver out of his chest. The dog took out to the knoll; he knew that foes were there. He began at them. A message came in to Fionn that the dog was doing much harm to the people without. "Come," said Fionn to one of the gillies, "and check the dog." The gillie went out, and (was) together with the dog; a message came in that the gillie was working worse than the dog. From man to man they went out till Fionn was left within alone. The Feen killed the people of Danan altogether. The lads of the Feen went out altogether, and they did not remember that they had left Fionn within. When the children of the king saw that the rest were gone, they said that they would get the head of Fionn and his heart. They began at him, and they drove him backwards till he reached a crag of rock. At the end of the house he set his back to it, and he was keeping them off. Now he remembered the dream. He was tightly tried. Fionn had the "Ord Fianna," and when he was in extremity it would sound of itself, and it would be heard in the five-fifths of Eirinn. The gillies heard it; they gathered and returned. He was alive, and he was no more. They raised him on the point of their spears: he got better. They killed the sons of the king, and all that were alive of the people, and they got the chase as it ever was.

Conall

T HERE WAS AN OLD KING before now in Erin, and a sister of his, whose name was Maobh, had three sons. The eldest of them was Ferghus, the middlemost Lagh an Laidh, and the youngest one Conall.

He thought he would make an heir of the eldest one, Ferghus. He gave him the schooling of the son of a king and a 'ridere,' and when he was satisfied with school and learning he brought him home to the palace. Now they were in the palace.

Said the king, "I have passed this year well; the end of the year is coming now, and trouble and care are coming on with it."

"What trouble or care is coming on thee?" said the young man. "The vassals of the country are coming to reckon with me to-day." "Thou hast no need to be in trouble. It is proclaimed that I am the young heir, and it is set down in papers and in letters in each end of the realm. I will build a fine castle in front of the palace for thee. I will get carpenters, and stonemasons, and smiths to build that castle."

"Is that thy thought, son of my sister?" said the king. "Thou hadst neither claim nor right to the realm unless I myself had chosen to give it to thee with my own free will. Thou wilt not see thyself handling Erin till I go first under the mould."

"There will be a day of battle and combat before I let this go on," said the young man.

He went away, and he sailed to Alba. A message was sent up to the king of Alba that the young king of Erin was come to Alba to see him. He was taken up on the deadly points. Meat was set in the place for eating; drink in the place for drinking; and music in the place for hearing; and they were plying the feast and the company.

"Oh! young king of Erin," said the king of Alba, "it was not without the beginning of some matter that thou art come to Alba."

"I should not wish to let out the knowledge of my matter till I should first know whether I may get it."

"Anything I have thou gettest it, for if I were seeking help, perhaps I would go to thee to get it."

"There came a word with trouble between me and my mother's brother. It was proclaimed out that I was king of Erin; and he said to me that I should have nothing to do with anything till a clod should first go on him. I wish to stand my right, and to get help from thee."

"I will give thee that," said the king; "three hundred swift heroes, three hundred brave heroes, three hundred full heroes; and that is not bad helping."

"I am without a chief over them, and I am as ill off as I was before; but I have another small request, and if I might get it, I would wish to let it out."

"Anything I have that I can part from, thou shalt get it," said the king; "but the thing I have not, I cannot give it to thee. Let out thy speech, and thou shalt have it."

"It is Boinne Breat, thy son, at their head."

"My torture to thee! had I not promised him to thee, thou hadst not got him. But there were not born in Alba, nor in Erin, nor in Sassun, nor in any one place (those) who would gain victory over my son if they keep to fair play. If my son does not come back as be went, the word of an Eriannach is never again to be taken, for it is by treachery he will be overcome."

They went away on the morrow, and they sailed to the king of Sassun. A message went up to the king of Sassun that the young king of Erin had come to the place. The king of Sassun took out to meet him. He was taken up on the deadly points; music was raised, and lament laid down in the palace of the king of Sassun; meat was set in the place for eating; drink in the place for drinking; music in the place of hearing; and they were plying the feast and the company with joy and pleasure of mind.

"Oh! young king of Erin," said the king of Sassun, "it is not without the end of a matter that thou art come here."

"I got the schooling of the son of a king and a ridere. My mother's brother took me home. He began to speak about the vassals of the country and the people of the realm; that care and trouble were on him; and that he had rather the end of the year had not come at all. Said I to him, 'I will build thee a palace, so that thou shalt have but to wash thy face, and stretch thy feet in thy shoes.' Said he, 'My sister's son, thou hadst no right to the realm, and thou gettest it not till a clod goes on me, in spite of everything.' Said I, 'There will be a day of battle and combat between thee and me, before the matter is so.' I went away; I took my ship; I took a skipper with me; and I sailed to Alba. I reached Alba, and I got three hundred swift heroes, three hundred brave heroes, and three hundred full heroes; now I am come to thee to see what help thou wilt give me."

"I will give thee as many more, and a hero at their head," said the king of Sassun.

They went away, and they sailed to Erin. They went on shore on a crag in Erin, and the name of Carrig Fhearghuis is on that rock still. He reached the king. "Brother of my mother, art thou now ready?" – "Well, then, Fhearghuis, though I said that, I thought thou wouldst not take anger; but I have not gathered my lot of people yet." – "That is no answer for me. Thou hast Erin under thy rule. I am here with my men, and I have neither place, nor meat, nor drink for them."

"Oo!" said the king, "the storehouses of Erin are open beneath thee, and I will go away and gather my people."

He went away. He went all round Erin. He came to a place which they called 'An t' Iubhar' (Newry). There was but one man in Iubhar, who was called Goibhlean Gobba (Goivlan Smith). He thought to go in, for thirst was on him; and that he would quench his thirst, and breathe a while. He went in. There was within but the smith's daughter. She brought him a chair in which he might sit. He asked for a drink. The smith's daughter did not know what she should do, for the smith had but one cow, which was called the Glas Ghoibhlean (Grey Goivlan), with the vessel he had for the milk of the cow; three times in the day it would go beneath the cow; three times in the day thirst would be on him; and he would drink the vessel each time, and unless the daughter had the vessel full she was not to get off. She was afraid, when the king asked for a drink, that unless she had the vessel full her head would be taken off. It was so that she thought the vessel should be set before the king at all hazards. She brought down the vessel, and she set it before him. He drank a draught; he took out the fourth part, and he left three quarters in it. "I would rather you should take it out altogether than leave it. My father has made an oath that unless I have the vessel full, I have but to die."

"Well, then," said the king, "it is a spell of my spells to leave the vessel as full as it was before."

He set the vessel on the board, he struck his palm on it, and he struck off as much as was above the milk, and the vessel was full; and before he went away, the girl was his own.

"Now, thou art going, oh king of Erin, and I am shamed; what wilt thou leave with me?"

"I would give thee a thousand of each hue, a thousand of each kind, a thousand of each creature."

"What should I do with that, for I wilt not find salt in Erin to salt them?"

"I would give thee glens and high moors to feed them from year to year."

"What should I do with that? for if Fearghus should kill you, he will take it from me, unless I have it with writing, and a drop of blood to bind it."

"I am in haste this night, but go to-morrow to the camp to Croc Maol Nam Muc," said the king; and he left his blessing with her.

Her father came.

"Far from thee – far from thee be it, my daughter! I think that a stranger has been to see thee here this day."

"How dost thou know that?

"Thou hadst a maiden's slow eyelash when I went out; thou hast the brisk eyelash of a wife now."

"Whom wouldst thou rather had been here?"

"I never saw the man I would rather be here than the king of Erin."

"Well, it was he; he left me a thousand of each hue, a thousand of each kind, a thousand of each creature.

"'What,' said I, 'shall I do with them, as I cannot get in Erin as much salt as will salt them?'

"Said he, 'I would give thee glens and high moors to feed them from year to year.'

"'What shall I do if Fearghus should kill you? I will not get them.'

"He said, 'I should have writing and a drop of his own blood to bind it.'"

They slept that night as they were. If it was early that the day came, it was earlier that the smith arose. "Come, daughter, and let us be going." She went, herself and the smith, and they reached the king in his camp.

"Wert thou not in the Iubhar yesterday?" said the smith to the king, "I was; and hast thou mind of thy words to the girl?"

"I have; but the battle will not be till to-morrow. I will give thee, as I said, to the girl; but leave her."

The smith got that, and he went away.

That night, when she had slept a while, she awoke, for she had seen a dream. "Art thou waking?"

"I am; what wilt thou with me? I saw a dream there: a shoot of fir growing from the heart of the king, one from my own heart, and they were twining about each other." "That is our babe son." They slept, and it was not long till she saw the next dream.

"Art thou waking, king of Erin?" "I am; what wilt thou with me?" "I saw another dream. Fearghus, coming down, and taking the head and the neck out of me."

"That is, Fearghus killing me, and taking out my head and neck."

She slept again, and she saw another dream.

"Art thou sleeping, king of Erin?"

35

"I am not; what wilt thou with me now?

"I saw Erin, from side to side, and from end to end, covered with sheaves of barley and oats. There came a blast of wind from the east, from the west, from the north; every tree was swept away, and no more of them were seen."

"Fearghus will kill me, and he will take the head and neck out of me. As quickly as ever thou didst (anything), seize my set of arms, and keep them. A baby boy is begotten between thee and me. Thou shalt suckle and nurse him, and thou shalt set him in order. Keep the arms. When thou seest that he has speech, and can help himself, thou shalt send him away through the world a wandering, till he find out who he is. He will get to be king over Erin; his son will be king over Erin; his grandson will be king over Erin. His race will be kings over Erin till it reaches the ninth knee. A child will be born from that one. A farmer will come in with a fish; he will cook the fish; a bone will stick in his throat, and he will be choked."

Maobh, the king's sister, the mother of Fearghus, had two other sons, and the battle was to be on the morrow. Lagh an Laidh and Connal; and Lagh an Laidh was the eldest.

"Whether," said Lagh an Laidh, "shall we be with our mother's brother or with Fearghus?"

"I know not. If our mother's brother wins, and we are with Fearghus, it is a stone in our shoe for ever; but if Fearghus wins, he will turn his back to us, because we were on the other side."

"Well, then, it is not thus it shall be; but be thou with Fearghus, and I will be with our mother's brother."

"It shall not be so; we will leave it to our mother."

"Were I a man," said Maobh, "I would set the field with my own brother."

"Well, then, I will be with Fearghus," said Lagh an Laidh, "and be thou with Fearghus, oh Connal!"

Fearghus went to Fionn; he blessed him in calm, soft words. Fionn blessed him in better words; and if no better, they were no worse.

"I heard that there was a day of battle and combat between thyself and thy mother's brother," said he.

"That is to be, and I came to you for help."

"It is but bold for me to go against thy mother's brother, since it was on his land that I got my keep. If thy mother's brother should win, we shall get neither furrow nor clod of the land of Erin as long as we live. I will do thus. I will not strike a blow with thee, and I will not strike a blow against thee."

Fearghus went home on the morrow, and they set in order for the battle. The king's company was on one side, and the company of Fearghus on the other. Fearghus had no Gaisgich heroes but Boinne Breat and his company. The great Saxon hero and his company, and Lagh an Laidh. Boinne Breat drew out to the skirt of the company; he put on his harness of battle and hard combat. He set his silken netted coat above his surety shirt; a booming shield on his left side; how many deaths were in his tanned sheath!

He strode out on the stern steps like a sudden blaze; each pace he put from him was less than a hill, and greater than a knoll on the mountain side. He turned on them, cloven and cringing. Three ranks would he drive of them, dashing them from their shields, to their blood and their flesh in the skies. Would he not leave one to tell the tale, or report bad news; to put in a land of holes or a shelf of rock. There was one little one-eyed russet man, one-eyed, and on one knee and one handed. "Thou shalt not be to tell a tale of me;" he went and he took his head off. Then Boinne Breat shunned the fight, and he took his armour off.

"Go down, Fearghus, and take off the head of thy mother's brother, or I will take it off."

Fearghus went down, he caught hold of his mother's brother, and he took his head off. The smith's daughter went to the arms, and she took them with her.

Lagh an Laidh kept on his armour. When he saw Fearghus going to take off the head of his mother's brother, he took a frenzy. Lagh and Laidh went about the hill to try if he could see Boinne Breat, who was unarmed. Boinne Breat thought that man was drunk with battle. He thought that he would turn on the other side of the hill to try if he could come to his own place. Lagh an Laidh turned on the other side against him. He thought to turn again to try if the battle frenzy would abate. The third time he said he would not turn for all who were in Albuin, or Eirinn, or Sassun. "It is strange thou, man, that wert with me throughout the battle, to be against me?" "I will not believe but that thou hast taken the drunkenness of battle," said Boinne Breat.

"I am quite beside myself."

"Well, then," said he, "though I am unarmed, and thou under arms, remember that thou art no more to me than what I can hold between these two fingers."

"I will not be a traiter to thee, there behind thee are three of the best heroes in Albuin, or Eirinn, or Sassun."

He gave a turn to see the three heroes, and when he turned Lagh an Laigh struck off his head.

"My torture," said Fearghus, "I had rather my own head were there. An Eireannach is not to be taken at his word as long as a man shall live. It is a stone in thy shoe every day for ever, and a pinch of the land of Eirinn thou shalt not have."

Lagh and Laidh went away and he went to the mountain. He made a castle for himself there, and he stayed in it.

The smith's daughter came on well till she bore a babe-son. She gave him the name of Conal Mac Righ Eirinn. She nourished him well, and right well. When speech came and he could walk well, she took him with her on a wet misty day to the mountain amongst high moors and forests. She left him there astray to make out a way for himself, and she went home.

He did not know in the world what he should do, as he did not know where to go, but he found a finger of a road. He followed the road. What should he see but a little hut at the evening of the day at the wayside. He went into the hut: there was no man within: he let himself down at the fireside. There he was till a woman came at the end of the night, and she had six sheep. She saw a great slip of a man beside the fire, who seemed to be a fool. She took great wonder when she saw him, and she said that he had better go out of that, and go down to the king's house, and that he would get something amongst the servants in the kitchen. He said he would not go, but if she would give him something that he might eat, that he would go to herd the sheep for herself. What should be the name of the woman but Caomhag Gentle. "If I thought that, I would give thee meat and drink," said she. On the morrow he went away with the sheep. "I have not a bite of grass for them," said she, "but a road; and thou shalt keep them at the edge of the road, and thou shalt not let them off it."

At the time of night he came home with them; on the morrow he went away with the sheep. There were near to the place where he was with them three fields of wheat that belonged to three gentlemen. The sheep were wearing him out. He went and he levelled the dyke, and he let them in from one to the other till they had eaten the three fields. On a day of days, the three gentlemen gathered. When they came, he had let the fields be eaten by the sheep.

"Who art thou? Thou hast eaten the fields?"

"It was not I that ate them at all; it was the sheep that ate them."

"We will not be talking to him at all; he is but a fool. We will reach Caomhag to see if the sheep are hers."

They reached Caomhag. They took her with them to the court. This was the first court that Fearghus had made after he got the crown.

The kings had a heritage at that time. When they did not know how to split justice properly, the judgment-seat would begin to kick, and the king's neck would take a twist when he did not do justice as he ought.

"I can make nothing of it," said the king, "but that they should have the tooth that did the damage."

The judgment-seat would begin to kick, and the king's neck took a turn. "Come here one of you and loose me; try if you can do justice better than that." Though there were thousands within, none would go in the king's place. They would not give the king such bad respect, as that any one of them would go before him.

"Is there a man that will loose me?"

"There is not, unless the herd of Caomhag himself will loose thee."

Caomhag's herd was set down.

"Loose for me, my little hero, and do justice as it should (be done), and let me out of this."

"(Nor) right nor justice will I do before I get something that I may eat."

Then he got something which he ate.

"What justice didst thou do thyself?" said he.

"I did but (doom) the tooth that did the damage to be theirs."

"What was in the way that thou didst not give death to Caomhag? This is what I would do: Caomhag has six sheep, and though the six sheep were taken from her, they would not pay the gentlemen. Caomhag will have six lambs, the gentlemen shall have the six lambs, and she herself shall have the sheep to keep."

The turn went out of the king's neck. He went away, and they did not ask who he was, and he got no skaith.

There was another gentleman, and he had a horse, and he sent him to a smithy to be shod. The smith had a young son and a nurse under the child. What should it be but a fine day, and it was without that the horse was being shod, and she never saw a horse shod before; and she went out to see the shoeing of the horse. She sat opposite to the horse, and he took the nail and the shoe, and he did not hit the hoof with the nail but he put it in the flesh, and the horse struck the child, and drove the cup of his head off. They had but to go to justice again to the king, and the justice the king made for them was, that the leg should be taken off the horse. The judgment-seat began to kick again, and the king's neck took a twist. The herd of Caomhag was there, and they asked him to loose the king. He said that he would not do a thing till he should first get something to eat.

He got that. He went where the king was.

"What law didst thou make?"

"The leg to be taken off the horse?

"That will not pay the smith. Send hither to me the groom that broke the horse, and the gentleman to whom he belongs. Send over here the smith and the nurse."

The gentleman and the groom came.

"Well then, my gentleman, didst thou make this groom break this horse as he should?"

The groom said that he had done that as well as he knew (how to do it).

"No more could be asked of thee. Well, smith, didst thou give an order to the nurse to stay within without coming out of her chamber?"

"I did not give it," said the smith, "but (she might do) as she chose herself."

"My gentleman," said he, "since thou art best kept, I will put a third of the Eiric of the smith's son on thee, and another third on the smith himself, because he did not measure the nail before he put it to use, and another third on the nurse and the groom because she did not stay within in her chamber, and in case he left some word or other untaught to the horse."

The gentleman went away and the smith; the judgment-seat stopped, and she hadn't a kick; the turn came out of the king's neck, and they let him go as usual.

Said the king – "If he has travelled over the universe and the world, there is a drop of king's blood in that lad; he could not split the law so well as that if it were not in him. Let the three best heroes I have go, and let them bring me his head."

They went after him. He gave a glance from him and what should he see coming but they. They came where he was. "Where are you going?" – "We are going to kill thyself. The king sent us to thee."

"Well, then, that was but a word that came into his mouth, and it is not worth your while to kill me."

"He is but a fool," said they.

"Since he sent you to kill me, why don't you kill me?"

"Wilt thou thyself kill thyself, my little hero?" said they.

"How shall I kill myself?"

"Here's for thee a sword and strike it on thee about the neck, and cast the head off thyself," said they.

He seized on the sword, and gave it a twirl in his fist. "Fall to killing thyself, my little hero."

"Begone," said he, "and return home, and do not hide from the king that you did not kill me."

"Well, then, give me the sword," said one of them.

"I will not give it; there are not in Erin as many as will take it from my fist," said he.

They went and they returned home. As he was going by himself, he said, "I was not born without a mother, and I was not begotten without a father. I have no mind (of) ever coming to Erin, and I know that it was in Erin I was born. I will not leave a house in which there is smoke or fire in Erin till I know who (am)."

He went to the Iubhar. What was it but a fine warm day. Whom did he see but his mother washing. He was coming to a sort of understanding, so that he was thinking that it was his mother who was there. He went and he went behind her, and he put his hand on her breast. "Indeed," said he, "a, foster son of thy right breast am I." She gave her head a toss. "Thy like of a tarlaid drudge, I never had as a son or a foster son."– "My left hand is behind thy head, and a sword in my right hand, and I will strike off thy head unless thou tell me who I am." – "Still be thy hand, Conall, son of the king of Erin."

"I knew myself I was that, and that there was a drop of the blood of a king's son in me; but who killed my father?"

Fearghus killed him; and a loss as great as thy father was slain on the same day – that was Boinne Breat, son of the king of Alba."

"Who slew Boinne Breat?" – "It is a brother of Fearghus, whom they call Lagh an Laidh."

And where is that man dwelling?

He could not get a bit on the land of Erin when once he had slain Boinne Breat; he went to the hills, and he made him a 'còs' in the forest, amongst 'uille biaste,' monsters, and untamed creatures."

"Who kept my father's arms?" – "It is I."

"Go fetch them, and bring them hither to me." She brought them.

He went and put the arms on him, and they became him as well as though they had been made for himself.

"I eat not a bit, and I drink not a draught, and I make no stop but this night, until I reach where that man is, wheresoever he may be."

He passed that night where he was. In the morning, on the morrow he went away; he went on till there was black upon his soles and holes in his shoes. The white clouds of day were going, and the black clouds of night coming, and without his finding a place of staying or rest for him. There he saw a great wood. He made a 'còs,' in one of the trees above in which he might stay that night. In the morning, on the morrow he cast a glance from him. What should he see but the very uile bheist, whose like was never seen under the sun, stretched without clothing, without foot coverings, or head covering, hair and beard gone over him. He thought, though he should go down, that he could not do for him. He put an arrow in a 'crois,' and he fired at him. He struck him with it on the right fore-arm, and the one who was below gave a start. "Move not a sinew of thy sinews, nor a vein of thy veins, nor a bit of thy flesh, nor a hair of thy locks, till thou promise to see me a king over Erin, or I will send down of slender oaken darts enough to sew thee to the earth." The uile bheist did not give him yielding for that. He went and he fired again, and he struck him in the left fore-arm. "Did I not tell thee before, not to stir a vein of thy veins nor a bit of thy flesh, nor a hair of thy locks till thou shouldst promise to see me king over Erin." – "Come down then, and I will see thyself or myself that before this time to morrow night." He came down.

"If I had known that it was thy like of a drudge that should dictate thus to me, I would not do it for thee for anything; but since I promised thee I will do it, and we will be going."

They went to the palace of the king. They shouted Battle or Combat to be sent out, or else the head of Fearghus, or himself a captive.

Battle and combat they should get, and not his head at all, and they could not get himself a captive.

There were sent out four hundred swift heroes, four hundred full heroes, and four hundred strong heroes.

They began at them. The one could not put from the other's hand as they were killed.

They shouted battle or combat again, or else the head of Fearghus to be sent out, or himself a captive.

"It is battle and combat thou shalt have, and not at all my head, and no more shalt thou get myself a captive."

There were sent out twelve hundred swift heroes, twelve hundred full heroes, and twelve hundred stout heroes.

The one could not put from the other's hand as they killed of them.

They shouted battle and combat, or else the head of Fearghus, or himself a captive.

Battle and combat they should have, and not the head of Fearghus at all, nor himself a captive.

There were sent out four hundred score to them. The one could not put from the other as they killed.

They shouted battle and combat.

"Those who are without," said Fearghus, "are so hard (to please) that they will take but my head, and unless they get (it) they will kill all there are in Erin and myself after them. Take one of you a head from one of those who were slain, and when Lagh an Laidh comes and asks my head, or myself a captive, give it to him, and he will think it is my head."

The head was given to Lagh an Laidh. He went where Conall was with it.

"What hast thou there?" said Conall.

"The head of Fearghus."

"That is not the head of Fearghus yet. I saw him a shorter (time) than thyself, but turn and bring hither to me the head of Fearghus."

Lagh an Laidh returned.

Let another go to meet him in the king's stead, and say that it is his head he shall get, not himself a captive.

This one went to meet Lagh an Laidh. He seized him and took the head out of his neck.

He reached Conall. "What hast thou there?" – "The head of Fearghus."

"That is not the head of Fearghus yet; turn and bring to me the head of Fearghus."

Lagh an Laidh returned.

"The one who is without is so watchful, and the other is so blind, that there is no man in Erin but they will kill unless they get. myself."

"Where art thou going, Lagh an Laidh?" said Fearghus.

"I am going to seek thy head, or thyself as a captive."

"It's my head thou shalt get, and not myself as a captive; but what kindness art thou giving thy brother?"

"The kindness that thou gavest thyself to me, I will give it to thee."

He took the head out of his neck, and he took it with him. He came where Conall was.

"What hast thou there?" – "The head of Fearghus." – "It is not." – "Truly it is." – "Let me see it."

He gave it to him. He drew it, and he struck him with it, and he made two heads of the one. Then they began at each other.

They would make a bog on the rock, and a rock on the bog. In the place where the least they would sink, they would sink to the knees, in the place where the most they would sink, they would sink to the eyes.

Conall thought it would be ill for him to fall after he had got so near the matter.

He drew his sword, and he threw the head off Lagh an Laidh.

"Now I am king over Erin, as I myself had a right to be."

He took his mother and her father from the Iubhar, and took them to the palace; and his race were in it till the ninth knee. The last one was choked, as a babe, with a splinter of bone that went crosswise into his throat, and another tribe came in on Eirinn.

The Poor Brother and the Rich

THERE WAS A POOR BROTHER and a rich brother before now. The work that the poor one had, was to be at drains; he hired a gillie, and they had nothing with their mealtime but to take it without sauce. "Hadn't we better," said the gillie, "steal a cow of thy brother's lot?" They went and they did this.

The rich brother was taking a notion that it was they who stole his cow; and he did not know in what way he could contrive to find out if it were they who stole her. He went and he put his mother-in-law in a kist, and he came to seek room for the kist in his brother's house; he put bread and cheese with the crone in the kist; and there was a hole in it, in order that she might find out everything. The gillie found out that the crone was in the kist; he wetted sacks and put them on top of the kist; the water was streaming out of the sacks on the crone, and she was not hearing a word. He went, in the night, where the crone was, and he said to her, "Was she hearing?" "I am not," said she." "Art thou eating a few?" "I am not." "Give me a piece of the cheese, and I will cut it for thee." He cut the cheese, and he stuffed it into her throat till she was choked. The kist was taken home, and the dead crone in it. They buried the crone, and they laid out but little on her.

In the night, said the poor man's gillie to his master, "Is it not lamentable that such and such linen should go with the crone to the cell, while the children are so much in want of shirts?" He went, and he took a spade with him, and he reached the church-yard. He dug the grave, and he took the crone from the coffin; he took off her the tais dress, he threw her on his back, and he came to the house of the rich brother; he went in with her, and he placed her seated at the fireside, and the tongs between her two feet. When the maid servant rose in the morning, she fell in a faint when she saw the crone before her. The rich brother thrashed his wife because of her mother saying, "that she was about to bring him to bare ruin." He went to the house of his poor brother and told that the crone had come home. "Ah ha!" said the gillie, "because thou didst not spend enough on her living, thou wilt spend it on her dead; I saw the like of this before; thou must lay out a good deal on her."

They bought a good lot of things for the funeral, and they left the one half of it in the house of the poor brother and they buried the crone again. "Is it not lamentable," said the poor brother's gillie to his master, "that such a lot of linen should go on the crone, while thou art so much in want of a shirt thyself?" He went to the cell that night again, he raised the crone, he took off her the tais clothes, and he took her with him on his back; he went into the house of the rich brother, as was usual, and be set the crone standing at the end of the dresser, with her claw full of seeds from the dish of sowens, as if she were eating it. When the man of the house saw her back in the morning, he thrashed his wife soundly, because of her mother. He went then to the house of his poor brother, and he told that the crone had come home again. "Aha!" said the gillie, "because thou didst not spend money on her living, thou wilt spend it on her dead; I saw the like of this before." "Go thou, then, and lay out a good deal on her, for I am tired of her," said the man. He bought a good lot for the crone's funeral, and he took the one half to his master's house. They buried the crone. In the night, said the gillie to his master, "Is it not lamentable that such linen should go with the crone to the cell, while I myself am in such want of a shirt."He took himself to the cell, he raised the crone, he took off her the tais dress, he put her on top of him, and he reached the rich brother's house. He did not get in this journey, so he went with her to the stable, and he tied her on top of a year-old colt. When they rose in the morning, they were well pleased when they did not see the crone before them. He was going from home; he went out to the stable, and he took the mare with him; but he never perceived that the crone was on top of the year-old. When he went away on top of the mare, after him went the year-old with the crone clattering on top of him. He turned back when he saw the crone, and he was like to kill his wife this time. He went to his brother's house and he told that the crone had come back again.

"As thou didst not spend money on her living," said the gillie, "thou must spend it on her dead."

"Go and lay out as thou wilt on her," said he to the gillie, "but keep her away."

He went this time and he bought a good lot for the crone's funeral, and he invited every one in the place.

They buried the crone again; and the poor brother was as wealthy as the other, by reason of the funerals.

A Puzzle

THERE WAS A CUSTOM ONCE through the Gældom, when a man would die, that the whole people of the place would gather together to the house in which the dead man was – Tigh aire faire (the shealing of watching), and they would be at drinking, and singing, and telling tales, till the white day should come.

At this time they were gathered together in the house of watching, and there was a man in this house, and when the tale went about, he had neither tale nor song, and as he had not, he was put out at the door. When he was put out he stood at the end of the barn; he was afraid to go farther. He was but a short time standing when he saw nine, dressed in red garments, going past, and shortly after that he saw other nine going past in green dresses; shortly after this he saw other nine going past in blue dresses. A while after that came a horse, and a woman and a man on him. Said the woman to the man, "I will go to speak to that man who is there at the end of the barn." She asked him what he was doing standing there? He told her? "Sawest thou any man going past since the night fell?" said she. He said that he had; he told her all he had seen. "Thou sawest all that went past since the night fell," said she. "Well then," said she, "the first nine thou sawest, these were brothers of my father, and the second nine brothers of my mother, and the third nine, these were my own sons, and they are altogether sons to that man who is on the horse. That is my husband; and there is no law in Eirinn, nor in Alaba, nor in Sasunn that can find fault with us. Go thou in, and I myself will not believe but that a puzzle is on them till day;" and she went and she left him.

The Two Shepherds

THERE WERE OUT BETWEEN LOCHABER and Baideanach two shepherds who were neighbours to each other, and the one would often be going to see the other. One was on the east side of a river, and another on the west. The one who was on the west side of the river came to the house of the one who was on the east of it on an evening visit. He staid till it was pretty late, and then he wished to go home. "It is time to go home," said he. "It is not that which thou shalt do, but thou shalt stay to-night," said the other, "since it is so long in the night." "I will not stay at all events; if I were over the river I don't care more."

The houseman had a pretty strong son, and he said, "I will go with thee, and I will set thee over the river, but thou hadst better stay." – "I will not stay at all events." – "If thou wilt not stay I will go with thee." The son of the houseman called a dog which he had herding. The dog went with him. When he set the man on the other side of the river, the man said to him, "Be returning now, I am far in thy debt." The strong lad returned, and the dog with him. When he reached the river as he was returning back home, he was thinking whether he should take the stepping-stones, or put off his foot-clothes and take below. He put off his foot-clothes for fear of taking the stepping-stones, and when he was over there in the river, the dog that was with him leaped at the back of his head. He threw her off him; she leaped again; he did the same thing. When he was on the other side of the river, he put his hand on his head, and there was not a bit of a bonnet on it. He was saying, whether should he return to seek the bonnet, or should he go home without it. "It's disgusting for me to return home without my bonnet; I will return over yet to the place where I put my foot-clothes off me; I doubt it is there that I left it." So he returned to the other side of the river. He saw a right big man seated where he had been, and his own bonnet in his hand. He caught hold of the bonnet, and he took it from him. "What business hast thou there with that? – It is mine, and thou hadst no business to take it from me, though thou hast got it." Over the river then they went, without a word for each other, fiercely, hatingly. When they went over, then, on the river, the big man put his hand under the arm of the shepherd, and he began to drag the lad down to a loch that was there, against his will and against his strength. They stood front to front, bravely, firmly on either side. In spite of the strength of the shepherd's son, the big man was about to conquer. It was so that the shepherd's son thought of putting his hand about an oak tree that was in the place. The big man was striving to take him with him, and the tree was bending and twisting. At last the tree was loosening in the earth. She loosened all but one of her roots. At the time when the last root of the tree slipped, the cocks that were about the wood crowed. The shepherd's son understood that when he heard the cocks crowing that it was on the short side of day. When they heard between them the cocks crowing, the big man said, "Thou has stood well, and thou hadst need, or thy bonnet had been dear for thee." The big man left him, and they never more noticed a thing near the river.

Thomas of the Thumb

THERE WAS ONE BEFORE NOW whose name was Tómas na h òrdaig, and he was no bigger than the thumb of a stalwart man. Tómas went once to take a walk, and there came a coarse shower of hailstones, and Tómas went in under a dock leaf; and there came a great drove of cattle past, and there was a great brindled bull amongst them, and he was eating about the docken, and he ate Tómas of the Thumb. His mother and his father missed him, and they went to seek him. They were going past the brindled bull, and quoth Tómas na h òrdaig,

> "Ye are there a seeking me,
> Through smooth places, and moss places;
> And here am I a lonely one,
> Within the brindled bull."

Then they killed the brindled bull, and they sought Tómas na h òrdaig amongst the paunches and entrails of the bull, but they threw away the great gut in which he was.

There came a carlin the way, and she took the great gut, and as she was going along she went over a bog.

Tómas said something to her, and the old wife threw away the great gut from her in a fright.

There came a fox the way, and he took with him the gut, and Tómas shouted "Bies taileù! the fox. Bis taileù! the fox."

Then the dogs ran after the fox, and they caught him, and they ate him and though they ate the gut they did not touch Tómas na h òrdaig.

Tómas went home, where his mother and his father were, and he it was indeed that had the queer story for them.

The Story of the Lay of the Great Fool

THERE WERE TWO BROTHERS ONCE in Eirinn, and one of them was a king and the other a 'ridire.' They were both married. On the knight there was a track (that is, the knight had children), and there were no children at all to the king. It was a source of insult to the knight and his lot of sons, that the king should have the realm at all. The thing that happened was, that they gathered armies, both of them, on each side. On the day of the battle that they gave, the knight and his three sons were slain.

The wife of the knight was heavy, and the king sent word that if she were to have a babe son to slay him, but that if it were a baby daughter to keep her alive, and keep her. It was a lad that she had, and there was a kitchen wench within who had a love son. Braomall was her name, and Domhnull was the name of her son.

When the son of the knight was born, this one fled with the two, the knight's son and her own son. They were being fed at the cost of the knight's wife. She was there on a day, and for fear they should be hungry, she went to a town land to seek food for them. They were hungry, and she was not coming, and they saw three deer coming towards the bothy. The knight's son was where the other was, and he asked what creatures were there. He told him there were creatures on which there was meat and clothing.

"If we were the better for it I would catch them," said he.

He ran and he caught the three deer, and they were before his 'muime' when she came. She flayed them, and they ate, and she made a dress for him of the deer's hides. Thus they were in a good way till the deer failed, and hunger came upon them again, and she went again to the town land. There came a great horse that belonged to the king – a wild horse – to the place where they were. He asked of Donald what beast was that.

"That is a beast on which sport is done, one is upon him riding him."

"If we were the better for him I would catch him," said he.

"Thou ill-conditioned tatterdemalion! to catch that beast! It would discomfit any man in the realm to catch him." He did not bear any more chatter, but he came round about, and he struck his fist on Donald, and he drove his brains out. He put an oaken skewer through his ear, and he hung him up against the door of the bothy. "Be there thou fifty beyond the worst," said he.

Then he stretched out after the horse, and the hides were trailing behind him. He caught the horse, and he mounted him; and the horse that had never borne to see a man, he betook himself to the stable for fear. His father's brother had got a son by another wife. When he saw the palace he went up with wonder to look at the palace of his father's brother.

His muime never had called him anything but 'the great fool' and 'Creud orm.' When he perceived the son of his father's brother playing shinty, he went where he was, and, "Creud orm," said he.

"Who art thou," said the king's son – "of the gentles or ungentles of the realm, that has the like of that speech?"

"I am the great fool, the son of the knight's wife, the nursling of the nurse, and the foster-brother of Donald the nurse's son, going to do folly for myself, and if need were, it is I that could make a fool of thee also."

"Thou ill-conditioned tatterdemalion! make a fool of me?" said the king's son.

He put over the fist and he drove the brain out of him. "Be there, then, thou fifty over worse, as is Donald the nurse's son, with an oaken skewer through his ear."

He went in where the king was. "Creud orm," said he.

"Who art thou," said the king – "of the gentles or ungentles of the realm, that hast such a speech?"

"I am the great fool, the son of the knight's wife, the nursling of the nurse, and the foster-brother of the nurse's son, going to make folly for myself, and if need were, it is I that could make a fool of thee also."

"Well, then, it is not thou that made me that, but my counsellor, on the day that I slew thy father, and did not slay thy mother."

Then the king went with him. Every one, then, that he fell in with in the town, they were going with him, and that was their blessing, "Creud orm."

There was a splendid woman in the realm, and there was a great 'Fachnach,' that had taken her away. The people thought, if they could bring him to the presence of this woman, that be would set his head upon her, and that he would let the people away; that it was likely they would come between himself and the Fachach, and that the Fachach would kill him. That time he was an utter fool.

The Hoodie and the Fox

THE HOODIE AND THE FOX were good at early rising, and they laid a wager with each other, for which should soonest get up in the morning. The hoodie went into a tree top, and she slept; and the fox staid at the foot of the tree, looking aloft (to see) when the day would come. As soon as he perceived the day he cried,

"Sê-n-lAbAn-ê." It is bright day.

The hoodie had never stirred all the night, and then she awoke with the cry, and she answered, "SAd-o-bê-ê, SAd-o-bê-ê." It's long since it was. Then the fox lost the wager and the hoodie won.

The Reason Why the Dallag (Dog-Fish) is Called the King's Fish

WHAT BUT THAT THE KING of Lochlann should come to the King of Eirinn to be a while along with him.

The King of Lochlann and Fionn went on a day to fish, and they had a little boat, and they had no man but themselves.

They spent the greatest part of the day fishing, and they did not get a thing.

Then there laid a beast on (the hook of) Fionn, and he fell to fishing, so that he put the hook into him. He took in the fish; and what fish was it but a dog-fish. The hook of the King of Lochlann was in her maw, under the hook of Fionn, and the hook of Fionn was in the outer mouth. Then the King of Lochlann fell to at taking out the dog-fish, since it was his hook that was farthest down in her. They fell to arguing with each other, and Fionn would not yield a bit till they should go to law.

Then they went to land with the boat, and they went to law, and the law made (over) the fish to Fionn; and that there should be a fine laid upon the King of Lochlann, since he had not felt the fish when first it struck him.

With the rage that the King of Lochlann took he went home to Lochlann, and he told to his muime and his oide (his foster parents) how it had happened.

The Muilearteach was his muime, and the Smith of Songs, who was married to her, was his foster-father.

She said that it was she who would bring out the recompense for that.

Then she came till she reached Eirinn, and the King of Lochlann with her, and the Smith of Songs.

The Dallag was never said after that but the king's fish.

Canonbie Dick and Thomas of Ercildoune

I
T CHANCED, LONG YEARS AGO, that a certain horse-dealer
lived in the South of Scotland, near the Border, not very far
from Longtown. He was known as Canonbie Dick; and as he
went up and down the country, he almost always had a long
string of horses behind him, which he bought at one fair and
sold at another, generally managing to turn a good big penny by
the transaction.

He was a very fearless man, not easily daunted; and the people who knew
him used to say that if Canonbie Dick dare not attempt a thing, no one
else need be asked to do it.

One evening, as he was returning from a fair at some distance from
his home with a pair of horses which he had not succeeded in selling, he
was riding over Bowden Moor, which lies to the west of the Eildon Hills.
These hills are, as all men know, the scene of some of the most famous
of Thomas the Rhymer's prophecies; and also, so men say, they are the
sleeping-place of King Arthur and his Knights, who rest under the three
high peaks, waiting for the mystic call that shall awake them.

But little recked the horse-dealer of Arthur and his Knights, nor yet of
Thomas the Rhymer. He was riding along at a snail's pace, thinking over
the bargains which he had made at the fair that day, and wondering when
he was likely to dispose of his two remaining horses.

All at once he was startled by the approach of a venerable man, with
white hair and an old-world dress, who seemed almost to start out of the
ground, so suddenly did he make his appearance.

When they met, the stranger stopped, and, to Canonbie Dick's great
amazement, asked him for how much he would be willing to part with
his horses.

The wily horse-dealer thought that he saw a chance of driving a good
bargain, for the stranger looked a man of some consequence; so he
named a good round sum.

The old man tried to bargain with him; but when he found that he had not much chance of succeeding – for no one ever did succeed in inducing Canonbie Dick to sell a horse for a less sum than he named for it at first – he agreed to buy the animals, and, pulling a bag of gold from the pocket of his queerly cut breeches, he began to count out the price.

As he did so, Canonbie Dick got another shock of surprise, for the gold that the stranger gave him was not the gold that was in use at the time, but was fashioned into Unicorns, and Bonnet-pieces, and other ancient coins, which would be of no use to the horse-dealer in his everyday transactions. But it was good, pure gold; and he took it gladly, for he knew that he was selling his horses at about half as much again as they were worth. "So," thought he to himself, "surely I cannot be the loser in the long run."

Then the two parted, but not before the old man had commissioned Dick to get him other good horses at the same price, the only stipulation he made being that Dick should always bring them to the same spot, after dark, and that he should always come alone.

And, as time went on, the horse-dealer found that he had indeed met a good customer.

For, whenever he came across a suitable horse, he had only to lead it over Bowden Moor after dark, and he was sure to meet the mysterious, white-headed stranger, who always paid him for the animal in old-fashioned golden pieces.

And he might have been selling horses to him yet, for aught I know, had it not been for his one failing.

Canonbie Dick was apt to get very thirsty, and his ordinary customers, knowing this, took care always to provide him with something to drink. The old man never did so; he paid down his money and led away his horses, and there was an end of the matter.

But one night, Dick, being even more thirsty than usual, and feeling sure that his mysterious friend must live somewhere in the neighbourhood, seeing that he was always wandering about the hillside when everyone else was asleep, hinted that he would be very glad to go home with him and have a little refreshment.

"He would need to be a brave man who asks to go home with me," returned the stranger; "but, if thou wilt, thou canst follow me. Only, remember this – if thy courage fail thee at that which thou wilt behold, thou wilt rue it all thy life."

Canonbie Dick laughed long and loud. "My courage hath never failed me yet," he cried. "Beshrew me if I will let it fail now. So lead on, old man, and I will follow."

Without a word the stranger turned and began to ascend a narrow path which led to a curious hillock, which from its shape, was called by the country-folk the 'Lucken Hare.'

It was supposed to be a great haunt of Witches; and, as a rule, nobody passed that way after dark, if they could possibly help it.

Canonbie Dick was not afraid of Witches, however, so he followed his guide with a bold step up the hillside; but it must be confessed that he felt a little startled when he saw him turn down what seemed to be an entrance to a cavern, especially as he never remembered having seen any opening in the hillside there before.

He paused for a moment, looking round him in perplexity, wondering where he was being taken; and his conductor glanced at him scornfully.

"You can go back if you will," he said. "I warned thee thou wert going on a journey that would try thy courage to the uttermost." There was a jeering note in his voice that touched Dick's pride.

"Who said that I was afraid?" he retorted. "I was just taking note of where this passage stands on the hillside, so as to know it another time."

The stranger shrugged his shoulders. "Time enough to look for it when thou wouldst visit it again," he said. And then he pursued his way, with Dick following closely at his heels.

After the first yard or two they were enveloped in thick darkness, and the horse-dealer would have been sore put to it to keep near his guide had not the latter held out his hand for him to grasp. But after a little space a faint glimmering of light began to appear, which grew clearer and clearer, until at last they found themselves in an enormous cavern lit by flaming torches, which were stuck here and there in sconces in the rocky walls, and which, although they served to give light enough to see by, yet threw such ghostly shadows on the floor that they only seemed to intensify the gloom that hung over the vast apartment.

And the curious thing about this mysterious cave was that, along one side of it, ran a long row of horse stalls, just like what one would find in a stable, and in each stall stood a coal-black charger, saddled and bridled, as if ready for the fray; and on the straw, by every horse's side, lay the gallant figure of a knight, clad from head to foot in coal-black armour, with a drawn sword in his mailed hand.

But not a horse moved, not a chain rattled. Knights and steeds alike were silent and motionless, looking exactly as if some strange enchantment had been thrown over them, and they had been suddenly turned into black marble.

There was something so awesome in the still, cold figures and in the unearthly silence that brooded over everything that Canonbie Dick, reckless and daring though he was, felt his courage waning and his knees beginning to shake under him.

In spite of these feelings, however, he followed the old man up the hall to the far end of it, where there was a table of ancient workmanship, on which was placed a glittering sword and a curiously wrought hunting-horn.

When they reached this table the stranger turned to him, and said, with great dignity, "Thou hast heard, good man, of Thomas of Ercildoune – Thomas the Rhymer, as men call him – he who went to dwell for a time with the Queen of Fairy-land, and from her received the Gifts of Truth and Prophecy?"

Canonbie Dick nodded; for as the wonderful Soothsayer's name fell on his ears, his heart sank within him and his tongue seemed to cleave to the roof of his mouth. If he had been brought there to parley with Thomas the Rhymer, then had he laid himself open to all the eldrich Powers of Darkness.

"I that speak to thee am he," went on the white-haired stranger. "And I have permitted thee thus to have thy desire and follow me hither in order that I may try of what stuff thou art made. Before thee lies a Horn and a Sword. He that will sound the one, or draw the other, shall, if his courage fail not, be King over the whole of Britain. I, Thomas the Rhymer, have spoken it, and, as thou knowest, my tongue cannot lie. But list ye, the outcome of it all depends on thy bravery; and it will be a light task, or a heavy, according as thou layest hand on Sword or Horn first."

Now Dick was more versed in giving blows than in making music, and his first impulse was to seize the Sword, then, come what might, he had something in his hand to defend himself with. But just as he was about to lift it the thought struck him that, if the place were full of spirits, as he felt sure that it must be, this action of him might be taken to mean defiance, and might cause them to band themselves together against him.

So, changing his mind, he picked up the Horn with a trembling hand, and blew a blast upon it, which, however, was so weak and feeble that it could scarce be heard at the other end of the hall.

The result that followed was enough to appal the stoutest heart. Thunder rolled in crashing peals through the immense hall. The charmed Knights and their horses woke in an instant from their enchanted sleep. The Knights sprang to their feet and seized their swords, brandishing them round their heads, while their great black chargers stamped, and snorted, and ground their bits, as if eager to escape from their stalls. And where a moment before all had been stillness and silence, there was now a scene of wild din and excitement.

Now was the time for Canonbie Dick to play the man. If he had done so all the rest of his life might have been different.

But his courage failed him, and he lost his chance. Terrified at seeing so many threatening faces turned towards him, he dropped the Horn and made one weak, undecided effort to pick up the Sword.

But, ere he could do so, a mysterious voice sounded from somewhere in the hall, and these were the words that it uttered:

> *"Woe to the coward, that ever he was born,*
> *Who did not draw the Sword before he blew the Horn."*

And, before Dick knew what he was about, a perfect whirlwind of cold, raw air tore through the cavern, carrying the luckless horse-dealer along with it; and, hurrying him along the narrow passage through which he had entered, dashed him down outside on a bank of loose stones and shale. He fell right to the bottom, and was found, with little life left in him, next morning, by some shepherds, to whom he had just strength enough left to whisper the story of his weird and fearful adventure.

Gold-Tree and Silver-Tree

I N BYGONE DAYS THERE LIVED a little Princess named
Gold-Tree, and she was one of the prettiest children in the
whole world.

Although her mother was dead, she had a very happy life, for her father loved
her dearly, and thought that nothing was too much trouble so long as it gave
his little daughter pleasure. But by and by he married again, and then the
little Princess's sorrows began.

For his new wife, whose name, curious to say, was Silver-Tree, was very
beautiful, but she was also very jealous, and she made herself quite miserable
for fear that, some day, she should meet someone who was better looking
than she was herself.

When she found that her step-daughter was so very pretty, she took a dislike
to her at once, and was always looking at her and wondering if people would
think her prettier than she was. And because, in her heart of hearts, she was
afraid that they would do so, she was very unkind indeed to the poor girl.

At last, one day, when Princess Gold-Tree was quite grown up, the two
ladies went for a walk to a little well which lay, all surrounded by trees, in the
middle of a deep glen.

Now the water in this well was so clear that everyone who looked into it
saw his face reflected on the surface; and the proud Queen loved to come
and peep into its depths, so that she could see her own picture mirrored in
the water.

But to-day, as she was looking in, what should she see but a little trout, which
was swimming quietly backwards and forwards not very far from the surface.

"Troutie, troutie, answer me this one question," said the Queen. "Am not I
the most beautiful woman in the world?"

"No, indeed, you are not," replied the trout promptly, jumping out of the
water, as he spoke, in order to swallow a fly.

"Who is the most beautiful woman, then?" asked the disappointed Queen,
for she had expected a far different answer.

"Thy step-daughter, the Princess Gold-Tree, without a doubt," said the little fish; then, frightened by the black look that came upon the jealous Queen's face, he dived to the bottom of the well.

It was no wonder that he did so, for the Queen's expression was not pleasant to look at, as she darted an angry glance at her fair young step-daughter, who was busy picking flowers some little distance away.

Indeed, she was so annoyed at the thought that anyone should say that the girl was prettier than she was, that she quite lost her self-control; and when she reached home she went up, in a violent passion, to her room, and threw herself on the bed, declaring that she felt very ill indeed.

It was in vain that Princess Gold-Tree asked her what the matter was, and if she could do anything for her. She would not let the poor girl touch her, but pushed her away as if she had been some evil thing. So at last the Princess had to leave her alone, and go out of the apartment, feeling very sad indeed.

By and by the King came home from his hunting, and he at once asked for the Queen. He was told that she had been seized with sudden illness, and that she was lying on her bed in her own room, and that no one, not even the Court Physician, who had been hastily summoned, could make out what was wrong with her. In great anxiety – for he really loved her – the King went up to her bedside, and asked the Queen how she felt, and if there was anything that he could do to relieve her.

"Yes, there is one thing that thou couldst do," she answered harshly, "but I know full well that, even although it is the only thing that will cure me, thou wilt not do it."

"Nay," said the King, "I deserve better words at thy mouth than these; for thou knowest that I would give thee aught thou carest to ask, even if it be the half of my Kingdom."

"Then give me thy daughter's heart to eat," cried the Queen, "for unless I can obtain that, I will die, and that speedily."

She spoke so wildly, and looked at him in such a strange fashion, that the poor King really thought that her brain was turned, and he was at his wits' end what to do. He left the room, and paced up and down the corridor in great distress, until at last he remembered that that very morning the son of a great King had arrived from a country far over the sea, asking for his daughter's hand in marriage.

"Here is a way out of the difficulty," he said to himself. "This marriage pleaseth me well, and I will have it celebrated at once. Then, when my daughter is safe out of the country, I will send a lad up the hillside, and he shall kill a he-goat, and I will have its heart prepared and dressed, and send it up to my wife. Perhaps the sight of it will cure her of this madness."

So he had the strange Prince summoned before him, and told him how the Queen had taken a sudden illness that had wrought on her brain, and had caused her to take a dislike to the Princess, and how it seemed as if it would be a good thing if, with the maiden's consent, the marriage could take place at once, so that the Queen might be left alone to recover from her strange malady.

Now the Prince was delighted to gain his bride so easily, and the Princess was glad to escape from her step-mother's hatred, so the marriage took place at once, and the newly wedded pair set off across the sea for the Prince's country.

Then the King sent a lad up the hillside to kill a he-goat; and when it was killed he gave orders that its heart should be dressed and cooked, and sent to the Queen's apartment on a silver dish. And the wicked woman tasted it, believing it to be the heart of her step-daughter; and when she had done so, she rose from her bed and went about the Castle looking as well and hearty as ever.

I am glad to be able to tell you that the marriage of Princess Gold-Tree, which had come about in such a hurry, turned out to be a great success; for the Prince whom she had wedded was rich, and great, and powerful, and he loved her dearly, and she was as happy as the day was long.

So things went peacefully on for a year. Queen Silver-Tree was satisfied and contented, because she thought that her step-daughter was dead; while all the time the Princess was happy and prosperous in her new home.

But at the end of the year it chanced that the Queen went once more to the well in the little glen, in order to see her face reflected in the water.

And it chanced also that the same little trout was swimming backwards and forwards, just as he had done the year before. And the foolish Queen determined to have a better answer to her question this time than she had last.

"Troutie, troutie," she whispered, leaning over the edge of the well, "am not I the most beautiful woman in the world?"

"By my troth, thou art not," answered the trout, in his very straightforward way.

"Who is the most beautiful woman, then?" asked the Queen, her face growing pale at the thought that she had yet another rival.

"Why, your Majesty's step-daughter, the Princess Gold-Tree, to be sure," answered the trout.

The Queen threw back her head with a sigh of relief. "Well, at any rate, people cannot admire her now," she said, "for it is a year since she died. I ate her heart for my supper."

"Art thou sure of that, your Majesty?" asked the trout, with a twinkle in his eye. "Methinks it is but a year since she married the gallant young Prince who came from abroad to seek her hand, and returned with him to his own country."

When the Queen heard these words she turned quite cold with rage, for she knew that her husband had deceived her; and she rose from her knees and went straight home to the Palace, and, hiding her anger as best she could, she asked him if he would give orders to have the Long Ship made ready, as she wished to go and visit her dear step-daughter, for it was such a very long time since she had seen her.

The King was somewhat surprised at her request, but he was only too glad to think that she had got over her hatred towards his daughter, and he gave orders that the Long Ship should be made ready at once.

Soon it was speeding over the water, its prow turned in the direction of the land where the Princess lived, steered by the Queen herself; for she knew the course that the boat ought to take, and she was in such haste to be at her journey's end that she would allow no one else to take the helm.

Now it chanced that Princess Gold-Tree was alone that day, for her husband had gone a-hunting. And as she looked out of one of the Castle windows she saw a boat coming sailing over the sea towards the landing place. She recognised it as her father's Long Ship, and she guessed only too well whom it carried on board.

She was almost beside herself with terror at the thought, for she knew that it was for no good purpose that Queen Silver-Tree had taken the trouble to set out to visit her, and she felt that she would have given almost anything she possessed if her husband had but been at home. In her distress she hurried into the servants' hall.

"Oh, what shall I do, what shall I do?" she cried, "for I see my father's Long Ship coming over the sea, and I know that my step-mother is on board. And if she hath a chance she will kill me, for she hateth me more than anything else upon earth."

Now the servants worshipped the ground that their young Mistress trod on, for she was always kind and considerate to them, and when they saw how frightened she was, and heard her piteous words, they crowded round her, as if to shield her from any harm that threatened her.

"Do not be afraid, your Highness," they cried; "we will defend thee with our very lives if need be. But in case thy Lady Step-Mother should have the power to throw any evil spell over thee, we will lock thee in the great Mullioned Chamber, then she cannot get nigh thee at all."

Now the Mullioned Chamber was a strong-room, which was in a part of the castle all by itself, and its door was so thick that no one could possibly break through it; and the Princess knew that if she were once inside the room, with its stout oaken door between her and her step-mother, she would be perfectly safe from any mischief that that wicked woman could devise.

So she consented to her faithful servants' suggestion, and allowed them to lock her in the Mullioned Chamber.

So it came to pass that when Queen Silver-Tree arrived at the great door of the Castle, and commanded the lackey who opened it to take her to his Royal Mistress, he told her, with a low bow, that that was impossible, because the Princess was locked in the strong-room of the Castle, and could not get out, because no one knew where the key was.

(Which was quite true, for the old butler had tied it round the neck of the Prince's favourite sheep-dog, and had sent him away to the hills to seek his master.)

"Take me to the door of the apartment," commanded the Queen. "At least I can speak to my dear daughter through it." And the lackey, who did not see what harm could possibly come from this, did as he was bid.

"If the key is really lost, and thou canst not come out to welcome me, dear Gold-Tree," said the deceitful Queen, "at least put thy little finger through the keyhole that I may kiss it."

The Princess did so, never dreaming that evil could come to her through such a simple action. But it did. For instead of kissing the tiny finger, her step-mother stabbed it with a poisoned needle, and, so deadly was the poison, that, before she could utter a single cry, the poor Princess fell, as one dead, on the floor.

When she heard the fall, a smile of satisfaction crept over Queen Silver-Tree's face. "Now I can say that I am the handsomest woman in the world," she whispered; and she went back to the lackey who stood waiting at the end of the passage, and told him that she had said all that she had to say to her daughter, and that now she must return home.

So the man attended her to the boat with all due ceremony, and she set sail for her own country; and no one in the Castle knew that any harm had befallen their dear Mistress until the Prince came home from his hunting with the key of the Mullioned Chamber, which he had taken from his sheep-dog's neck, in his hand.

He laughed when he heard the story of Queen Silver-Tree's visit, and told the servants that they had done well; then he ran upstairs to open the door and release his wife.

But what was his horror and dismay, when he did so, to find her lying dead at his feet on the floor.

He was nearly beside himself with rage and grief; and, because he knew that a deadly poison such as Queen Silver-Tree had used would preserve the Princess's body so that it had no need of burial, he had it laid on a silken couch and left in the Mullioned Chamber, so that he could go and look at it whenever he pleased.

He was so terribly lonely, however, that in a little time he married again, and his second wife was just as sweet and as good as the first one had been. This new wife was very happy, there was only one little thing that caused her any trouble at all, and she was too sensible to let it make her miserable.

That one thing was that there was one room in the Castle – a room which stood at the end of a passage by itself – which she could never enter, as her husband always carried the key. And as, when she asked him the reason of this, he always made an excuse of some kind, she made up her mind that she would not seem as if she did not trust him, so she asked no more questions about the matter.

But one day the Prince chanced to leave the door unlocked, and as he had never told her not to do so, she went in, and there she saw Princess Gold-Tree lying on the silken couch, looking as if she were asleep.

"Is she dead, or is she only sleeping?" she said to herself, and she went up to the couch and looked closely at the Princess. And there, sticking in her little finger, she discovered a curiously shaped needle.

"There hath been evil work here," she thought to herself. "If that needle be not poisoned, then I know naught of medicine." And, being skilled in leechcraft, she drew it carefully out.

In a moment Princess Gold-Tree opened her eyes and sat up, and presently she had recovered sufficiently to tell the Other Princess the whole story.

Now, if her step-mother had been jealous, the Other Princess was not jealous at all; for, when she heard all that had happened, she clapped her little hands, crying, "Oh, how glad the Prince will be; for although he hath married again, I know that he loves thee best."

That night the Prince came home from hunting looking very tired and sad, for what his second wife had said was quite true. Although he loved her very much, he was always mourning in his heart for his first dear love, Princess Gold-Tree.

"How sad thou art!" exclaimed his wife, going out to meet him. "Is there nothing that I can do to bring a smile to thy face?"

"Nothing," answered the Prince wearily, laying down his bow, for he was too heart-sore even to pretend to be gay.

"Except to give thee back Gold-Tree," said his wife mischievously. "And that can I do. Thou wilt find her alive and well in the Mullioned Chamber."

Without a word the Prince ran upstairs, and, sure enough, there was his dear Gold-Tree, sitting on the couch ready to welcome him.

He was so overjoyed to see her that he threw his arms round her neck and kissed her over and over again, quite forgetting his poor second wife, who had followed him upstairs, and who now stood watching the meeting that she had brought about.

She did not seem to be sorry for herself, however. "I always knew that thy heart yearned after Princess Gold-Tree," she said. "And it is but right that it should be so. For she was thy first love, and, since she hath come to life again, I will go back to mine own people."

"No, indeed thou wilt not," answered the Prince, "for it is thou who hast brought me this joy. Thou wilt stay with us, and we shall all three live happily together. And Gold-Tree and thee will become great friends."

And so it came to pass. For Princess Gold-Tree and the Other Princess soon became like sisters, and loved each other as if they had been brought up together all their lives.

In this manner another year passed away, and one evening, in the old country, Queen Silver-Tree went, as she had done before, to look at her face in the water of the little well in the glen.

And, as had happened twice before, the trout was there. "Troutie, troutie," she whispered, "am not I the most beautiful woman in the world?"

"By my troth, thou art not," answered the trout, as he had answered on the two previous occasions.

"And who dost thou say is the most beautiful woman now?" asked the Queen, her voice trembling with rage and vexation.

"I have given her name to thee these two years back," answered the trout. "The Princess Gold-Tree, of course."

"But she is dead," laughed the Queen. "I am sure of it this time, for it is just a year since I stabbed her little finger with a poisoned needle, and I heard her fall down dead on the floor."

"I would not be so sure of that," answered the trout, and without saying another word he dived straight down to the bottom of the well.

After hearing his mysterious words the Queen could not rest, and at last she asked her husband to have the Long Ship prepared once more, so that she could go and see her step-daughter.

The King gave the order gladly; and it all happened as it had happened before.

She steered the Ship over the sea with her own hands, and when it was approaching the land it was seen and recognised by Princess Gold-Tree.

The Prince was out hunting, and the Princess ran, in great terror, to her friend, the Other Princess, who was upstairs in her chamber.

"Oh, what shall I do, what shall I do?" she cried, "for I see my father's Long Ship coming, and I know that my cruel step-mother is on board, and she will try to kill me, as she tried to kill me before.

"Oh! come, let us escape to the hills."

"Not at all," replied the Other Princess, throwing her arms round the trembling Gold-Tree. "I am not afraid of thy Lady Step-Mother. Come with me, and we will go down to the sea shore to greet her."

So they both went down to the edge of the water, and when Queen Silver-Tree saw her step-daughter coming she pretended to be very glad, and sprang out of the boat and ran to meet her, and held out a silver goblet full of wine for her to drink.

"'Tis rare wine from the East," she said, "and therefore very precious. I brought a flagon with me, so that we might pledge each other in a loving cup."

Princess Gold-Tree, who was ever gentle and courteous, would have stretched out her hand for the cup, had not the Other Princess stepped between her and her step-mother.

"Nay, Madam," she said gravely, looking the Queen straight in the face; "it is the custom in this land for the one who offers a loving cup to drink from it first herself."

"I will follow the custom gladly," answered the Queen, and she raised the goblet to her mouth. But the Other Princess, who was watching for closely, noticed that she did not allow the wine that it contained to touch her lips. So she stepped forward and, as if by accident, struck the bottom of the goblet with her shoulder. Part of its contents flew into the Queen's face, and part, before she could shut her mouth, went down her throat.

So, because of her wickedness, she was, as the Good Book says, caught in her own net. For she had made the wine so poisonous that, almost before she had swallowed it, she fell dead at the two Princesses' feet.

No one was sorry for her, for she really deserved her fate; and they buried her hastily in a lonely piece of ground, and very soon everybody had forgotten all about her.

As for Princess Gold-Tree, she lived happily and peacefully with her husband and her friend for the remainder of her life.

The Three Widows

THERE WERE THREE WIDOWS, and every one of them had a son apiece. Dòmhnull was the name of the son of one of them.

Dòmhnull had four stots, and the rest had but two each. They were always scolding, saying that he had more grass than they had themselves. On a night of the nights they went to the fold, and they seized on the stots of Dòmhnull and they killed them. When Dòmhnull rose and went out in the morning to see the stots, he found them dead.

He flayed the stots, and he salted them, and he took one of the hides with him to the big town to sell. The way was so long, that the night came on him before he reached the big town. He went into a wood and he put the hide about his head. There came a heap of birds, and they lighted on the hide; he put out his hand and he seized on one of them. About the brightening of day he went away; he betook himself to the house of a gentleman.

The gentleman came to the door, and he asked what he had there in his oxter. He said that he had a soothsayer. "What divination will he be doing?"

"He will be doing every sort of divination," said Dòmhnull. "Make him do divination," said the gentleman.

He went and he wrung him, and the bird gave a ran. "What is he saying?" said the gentleman. "He says that thou hast a wish to buy him, and that thou wilt give two hundred pounds Saxon for him," said Dòmhnull. "Well, surely! – it is true, doubtless; and if I were thinking that he would do divination, I would give that for him," said the gentleman.

So now the gentleman bought the bird from Dòmhnull, and he gave him two hundred pounds Saxon for him.

"Try that thou do not sell him to any man, and that there is no knowing that I might not come myself to seek him yet. I would not give him to thee for three thousand pounds Saxon were it not that I am in extremity."

Dòmhnull went home, and the bird did not do a pinch of divination ever after.

When he took his meat he began at counting the money. Who were looking at him but those who killed the stots. They came in.

"Ah, Dòmhnull," said they, "How didst thou get all the money that is there?"

"I got it as you may get it too. It's I that am pleased that you killed the stots for me," said be. "Kill you your own stots and flay them, and take with you' the hides to the big town, and be shouting, 'Who will buy a stot's hide,' and you will get plenty of money."

They killed the stots, and they flayed them. They took with them the hides to the big town, and they began at shouting, "Who will buy a stot's hide." They were at that work the length of the day; and when the people of the big town were tired making sport of them, they returned home. Now they did not know what they should do. They were vexed because of the stots that were killed. They saw the mother of Dòmhnull going to the well, and they seized on her and they choked her.

When Dòmhnull was taking sorrow, so long was his mother coming, he looked out to try if he could see her. He reached the well, and he found her dead there. He did not know what he should do. Then he took her with him home. On the morrow he arrayed her in the best clothes she had, and he took her to the big town. He walked up to the king's house with her on the top of him. When he came to the king's house he met with a large well. He went and he stuck the stick into the bank of the well, and he set her standing with her chest on the stick. He reached the door and he struck at it, and the maidservant came down.

"Say to the king," said he, "that there is a respectable woman yonder, and that she has business with him."

The maidservant told that to the king. "Say to him to say to her to come over," said the king.

"The king is asking thee to say to her to come over," said the maidservant to Dòmhnull.

"I won't go there; go there thyself; I am tired enough."

The maid went up, and she told the king that not a bit of the man would go there. "Go there thyself," said the king.

"If she will not answer thee," said Dòmhnull to the maidservant, "thou shalt push her; she is deaf."

The maidservant reached where she was. "Good woman," said the maidservant to her, "the king is asking yourself to come over." She took no notice. She pushed her and she said not a word. Dòmhnull was seeing how it was without.

"Draw the stick from her chest," said Dòmhnull; "it's asleep she is."

She drew the stick from her chest, and there she went head foremost into the well. Then he shouted out, "Oh my cattle! my cattle! my mother drowned in the well! What shall I do this day?" Then he struck his two palms against each other, and there was no howl he gave that could not be heard at three miles' distance.

The king came out. "Oh, my lad, never give it voice for ever, and I will pay for thy mother. How much wilt thou be asking for thy mother?"

"Five hundred pounds Saxon," said Dòmhnull.

"Thou shalt get that within the minute," said the king.

Dòmhnull got the five hundred Saxon pounds. He went where his mother was; he took the clothes off that were on her, and he threw her into the well.

He came home, and he was counting the money. They came – the two – where he was, to see if he should be lamenting his mother. They put a question to him – "Where had he got all the money that was there?"

"I got it," said he, "where you may get it if you yourselves should choose."

"How shall we get it?"

"Kill you your mothers, and take them with you on top of you, and take them about the big town, and be shouting, 'Who will buy old dead carlins?' and you get your fortunes."

When they heard that they went home, and each one of them began upon his mother with a stone in a stocking till he killed her.

They went on the morrow to the big town. They began at shouting, "Who will buy old carlins dead?" And there was no man who would buy that.

When the people of the big town were tired making sport of them, they set the dogs at them home.

When they came home that night they laid down and they slept. On the morrow, when they rose, they went where Dòmhnull was, and they seized on him and they put him into a barrel. They went with it to reel it down from a peak of rock. They were thus, and they had time about carrying it. The one said to the other, "Since the way was so long, and the day so hot, that they should go in to take a dram." They went in, and they left him in the barrel on the great road without. He heard a 'Tristrich' coming, and who was there but the shepherd, and a hundred sheep with him. He came down, and he began to play a 'trump' (Jew's harp) which he had in the barrel. The shepherd struck a stroke of his stick on a barrel. "Who's in here?" said he. "It's me," said Dòmhnull. "What art thou doing in it?" said the shepherd. "I am making a fortune in it," said Dòmhnull, "and no man ever saw such a place with gold and silver. I have just filled a thousand purses here, and the fortune is nearly made." "It's a pity," said the shepherd, "that thou shouldest not let myself in a while."

"I won't let thee. It is much that would make me."

"And wilt thou let me in? Mightest thou not let me in for one minute, and mightest thou not have enough thyself nevertheless?"

"By the books, poor man, since thou art needful, I will not let thee in. (Do) thou thyself drive the head out of the barrel and come here; but thou shalt not get (leave) to be long in it," said Dòmhnull.

The shepherd took the head out of the barrel, and he came out; he seized on the shepherd by the two shanks, and he set him head foremost in the barrel.

"There is neither silver nor gold here," said the shepherd.

"Thou wilt not see a thing till the head goes on the barrel," said Dòmhnull.

"Oh, I don't see a shadow in here," said he.

"If thou seest not, so be it with thee," said Dòmhnull.

Dòmhnull went and he put on the plaid that the shepherd had, and when he put on the plaid the dog followed him. Then they came out and they seized the barrel, and they raised it on their shoulders. They went away with it.

The shepherd would say at the end of every minute, "It's me that's in it – it's me that's in it." "Oh, it's thou, roguey! belike it's thou?"

They reached the peak of the rock, and they let down the barrel with the rock and shepherd in its inside.

When they returned, whom did they see but Dòmhnull, with his plaid and his dog, and his hundred of sheep with him in a park.

They went over to him.

"Oh, Dòmhnull," said they, "how gottest thou to come hither?"

"I got as you might get if you would try it. After that I had reached the world over yonder, they said to me that I had plenty of time for going over there, and they set me over here, and a hundred sheep with me to make money for myself."

"And would they give the like of that to us if we should go there?" said they.

"They would give (that.) It's they that would give," said Dòmhnull.

"(By) what means shall we get going there?" said they.

"Exactly the very means by which you yourselves sent me there," said he.

They went and they took with them two barrels to set themselves into up above.

When they reached the place one of them went into one of the barrels, and the other sent him down with the rock. That one gave a roar below, and his brains just after going out with the blow he got.

The other one asked Dòmhnull. what he was saying?

"He is shouting. 'Cattle and sheep, wealth and profit,'" said Dòmhnull.

"Down with me, down with me!" said the other one.

He did not stay to go into the barrel. He cut a caper down, and the brains went out of him.

Dòmhnull went home, and he had the land to himself.

Tales of
Fairy Folk

We look in vain in Scotland's 'fairy' tales for pretty nymphs with butterfly wings and starry wands; even for engaging 'little people'. More typical is the grotesque 'gruagach' in 'The Young King of Easaidh Ruadh'; the shape-shifting crow-man in 'The Tale of the Hoodie'; or the dark-dwelling marauders of 'The Page-Boy and the Silver Goblet'. Or, for that matter, the outwardly ordinary – yet, oddly, just as menacing – 'Woman of Peace' who bothers the housewife in 'Sanntraigh'.

The 'brownie' (which, incidentally, is also sometimes referred to as a 'gruagach', that word sometimes meaning a 'spectre of the class of Brownies to which the Highland dairymaids made frequent libations of milk' and 'rarely the chief of a place', but also a creature 'who did odd jobs about the house for the maids'), while ugly and hairy, can at least be described as a kind of benevolent fairy, with its unerring drive to serve the family whose home it inhabits.

Really, though, what the fairy tradition represents in Scotland's folk tales is the permeability of the border between everyday reality and a life beyond that is mysterious and magical – albeit as often in a sinister way as in an agreeably 'enchanting' one.

The Brownie

The Scottish Brownie formed a class of being distinct in habit and disposition from the freakish and mischievous elves. He was meagre, shaggy, and wild in his appearance. In the day-time he lurked in remote recesses of the old houses which he delighted to haunt, and in the night sedulously employed himself in discharging any laborious task which he thought might be acceptable to the family to whose service he had devoted himself. But the Brownie does not drudge from the hope of recompense. On the contrary, so delicate is his attachment that the offer of reward, but particularly of food, infallibly occasions his disappearance for ever.

It is told of a Brownie, who haunted a border family now extinct, that the lady having fallen unexpectedly ill, and the servant, who was ordered to ride to Jedburgh for the *sage-femme*, showing no great alertness in setting out, the familiar spirit slipped on the greatcoat of the lingering domestic, rode to the town on the laird's best horse, and returned with the midwife *en croupe*. During the short space of his absence, the Tweed, which they must necessarily ford, rose to a dangerous height. Brownie, who transported his charge with all the rapidity of the ghostly lover of Lenore, was not to be stopped by the obstacle. He plunged in with the terrified old lady, and landed her in safety where her services were wanted. Having put the horse into the stable (where it was afterwards found in a woeful plight), he proceeded to the room of the servant, whose duty he had discharged, and finding him just in the act of drawing on his boots, he administered to him a most merciless drubbing with his own horsewhip. Such an important service excited the gratitude of the laird, who, understanding that Brownie had been heard to express a wish to have a green coat, ordered a vestment of the colour to be made, and left in his haunts. Brownie took away the green coat, but was never seen more. We may suppose that, tired of his domestic drudgery, he went in his new livery to join the fairies.

The last Brownie known in Ettrick Forest resided in Bodsbeck, a wild and solitary spot, near the head of Moffat Water, where he exercised his functions undisturbed, till the scrupulous devotion of an old lady induced her to "hire him away," as it was termed, by placing in his haunt a porringer of milk and a piece of money. After receiving this hint to depart, he was heard the whole night to howl and cry, "Farewell to bonnie Bodsbeck!" which he was compelled to abandon for ever.

The Young King of Easaidh Ruadh

THE YOUNG KING OF EASAIDH RUADH, after he got the heirship to himself, was at much merry making, looking out what would suit him, and what would come into his humour. There was a gruagach near his dwelling, who was called Gruagach carsalach donn (The brown curly long-haired one.)

He thought to himself that he would go to play a game with him. He went to the Seanagal (soothsayer) and he said to him – "I am made up that I will go to game with the Gruagach carsalach donn." "Aha!" said the Seanagal, "art thou such a man? Art thou so insolent that thou art going to play a game against the Gruagach carsalach donn? 'Twere my advice to thee to change thy nature and not to go there." "I wont do, that," said he. "'Twere my advice to thee, if thou shouldst win of the Gruagach carsalach donn, to get the cropped rough-skinned maid that is behind the door for the worth of thy gaming, and many a turn will he put off before thou gettest her." He lay down that night, and if it was early that the day came, 'twas earlier than that that the king arose to hold gaming against the Gruagach. He reached the Gruagach, he blessed the Gruagach, and the Gruagach blessed him. Said, the Gruagach to him, "Oh young king of Easaidh Ruadh, what brought thee to me to-day? Wilt thou game with me?" They began and they played the game. The king won. "Lift the stake of thy gaming so that I may get (leave) to be moving." "The stake of my gaming is to give me the cropped rough-skinned girl thou hast behind the door." "Many a fair woman have I within besides her," said the Gruagach. "I will take none but that one." "Blessing to thee and cursing to thy teacher of learning." They went to the house of the Gruagach, and the Gruagach set in order twenty young girls. "Lift now thy choice from amongst these." One was coming out after another, and every one that would come out she would say, "I am she; art thou not silly that art not taking me with thee?" But the Seanagal had asked him to take none but the last one that would come out. When the last one came out, he said, "This is mine." He went with her, and when they were a bit from the house, her form altered, and she is the loveliest woman that was on earth. The king was going home full of joy at getting such a charming woman.

He reached the house, and he went to rest. If it was early that the day arose, it was earlier than that that the king arose to go to game with the Gruagach. "I must absolutely go to game against the Gruagach to-day," said he to his wife. "Oh!" said she, "that's my father, and if thou goest to game with him, take nothing for the stake of thy play but the dun shaggy filly that has the stick saddle on her."

The king went to encounter the Gruagach, and surely the blessing of the two to each other was not beyond what it was before. "Yes!" said the Gruagach, "how did thy young bride please thee yesterday?" "She pleased fully." "Hast thou come to game with me to-day?" "I came." They began at the gaming, and the king won from the Gruagach on that day. "Lift the stake of thy gaming, and be sharp about it." "The stake of my gaming is the dun shag filly on which is the stick saddle."

They went away together. They reached the dun shaggy filly. He took her out from the stable, and the king put his leg over her and she was the swift heroine! He went home. His wife had her hands spread before him, and they were cheery together that night. "I would rather myself," said his wife, "that thou shouldest not go to game with the Gruagach any more, for if he wins he will put trouble on thy head." "I won't do that," said he, "I will go to play with him to-day."

He went to play with the Gruagach. When he arrived, he thought the Gruagach was seized with joy. "Hast thou come?" he said. "I came." They played the game, and, as a cursed victory for the king, the Gruagach won that day. "Lift the stake of thy game," said the young king of Easaidh Ruadh, "and be not heavy on me, for I cannot stand to it." "The stake of my play is," said he, "that I lay it as crosses and as spells on thee, and as the defect of the year, that the cropped rough-skinned creature, more uncouth and unworthy than thou thyself, should take thy head, and thy neck, and thy life's look off, if thou dost not get for me the Glaive of Light of the king of the oak windows." The king went home, heavily, poorly, gloomily. The young queen came meeting him, and she said to him, "Mohrooai! my pity! there is nothing with thee tonight." Her face and her splendour gave some pleasure to the king when he looked on her brow, but when he sat on a chair to draw her towards him, his heart was so heavy that the chair broke under him.

"What ails thee, or what should ail thee, that thou mightest not tell it to me?" said the queen. The king told how it happened. "Ha!" said she, "what should'st thou mind, and that thou hast the best wife in Erin, and the second best horse in Erin. If thou takest my advice, thou wilt come (well) out of all these things yet."

If it was early that the day came, it was earlier than that that the queen arose, and she set order in everything, for the king was about to go on his journey. She set in order the dun shaggy filly, on which was the stick saddle, and though he saw it as wood, it was full of sparklings with gold and silver. He got on it; the queen kissed him, and she wished him victory of battlefields. "I need not be telling thee anything. Take thou the advice of thine own she comrade, the filly, and she will tell thee what thou shouldest do." He set out on his journey, and it was not dreary to be on the dun steed. She would catch the swift March wind that would be before, and the swift March wind would not catch her. They came at the mouth of dusk and lateness, to the court and castle of the king of the oak windows.

Said the dun shaggy filly to him, "We are at the end of the journey, and we have not to go any further; take my advice, and I will take thee where the sword of light of the king of the oak windows is, and if it comes with thee without scrape or creak, it is a good mark on our journey. The king is now at his dinner, and the sword of light is in his own chamber. There is a knob on its end, and when thou catchest the sword, draw it softly out of the window 'case.'" He came to the window where the sword was. He caught the sword and it came with him softly till it was at its point, and then it gave a sort of a "sgread." "We will now be going," said the filly. "It is no stopping time for us.

I know the king has felt us taking the sword out." He kept his sword in his hand, and they went away, and when they were a bit forward, the filly said, "We will stop now, and look thou whom thou seest behind thee." "I see" said he, "a swarm of brown horses coming madly." "We are swifter ourselves than these yet," said the filly. They went, and when they were a good distance forward, "Look now," said she; "whom seest thou coming?" "I see a swarm of black horses, and. one white-faced black horse, and he is coming and coming in madness, and a man on him." "That is the best horse in Erin; it is my brother, and he got three months more nursing than I, and he will come past me with a whirr, and try if thou wilt be so ready, that when he comes past me, thou wilt take the head off the man who is on him; for in the time of passing he will look at thee, and there is no sword in his court wilt take off his head but the very sword that is in thy hand." When this man was going past, he gave his head a turn to look at him, he drew the sword and he took his head off, and the shaggy dun filly caught it in her mouth.

This was the king of the oak windows. "Leap on the black horse," said she, "and leave the carcass there, and be going home as fast as he will take thee home, and I will be coming as best I may after thee." He leaped on the black horse, and, "Moirë!" he was the swift hero, and they reached the house long before day. The queen was without rest till he arrived. They raised music, and they laid down woe. On the morrow, he said, "I am obliged to go to see the Gruagach to-day, to try if my spells will be loose." "Mind that it is not as usual the Gruagach will meet thee. He will meet thee furiously, wildly, and he will say to thee, didst thou get the sword? and say thou that thou hast got it; he will say, how didst thou get it? and thou shalt say, if it were not the knob that was on its end I had not got it. He will ask thee again, how didst thou get the sword? and thou wilt say, if it were not the knob that was on its end, I had not got it. Then he will give himself a lift to look what knob is on the sword, and thou wilt see a mole on the right side of his neck, and stab the point of the sword in the mole; and if thou dost not hit the mole, thou and I are done. His brother was the king of the oak windows, and he knows that till the other had lost his life, he would not part with the sword. The death of the two is in the sword, but there is no other sword that will touch them but it." The queen kissed him, and she called on victory of battlefields (to be) with him, and he went away.

The Gruagach met him in the very same place where he was before. "Didst thou get the sword?" "I got the sword." "How didst thou get the sword?" "If it were not the knob that was on its end I had not got it," said he. "Let me see the sword." "It was not laid on me to let thee see it." "How didst thou get the sword?" "If it were not the knob that was on its end, I got it not." The Gruagach gave his head a lift to look at the sword; he saw the mole; he was sharp and quick, and he thrust the sword into the mole, and the Gruagach fell down dead.

He returned home, and when he returned home, he found his set of keepers and watchers tied back to back, without wife, or horse, or sweetheart of his, but was taken away.

When he loosed them, they said to him, "A great giant came and he took away thy wife and thy two horses." "Sleep will not come on mine eyes nor rest on mine head till I get my wife and my two horses back." In saying this, he went on his journey. He took the side that the track of the horses was, and he followed them diligently. The dusk and lateness were coming on him, and no stop did he make until he reached the side of the green wood. He saw where there was the forming of the site of a fire, and he thought that he would put fire upon it, and thus he would put the night past there.

He was not long here at the fire, when 'Cu Seang' of the green wood came on him.

He blessed the dog, and the dog blessed him.

"Oov! oov!" said the dog, "Bad was the plight of thy wife and thy two horses here last night with the big giant." "It is that which has set me so pained and pitiful on their track to-night; but there is no help for it." "Oh! king," said the dog, "thou must not be without meat." The dog went into the wood. He brought out creatures, and they made them meat contentedly. "I rather think myself," said the king, "that I may turn home; that I cannot go near that giant." "Don't do that," said the dog. "There's no fear of thee, king. Thy matter will grow with thee. Thou must not be here without sleeping." "Fear will not let me sleep without a warranty." "Sleep thou," said the dog, "and I will warrant thee." The king let himself down, stretched out at the side of the fire, and he slept. When the watch broke, the dog said to him, "Rise up, king, till thou gettest a morsel of meat that will strengthen thee, till thou wilt be going on thy journey. Now," said the dog, "if hardship or difficulty comes on thee, ask my aid, and I will be with thee in an instant." They left a blessing with each other, and he went away. In the time of dusk and lateness, he came to a great precipice of rock, and there was the forming of the site of a fire.

He thought he would gather dry fuel, and that he would set on fire. He began to warm himself, and he was not long thus when the hoary hawk of the grey rock came on him. "Oov! oov!" said she, "Bad was the plight of thy wife and thy two horses last night with the big giant." "There is no help for it," said be. "I have got much of their trouble and little of their benefit myself." "Catch courage," said she. "Thou wilt get something of their benefit yet. Thou must not be without meat here," said she. There is no contrivance for getting meat," said he. "We will not be long getting meat," said the falcon. She went, and she was not long when she came with three ducks and eight blackcocks in her mouth. They set their meat in order, and they took it. "Thou must not be without sleep," said the falcon. "How shall I sleep without a warranty over me, to keep me from any one evil that is here." "Sleep thou, king, and I will warrant thee." He let himself down, stretched out, and he slept.

In the morning, the falcon set him on foot. "Hardship or difficulty that comes on thee, mind, at any time, that thou wilt get my help." He went swiftly, sturdily. The night was coming, and the little birds of the forest of branching bushy trees, were talking about the briar roots and the twig tops; and if they were, it was stillness, not peace for him, till he came to the side of a great river that was there, and at the bank of the river there was the forming of the site of a fire. The king blew a heavy, little spark of fire. He was not long here when there came as company for him the brown otter of the river. "Och! och!" said the otter, "Bad was the plight of thy wife and thy two horses last night with the giant." "There is no help for it. I got much of their trouble and little of their benefit." "Catch courage, before mid-day to-morrow thou wilt see thy wife. Oh! king, thou must not be without meat," said the otter. "How is meat to be got here?" said the king. The otter went through the river, and she came and three salmon with her, that were splendid. They made meat, and they took it. Said the otter to the king, "Thou must sleep." How can I sleep without any warranty over me? Sleep thou, and I will warrant thee." The king slept. In the morning, the otter said to him, "Thou wilt be this night in presence of thy wife." He left blessing with the otter. "Now," said the otter, "if difficulty be on thee, ask my aid and thou shalt get it." The king went till he reached a rock, and he looked down into a chasm that was in the rock, and at the bottom he saw his wife and his two horses, and he did not know how be should get where they were. He went round till he came to the foot of the rock, and there was a fine road for going in. He went in, and if he went it was then she began crying. "Ud! ud!" said he, "this is bad! If thou art crying now when I myself have got so much trouble coming about thee." "Oo!" said the horses, "set him in front of us, and there is no fear for him, till we leave this." She made meat for him, and she set him to rights, and when they were a while together, she put him in front of the horses. When the giant came, he said, "The smell of the stranger is within." Says she, "My treasure! My joy and my cattle! there is nothing but the smell of the litter of the horses." At the end of a while he went to give meat to the horses, and the horses began at him, and they all but killed him, and he hardly crawled from them. "Dear thing," said she, "they are like to kill thee." "If I myself had my soul to keep, it's long since they had killed me," said he. "Where, dear, is thy soul? By the books I will take care of it." "It is," said he, "in the Bonnach stone." When he went on the morrow, she set the Bonnach stone in order exceedingly. In the time of dusk and lateness, the giant came home. She set her man in front of the horses. The giant went to give the horses meat and they mangled him more and more. "What made thee set the Bonnach stone in order like that?" said he. "Because thy soul is in it." "I perceive that if thou didst know where my soul is, thou wouldst give it much respect." "I would give (that)," said she. "It is not there," said he, "my soul is; it is in the threshold." She set in order the threshold finely on the morrow. When the giant returned, he went to give meat to the horses, and the horses mangled him more and more. "What brought thee to set the threshold in order like that?" "Because thy soul is in it." "I perceive if thou knewest where my soul is, that thou wouldst take care of it." "I would take that," said she. "It is not there that my soul is," said he. "There is a great flagstone under the threshold. There is a wether under the flag. There is a duck in the wether's belly, and an egg in the belly of the duck, and it is in the egg that my soul is." When the giant went away on the morrow's day, they raised the flagstone and out went the wether. "If I had the slim dog of the greenwood, he would not be long bringing the wether to me." The slim dog of the greenwood came with the wether in his mouth. When they opened the wether, out was the duck on the wing with the other ducks.

"If I had the Hoary Hawk of the grey rock, she would not be long bringing the duck to me." The Hoary Hawk of the grey rock came with the duck in her mouth; when they split the duck to take the egg from her belly, out went the egg into the depth of the ocean. "If I had the brown otter of the river, he would not be long bringing the egg to me." The brown otter came and the ego, in her mouth, and the queen caught the egg, and she crushed it between her two hands. The giant was coming in the lateness, and when she crushed the egg, he fell down dead, and he has never yet moved out of that. They took with them a great deal of his gold and silver. They passed a cheery night with the brown otter of the river, a night with the hoary falcon of the grey rock, and a night with the slim dog of the greenwood. They came home and they set in order "a Cuirm Curaidh Cridheil," a hearty hero's feast, and they were lucky and well pleased after that.

The Tale of the Hoodie

THERE WAS ERE NOW A FARMER, and he had three daughters. They were waulking clothes at a river. A hoodie came round and he said to the eldest one, 'M-pos-u-mi, "Wilt thou wed me, farmer's daughter?" "I won't wed thee, thou ugly brute. An ugly brute is the hoodie," said she. He came to the second one on the morrow, and he said to her, "M-pos-u-mi, wilt thou wed me?" "Not I, indeed," said she; "an ugly brute is the hoodie." The third day he said to the youngest, M-pos-u-mi, "Wilt thou wed me, farmer's daughter?," "I will wed thee," said she; "a pretty creature is the hoodie," and on the morrow they married.

The hoodie said to her, "Whether wouldst thou rather that I should be a hoodie by day, and a man at night; or be a hoodie at night, and a man by day?" "I would rather that thou wert a man by day, and a hoodie at night," says she. After this he was a splendid fellow by day, and a hoodie at night. A few days after they married he took her with him to his own house.

At the end of three quarters they had a son. In the night there came the very finest music that ever was heard about the house. Every man slept, and the child was taken away. Her father came to the door in the morning, and he asked how were all there. He was very sorrowful that the child should be taken away, for fear that he should be blamed for it himself.

At the end of three quarters again they had another son. A watch was set on the house. The finest of music came, as it came before, about the house; every man slept, and the child was taken away. Her father came to the door in the morning. He asked if every thing was safe; but the child was taken away, and he did not know what to do for sorrow.

Again, at the end of three quarters they had another son. A watch was set on the house as usual. Music came about the house as it came before; every one slept, and the child was taken away. When they rose on the morrow they went to another place of rest that they had, himself and his wife, and his sister-in-law. He said to them by the way, "See that you have not forgotten any thing." The wife said, "I forgot my coarse comb." The coach in which they were fell a withered faggot, and he went away as a hoodie.

Her two sisters returned home, and she followed after him. When he would be on a hill top, she would follow to try and catch him; and when she would reach the top of a hill, he would be in the hollow on the other side. When night came, and she was tired, she had no place of rest or dwelling; she saw a little house of light far from her, and though far from her she was not long in reaching it.

When she reached the house she stood deserted at the door. She saw a little laddie about the house, and she yearned to him exceedingly. The housewife told her to come up, that she knew her cheer and travel. She laid down, and no sooner did the day come than she rose. She went out, and when she was out, she was going from hill to hill to try if she could see a hoodie. She saw a hoodie on a hill, and when she would get on the hill the hoodie would be in the hollow, when she would go to the hollow, the hoodie would be on another hill. When the night came she had no place of rest or dwelling. She saw a little house of light far from her, and if far from her she, was not long reaching it. She went to the door. She saw a laddie on the floor to whom she yearned right much. The, housewife laid her to rest. No earlier came the day than she took out as she used. She passed this day as the other days. When the night came she reached a house. The housewife told her to come up, that she knew her cheer and travel, that her man had but left the house a little while, that she should be clever, that this was the last night she would see him, and not to sleep, but to strive to seize him. She slept, he came where she was, and he let fall a ring on her right hand. Now when she awoke she tried to catch hold of him, and she caught a feather of his wing. He left the feather with her, and he went away. When she rose in the morning she did not know what she should do. The housewife said that he had gone over a hill of poison over which she could not go without horseshoes on her hands and feet. She gave her man's clothes, and she told her to go to learn smithying till she should be able to make horse shoes for herself.

She learned smithying so well that she made horseshoes for her hands and feet. She went over the hill of poison. That same day after she had gone over the hill of poison, her man was to be married to the daughter of a great gentleman that was in the town.

There was a race in the town that day, and every one was to be at the race but the stranger that had come over to poison hill. The cook came to her, and he said to her, Would she go in his place to make the wedding meal, and that he might get to the race.

She said she would go. She was always watching where the bridegroom would be sitting.

She let fall the ring and the feather in the broth that was before him. With the first spoon he took up the ring, with the next he took up the feather. When the minister came to the fore to make the marriage, he would not marry till he should find out who had made ready the meal. They brought up the cook of the gentleman, and he said that this was not the cook who made ready the meal.

They brought up now the one who had made ready the meal. He said, "That now was his married wife." The spells went off him. They turned back over the hill of poison, she throwing the horse shoes behind her to him, as she went a little bit forward, and he following her. When they came, back over the hill, they went to the three houses in which she had been. These were the houses of his sisters, and they took with them the three sons, and they came home to their own house, and they were happy.

The Girl and the Dead Man

THERE WAS BEFORE NOW A poor woman, and she had a leash of daughters. Said the eldest one of them to her mother, "I had better go myself and seek for fortune." "I had better," said her mother, "bake a bannock for thee." When the bannock was ready, her mother said to her, "Whether wouldst thou like best the bit and my blessing, or the big bit and my curse?" "I would rather," said she, "the big bit and thy curse." She went away, and when the night was wreathing round her, she sat at the foot of a wall to eat the bannock. There gathered the sreath chuileanach and her twelve puppies, and the little birds of the air about her, for a part of the bannock. "Wilt thou give us a part of the bannock," said they. "I won't give it, you ugly brutes; I have not much for myself." "My curse will be thine, and the curse of my twelve birds; and thy mother's curse is the worst of all."

She rose and she went away, and she had not half enough with the bit of the bannock. She saw a little house a long way from her; and if a long way from her, she was not long reaching it. She struck in the door. "Who's there?" "A good maid seeking a master." "We want that," said they, and she got in. She had now a peck of gold and a peck of silver to get; and she was to be awake every night to watch a dead man, brother of the housewife, who was under spells. She had besides, of nuts as she broke, of needles as she lost, of thimbles as she pierced, of thread as she used, of candles as she burned, a bed of green silk over her, a bed of green silk under her, sleeping by day and watching by night. The first night when she was watching she fell asleep; the mistress came in, she struck the magic club on her, she fell down dead, and she threw her out at the back of the midden.

Said the middle one to her mother, "I had better go seek fortune and follow my sister." Her mother baked her a bannock; and she chose the big half and her mother's curse, as her elder sister did, and it happened to her as it happened to her sister.

Said the youngest one to her mother, "I had better myself go to seek fortune too, and follow my sisters." "I had better bake a bannock," said her mother. "Whether wouldst thou rather the little bit and my blessing, or the big bit and my curse?

"I would rather the little bit and your blessing." She went, and the night was wreathing round her, and she sat at the foot of a wall to eat the bannock. There gathered the sreath chuileanach and the twelve puppies, and the little birds of the air about her. "Wilt thou give us some of that?" "I will give, you pretty creatures, if you will keep me company." She gave them some of the bannock; they ate and they had plenty, and she had enough. They clapped their wings about her till she was snug with the warmth. She went, she saw a little house a long way from her; and if it was a long way from her, she was not long reaching it. She struck in the door. "Who's there?" "A good maid seeking a master." "We have need of that." The wages she had were a peck of gold and a peck of silver; of nuts as she broke, of needles as she lost, of thimbles as she pierced, of thread as she used, of candles as she burned, a bed of the green silk over her, and a bed of the green silk under her. She sat to watch the dead man, and she was sewing; on the middle of night he rose up, and screwed up a grin. "If thou dost not lie down properly, I will give thee the one leathering with a stick." He lay down. At the end of a while, he rose on one elbow, and screwed up a grin; and the third time he rose and screwed up a grin. When he rose the third time, she struck him a lounder of the stick; the stick stuck to the dead man, and the hand stuck to the stick; and out they were. They went forward till they were going through a wood; when it was low for her it was high for him; and when it was high for him it was low for her. The nuts were knocking their eyes out, and the sloes taking their ears off, till they got through the wood. After going through the wood they returned home. She got a peck of gold and a peck of silver, and the vessel of cordial. She rubbed the vessel of cordial to her two sisters, and brought them alive. They returned home; they left me sitting here, and if they were well, 'tis well; and if they were not, let them be.

Sanntraigh

❀

THERE WAS A HERD'S WIFE in the island of Sanntraigh, and she had a kettle. A woman of peace (fairy) would come every day to seek the kettle. She would not say a word when she came, but she would catch hold of the kettle. When she would catch the kettle, the woman of the house would say –

> *A smith is able to make*
> *Cold iron hot with coal.*
> *The due of a kettle is bones,*
> *And to bring it back again whole.*

The woman of peace would come back every day with the kettle and flesh and bones in it. On a day that was there, the housewife was for going over the ferry to Baile a Chaisteil, and she said to her man, "If thou wilt say to the woman of peace as I say, I will go to Baile Castle." "Oo! I will say it. Surely it's I that will say it." He was spinning a heather rope to be set on the house. He saw a woman coming and a shadow from her feet, and he took fear of her. He shut the door. He stopped his work. When she came to the door she did not find the door open, and he did not open it for her. She went above a hole that was in the house. The kettle gave two jumps, and at the third leap it went out at the ridge of the house. The night came, and the kettle came not. The wife came back over the ferry, and she did not see a bit of the kettle within, and she asked, "Where was the kettle?" "Well then I don't care where it is," said the man; "I never took such a fright as I took at it. I shut the door, and she did not come any more with it." "Good-for-nothing wretch, what didst thou do? There are two that will be ill off – thyself and I." "She will come to-morrow with it." "She will not come."

She hasted herself and she went away. She reached the knoll, and there was no man within. It was after dinner, and they were out in the mouth of the night. She went in. She saw the kettle, and she lifted it with her. It was heavy for her with the remnants that they left in it. When the old carle that was within saw her going out, he said,

Silent wife, silent wife,
That came on us from the land of chase,
Thou man on the surface of the "Bruth,"
Loose the black, and slip the Fierce.

The two dogs were let loose; and she was not long away when she heard the clatter of the dogs coming. She kept the remnant that was in the kettle, so that if she could get it with her, well, and if the dogs should come that she might throw it at them. She perceived the dogs coming. She put her hand in the kettle. She took the board out of it, and she threw at them a quarter of what was in it. They noticed it there for a while. She perceived them again, and she threw another piece at them when they closed upon her. She went away walking as well as she might; when she came near the farm, she threw the mouth of the pot downwards, and there she left them all that was in it. The dogs of the town struck (up) a barking when they saw the dogs of peace stopping. The woman of peace never came more to seek the kettle.

Cailliach Mhor Chlibhrich

T HIS CELEBRATED WITCH WAS ACCUSED of having enchanted the deer of the Reay forest, so that they avoided pursuit. Lord Reay was exceedingly angry, but at a loss how to remedy the evil. His man, William (the same who braved the witch and sat down in her hut) promised to find out if this was the case.

He watched her for a whole night, and by some counter enchantments managed to be present when in the early morning she was busy milking the hinds. They were standing all about the door of the hut till one of them ate a hank of blue worsted hanging from a nail in it. The witch struck the animal, and said, "The spell is off you; and Lord Reay's bullet will be your death to-day." William repeated this to his master to confirm the tale of his having passed the night in the hut of the great hag, which no one would believe. And the event justified it, for a fine yellow hind was killed that day, and the hank of blue yarn was found in its stomach.

The Smith and the Fairies

YEARS AGO THERE LIVED IN Crossbrig a smith of the name of MacEachern. This man had an only child, a boy of about thirteen or fourteen years of age, cheerful, strong, and healthy. All of a sudden he fell ill; took to his bed and moped whole days away. No one could tell what was the matter with him, and the boy himself could not, or would not, tell how he felt. He was wasting away fast; getting thin, old, and yellow; and his father and all his friends were afraid that he would die.

At last one day, after the boy had been lying in this condition for a long time, getting neither better nor worse, always confined to bed, but with an extraordinary appetite, – one day, while sadly revolving these things, and standing idly at his forge, with no heart to work, the smith was agreeably surprised to see an old man, well known to him for his sagacity and knowledge of out-of-the-way things, walk into his workshop. Forthwith he told him the occurrence which had clouded his life.

The old man looked grave as he listened; and after sitting a long time pondering over all he had heard, gave his opinion thus – "It is not your son you have got. The boy has been carried away by the 'Daoine Sith,' and they have left a Sibhreach in his place." "Alas! and what then am I to do?" said the smith. "How am I ever to see my own son again?" "I will tell you how," answered the old man. "But, first, to make sure that it is not your own son you have got, take as many empty egg shells as you can get, go with them into the room, spread them out carefully before his sight, then proceed to draw water with them, carrying them two and two in your hands as if they were a great weight, and arrange when full, with every sort of earnestness round the fire." The smith accordingly gathered as many broken egg-shells as he could get, went into the room, and proceeded to carry out all his instructions.

He had not been long at work before there arose from the bed a shout of laughter, and the voice of the seeming sick boy exclaimed, "I am now 800 years of age, and I have never seen the like of that before."

The smith returned and told the old man. "Well, now," said the sage to him, "did I not tell you that it was not your son you had: your son is in Brorra-cheill in a digh there (that is, a round green hill frequented by fairies). Get rid as soon as possible of this intruder, and I think I may promise you your son."

"You must light a very large and bright fire before the bed on which this stranger is lying. He will ask you 'What is the use of such a fire as that?' Answer him at once, 'You will see that presently!' and then seize him, and throw him into the middle of it. If it is your own son you have got, he will call out to save him; but if not, this thing will fly through the roof."

The smith again followed the old man's advice, kindled a large fire, answered the question put to him as he had been directed to do, and seizing the child flung him in without hesitation. The 'Sibhreach' gave an awful yell, and sprung through the roof, where a hole was left to let the smoke out.

On a certain night the old man told him the green round hill, where the fairies kept the boy, would be open. And on that night the smith, having provided himself with a bible, a dirk, and a crowing cock, was to proceed to the hill. He would hear singing and dancing and much merriment going on, but he was to advance boldly; the bible he carried would be a certain safeguard to him against any danger from the fairies. On entering the hill he was to stick the dirk in the threshold, to prevent the hill from closing upon him; "and then," continued the old man, "on entering you will see a spacious apartment before you, beautifully clean, and there, standing far within, working at a forge, you will also see your own son. When you are questioned, say you come to seek him, and will not go without him."

Not long after this, the time came round, and the smith sallied forth, prepared as instructed. Sure enough as he approached the hill, there was a light where light was seldom seen before. Soon after a sound of piping, dancing, and joyous merriment reached the anxious father on the night wind.

Overcoming every impulse to fear, the smith approached the threshold steadily, stuck the dirk into it as directed, and entered. Protected by the bible he carried on his breast, the fairies could not touch him; but they asked him, with a good deal of displeasure, what he wanted there. He answered, "I want my son, whom I see down there, and I will not go without him."

Upon hearing this, the whole company before him gave a loud laugh, which wakened up the cock he carried dozing in his arms, who at once leaped up on his shoulders, clapped his wings lustily, and crowed loud and long.

The fairies, incensed, seized the smith and his son, and throwing them out of the hill, flung the dirk after them, "and in an instant a' was dark."

For a year and a day the boy never did a turn of work, and hardly ever spoke a word; but at last one day, sitting by his father and watching him finishing a sword he was making for some chief, and which he was very particular about, he suddenly exclaimed, "That is not the way to do it;" and taking the tools from his father's hands he set to work himself in his place, and soon fashioned a sword, the like of which was never seen in the country before.

From that day the young man wrought constantly with his father, and became the inventor of a peculiarly fine and well-tempered weapon, the making of which kept the two smiths, father and son, in constant employment, spread their fame far and wide, and gave them the means in abundance, as they before had the disposition to live content with all the world and very happily with one another.

Man

THE MANKS FAIRY CREED is the same as elsewhere in Scotland. Such beings are supposed to exist, and are known by the name of Ferish, which a Manksman assured me was a genuine Manks word. If so, fairy may be old Celtic, and derived from the same root as Peri, instead of being derived from it.

The fairies in the Isle of Man are believed to be spirits. They are not supposed to throw arrows as they are said still to do in the Highlands. None of the old peasants seemed to take the least interest in 'elf shots,' the flint arrows, which generally lead to a story when shown elsewhere. One old man said, "The ferish have no body, no bones and scorned the arrow heads. It is stated in Train's history, that no flint-arrow heads have ever been found in the Isle of Man; but as there are numerous barrows, flint weapons may yet be discovered when some one looks for them.

Still these Manks fairies are much the same as their neighbours on the main land. They go into mills at night and grind stolen corn; they steal milk from the cattle; they live in green mounds; in short, they are like little mortals invested with supernatural power, thus: There was a man who lived not long ago near Port Erin, who had a Lhiannan Rhee. "He was like other people, but he had a fairy sweetheart; but he noticed her, and they do not like being noticed, the fairies, and so he lost his mind. Well, he was quite quiet like other people, but at night he slept in the barn; and they used to hear him talking to his sweetheart, and scolding her sometimes; but if any one made a noise he would be quiet at once."

Now, the truth of this story is clear enough; the man went mad; but this madness took the form of the popular belief, and that again attributed his madness to the fairy mistress. I am convinced that this was believed to be a case of genuine fairy intercourse; and it shows that the fairy creed still survives in the Isle of Man.

Thomas the Rhymer

OF ALL THE YOUNG GALLANTS in Scotland in the thirteenth century, there was none more gracious and debonair than Thomas Learmont, Laird of the Castle of Ercildoune, in Berwickshire.

He loved books, poetry, and music, which were uncommon tastes in those days; and, above all, he loved to study nature, and to watch the habits of the beasts and birds that made their abode in the fields and woods round about his home.

Now it chanced that, one sunny May morning, Thomas left his Tower of Ercildoune, and went wandering into the woods that lay about the Huntly Burn, a little stream that came rushing down from the slopes of the Eildon Hills. It was a lovely morning – fresh, and bright, and warm, and everything was so beautiful that it looked as Paradise might look.

The tender leaves were bursting out of their sheaths, and covering all the trees with a fresh soft mantle of green; and amongst the carpet of moss under the young man's feet, yellow primroses and starry anemones were turning up their faces to the morning sky.

The little birds were singing like to burst their throats, and hundreds of insects were flying backwards and forwards in the sunshine; while down by the burnside the bright-eyed water-rats were poking their noses out of their holes, as if they knew that summer had come, and wanted to have a share in all that was going on.

Thomas felt so happy with the gladness of it all, that he threw himself down at the root of a tree, to watch the living things around him.

As he was lying there, he heard the trampling of a horse's hooves, as it forced its way through the bushes; and, looking up, he saw the most beautiful lady that he had ever seen coming riding towards him on a grey palfrey.

She wore a hunting dress of glistening silk, the colour of the fresh spring grass; and from her shoulders hung a velvet mantle, which matched the riding-skirt exactly. Her yellow hair, like rippling gold, hung loosely round her shoulders, and on her head sparkled a diadem of precious stones, which flashed like fire in the sunlight.

Her saddle was of pure ivory, and her saddle-cloth of blood-red satin, while her saddle girths were of corded silk and her stirrups of cut crystal. Her horse's reins were of beaten gold, all hung with little silver bells, so that, as she rode along, she made a sound like fairy music.

Apparently she was bent on the chase, for she carried a hunting-horn and a sheaf of arrows; and she led seven greyhounds along in a leash, while as many scenting hounds ran loose at her horse's side.

As she rode down the glen, she lilted a bit of an old Scotch song; and she carried herself with such a queenly air, and her dress was so magnificent, that Thomas was like to kneel by the side of the path and worship her, for he thought that it must be the Blessed Virgin herself.

But when the rider came to where he was, and understood his thoughts, she shook her head sadly.

"I am not that Blessed Lady, as thou thinkest," she said. "Men call me Queen, but it is of a far other country; for I am the Queen of Fairy-land, and not the Queen of Heaven."

And certainly it seemed as if what she said were true; for, from that moment, it was as if a spell were cast over Thomas, making him forget prudence, and caution, and common-sense itself.

For he knew that it was dangerous for mortals to meddle with Fairies, yet he was so entranced with the Lady's beauty that he begged her to give him a kiss. This was just what she wanted, for she knew that if she once kissed him she had him in her power.

And, to the young man's horror, as soon as their lips had met, an awful change came over her. For her beautiful mantle and riding-skirt of silk seemed to fade away, leaving her clad in a long grey garment, which was just the colour of ashes. Her beauty seemed to fade away also, and she grew old and wan; and, worst of all, half of her abundant yellow hair went grey before his very eyes. She saw the poor man's astonishment and terror, and she burst into a mocking laugh.

"I am not so fair to look on now as I was at first," she said, "but that matters little, for thou hast sold thyself, Thomas, to be my servant for seven long years. For whoso kisseth the Fairy Queen must e'en go with her to Fairy-land, and serve her there till that time is past."

When he heard these words poor Thomas fell on his knees and begged for mercy. But mercy he could not obtain. The Elfin Queen only laughed in his face, and brought her dapple-grey palfrey close up to where he was standing.

"No, no," she said, in answer to his entreaties. "Thou didst ask the kiss, and now thou must pay the price. So dally no longer, but mount behind me, for it is full time that I was gone."

So Thomas, with many a sigh and groan of terror, mounted behind her; and as soon as he had done so, she shook her bridle rein, and the grey steed galloped off.

On and on they went, going swifter than the wind; till they left the land of the living behind, and came to the edge of a great desert, which stretched before them, dry, and bare, and desolate, to the edge of the far horizon.

At least, so it seemed to the weary eyes of Thomas of Ercildoune, and he wondered if he and his strange companion had to cross this desert; and, if so, if there were any chance of reaching the other side of it alive.

But the Fairy Queen suddenly tightened her rein, and the grey palfrey stopped short in its wild career.

"Now must thou descend to earth, Thomas," said the Lady, glancing over her shoulder at her unhappy captive, "and lout down, and lay thy head on my knee, and I will show thee hidden things, which cannot be seen by mortal eyes."

So Thomas dismounted, and louted down, and rested his head on the Fairy Queen's knee; and lo, as he looked once more over the desert, everything seemed changed. For he saw three roads leading across it now, which he had not noticed before, and each of these three roads was different.

One of them was broad, and level, and even, and it ran straight on across the sand, so that no one who was travelling by it could possibly lose his way.

And the second road was as different from the first as it well could be. It was narrow, and winding, and long; and there was a thorn hedge on one side of it, and a briar hedge on the other; and those hedges grew so high, and their branches were so wild and tangled, that those who were travelling along that road would have some difficulty in persevering on their journey at all.

And the third road was unlike any of the others. It was a bonnie, bonnie road, winding up a hillside among brackens, and heather, and golden-yellow whins, and it looked as if it would be pleasant travelling, to pass that way.

"Now," said the Fairy Queen, "an' thou wilt, I shall tell thee where these three roads lead to. The first road, as thou seest, is broad, and even, and easy, and there be many that choose it to travel on. But though it be a good road, it leadeth to a bad end, and the folk that choose it repent their choice for ever.

"And as for the narrow road, all hampered and hindered by the thorns and the briars, there be few that be troubled to ask where that leadeth to. But did they ask, perchance more of them might be stirred up to set out along it. For that is the Road of Righteousness; and, although it be hard and irksome, yet it endeth in a glorious City, which is called the City of the Great King.

"And the third road – the bonnie road – that runs up the brae among the ferns, and leadeth no mortal kens whither, but I ken where it leadeth, Thomas – for it leadeth unto fair Elf-land; and that road take we.

"And, mark 'ee, Thomas, if ever thou hopest to see thine own Tower of Ercildoune again, take care of thy tongue when we reach our journey's end, and speak no single word to anyone save me – for the mortal who openeth his lips rashly in Fairy-land must bide there for ever."

Then she bade him mount her palfrey again, and they rode on. The ferny road was not so bonnie all the way as it had been at first, however. For they had not ridden along it very far before it led them into a narrow ravine, which seemed to go right down under the earth, where there was no ray of light to guide them, and where the air was dank and heavy. There was a sound of rushing water everywhere, and at last the grey palfrey plunged right into it; and it crept up, cold and chill, first over Thomas's feet, and then over his knees.

His courage had been slowly ebbing ever since he had been parted from the daylight, but now he gave himself up for lost; for it seemed to him certain that his strange companion and he would never come safe to their journey's end.

He fell forward in a kind of swoon; and, if it had not been that he had tight hold of the Fairy's ash-grey gown, I warrant he had fallen from his seat, and had been drowned.

But all things, be they good or bad, pass in time, and at last the darkness began to lighten, and the light grew stronger, until they were back in broad sunshine.

Then Thomas took courage, and looked up; and lo, they were riding through a beautiful orchard, where apples and pears, dates and figs and wine-berries grew in great abundance. And his tongue was so parched and dry, and he felt so faint, that he longed for some of the fruit to restore him.

He stretched out his hand to pluck some of it; but his companion turned in her saddle and forbade him.

"There is nothing safe for thee to eat here," she said, "save an apple, which I will give thee presently. If thou touch aught else thou art bound to remain in Fairy-land for ever."

So poor Thomas had to restrain himself as best he could; and they rode slowly on, until they came to a tiny tree all covered with red apples. The Fairy Queen bent down and plucked one, and handed it to her companion.

"This I can give thee," she said, "and I do it gladly, for these apples are the Apples of Truth; and whoso eateth them gaineth this reward, that his lips will never more be able to frame a lie."

Thomas took the apple, and ate it; and for evermore the Grace of Truth rested on his lips; and that is why, in after years, men called him 'True Thomas.'

They had only a little way to go after this, before they came in sight of a magnificent Castle standing on a hillside.

"Yonder is my abode," said the Queen, pointing to it proudly. "There dwelleth my Lord and all the Nobles of his court; and, as my Lord hath an uncertain temper and shows no liking for any strange gallant whom he sees in my company, I pray thee, both for thy sake and mine, to utter no word to anyone who speaketh to thee; and, if anyone should ask me who and what thou art, I will tell them that thou art dumb. So wilt thou pass unnoticed in the crowd."

With these words the Lady raised her hunting-horn, and blew a loud and piercing blast; and, as she did so, a marvellous change came over her again; for her ugly ash-covered gown dropped off her, and the grey in her hair vanished, and she appeared once more in her green riding-skirt and mantle, and her face grew young and fair.

And a wonderful change passed over Thomas also; for, as he chanced to glance downwards, he found that his rough country clothes had been transformed into a suit of fine brown cloth, and that on his feet he wore satin shoon.

Immediately the sound of the horn rang out, the doors of the Castle flew open, and the King hurried out to meet the Queen, accompanied by such a number of Knights and Ladies, Minstrels and Page-boys, that Thomas, who had slid from his palfrey, had no difficulty in obeying her wishes and passing into the Castle unobserved.

Everyone seemed very glad to see the Queen back again, and they crowded into the Great Hall in her train, and she spoke to them all graciously, and allowed them to kiss her hand. Then she passed, with her husband, to a dais at the far end of the huge apartment, where two thrones stood, on which the Royal pair seated themselves to watch the revels which now began.

Poor Thomas, meanwhile, stood far away at the other end of the Hall, feeling very lonely, yet fascinated by the extraordinary scene on which he was gazing.

For, although all the fine Ladies, and Courtiers, and Knights were dancing in one part of the Hall, there were huntsmen coming and going in another part, carrying in great antlered deer, which apparently they had killed in the chase, and throwing them down in heaps on the floor. And there were rows of cooks standing beside the dead animals, cutting them up into joints, and bearing away the joints to be cooked.

Altogether it was such a strange, fantastic scene that Thomas took no heed of how the time flew, but stood and gazed, and gazed, never speaking a word to anybody. This went on for three long days, then the Queen rose from her throne, and, stepping from the dais, crossed the Hall to where he was standing.

"'Tis time to mount and ride, Thomas," she said, "if thou wouldst ever see the fair Castle of Ercildoune again."

Thomas looked at her in amazement. "Thou spokest of seven long years, Lady," he exclaimed, "and I have been here but three days."

The Queen smiled. "Time passeth quickly in Fairy-land, my friend," she replied. "Thou thinkest that thou hast been here but three days. 'Tis seven years since we two met. And now it is time for thee to go. I would fain have had thy presence with me longer, but I dare not, for thine own sake. For every seventh year an Evil Spirit cometh from the Regions of Darkness, and carrieth back with him one of our followers, whomsoever he chanceth to choose. And, as thou art a goodly fellow, I fear that he might choose thee.

"So, as I would be loth to let harm befall thee, I will take thee back to thine own country this very night."

Once more the grey palfrey was brought, and Thomas and the Queen mounted it; and, as they had come, so they returned to the Eildon Tree near the Huntly Burn.

Then the Queen bade Thomas farewell; and, as a parting gift, he asked her to give him something that would let people know that he had really been to Fairy-land.

"I have already given thee the Gift of Truth," she replied. "I will now give thee the Gifts of Prophecy and Poesie; so that thou wilt be able to foretell the future, and also to write wondrous verses. And, besides these unseen gifts, here is something that mortals can see with their own eyes – a Harp that was fashioned in Fairy-land. Fare thee well, my friend. Some day, perchance, I will return for thee again."

With these words the Lady vanished, and Thomas was left alone, feeling a little sorry, if the truth must be told, at parting with such a radiant Being and coming back to the ordinary haunts of men.

After this he lived for many a long year in his Castle of Ercildoune, and the fame of his poetry and of his prophecies spread all over the country, so that people named him True Thomas, and Thomas the Rhymer.

I cannot write down for you all the prophecies which Thomas uttered, and which most surely came to pass, but I will tell you one or two.

He foretold the Battle of Bannockburn in these words:

> *"The Burn of Breid*
> *Shall rin fou reid,"*

which came to pass on that terrible day when the waters of the little Bannockburn were reddened by the blood of the defeated English.

He also foretold the Union of the Crowns of England and Scotland, under a Prince who was the son of a French Queen, and who yet bore the blood of Bruce in his veins.

> *"A French Quen shall bearre the Sonne;*
> *Shall rule all Britainne to the sea,*
> *As neere as is the ninth degree,"*

which thing came true in 1603, when King James, son of Mary, Queen of Scots, became Monarch of both countries.

Fourteen long years went by, and people were beginning to forget that Thomas the Rhymer had ever been in Fairy-land; but at last a day came when Scotland was at war with England, and the Scottish army was resting by the banks of the Tweed, not far from the Tower of Ercildoune.

And the Master of the Tower determined to make a feast, and invite all the Nobles and Barons who were leading the army to sup with him.

That feast was long remembered.

For the Laird of Ercildoune took care that everything was as magnificent as it could possibly be; and when the meal was ended he rose in his place, and, taking his Elfin Harp, he sang to his assembled guests song after song of the days of long ago.

The guests listened breathlessly, for they felt that they would never hear such wonderful music again. And so it fell out.

For that very night, after all the Nobles had gone back to their tents, a soldier on guard saw, in the moonlight, a snow-white Hart and Hind moving slowly down the road that ran past the camp.

There was something so unusual about the animals that he called to his officer to come and look at them. And the officer called to his brother officers, and soon there was quite a crowd softly following the dumb creatures, who paced solemnly on, as if they were keeping time to music unheard by mortal ears.

"There is something uncanny about this," said one soldier at last. "Let us send for Thomas of Ercildoune, perchance he may be able to tell us if it be an omen or no."

"Ay, send for Thomas of Ercildoune," cried every one at once. So a little page was sent in haste to the old Tower to rouse the Rhymer from his slumbers.

When he heard the boy's message, the Seer's face grew grave and wrapt.

"'Tis a summons," he said softly, "a summons from the Queen of Fairy-land. I have waited long for it, and it hath come at last."

And when he went out, instead of joining the little company of waiting men, he walked straight up to the snow-white Hart and Hind. As soon as he reached them they paused for a moment as if to greet him. Then all three moved slowly down a steep bank that sloped to the little river Leader, and disappeared in its foaming waters, for the stream was in full flood.

And, although a careful search was made, no trace of Thomas of Ercildoune was found; and to this day the country folk believe that the Hart and the Hind were messengers from the Elfin Queen, and that he went back to Fairy-land with them.

The Page-Boy and the Silver Goblet

THERE WAS ONCE A LITTLE page-boy, who was in service in a stately Castle. He was a very good-natured little fellow, and did his duties so willingly and well that everybody liked him, from the great Earl whom he served every day on bended knee, to the fat old butler whose errands he ran.

Now the Castle stood on the edge of a cliff overlooking the sea, and although the walls at that side were very thick, in them there was a little postern door, which opened on to a narrow flight of steps that led down the face of the cliff to the sea shore, so that anyone who liked could go down there in the pleasant summer mornings and bathe in the shimmering sea.

On the other side of the Castle were gardens and pleasure grounds, opening on to a long stretch of heather-covered moorland, which, at last, met a distant range of hills.

The little page-boy was very fond of going out on this moor when his work was done, for then he could run about as much as he liked, chasing bumble-bees, and catching butterflies, and looking for birds' nests when it was nesting time.

So one night, when everyone else was asleep, he crept out of the Castle by the little postern door, and stole down the stone steps, and along the sea shore, and up on to the moor, and went straight to the Fairy Knowe.

To his delight he found that what everyone said was true. The top of the Knowe was tipped up, and from the opening that was thus made, rays of light came streaming out.

His heart was beating fast with excitement, but, gathering his courage, he stooped down and slipped inside the Knowe.

He found himself in a large room lit by numberless tiny candles, and there, seated round a polished table, were scores of the Tiny Folk, Fairies, and Elves, and Gnomes, dressed in green, and yellow, and pink; blue, and lilac, and scarlet; in all the colours, in fact, that you can think of.

He stood in a dark corner watching the busy scene in wonder, thinking how strange it was that there should be such a number of these tiny beings living their own lives all unknown to men, at such a little distance from them, when suddenly someone – he could not tell who it was – gave an order.

"Fetch the Cup," cried the owner of the unknown voice, and instantly two little Fairy pages, dressed all in scarlet livery, darted from the table to a tiny cupboard in the rock, and returned staggering under the weight of a most beautiful silver cup, richly embossed and lined inside with gold.

He placed it in the middle of the table, and, amid clapping of hands and shouts of joy, all the Fairies began to drink out of it in turn. And the page could see, from where he stood, that no one poured wine into it, and yet it was always full, and that the wine that was in it was not always the same kind, but that each Fairy, when he grasped its stem, wished for the wine that he loved best, and lo! in a moment the cup was full of it.

"'Twould be a fine thing if I could take that cup home with me," thought the page. "No one will believe that I have been here except I have something to show for it." So he bided his time, and watched.

Presently the Fairies noticed him, and, instead of being angry at his boldness in entering their abode, as he expected that they would be, they seemed very pleased to see him, and invited him to a seat at the table. But by and by they grew rude and insolent, and jeered at him for being content to serve mere mortals, telling him that they saw everything that went on at the Castle, and making fun of the old butler, whom the page loved with all his heart. And they laughed at the food he ate, saying that it was only fit for animals; and when any fresh dainty was set on the table by the scarlet-clad pages, they would push the dish across to him, saying: "Taste it, for you will not have the chance of tasting such things at the Castle."

At last he could stand their teasing remarks no longer; besides, he knew that if he wanted to secure the cup he must lose no time in doing so.

So he suddenly stood up, and grasped the stem of it tightly in his hand. "I'll drink to you all in water," he cried, and instantly the ruby wine was turned to clear cold water.

He raised the cup to his lips, but he did not drink from it. With a sudden jerk he threw the water over the candles, and instantly the room was in darkness. Then, clasping the precious cup tightly in his arms, he sprang to the opening of the Knowe, through which he could see the stars glimmering clearly.

He was just in time, for it fell to with a crash behind him; and soon he was speeding along the wet, dew-spangled moor, with the whole troop of Fairies at his heels.

They were wild with rage, and from the shrill shouts of fury which they uttered, the page knew well that, if they overtook him, he need expect no mercy at their hands.

And his heart began to sink, for, fleet of foot though he was, he was no match for the Fairy Folk, who gained on him steadily.

All seemed lost, when a mysterious voice sounded out of the darkness:

> *"If thou wouldst gain the Castle door,*
> *Keep to the black stones on the shore."*

It was the voice of some poor mortal, who, for some reason or other, had been taken prisoner by the Fairies – who were really very malicious Little Folk – and who did not want a like fate to befall the adventurous page-boy; but the little fellow did not know this.

He had once heard that if anyone walked on the wet sands, where the waves had come over them, the Fairies could not touch him, and this mysterious sentence brought the saying into his mind.

So he turned, and dashed panting down to the shore. His feet sank in the dry sand, his breath came in little gasps, and he felt as if he must give up the struggle; but he persevered, and at last, just as the foremost Fairies were about to lay hands on him, he jumped across the water-mark on to the firm, wet sand, from which the waves had just receded, and then he knew that he was safe.

For the Little Folk could go no step further, but stood on the dry sand uttering cries of rage and disappointment, while the triumphant page-boy ran safely along the shore, his precious cup in his arms, and climbed lightly up the steps in the rock and disappeared through the postern. And for many years after, long after the little page-boy had grown up and become a stately butler, who trained other little page-boys to follow in his footsteps, the beautiful cup remained in the Castle as a witness of his adventure.

The Elfin Knight

THERE IS A LONE MOOR in Scotland, which, in times past, was said to be haunted by an Elfin Knight. This Knight was only seen at rare intervals, once in every seven years or so, but the fear of him lay on all the country round, for every now and then someone would set out to cross the moor and would never be heard of again.

And although men might search every inch of the ground, no trace of him would be found, and with a thrill of horror the searching party would go home again, shaking their heads and whispering to one another that he had fallen into the hands of the dreaded Knight.

So, as a rule, the moor was deserted, for nobody dare pass that way, much less live there; and by and by it became the haunt of all sorts of wild animals, which made their lairs there, as they found that they never were disturbed by mortal huntsmen.

Now in that same region lived two young earls, Earl St Clair and Earl Gregory, who were such friends that they rode, and hunted, and fought together, if need be.

And as they were both very fond of the chase, Earl Gregory suggested one day that they should go a-hunting on the haunted moor, in spite of the Elfin King.

"Certes, I hardly believe in him at all," cried the young man, with a laugh. "Methinks 'tis but an old wife's tale to frighten the bairns withal, lest they go straying amongst the heather and lose themselves. And 'tis pity that such fine sport should be lost because we – two bearded men – pay heed to such gossip."

But Earl St Clair looked grave. "'Tis ill meddling with unchancy things," he answered, "and 'tis no bairn's tale that travellers have set out to cross that moor who have vanished bodily, and never mair been heard of; but it is, as thou sayest, a pity that so much good sport be lost, all because an Elfin Knight choosest to claim the land as his, and make us mortals pay toll for the privilege of planting a foot upon it.

"I have heard tell, however, that one is safe from any power that the Knight may have if one wearest the Sign of the Blessed Trinity. So let us bind That on our arm and ride forth without fear."

Sir Gregory burst into a loud laugh at these words. "Dost thou think that I am one of the bairns," he said, "first to be frightened by an idle tale, and then to think that a leaf of clover will protect me? No, no, carry that Sign if thou wilt; I will trust to my good bow and arrow."

But Earl St Clair did not heed his companion's words, for he remembered how his mother had told him, when he was a little lad at her knee that whoso carried the Sign of the Blessed Trinity need never fear any spell that might be thrown over him by Warlock or Witch, Elf or Demon.

So he went out to the meadow and plucked a leaf of clover, which he bound on his arm with a silken scarf; then he mounted his horse and rode with Earl Gregory to the desolate and lonely moorland.

For some hours all went well; and in the heat of the chase the young men forgot their fears. Then suddenly both of them reined in their steeds and sat gazing in front of them with affrighted faces.

For a horseman had crossed their track, and they both would fain have known who he was and whence he came.

"By my troth, but he rideth in haste, whoever he may be," said Earl Gregory at last, "and tho' I always thought that no steed on earth could match mine for swiftness, I reckon that for every league that mine goeth, his would go seven. Let us follow him, and see from what part of the world he cometh."

"The Lord forbid that thou shouldst stir thy horse's feet to follow him," said Earl St Clair devoutly. "Why, man, 'tis the Elfin Knight! Canst thou not see that he doth not ride on the solid ground, but flieth through the air, and that, although he rideth on what seemeth a mortal steed, he is really carried by mighty pinions, which cleave the air like those of a bird? Follow him forsooth! It will be an evil day for thee when thou seekest to do that."

But Earl St Clair forgot that he carried a Talisman which his companion lacked, that enabled him to see things as they really were, while the other's eyes were holden, and he was startled and amazed when Earl Gregory said sharply, "Thy mind hath gone mad over this Elfin King. I tell thee he who passed was a goodly Knight, clad in a green vesture, and riding on a great black jennet. And because I love a gallant horseman, and would fain learn his name and degree, I will follow him till I find him, even if it be at the world's end."

And without another word he put spurs to his horse and galloped off in the direction which the mysterious stranger had taken, leaving Earl St Clair alone upon the moorland, his fingers touching the sacred Sign and his trembling lips muttering prayers for protection.

For he knew that his friend had been bewitched, and he made up his mind, brave gentleman that he was, that he would follow him to the world's end, if need be, and try to deliver him from the spell that had been cast over him.

Meanwhile Earl Gregory rode on and on, ever following in the wake of the Knight in green, over moor, and burn, and moss, till he came to the most desolate region that he had ever been in in his life; where the wind blew cold, as if from snow-fields, and where the hoar-frost lay thick and white on the withered grass at his feet.

And there, in front of him, was a sight from which mortal man might well shrink back in awe and dread. For he saw an enormous Ring marked out on the ground, inside of which the grass, instead of being withered and frozen, was lush, and rank, and green, where hundreds of shadowy Elfin figures were dancing, clad in loose transparent robes of dull blue, which seemed to curl and twist round their wearers like snaky wreaths of smoke.

These weird Goblins were shouting and singing as they danced, and waving their arms above their heads, and throwing themselves about on the ground, for all the world as if they had gone mad; and when they saw Earl Gregory halt on his horse just outside the Ring they beckoned to him with their skinny fingers.

"Come hither, come hither," they shouted; "come tread a measure with us, and afterwards we will drink to thee out of our Monarch's loving cup."

And, strange as it may seem, the spell that had been cast over the young Earl was so powerful that, in spite of his fear, he felt that he must obey the eldrich summons, and he threw his bridle on his horse's neck and prepared to join them.

But just then an old and grizzled Goblin stepped out from among his companions and approached him.

Apparently he dare not leave the charmed Circle, for he stopped at the edge of it; then, stooping down and pretending to pick up something, he whispered in a hoarse whisper:

"I know not whom thou art, nor from whence thou comest, Sir Knight, but if thou lovest thy life, see to it that thou comest not within this Ring, nor joinest with us in our feast. Else wilt thou be for ever undone."

But Earl Gregory only laughed. "I vowed that I would follow the Green Knight," he replied, "and I will carry out my vow, even if the venture leadeth me close to the nethermost world."

And with these words he stepped over the edge of the Circle, right in amongst the ghostly dancers.

At his coming they shouted louder than ever, and danced more madly, and sang more lustily; then, all at once, a silence fell upon them, and they parted into two companies, leaving a way through their midst, up which they signed to the Earl to pass.

He walked through their ranks till he came to the middle of the Circle; and there, seated at a table of red marble, was the Knight whom he had come so far to seek, clad in his grass-green robes. And before him, on the table, stood a wondrous goblet, fashioned from an emerald, and set round the rim with blood-red rubies.

And this cup was filled with heather ale, which foamed up over the brim; and when the Knight saw Sir Gregory, he lifted it from the table, and handed it to him with a stately bow, and Sir Gregory, being very thirsty, drank.

And as he drank he noticed that the ale in the goblet never grew less, but ever foamed up to the edge; and for the first time his heart misgave him, and he wished that he had never set out on this strange adventure.

But, alas! the time for regrets had passed, for already a strange numbness was stealing over his limbs, and a chill pallor was creeping over his face, and before he could utter a single cry for help the goblet dropped from his nerveless fingers, and he fell down before the Elfin King like a dead man.

Then a great shout of triumph went up from all the company; for if there was one thing which filled their hearts with joy, it was to entice some unwary mortal into their Ring and throw their uncanny spell over him, so that he must needs spend long years in their company.

But soon their shouts of triumphs began to die away, and they muttered and whispered to each other with looks of something like fear on their faces.

For their keen ears heard a sound which filled their hearts with dread. It was the sound of human footsteps, which were so free and untrammelled that they knew at once that the stranger, whoever he was, was as yet untouched by any charm. And if this were so he might work them ill, and rescue their captive from them.

And what they dreaded was true; for it was the brave Earl St Clair who approached, fearless and strong because of the Holy Sign he bore.

And as soon as he saw the charmed Ring and the eldrich dancers, he was about to step over its magic border, when the little grizzled Goblin who had whispered to Earl Gregory, came and whispered to him also.

"Alas! alas!" he exclaimed, with a look of sorrow on his wrinkled face, "hast thou come, as thy companion came, to pay thy toll of years to the Elfin King? Oh! if thou hast wife or child behind thee, I beseech thee, by all that thou holdest sacred, to turn back ere it be too late."

"Who art thou, and from whence hast thou come?" asked the Earl, looking kindly down at the little creature in front of him.

"I came from the country that thou hast come from," wailed the Goblin. "For I was once a mortal man, even as thou. But I set out over the enchanted moor, and the Elfin King appeared in the guise of a beauteous Knight, and he looked so brave, and noble, and generous that I followed him hither, and drank of his heather ale, and now I am doomed to bide here till seven long years be spent.

"As for thy friend, Sir Earl, he, too, hath drunk of the accursed draught, and he now lieth as dead at our lawful Monarch's feet. He will wake up, 'tis true, but it will be in such a guise as I wear, and to the bondage with which I am bound."

"Is there naught that I can do to rescue him!" cried Earl St Clair eagerly, "ere he taketh on him the Elfin shape? I have no fear of the spell of his cruel captor, for I bear the Sign of One Who is stronger than he. Speak speedily, little man, for time presseth."

"There is something that thou couldst do, Sir Earl," whispered the Goblin, "but to essay it were a desperate attempt. For if thou failest, then could not even the Power of the Blessed Sign save thee."

"And what is that?" asked the Earl impatiently.

"Thou must remain motionless," answered the old man, "in the cold and frost till dawn break and the hour cometh when they sing Matins in the Holy Church. Then must thou walk slowly nine times round the edge of the enchanted Circle, and after that thou must walk boldly across it to the red marble table where sits the Elfin King. On it thou wilt see an emerald goblet studded with rubies and filled with heather ale. That must thou secure and carry away; but whilst thou art doing so let no word cross thy lips. For this enchanted ground whereon we dance may look solid to mortal eyes, but in reality it is not so. 'Tis but a quaking bog, and under it is a great lake, wherein dwelleth a fearsome Monster, and if thou so much as utter a word while thy foot resteth upon it, thou wilt fall through the bog and perish in the waters beneath."

So saying the Grisly Goblin stepped back among his companions, leaving Earl St Clair standing alone on the outskirts of the charmed Ring.

There he waited, shivering with cold, through the long, dark hours, till the grey dawn began to break over the hill tops, and, with its coming, the Elfin forms before him seemed to dwindle and fade away.

And at the hour when the sound of the Matin Bell came softly pealing from across the moor, he began his solemn walk. Round and round the Ring he paced, keeping steadily on his way, although loud murmurs of anger, like distant thunder, rose from the Elfin Shades, and even the very ground seemed to heave and quiver, as if it would shake this bold intruder from its surface.

But through the power of the Blessed Sign on his arm Earl St Clair went on unhurt.

When he had finished pacing round the Ring he stepped boldly on to the enchanted ground, and walked across it; and what was his astonishment to find that all the ghostly Elves and Goblins whom he had seen, were lying frozen into tiny blocks of ice, so that he was sore put to it to walk amongst them without treading upon them.

And as he approached the marble table the very hairs rose on his head at the sight of the Elfin King sitting behind it, stiff and stark like his followers; while in front of him lay the form of Earl Gregory, who had shared the same fate.

Nothing stirred, save two coal-black ravens, who sat, one on each side of the table, as if to guard the emerald goblet, flapping their wings, and croaking hoarsely.

When Earl St Clair lifted the precious cup, they rose in the air and circled round his head, screaming with rage, and threatening to dash it from his hands with their claws; while the frozen Elves, and even their mighty King himself stirred in their sleep, and half sat up, as if to lay hands on this presumptuous intruder. But the Power of the Holy Sign restrained them, else had Earl St Clair been foiled in his quest.

As he retraced his steps, awesome and terrible were the sounds that he heard around him. The ravens shrieked, and the frozen Goblins screamed; and up from the hidden lake below came the sound of the deep breathing of the awful Monster who was lurking there, eager for prey.

But the brave Earl heeded none of these things, but kept steadily onwards, trusting in the Might of the Sign he bore. And it carried him safely through all the dangers; and just as the sound of the Matin Bell was dying away in the morning air he stepped on to solid ground once more, and flung the enchanted goblet from him.

And lo! every one of the frozen Elves vanished, along with their King and his marble table, and nothing was left on the rank green grass save Earl Gregory, who slowly woke from his enchanted slumber, and stretched himself, and stood up, shaking in every limb. He gazed vaguely round him, as if he scarce remembered where he was.

And when, after Earl St Clair had run to him and had held him in his arms till his senses returned and the warm blood coursed through his veins, the two friends returned to the spot where Earl St Clair had thrown down the wondrous goblet, they found nothing but a piece of rough grey whinstone, with a drop of dew hidden in a little crevice which was hollowed in its side.

The Witch of Fife

IN THE KINGDOM OF FIFE, in the days of long ago, there lived an old man and his wife. The old man was a douce, quiet body, but the old woman was lightsome and flighty, and some of the neighbours were wont to look at her askance, and whisper to each other that they sorely feared that she was a Witch.

And her husband was afraid of it, too, for she had a curious habit of disappearing in the gloaming and staying out all night; and when she returned in the morning she looked quite white and tired, as if she had been travelling far, or working hard.

He used to try and watch her carefully, in order to find out where she went, or what she did, but he never managed to do so, for she always slipped out of the door when he was not looking, and before he could reach it to follow her, she had vanished utterly.

At last, one day, when he could stand the uncertainty no longer, he asked her to tell him straight out whether she were a Witch or no. And his blood ran cold when, without the slightest hesitation, she answered that she was; and if he would promise not to let anyone know, the next time that she went on one of her midnight expeditions she would tell him all about it.

The Goodman promised; for it seemed to him just as well that he should know all about his wife's cantrips.

He had not long to wait before he heard of them. For the very next week the moon was new, which is, as everybody knows, the time of all others when Witches like to stir abroad; and on the first night of the new moon his wife vanished. Nor did she return till daybreak next morning.

And when he asked her where she had been, she told him, in great glee, how she and four like-minded companions had met at the old Kirk on the moor and had mounted branches of the green bay tree and stalks of hemlock, which had instantly changed into horses, and how they had ridden, swift as the wind, over the country, hunting the foxes, and the weasels, and the owls; and how at last they had swam the Forth and come to the top of Bell Lomond. And how there they had dismounted from their horses, and drunk beer that had been brewed in no earthly brewery, out of horn cups that had been fashioned by no mortal hands.

And how, after that, a wee, wee man had jumped up from under a great mossy stone, with a tiny set of bagpipes under his arm, and how he had piped such wonderful music, that, at the sound of it, the very trouts jumped out of the Loch below, and the stoats crept out of their holes, and the corby crows and the herons came and sat on the trees in the darkness, to listen. And how all the Witches danced until they were so weary that, when the time came for them to mount their steeds again, if they would be home before cock-crow, they could scarce sit on them for fatigue.

The Goodman listened to this long story in silence, shaking his head meanwhile, and, when it was finished, all that he answered was: "And what the better are ye for all your dancing? Ye'd have been a deal more comfortable at home."

At the next new moon the old wife went off again for the night; and when she returned in the morning she told her husband how, on this occasion, she and her friends had taken cockle-shells for boats, and had sailed away over the stormy sea till they reached Norway. And there they had mounted invisible horses of wind, and had ridden and ridden, over mountains and glens, and glaciers, till they reached the land of the Lapps lying under its mantle of snow.

And here all the Elves, and Fairies, and Mermaids of the North were holding festival with Warlocks, and Brownies, and Pixies, and even the Phantom Hunters themselves, who are never looked upon by mortal eyes. And the Witches from Fife held festival with them, and danced, and feasted, and sang with them, and, what was of more consequence, they learned from them certain wonderful words, which, when they uttered them, would bear them through the air, and would undo all bolts and bars, and so gain them admittance to any place soever where they wanted to be. And after that they had come home again, delighted with the knowledge which they had acquired.

"What took ye to siccan a land as that?" asked the old man, with a contemptuous grunt. "Ye would hae been a sight warmer in your bed."

But when his wife returned from her next adventure, he showed a little more interest in her doings.

For she told him how she and her friends had met in the cottage of one of their number, and how, having heard that the Lord Bishop of Carlisle had some very rare wine in his cellar, they had placed their feet on the crook from which the pot hung, and had pronounced the magic words which they had learned from the Elves of Lappland. And, lo and behold! they flew up the chimney like whiffs of smoke, and sailed through the air like little wreathes of cloud, and in less time than it takes to tell they landed at the Bishop's Palace at Carlisle.

And the bolts and the bars flew loose before them, and they went down to his cellar and sampled his wine, and were back in Fife, fine, sober, old women by cock-crow.

When he heard this, the old man started from his chair in right earnest, for he loved good wine above all things, and it was but seldom that it came his way.

"By my troth, but thou art a wife to be proud of!" he cried. "Tell me the words, Woman! and I will e'en go and sample his Lordship's wine for myself."

But the Goodwife shook her head. "Na, na! I cannot do that," she said, "for if I did, an' ye telled it over again, 'twould turn the whole world upside down. For everybody would be leaving their own lawful work, and flying about the world after other folk's business and other folk's dainties. So just bide content, Goodman. Ye get on fine with the knowledge ye already possess."

And although the old man tried to persuade her with all the soft words he could think of, she would not tell him her secret.

But he was a sly old man, and the thought of the Bishop's wine gave him no rest. So night after night he went and hid in the old woman's cottage, in the hope that his wife and her friends would meet there; and although for a long time it was all in vain, at last his trouble was rewarded. For one evening the whole five old women assembled, and in low tones and with chuckles of laughter they recounted all that had befallen them in Lappland. Then, running to the fireplace, they, one after another, climbed on a chair and put their feet on the sooty crook. Then they repeated the magic words, and, hey, presto! they were up the lum and away before the old man could draw his breath.

"I can do that, too," he said to himself; and he crawled out of his hiding-place and ran to the fire. He put his foot on the crook and repeated the words, and up the chimney he went, and flew through the air after his wife and her companions, as if he had been a Warlock born.

And, as Witches are not in the habit of looking over their shoulders, they never noticed that he was following them, until they reached the Bishop's Palace and went down into his cellar, then, when they found that he was among them, they were not too well pleased.

However, there was no help for it, and they settled down to enjoy themselves. They tapped this cask of wine, and they tapped that, drinking a little of each, but not too much; for they were cautious old women, and they knew that if they wanted to get home before cock-crow it behoved them to keep their heads clear.

But the old man was not so wise, for he sipped, and he sipped, until at last he became quite drowsy, and lay down on the floor and fell fast asleep.

And his wife, seeing this, thought that she would teach him a lesson not to be so curious in the future. So, when she and her four friends thought that it was time to be gone, she departed without waking him.

He slept peacefully for some hours, until two of the Bishop's servants, coming down to the cellar to draw wine for their Master's table, almost fell over him in the darkness. Greatly astonished at his presence there, for the cellar door was fast locked, they dragged him up to the light and shook him, and cuffed him, and asked him how he came to be there.

And the poor old man was so confused at being awakened in this rough way, and his head seemed to whirl round so fast, that all he could stammer out was, "that he came from Fife, and that he had travelled on the midnight wind."

As soon as they heard that, the men servants cried out that he was a Warlock, and they dragged him before the Bishop, and, as Bishops in those days had a holy horror of Warlocks and Witches, he ordered him to be burned alive.

When the sentence was pronounced, you may be very sure that the poor old man wished with all his heart that he had stayed quietly at home in bed, and never hankered after the Bishop's wine.

But it was too late to wish that now, for the servants dragged him out into the courtyard, and put a chain round his waist, and fastened it to a great iron stake, and they piled faggots of wood round his feet and set them alight.

As the first tiny little tongue of flame crept up, the poor old man thought that his last hour had come. But when he thought that, he forgot completely that his wife was a Witch.

For, just as the little tongue of flame began to singe his breeches, there was a swish and a flutter in the air, and a great Grey Bird, with outstretched wings, appeared in the sky, and swooped down suddenly, and perched for a moment on the old man's shoulder.

And in this Grey Bird's mouth was a little red pirnie, which, to everyone's amazement, it popped on to the prisoner's head. Then it gave one fierce croak, and flew away again, but to the old man's ears that croak was the sweetest music that he had ever heard.

For to him it was the croak of no earthly bird, but the voice of his wife whispering words of magic to him. And when he heard them he jumped for joy, for he knew that they were words of deliverance, and he shouted them aloud, and his chains fell off, and he mounted in the air – up and up – while the onlookers watched him in awestruck silence.

He flew right away to the Kingdom of Fife, without as much as saying good-bye to them; and when he found himself once more safely at home, you may be very sure that he never tried to find out his wife's secrets again, but left her alone to her own devices.

Farquhar MacNeill

ONCE UPON A TIME there was a young man named Farquhar MacNeill. He had just gone to a new situation, and the very first night after he went to it his mistress asked him if he would go over the hill to the house of a neighbour and borrow a sieve, for her own was all in holes, and she wanted to sift some meal.

Farquhar agreed to do so, for he was a willing lad, and he set out at once upon his errand, after the farmer's wife had pointed out to him the path that he was to follow, and told him that he would have no difficulty in finding the house, even though it was strange to him, for he would be sure to see the light in the window.

He had not gone very far, however, before he saw what he took to be the light from a cottage window on his left hand, some distance from the path, and, forgetting his Mistress's instructions that he was to follow the path right over the hill, he left it, and walked towards the light.

It seemed to him that he had almost reached it when his foot tripped, and he fell down, down, down, into a Fairy Parlour, far under the ground.

It was full of Fairies, who were engaged in different occupations.

Close by the door, or rather the hole down which he had so unceremoniously tumbled, two little elderly women, in black aprons and white mutches, were busily engaged in grinding corn between two flat millstones. Other two Fairies, younger women, in blue print gowns and white kerchiefs, were gathering up the freshly ground meal, and baking it into bannocks, which they were toasting on a girdle over a peat fire, which was burning slowly in a corner.

In the centre of the large apartment a great troop of Fairies, Elves, and Sprites were dancing reels as hard as they could to the music of a tiny set of bagpipes which were being played by a brown-faced Gnome, who sat on a ledge of rock far above their heads.

They all stopped their various employments when Farquhar came suddenly down in their midst, and looked at him in alarm; but when they saw that he was not hurt, they bowed gravely and bade him be seated. Then they went on with their work and with their play as if nothing had happened.

But Farquhar, being very fond of dancing, and being in no wise anxious to be seated, thought that he would like to have a reel first, so he asked the Fairies if he might join them. And they, although they looked surprised at his request, allowed him to do so, and in a few minutes the young man was dancing away as gaily as any of them.

And as he danced a strange change came over him. He forgot his errand, he forgot his home, he forgot everything that had ever happened to him, he only knew that he wanted to remain with the Fairies all the rest of his life.

And he did remain with them – for a magic spell had been cast over him, and he became like one of themselves, and could come and go at nights without being seen, and could sip the dew from the grass and honey from the flowers as daintily and noiselessly as if he had been a Fairy born.

Time passed by, and one night he and a band of merry companions set out for a long journey through the air. They started early, for they intended to pay a visit to the Man in the Moon and be back again before cock-crow.

All would have gone well if Farquhar had only looked where he was going, but he did not, being deeply engaged in making love to a young Fairy Maiden by his side, so he never saw a cottage that was standing right in his way, till he struck against the chimney and stuck fast in the thatch.

His companions sped merrily on, not noticing what had befallen him, and he was left to disentangle himself as best he could.

As he was doing so he chanced to glance down the wide chimney, and in the cottage kitchen he saw a comely young woman dandling a rosy-cheeked baby.

Now, when Farquhar had been in his mortal state, he had been very fond of children, and a word of blessing rose to his lips.

"God shield thee," he said, as he looked at the mother and child, little guessing what the result of his words would be.

For scarce had the Holy Name crossed his lips than the spell which had held him so long was broken, and he became as he had been before.

Instantly his thoughts flew to his friends at home, and to the new Mistress whom he had left waiting for her sieve; for he felt sure that some weeks must have elapsed since he set out to fetch it. So he made haste to go to the farm.

When he arrived in the neighbourhood everything seemed strange. There were woods where no woods used to be, and walls where no walls used to be. To his amazement, he could not find his way to the farm, and, worst of all, in the place where he expected to find his father's house he found nothing but a crop of rank green nettles.

In great distress he looked about for someone to tell him what it all meant, and at last he found an old man thatching the roof of a cottage.

This old man was so thin and grey that at first Farquhar took him for a patch of mist, but as he went nearer he saw that he was a human being, and, going close up to the wall and shouting with all his might, for he felt sure that such an ancient man would be deaf, he asked him if he could tell him where his friends had gone to, and what had happened to his father's dwelling.

The old man listened, then he shook his head. "I never heard of him," he answered slowly; "but perhaps my father might be able to tell you."

"Your father!" said Farquhar, in great surprise. "Is it possible that your father is alive?"

"Aye he is," answered the old man, with a little laugh. "If you go into the house you'll find him sitting in the arm-chair by the fire."

Farquhar did as he was bid, and on entering the cottage found another old man, who was so thin and withered and bent that he looked as if he must at least be a hundred years old. He was feebly twisting ropes to bind the thatch on the roof.

"Can ye tell me aught of my friends, or where my father's cottage is?" asked Farquhar again, hardly expecting that this second old man would be able to answer him.

"I cannot," mumbled this ancient person; "but perhaps my father can tell you."

"Your father!" exclaimed Farquhar, more astonished than ever. "But surely he must be dead long ago."

The old man shook his head with a weird grimace.

"Look there," he said, and pointed with a twisted finger, to a leathern purse, or sporran, which was hanging to one of the posts of a wooden bedstead in the corner.

Farquhar approached it, and was almost frightened out of his wits by seeing a tiny shrivelled face crowned by a red pirnie, looking over the edge of the sporran.

"Tak' him out; he'll no touch ye," chuckled the old man by the fire.

So Farquhar took the little creature out carefully between his finger and thumb, and set him on the palm of his left hand. He was so shrivelled with age that he looked just like a mummy.

"Dost know anything of my friends, or where my father's cottage is gone to?" asked Farquhar for the third time, hardly expecting to get an answer.

"They were all dead long before I was born," piped out the tiny figure. "I never saw any of them, but I have heard my father speak of them."

"Then I must be older than you!" cried Farquhar, in great dismay. And he got such a shock at the thought that his bones suddenly dissolved into dust, and he fell, a heap of grey ashes, on the floor.

The Minister and the Fairy

NOT LONG SINCE, A PIOUS clergyman was returning home, after administering spiritual consolation to a dying member of his flock. It was late of the night, and he had to pass through a good deal of uncanny land. He was, however, a good and a conscientious minister of the Gospel, and feared not all the spirits in the country.

On his reaching the end of a lake which stretched along the roadside for some distance, he was a good deal surprised at hearing the most melodious strains of music. Overcome by pleasure and curiosity, the minister coolly sat down to listen to the harmonious sounds, and try what new discoveries he could make with regard to their nature and source. He had not sat many minutes before he could distinguish the approach of the music, and also observe a light in the direction from whence it proceeded gliding across the lake towards him. Instead of taking to his heels, as any faithless wight would have done, the pastor fearlessly determined to await the issue of the phenomenon. As the light and music drew near, the clergyman could at length distinguish an object resembling a human being walking on the surface of the water, attended by a group of diminutive musicians, some of them bearing lights, and others instruments of music, from which they continued to evoke those melodious strains which first attracted his attention. The leader of the band dismissed his attendants, landed on the beach, and afforded the minister the amplest opportunities of examining his appearance. He was a little primitive-looking grey-headed man, clad in the most grotesque habit the clergyman had ever seen, and such as led him at once to suspect his real character. He walked up to the minister, whom he saluted with great grace, offering an apology for his intrusion. The pastor returned his compliments, and, without further explanation, invited the mysterious stranger to sit down by his side. The invitation was complied with, upon which the minister proposed the following question: – "Who art thou, stranger, and from whence?"

To this question the fairy, with downcast eye, replied that he was one of those sometimes called Doane Shee, or men of peace, or good men, though the reverse of this title was a more fit appellation for them. Originally angelic in his nature and attributes, and once a sharer of the indescribable joys of the regions of light, he was seduced by Satan to join him in his mad conspiracies; and, as a punishment for his transgression, he was cast down from those regions of bliss, and was now doomed, along with millions of fellow-sufferers, to wander through seas and mountains, until the coming of the Great Day. What their fate would be then they could not divine, but they apprehended the worst. "And," continued he, turning to the minister, with great anxiety, "the object of my present intrusion on you is to learn your opinion, as an eminent divine, as to our final condition on that dreadful day." Here the venerable pastor entered upon a long conversation with the fairy, touching the principles of faith and repentance. Receiving rather unsatisfactory answers to his questions, the minister desired the "sheech" to repeat after him the Paternoster, in attempting to do which, it was not a little remarkable that he could not repeat the word "art," but said "wert," in heaven. Inferring from every circumstance that their fate was extremely precarious, the minister resolved not to puff the fairies up with presumptuous, and, perhaps, groundless expectations. Accordingly, addressing himself to the unhappy fairy, who was all anxiety to know the nature of his sentiments, the reverend gentleman told him that he could not take it upon him to give them any hopes of pardon, as their crime was of so deep a hue as scarcely to admit of it. On this the unhappy fairy uttered a shriek of despair, plunged headlong into the loch, and the minister resumed his course to his home.

Habetrot the Spinstress

I N BYGONE DAYS, in an old farmhouse which stood by a river, there lived a beautiful girl called Maisie. She was tall and straight, with auburn hair and blue eyes, and she was the prettiest girl in all the valley. And one would have thought that she would have been the pride of her mother's heart.

But, instead of this, her mother used to sigh and shake her head whenever she looked at her. And why?

Because, in those days, all men were sensible; and instead of looking out for pretty girls to be their wives, they looked out for girls who could cook and spin, and who gave promise of becoming notable housewives.

Maisie's mother had been an industrious spinster; but, alas! to her sore grief and disappointment, her daughter did not take after her.

The girl loved to be out of doors, chasing butterflies and plucking wild flowers, far better than sitting at her spinning-wheel. So when her mother saw one after another of Maisie's companions, who were not nearly so pretty as she was, getting rich husbands, she sighed and said:

"Woe's me, child, for methinks no brave wooer will ever pause at our door while they see thee so idle and thoughtless." But Maisie only laughed.

At last her mother grew really angry, and one bright Spring morning she laid down three heads of lint on the table, saying sharply, "I will have no more of this dallying. People will say that it is my blame that no wooer comes to seek thee. I cannot have thee left on my hands to be laughed at, as the idle maid who would not marry. So now thou must work; and if thou hast not these heads of lint spun into seven hanks of thread in three days, I will e'en speak to the Mother at St Mary's Convent, and thou wilt go there and learn to be a nun."

Now, though Maisie was an idle girl, she had no wish to be shut up in a nunnery; so she tried not to think of the sunshine outside, but sat down soberly with her distaff.

But, alas! she was so little accustomed to work that she made but slow progress; and although she sat at the spinning-wheel all day, and never once went out of doors, she found at night that she had only spun half a hank of yarn.

The next day it was even worse, for her arms ached so much she could only work very slowly. That night she cried herself to sleep; and next morning, seeing that it was quite hopeless to expect to get her task finished, she threw down her distaff in despair, and ran out of doors.

Near the house was a deep dell, through which ran a tiny stream. Maisie loved this dell, the flowers grew so abundantly there.

This morning she ran down to the edge of the stream, and seated herself on a large stone. It was a glorious morning, the hazel trees were newly covered with leaves, and the branches nodded over her head, and showed like delicate tracery against the blue sky. The primroses and sweet-scented violets peeped out from among the grass, and a little water wagtail came and perched on a stone in the middle of the stream, and bobbed up and down, till it seemed as if he were nodding to Maisie, and as if he were trying to say to her, "Never mind, cheer up."

But the poor girl was in no mood that morning to enjoy the flowers and the birds. Instead of watching them, as she generally did, she hid her face in her hands, and wondered what would become of her. She rocked herself to and fro, as she thought how terrible it would be if her mother fulfilled her threat and shut her up in the Convent of St Mary, with the grave, solemn-faced sisters, who seemed as if they had completely forgotten what it was like to be young, and run about in the sunshine, and laugh, and pick the fresh Spring flowers.

"Oh, I could not do it, I could not do it," she cried at last. "It would kill me to be a nun."

"And who wants to make a pretty wench like thee into a nun?" asked a queer, cracked voice quite close to her.

Maisie jumped up, and stood staring in front of her as if she had been moonstruck. For, just across the stream from where she had been sitting, there was a curious boulder, with a round hole in the middle of it – for all the world like a big apple with the core taken out.

Maisie knew it well; she had often sat upon it, and wondered how the funny hole came to be there.

It was no wonder that she stared, for, seated on this stone, was the queerest little old woman that she had ever seen in her life. Indeed, had it not been for her silver hair, and the white mutch with the big frill that she wore on her head, Maisie would have taken her for a little girl, she wore such a very short skirt, only reaching down to her knees.

Her face, inside the frill of her cap, was round, and her cheeks were rosy, and she had little black eyes, which twinkled merrily as she looked at the startled maiden. On her shoulders was a black and white checked shawl, and on her legs, which she dangled over the edge of the boulder, she wore black silk stockings and the neatest little shoes, with great silver buckles.

In fact, she would have been quite a pretty old lady had it not been for her lips, which were very long and very thick, and made her look quite ugly in spite of her rosy cheeks and black eyes. Maisie stood and looked at her for such a long time in silence that she repeated her question.

"And who wants to make a pretty wench like thee into a nun? More likely that some gallant gentleman should want to make a bride of thee."

"Oh, no," answered Maisie, "my mother says no gentleman would look at me because I cannot spin."

"Nonsense," said the tiny woman. "Spinning is all very well for old folks like me – my lips, as thou seest, are long and ugly because I have spun so much, for I always wet my fingers with them, the easier to draw the thread from the distaff. No, no, take care of thy beauty, child; do not waste it over the spinning-wheel, nor yet in a nunnery."

"If my mother only thought as thou dost," replied the girl sadly; and, encouraged by the old woman's kindly face, she told her the whole story.

"Well," said the old Dame, "I do not like to see pretty girls weep; what if I were able to help thee, and spin the lint for thee?"

Maisie thought that this offer was too good to be true; but her new friend bade her run home and fetch the lint; and I need not tell you that she required no second bidding.

When she returned she handed the bundle to the little lady, and was about to ask her where she should meet her in order to get the thread from her when it was spun, when a sudden noise behind her made her look round.

She saw nothing; but what was her horror and surprise when she turned back again, to find that the old woman had vanished entirely, lint and all.

She rubbed her eyes, and looked all round, but she was nowhere to be seen. The girl was utterly bewildered. She wondered if she could have been dreaming, but no that could not be, there were her footprints leading up the bank and down again, where she had gone for the lint, and brought it back, and there was the mark of her foot, wet with dew, on a stone in the middle of the stream, where she had stood when she had handed the lint up to the mysterious little stranger.

What was she to do now? What would her mother say when, in addition to not having finished the task that had been given her, she had to confess to having lost the greater part of the lint also? She ran up and down the little dell, hunting amongst the bushes, and peeping into every nook and cranny of the bank where the little old woman might have hidden herself. It was all in vain; and at last, tired out with the search, she sat down on the stone once more, and presently fell fast asleep.

When she awoke it was evening. The sun had set, and the yellow glow on the western horizon was fast giving place to the silvery light of the moon. She was sitting thinking of the curious events of the day, and gazing at the great boulder opposite, when it seemed to her as if a distant murmur of voices came from it.

With one bound she crossed the stream, and clambered on to the stone. She was right.

Someone was talking underneath it, far down in the ground. She put her ear close to the stone, and listened.

The voice of the queer little old woman came up through the hole. "Ho, ho, my pretty little wench little knows that my name is Habetrot."

Full of curiosity, Maisie put her eye to the opening, and the strangest sight that she had ever seen met her gaze. She seemed to be looking through a telescope into a wonderful little valley. The trees there were brighter and greener than any that she had ever seen before and there were beautiful flowers, quite different from the flowers that grew in her country. The little valley was carpeted with the most exquisite moss, and up and down it walked her tiny friend, busily engaged in spinning.

She was not alone, for round her were a circle of other little old women, who were seated on large white stones, and they were all spinning away as fast as they could.

Occasionally one would look up, and then Maisie saw that they all seemed to have the same long, thick lips that her friend had. She really felt very sorry, as they all looked exceedingly kind, and might have been pretty had it not been for this defect.

One of the Spinstresses sat by herself, and was engaged in winding the thread, which the others had spun, into hanks. Maisie did not think that this little lady looked so nice as the others. She was dressed entirely in grey, and had a big hooked nose, and great horn spectacles. She seemed to be called Slantlie Mab, for Maisie heard Habetrot address her by that name, telling her to make haste and tie up all the thread, for it was getting late, and it was time that the young girl had it to carry home to her mother.

Maisie did not quite know what to do, or how she was to get the thread, for she did not like to shout down the hole in case the queer little old woman should be angry at being watched.

However, Habetrot, as she had called herself, suddenly appeared on the path beside her, with the hanks of thread in her hand.

"Oh, thank you, thank you," cried Maisie. "What can I do to show you how thankful I am?"

"Nothing," answered the Fairy. "For I do not work for reward. Only do not tell your mother who span the thread for thee."

It was now late, and Maisie lost no time in running home with the precious thread upon her shoulder. When she walked into the kitchen she found that her mother had gone to bed. She seemed to have had a busy day, for there, hanging up in the wide chimney, in order to dry, were seven large black puddings.

The fire was low, but bright and clear; and the sight of it and the sight of the puddings suggested to Maisie that she was very hungry, and that fried black puddings were very good.

Flinging the thread down on the table, she hastily pulled off her shoes, so as not to make a noise and awake her mother; and, getting down the frying-pan from the wall, she took one of the black puddings from the chimney, and fried it, and ate it.

Still she felt hungry, so she took another, and then another, till they were all gone. Then she crept upstairs to her little bed and fell fast asleep.

Next morning her mother came downstairs before Maisie was awake. In fact, she had not been able to sleep much for thinking of her daughter's careless ways, and had been sorrowfully making up her mind that she must lose no time in speaking to the Abbess of St Mary's about this idle girl of hers.

What was her surprise to see on the table the seven beautiful hanks of thread, while, on going to the chimney to take down a black pudding to fry for breakfast, she found that every one of them had been eaten. She did not know whether to laugh for joy that her daughter had been so industrious, or to cry for vexation because all her lovely black puddings – which she had expected would last for a week at least – were gone. In her bewilderment she sang out:

> *"My daughter's spun se'en, se'en, se'en,*
> *My daughter's eaten se'en, se'en, se'en,*
> *And all before daylight."*

Now I forgot to tell you that, about half a mile from where the old farmhouse stood, there was a beautiful Castle, where a very rich young nobleman lived. He was both good and brave, as well as rich; and all the mothers who had pretty daughters used to wish that he would come their way, some day, and fall in love with one of them. But he had never done so, and everyone said, "He is too grand to marry any country girl. One day he will go away to London Town and marry a Duke's daughter."

Well, this fine spring morning it chanced that this young nobleman's favourite horse had lost a shoe, and he was so afraid that any of the grooms might ride it along the hard road, and not on the soft grass at the side, that he said that he would take it to the smithy himself.

So it happened that he was riding along by Maisie's garden gate as her mother came into the garden singing these strange lines.

He stopped his horse, and said good-naturedly, "Good day, Madam; and may I ask why you sing such a strange song?"

Maisie's mother made no answer, but turned and walked into the house; and the young nobleman, being very anxious to know what it all meant, hung his bridle over the garden gate, and followed her.

She pointed to the seven hanks of thread lying on the table, and said, "This hath my daughter done before breakfast."

Then the young man asked to see the Maiden who was so industrious, and her mother went and pulled Maisie from behind the door, where she had hidden herself when the stranger came in; for she had come downstairs while her mother was in the garden.

She looked so lovely in her fresh morning gown of blue gingham, with her auburn hair curling softly round her brow, and her face all over blushes at the sight of such a gallant young man, that he quite lost his heart, and fell in love with her on the spot.

"Ah," said he, "my dear mother always told me to try and find a wife who was both pretty and useful, and I have succeeded beyond my expectations. Do not let our marriage, I pray thee, good Dame, be too long deferred."

Maisie's mother was overjoyed, as you may imagine, at this piece of unexpected good fortune, and busied herself in getting everything ready for the wedding; but Maisie herself was a little perplexed.

She was afraid that she would be expected to spin a great deal when she was married and lived at the Castle, and if that were so, her husband was sure to find out that she was not really such a good spinstress as he thought she was.

In her trouble she went down, the night before her wedding, to the great boulder by the stream in the glen, and, climbing up on it, she laid her head against the stone, and called softly down the hole, "Habetrot, dear Habetrot."

The little old woman soon appeared, and, with twinkling eyes, asked her what was troubling her so much just when she should have been so happy. And Maisie told her.

"Trouble not thy pretty head about that," answered the Fairy, "but come here with thy bridegroom next week, when the moon is full, and I warrant that he will never ask thee to sit at a spinning-wheel again."

Accordingly, after all the wedding festivities were over and the couple had settled down at the Castle, on the appointed evening Maisie suggested to her husband that they should take a walk together in the moonlight.

She was very anxious to see what the little Fairy would do to help her; for that very day he had been showing her all over her new home, and he had pointed out to her the beautiful new spinning-wheel made of ebony, which had belonged to his mother, saying proudly, "To-morrow, little one, I shall bring some lint from the town, and then the maids will see what clever little fingers my wife has."

Maisie had blushed as red as a rose as she bent over the lovely wheel, and then felt quite sick, as she wondered whatever she would do if Habetrot did not help her.

So on this particular evening, after they had walked in the garden, she said that she should like to go down to the little dell and see how the stream looked by moonlight. So to the dell they went.

As soon as they came to the boulder Maisie put her head against it and whispered, "Habetrot, dear Habetrot"; and in an instant the little old woman appeared.

She bowed in a stately way, as if they were both strangers to her, and said, "Welcome, Sir and Madam, to the Spinsters' Dell." And then she tapped on the root of a great oak tree with a tiny wand which she held in her hand, and a green door, which Maisie never remembered having noticed before, flew open, and they followed the Fairy through it into the other valley which Maisie had seen through the hole in the great stone.

All the little old women were sitting on their white chucky stones busy at work, only they seemed far uglier than they had seemed at first; and Maisie noticed that the reason for this was, that, instead of wearing red skirts and white mutches as they had done before, they now wore caps and dresses of dull grey, and instead of looking happy, they all seemed to be trying who could look most miserable, and who could push out their long lips furthest, as they wet their fingers to draw the thread from their distaffs.

"Save us and help us! What a lot of hideous old witches," exclaimed her husband. "Whatever could this funny old woman mean by bringing a pretty child like thee to look at them? Thou wilt dream of them for a week and a day. Just look at their lips"; and, pushing Maisie behind him, he went up to one of them and asked her what had made her mouth grow so ugly.

She tried to tell him, but all the sound that he could hear was something that sounded like spin-n-n.

He asked another one, and her answer sounded like this: span-n-n. He tried a third, and hers sounded like spun-n-n.

He seized Maisie by the hand and hurried her through the green door. "By my troth," he said, "my mother's spinning-wheel may turn to gold ere I let thee touch it, if this is what spinning leads to. Rather than that thy pretty face should be spoilt, the linen chests at the Castle may get empty, and remain so for ever!"

So it came to pass that Maisie could be out of doors all day wandering about with her husband, and laughing and singing to her heart's content. And whenever there was lint at the Castle to be spun, it was carried down to the big boulder in the dell and left there, and Habetrot and her companions spun it, and there was no more trouble about the matter.

The Fairy Boy of Leith

"ABOUT FIFTEEN YEARS SINCE, having business that detained me for some time at Leith, which is near Edinburgh, in the kingdom of Scotland, I often met some of my acquaintance at a certain house there, where we used to drink a glass of wine for our refection. The woman which kept the house was of honest reputation among the neighbours, which made me give the more attention to what she told me one day about a fairy boy (as they called him) who lived about that town. She had given me so strange an account of him, that I desired her I might see him the first opportunity, which she promised; and not long after, passing that way, she told me there was the fairy boy, but a little before I came by; and, casting her eye into the street, said, 'Look you, sir, yonder he is, at play with those other boys'; and pointing him out to me, I went, and by smooth words, and a piece of money, got him

to come into the house with me; where, in the presence of divers people, I demanded of him several astrological questions, which he answered with great subtlety; and, through all his discourse, carried it with a cunning much above his years, which seemed not to exceed ten or eleven.

"He seemed to make a motion like drumming upon the table with his fingers, upon which I asked him whether he could beat a drum? To which he replied, 'Yes, sir, as well as any man in Scotland; for every Thursday night I beat all points to a sort of people that used to meet under yonder hill' (pointing to the great hill between Edinburgh and Leith). 'How, boy?' quoth I, 'what company have you there?' 'There are, sir,' said he, 'a great company both of men and women, and they are entertained with many sorts of music besides my drum; they have, besides, plenty of variety of meats and wine, and many times we are carried into France or Holland in the night, and return again, and whilst we are there, we enjoy all the pleasures the country doth afford.' I demanded of him how they got under that hill? To which he replied that there was a great pair of gates that opened to them, though they were invisible to others, and that within there were brave large rooms, as well accommodated as most in Scotland. I then asked him how I should know what he said to be true? Upon which he told me he would read my fortune, saying, I should have two wives, and that he saw the forms of them over my shoulders; and both would be very handsome women.

"The woman of the house told me that all the people in Scotland could not keep him from the rendezvous on Thursday night; upon which, by promising him some more money, I got a promise of him to meet me at the same place in the afternoon, the Thursday following, and so dismissed him at that time. The boy came again at the place and time appointed, and I had prevailed with some friends to continue with me (if possible) to prevent his moving that night. He was placed between us, and answered many questions, until, about eleven of the clock, he was got away unperceived by the company; but I, suddenly missing him, hastened to the door, and took hold of him, and so returned him into the same room. We all watched him, and, of a sudden, he was again got out of doors; I followed him close, and he made a noise in the street, as if he had been set upon, and from that time I could never see him."

SPIRITS, MONSTERS & GHOSTLY TALES

Spirits, Monsters & Ghostly Tales

Tourists today are drawn to the 'Dark Sky Park' of deepest Galloway to experience its spectacular show of stars. In past centuries, though, Scotland's nights were frightening. Huddled anxiously around their hearths, people could not but be conscious of how tiny their lives were against the vast unknown-ness of the universe.

What terrors did the darkness hold? We see that clearly in stories of the cruel kelpie, like 'The Doomed Rider', the mischievous spectres of the 'Bogle' stories, or the kind of monstrous giant we find in 'Peerifool'. But such stories could be more subtle, too, exploring the limits of what mortal love could hope to attain, as we see in the haunting tale of 'The Mermaid Wife'.

The Mermaid Wife

A STORY IS TOLD of an inhabitant of Unst, who, in walking on the sandy margin of a voe, saw a number of mermen and mermaids dancing by moonlight, and several seal-skins strewed beside them on the ground.

At his approach they immediately fled to secure their garbs, and, taking upon themselves the form of seals, plunged immediately into the sea. But as the Shetlander perceived that one skin lay close to his feet, he snatched it up, bore it swiftly away, and placed it in concealment. On returning to the shore he met the fairest damsel that was ever gazed upon by mortal eyes, lamenting the robbery, by which she had become an exile from her submarine friends, and a tenant of the upper world. Vainly she implored the restitution of her property; the man had drunk deeply of love, and was inexorable; but he offered her protection beneath his roof as his betrothed spouse. The merlady, perceiving that she must become an inhabitant of the earth, found that she could not do better than accept of the offer. This strange attachment subsisted for many years, and the couple had several children. The Shetlander's love for his merwife was unbounded, but his affection was coldly returned. The lady would often steal alone to the desert strand, and, on a signal being given, a large seal would make his appearance, with whom she would hold, in an unknown tongue, an anxious conference. Years had thus glided away, when it happened that one of the children, in the course of his play, found concealed beneath a stack of corn a seal's skin; and, delighted with the prize, he ran with it to his mother. Her eyes glistened with rapture – she gazed upon it as her own – as the means by which she could pass through the ocean that led to her native home. She burst forth into an ecstasy of joy, which was only moderated when she beheld her children, whom she was now about to leave; and, after hastily embracing them, she fled with all speed towards the sea-side. The husband immediately returned, learned the discovery that had taken place, ran to overtake his wife, but only arrived in time to see her transformation of shape completed – to see her, in the form of a seal, bound from the ledge of a rock into the sea. The large animal of the same kind with whom she had held a secret converse soon appeared, and evidently congratulated her, in the most tender manner, on her escape. But before she dived to unknown depths, she cast a parting glance at the wretched Shetlander, whose despairing looks excited in her breast a few transient feelings of commiseration.

"Farewell!" said she to him, "and may all good attend you. I loved you very well when I resided upon earth, but I always loved my first husband much better."

Peerifool

❁

THERE WAS ONCE A KING and a Queen in Rousay who had three daughters. When the young Princesses were just grown up, the King died, and the Crown passed to a distant cousin, who had always hated him, and who paid no heed to the widowed Queen and her daughters.

So they were left very badly off, and they went to live in a tiny cottage, and did all the housework themselves. They had a kailyard in front of the cottage, and a little field behind it, and they had a cow that grazed in the field, and which they fed with the cabbages that grew in the kailyard. For everyone knows that to feed cows with cabbages makes them give a larger quantity of milk.

But they soon discovered that some one was coming at night and stealing the cabbages, and, of course, this annoyed them very much. For they knew that if they had not cabbages to give to the cow, they would not have enough milk to sell.

So the eldest Princess said she would take out a three-legged stool, and wrap herself in a blanket, and sit in the kailyard all night to see if she could catch the thief. And, although it was very cold and very dark, she did so.

At first it seemed as if all her trouble would be in vain, for hour after hour passed and nothing happened. But in the small hours of the morning, just as the clock was striking two, she heard a stealthy trampling in the field behind, as if some very heavy person were trying to tread very softly, and presently a mighty Giant stepped right over the wall into the kailyard.

He carried an enormous creel on his arm, and a large, sharp knife in his hand; and he began to cut the cabbages, and to throw them into the creel as fast as he could.

Now the Princess was no coward, so, although she had not expected to face a Giant, she gathered up her courage, and cried out sharply, "Who gave thee liberty to cut our cabbages? Leave off this minute, and go away."

The Giant paid no heed, but went on steadily with what he was doing.

"Dost thou not hear me?" cried the girl indignantly; for she was the Princess Royal, and had always been accustomed to be obeyed.

"If thou be not quiet I will take thee too," said the Giant grimly, pressing the cabbages down into the creel.

"I should like to see thee try," retorted the Princess, rising from her stool and stamping her foot; for she felt so angry that she forgot for a moment that she was only a weak maiden and he was a great and powerful Giant.

And, as if to show her how strong he was, he seized her by her arm and her leg, and put her in his creel on the top of the cabbages, and carried her away bodily.

When he reached his home, which was in a great square house on a lonely moor, he took her out, and set her down roughly on the floor.

"Thou wilt be my servant now," he said, "and keep my house, and do my errands for me. I have a cow, which thou must drive out every day to the hillside; and see, here is a bag of wool, when thou hast taken out the cow, thou must come back and settle thyself at home, as a good housewife should, and comb, and card it, and spin it into yarn, with which to weave a good thick cloth for my raiment. I am out most of the day, but when I come home I shall expect to find all this done, and a great bicker of porridge boiled besides for my supper."

The poor Princess was very dismayed when she heard these words, for she had never been accustomed to work hard, and she had always had her sisters to help her; but the Giant took no notice of her distress, but went out as soon as it was daylight, leaving her alone in the house to begin her work.

As soon as he had gone she drove the cow to the pasture, as he had told her to do; but she had a good long walk over the moor before she reached the hill, and by the time that she got back to the house she felt very tired.

So she thought that she would put on the porridge pot, and make herself some porridge before she began to card and comb the wool. She did so, and just as she was sitting down to sup them the door opened, and a crowd of wee, wee Peerie Folk came in.

They were the tiniest men and women that the Princess had ever seen; not one of them would have reached half-way to her knee; and they were dressed in dresses fashioned out of all the colours of the rainbow – scarlet and blue, green and yellow, orange and violet; and the funny thing was, that every one of them had a shock of straw-coloured yellow hair.

They were all talking and laughing with one another; and they hopped up, first on stools, then on chairs, till at last they reached the top of the table, where they clustered round the bowl, out of which the Princess was eating her porridge.

"We be hungry, we be hungry," they cried, in their tiny shrill voices. "Spare a little porridge for the Peerie Folk."

But the Princess was hungry also; and, besides being hungry, she was both tired and cross; so she shook her head and waved them impatiently away with her spoon,

> *"Little for one, and less for two,*
> *And never a grain have I for you."*

she said sharply, and, to her great delight, for she did not feel quite comfortable with all the Peerie Folk standing on the table looking at her, they vanished in a moment.

After this she finished her porridge in peace; then she took the wool out of the bag, and she set to work to comb and card it. But it seemed as if it were bewitched; it curled and twisted and coiled itself round her fingers so that, try as she would, she could not do anything with it. And when the Giant came home he found her sitting in despair with it all in confusion round her, and the porridge, which she had left for him in the pot, burned to a cinder.

As you may imagine, he was very angry, and raged, and stamped, and used the most dreadful words; and at last he took her by the heels, and beat her until all her back was skinned and bleeding; then he carried her out to the byre, and threw her up on the joists among the hens. And, although she was not dead, she was so stunned and bruised that she could only lie there motionless, looking down on the backs of the cows.

Time went on, and in the kailyard at home the cabbages were disappearing as fast as ever. So the second Princess said that she would do as her sister had done, and wrap herself in a blanket, and go and sit on a three-legged stool all night, to see what was becoming of them.

She did so, and exactly the same fate befell her that had befallen her elder sister. The Giant appeared with his creel, and he carried her off, and set her to mind the cow and the house, and to make his porridge and to spin; and the little yellow-headed Peerie Folk appeared and asked her for some supper, and she refused to give it to them; and after that, she could not comb or card her wool, and the Giant was angry, and he scolded her, and beat her, and threw her up, half dead, on the joists beside her sister and the hens.

Then the youngest Princess determined to sit out in the kailyard all night, not so much to see what was becoming of the cabbages, as to discover what had happened to her sisters.

And when the Giant came and carried her off, she was not at all sorry, but very glad, for she was a brave and loving little maiden; and now she felt that she had a chance of finding out where they were, and whether they were dead or alive.

So she was quite cheerful and happy, for she felt certain that she was clever enough to outwit the Giant, if only she were watchful and patient; so she lay quite quietly in her creel above the cabbages, but she kept her eyes very wide open to see by which road he was carrying her off.

And when he set her down in his kitchen, and told her all that he expected her to do, she did not look downcast like her sisters, but nodded her head brightly, and said that she felt sure that she could do it.

And she sang to herself as she drove the cow over the moor to pasture, and she ran the whole way back, so that she should have a good long afternoon to work at the wool, and, although she would not have told the Giant this, to search the house.

Before she set to work, however, she made herself some porridge, just as her sisters had done; and, just as she was going to sup them, all the little yellow-haired Peerie Folk trooped in, and climbed up on the table, and stood and stared at her.

"We be hungry, we be hungry," they cried. "Spare a little porridge for the Peerie Folk."

"With all my heart," replied the good-natured Princess. "If you can find dishes little enough for you to sup out of, I will fill them for you. But, methinks, if I were to give you all porringers, you would smother yourselves among the porridge."

At her words the Peerie Folk shouted with laughter, till their straw-coloured hair tumbled right over their faces; then they hopped on to the floor and ran out of the house, and presently they came trooping back holding cups of blue-bells, and foxgloves, and saucers of primroses and anemones in their hands; and the Princess put a tiny spoonful of porridge into each saucer, and a tiny drop of milk into each cup, and they ate it all up as daintily as possible with neat little grass spoons, which they had brought with them in their pockets.

When they had finished they all cried out, "Thank you! Thank you!" and ran out of the kitchen again, leaving the Princess alone. And, being alone, she went all over the house to look for her sisters, but, of course, she could not find them.

"Never mind, I will find them soon," she said to herself. "To-morrow I will search the byre and the outhouses; in the meantime, I had better get on with my work." So she went back to the kitchen, and took out the bag of wool, which the Giant had told her to make into cloth.

But just as she was doing so the door opened once more, and a Yellow-Haired Peerie Boy entered. He was exactly like the other Peerie Folk who had eaten the Princess's porridge, only he was bigger, and he wore a very rich dress of grass-green velvet. He walked boldly into the middle of the kitchen and looked round him.

"Hast thou any work for me to do?" he asked. "I ken grand how to handle wool and turn it into fine thick cloth."

"I have plenty of work for anybody who asks it," replied the Princess; "but I have no money to pay for it, and there are but few folk in this world who will work without wages."

"All the wages that I ask is that thou wilt take the trouble to find out my name, for few folk ken it, and few folk care to ken. But if by any chance thou canst not find it out, then must thou pay toll of half of thy cloth."

The Princess thought that it would be quite an easy thing to find out the Boy's name, so she agreed to the bargain, and, putting all the wool back into the bag, she gave it to him, and he swung it over his shoulder and departed.

She ran to the door to see where he went, for she had made up her mind that she would follow him secretly to his home, and find out from the neighbours what his name was.

But, to her great dismay, though she looked this way and that, he had vanished completely, and she began to wonder what she should do if the Giant came back and found that she had allowed someone, whose name she did not even know, to carry off all the wool.

And, as the afternoon wore on, and she could think of no way of finding out who the boy was, or where he came from, she felt that she had made a great mistake, and she began to grow very frightened.

Just as the gloaming was beginning to fall a knock came at the door, and, when she opened it, she found an old woman standing outside, who begged for a night's lodging.

Now, as I have told you, the Princess was very kind-hearted, and she would fain have granted the poor old Dame's request, but she dared not, for she did not know what the Giant would say. So she told the old woman that she could not take her in for the night, as she was only a servant, and not the mistress of the house; but she made her sit down on a bench beside the door, and brought her out some bread and milk, and gave her some water to bathe her poor, tired feet.

She was so bonnie, and gentle, and kind, and she looked so sorry when she told her that she would need to turn her away, that the old woman gave her her blessing, and told her not to vex herself, as it was a fine, dry night, and now that she had had a meal she could easily sit down somewhere and sleep in the shelter of the outhouses.

And, when she had finished her bread and milk, she went and laid down by the side of a green knowe, which rose out of the moor not very far from the byre door.

And, strange to say, as she lay there she felt the earth beneath her getting warmer and warmer, until she was so hot that she was fain to crawl up the side of the hillock, in the hope of getting a mouthful of fresh air.

And as she got near the top she heard a voice, which seemed to come from somewhere beneath her, saying, "tease, teasens, tease; card, cardens, card; spin, spinners, spin; for Peerifool Peerifool, Peerifool is what men call me." And when she got to the very top, she found that there was a crack in the earth, through which rays of light were coming; and when she put her eye to the crack, what should she see down below her but a brilliantly lighted chamber, in which all the Peerie Folk were sitting in a circle, working away as hard as they could.

Some of them were carding wool, some of them were combing it, some of them were spinning it, constantly wetting their fingers with their lips, in order to twist the yarn fine as they drew it from the distaff, and some of them were spinning the yarn into cloth.

While round and round the circle, cracking a little whip, and urging them to work faster, was a Yellow-Haired Peerie Boy.

"This is a strange thing, and these be queer on-goings," said the old woman to herself, creeping hastily down to the bottom of the hillock again. "I must e'en go and tell the bonnie lassie in the house yonder. Maybe the knowledge of what I have seen will stand her in good stead some day. When there be Peerie Folk about, it is well to be on one's guard."

So she went back to the house and told the Princess all that she had seen and heard, and the Princess was so delighted with what she had told her that she risked the Giant's wrath and allowed her to go and sleep in the hayloft.

It was not very long after the old woman had gone to rest before the door opened, and the Peerie Boy appeared once more with a number of webs of cloth upon his shoulder. "Here is thy cloth," he said, with a sly smile, "and I will put it on the shelf for thee the moment that thou tellest me what my name is."

Then the Princess, who was a merry maiden, thought that she would tease the little fellow for a time ere she let him know that she had found out his secret.

So she mentioned first one name and then another, always pretending to think that she had hit upon the right one; and all the time the Peerie Boy jumped from side to side with delight, for he thought that she would never find out the right name, and that half of the cloth would be his.

But at last the Princess grew tired of joking, and she cried out, with a little laugh of triumph, "Dost thou by any chance ken anyone called Peerifool, little Mannikin?"

Then he knew that in some way she had found out what men called him, and he was so angry and disappointed that he flung the webs of cloth down in a heap on the floor, and ran out at the door, slamming it behind him.

Meanwhile the Giant was coming down the hill in the darkening, and, to his astonishment, he met a troop of little Peerie Folk toiling up it, looking as if they were so tired that they could hardly get along. Their eyes were dim and listless, their heads were hanging on their breasts, and their lips were so long and twisted that the poor little people looked quite hideous.

The Giant asked how this was, and they told him that they had to work so hard all day, spinning for their Master that they were quite exhausted; and that the reason why their lips were so distorted was that they used them constantly to wet their fingers, so that they might pull the wool in very fine strands from the distaff.

"I always thought a great deal of women who could spin," said the Giant, "and I looked out for a housewife that could do so. But after this I will be more careful, for the housewife that I have now is a bonnie little woman, and I would be loth to have her spoil her face in that manner."

And he hurried home in a great state of mind in case he should find that his new servant's pretty red lips had grown long and ugly in his absence.

Great was his relief to see her standing by the table, bonnie and winsome as ever, with all the webs of cloth in a pile in front of her.

"By my troth, thou art an industrious maiden," he said, in high good humour, "and, as a reward for working so diligently, I will restore thy sisters to thee." And he went out to the byre, and lifted the two other Princesses down from the rafters, and brought them in and laid them on the settle.

Their little sister nearly screamed aloud when she saw how ill they looked and how bruised their backs were, but, like a prudent maiden, she held her tongue, and busied herself with applying a cooling ointment to their wounds, and binding them up, and by and by her sisters revived, and, after the Giant had gone to bed, they told her all that had befallen them.

"I will be avenged on him for his cruelty," said the little Princess firmly; and when she spoke like that her sisters knew that she meant what she said.

So next morning, before the Giant was up, she fetched his creel, and put her eldest sister into it, and covered her with all the fine silken hangings and tapestry that she could find, and on the top of all she put a handful of grass, and when the Giant came downstairs she asked him, in her sweetest tone, if he would do her a favour.

And the Giant, who was very pleased with her because of the quantity of cloth which he thought she had spun, said that he would.

"Then carry that creelful of grass home to my mother's cottage for her cow to eat," said the Princess. "'Twill help to make up for all the cabbages which thou hast stolen from her kailyard."

And, wonderful to relate, the Giant did as he was bid, and carried the creel to the cottage.

Next morning she put her second sister into another creel, and covered her with all the fine napery she could find in the house, and put an armful of grass on the top of it, and at her bidding the Giant, who was really getting very fond of her, carried it also home to her mother.

The next morning the little Princess told him that she thought that she would go for a long walk after she had done her housework, and that she might not be in when he came home at night, but that she would have another creel of grass ready for him, if he would carry it to the cottage as he had done on the two previous evenings. He promised to do so; then, as usual, he went out for the day.

In the afternoon the clever little maiden went through the house, gathering together all the lace, and silver, and jewellery that she could find, and brought them and placed them beside the creel. Then she went out and cut an armful of grass, and brought it in and laid it beside them.

Then she crept into the creel herself, and pulled all the fine things in above her, and then she covered everything up with the grass, which was a very difficult thing to do, seeing she herself was at the bottom of the basket. Then she lay quite still and waited.

Presently the Giant came in, and, obedient to his promise, he lifted the creel and carried it off to the old Queen's cottage.

No one seemed to be at home, so he set it down in the entry, and turned to go away. But the little Princess had told her sisters what to do, and they had a great can of boiling water ready in one of the rooms upstairs, and when they heard his steps coming round that side of the house, they threw open the window and emptied it all over his head; and that was the end of him.

The Doomed Rider

"**T**HE CONAN IS AS BONNY a river as we hae in a' the north country. There's mony a sweet sunny spot on its banks, an' mony a time an' aft hae I waded through its shallows, whan a boy, to set my little scautling-line for the trouts an' the eels, or to gather the big pearl-mussels that lie sae thick in the fords.**

But its bonny wooded banks are places for enjoying the day in – no for passing the nicht. I kenna how it is; it's nane o' your wild streams that wander desolate through a desert country, like the Aven, or that come rushing down in foam and thunder, ower broken rocks, like the Foyers, or that wallow in darkness, deep, deep in the bowels o' the earth, like the fearfu' Auldgraunt; an' yet no ane o' these rivers has mair or frightfuller stories connected wi' it than the Conan. Ane can hardly saunter ower half-a-mile in its course, frae where it leaves Coutin till where it enters the sea, without passing ower the scene o' some frightful auld legend o' the kelpie or the waterwraith. And ane o' the most frightful looking o' these places is to be found among the woods o' Conan House. Ye enter a swampy meadow that waves wi' flags an' rushes like a corn-field in harvest, an' see a hillock covered wi' willows rising like an island in the midst. There are thick mirk-woods on ilka side; the river, dark an' awesome, an' whirling round an' round in mossy eddies, sweeps away behind it; an' there is an auld burying-ground, wi' the broken ruins o' an auld Papist kirk, on the tap. Ane can see amang the rougher stanes the rose-wrought mullions of an arched window, an' the trough that ance held the holy water. About twa hunder years ago – a wee mair maybe, or a wee less, for ane canna be very sure o' the date o' thae old stories – the building was entire; an' a spot near it, whar the wood now grows thickest, was laid out in a corn-field. The marks o' the furrows may still be seen amang the trees.

"A party o' Highlanders were busily engaged, ae day in harvest, in cutting down the corn o' that field; an' just aboot noon, when the sun shone brightest an' they were busiest in the work, they heard a voice frae the river exclaim: 'The hour but not the man has come.' Sure enough, on looking round, there was the kelpie stan'in' in what they ca' a fause ford, just fornent the auld kirk. There is a deep black pool baith aboon an' below, but i' the ford there's a bonny ripple, that shows, as ane might think, but little depth o' water; an' just i' the middle o' that, in a place where a horse might swim, stood the kelpie. An' it again repeated its words: 'The hour but not the man has come,' an' then flashing through the water like a drake, it disappeared in the lower pool. When the folk stood wondering what the creature might mean, they saw a man on horseback come spurring down the hill in hot haste, making straight for the fause ford. They could then understand her words at ance; an' four o' the stoutest o' them sprang oot frae amang the corn to warn him o' his danger, an' keep him back. An' sae they tauld him what they had seen an' heard, an' urged him either to turn back an' tak' anither road, or stay for an hour or sae where he was. But he just wadna hear them, for he was baith unbelieving an' in haste, an' wauld hae taen the ford for a' they could say, hadna the Highlanders, determined on saving him whether he would or no, gathered round him an' pulled him frae his horse, an' then, to mak' sure o' him, locked him up in the auld kirk. Weel, when the hour had gone by – the fatal hour o' the kelpie – they flung open the door, an' cried to him that he might noo gang on his journey. Ah! but there was nae answer, though; an' sae they cried a second time, an' there was nae answer still; an' then they went in, an' found him lying stiff an' cauld on the floor, wi' his face buried in the water o' the very stone trough that we may still see amang the ruins.

His hour had come, an' he had fallen in a fit, as 'twould seem, head-foremost amang the water o' the trough, where he had been smothered, – an' sae ye see, the prophecy o' the kelpie availed naething."

Michael Scott

I N THE EARLY PART OF Michael Scott's life he was in the habit of
emigrating annually to the Scottish metropolis, for the purpose
of being employed in his capacity of mason. One time as he and
two companions were journeying to the place of their destination
for a similar object, they had occasion to pass over a high hill, the
name of which is not mentioned, but which is supposed to have
been one of the Grampians, and being fatigued with climbing,
they sat down to rest themselves. They had no sooner done so than
they were warned to take to their heels by the hissing of a large
serpent, which they observed revolving itself towards them with
great velocity. Terrified at the sight, Michael's two companions fled,
while he, on the contrary, resolved to encounter the reptile.

The appalling monster approached Michael Scott with distended mouth and
forked tongue; and, throwing itself into a coil at his feet, was raising its head
to inflict a mortal sting, when Michael, with one stroke of his stick, severed
its body into three pieces. Having rejoined his affrighted comrades, they
resumed their journey; and, on arriving at the next public-house, it being
late, and the travellers being weary, they took up their quarters at it for the
night. In the course of the night's conversation, reference was naturally made
to Michael's recent exploit with the serpent, when the landlady of the house,
who was remarkable for her 'arts,' happened to be present. Her curiosity
appeared much excited by the conversation; and, after making some inquiries
regarding the colour of the serpent, which she was told was white, she
offered any of them that would procure her the middle piece such a tempting
reward, as induced one of the party instantly to go for it. The distance was
not very great; and on reaching the spot, he found the middle and tail piece
in the place where Michael left them, but the head piece was gone.

The landlady on receiving the piece, which still vibrated with life, seemed
highly gratified at her acquisition; and, over and above the promised
reward, regaled her lodgers very plentifully with the choicest dainties in her

house. Fired with curiosity to know the purpose for which the serpent was intended, the wily Michael Scott was immediately seized with a severe fit of indisposition, which caused him to prefer the request that he might be allowed to sleep beside the fire, the warmth of which, he affirmed, was in the highest degree beneficial to him.

Never suspecting Michael Scott's hypocrisy, and naturally supposing that a person so severely indisposed would feel very little curiosity about the contents of any cooking utensils which might lie around the fire, the landlady allowed his request. As soon as the other inmates of the house were retired to bed, the landlady resorted to her darling occupation; and, in his feigned state of indisposition, Michael had a favourable opportunity of watching most scrupulously all her actions through the keyhole of a door leading to the next apartment where she was. He could see the rites and ceremonies with which the serpent was put into the oven, along with many mysterious ingredients. After which the unsuspicious landlady placed the dish by the fireside, where lay the distressed traveller, to stove till the morning.

Once or twice in the course of the night the 'wife of the change-house,' under the pretence of inquiring for her sick lodger, and administering to him some renovating cordials, the beneficial effects of which he gratefully acknowledged, took occasion to dip her finger in her saucepan, upon which the cock, perched on his roost, crowed aloud. All Michael's sickness could not prevent him considering very inquisitively the landlady's cantrips, and particularly the influence of the sauce upon the crowing of the cock. Nor could he dissipate some inward desires he felt to follow her example. At the same time, he suspected that Satan had a hand in the pie, yet he thought he would like very much to be at the bottom of the concern; and thus his reason and his curiosity clashed against each other for the space of several hours. At length passion, as is too often the case, became the conqueror. Michael, too, dipped his finger in the sauce, and applied it to the tip of his tongue, and immediately the cock perched on the spardan announced the circumstance in a mournful clarion. Instantly his mind received a new light to which he was formerly a stranger, and the astonished dupe of a landlady now found it her interest to admit her sagacious lodger into a knowledge of the remainder of her secrets.

Endowed with the knowledge of 'good and evil,' and all the 'second sights' that can be acquired, Michael left his lodgings in the morning, with the philosopher's stone in his pocket. By daily perfecting his supernatural attainments, by new series of discoveries, he became more than a match for Satan himself. Having seduced some thousands of Satan's best workmen into his employment, he trained them up so successfully to the architective business, and inspired them with such industrious habits, that he was more than sufficient for all the architectural work of the empire. To establish this assertion, we need only refer to some remains of his workmanship still existing north of the Grampians, some of them, stupendous bridges built by him in one short night, with no other visible agents than two or three workmen.

On one occasion work was getting scarce, as might have been naturally expected, and his workmen, as they were wont, flocked to his doors, perpetually exclaiming, "Work! work! work!" Continually annoyed by their incessant entreaties, he called out to them in derision to go and make a dry road from Fortrose to Ardersier, over the Moray Firth. Immediately their cry ceased, and as Scott supposed it wholly impossible for them to execute his order, he retired to rest, laughing most heartily at the chimerical sort of employment he had given to his industrious workmen. Early in the morning, however, he got up and took a walk at the break of day down to the shore to divert himself at the fruitless labours of his zealous workmen. But on reaching the spot, what was his astonishment to find the formidable piece of work allotted to them only a few hours before already nearly finished. Seeing the great damage the commercial class of the community would sustain from the operation, he ordered the workmen to demolish the most part of their work; leaving, however, the point of Fortrose to show the traveller to this day the wonderful exploit of Michael Scott's fairies.

On being thus again thrown out of employment, their former clamour was resumed, nor could Michael Scott, with all his sagacity, devise a plan to keep them in innocent employment. He at length discovered one. "Go," says he, "and manufacture me ropes that will carry me to the back of the moon, of these materials – miller's-sudds and sea-sand." Michael Scott here obtained rest from his active operators; for, when other work failed them, he always despatched them to their rope manufactory. But though these agents could never make proper ropes of those materials, their efforts to that effect are far from being contemptible, for some of their ropes are seen by the sea-side to this day.

We shall close our notice of Michael Scott by reciting one anecdote of him in the latter part of his life.

In consequence of a violent quarrel which Michael Scott once had with a person whom he conceived to have caused him some injury, he resolved, as the highest punishment he could inflict upon him, to send his adversary to that evil place designed only for Satan and his black companions. He accordingly, by means of his supernatural machinations, sent the poor unfortunate man thither; and had he been sent by any other means than those of Michael Scott, he would no doubt have met with a warm reception. Out of pure spite to Michael, however, when Satan learned who was his billet-master, he would no more receive him than he would receive the Wife of Beth; and instead of treating the unfortunate man with the harshness characteristic of him, he showed him considerable civilities. Introducing him to his 'Ben Taigh,' he directed her to show the stranger any curiosities he might wish to see, hinting very significantly that he had provided some accommodation for their mutual friend, Michael Scott, the sight of which might afford him some gratification. The polite housekeeper accordingly conducted the stranger through the principal apartments in the house, where he saw fearful sights. But the bed of Michael Scott! – his greatest enemy could not but feel satiated with revenge at the sight of it. It was a place too horrid to be described, filled promiscuously with all the awful brutes imaginable. Toads and lions, lizards and leeches, and, amongst the rest, not the least conspicuous, a large serpent gaping for Michael Scott, with its mouth wide open. This last sight having satisfied the stranger's curiosity, he was led to the outer gate, and came away. He reached his friends, and, among other pieces of news touching his travels, he was not backward in relating the entertainment that awaited his friend Michael Scott, as soon as he would 'stretch his foot' for the other world. But Michael did not at all appear disconcerted at his friend's intelligence. He affirmed that he would disappoint all his enemies in their expectations – in proof of which he gave the following signs: "When I am just dead," says he, "open my breast and extract my heart. Carry it to some place where the public may see the result. You will then transfix it upon a long pole, and if Satan will have my soul, he will come in the likeness of a black raven and carry it off; and if my soul will be saved it will be carried off by a white dove."

His friends faithfully obeyed his instructions. Having exhibited his heart in the manner directed, a large black raven was observed to come from the east with great fleetness, while a white dove came from the west with equal velocity. The raven made a furious dash at the heart, missing which, it was unable to curb its force, till it was considerably past it; and the dove, reaching the spot at the same time, carried off the heart amidst the rejoicing and ejaculations of the spectators.

The Battle of the Birds

THERE WAS ONCE A TIME when every creature and bird was gathering to battle. The son of the king of Tethertown said, that he would go to see the battle, and that he would bring sure word home to his father the king, who would be king of the creatures this year. The battle was over before he arrived all but one (fight), between a great black raven and a snake, and it seemed as if the snake would get the victory over the raven. When the King's son saw this, he helped the raven, and with one blow takes the head off the snake. When the raven had taken breath, and saw that the snake was dead, he said, "For thy kindness to me this day, I will give thee a sight. Come up now on the root of my two wings." The king's son mounted upon the raven, and, before he stopped, he took him over seven Bens, and seven Glens, and seven Mountain Moors.

"Now," said the raven, "seest thou that house yonder? Go now to it. It is a sister of mine that makes her dwelling in it; and I will go bail that thou art welcome. And if she asks thee, Wert thou at the battle of the birds? say thou that thou wert. And if she asks, Didst thou see my likeness? say that thou sawest it. But be sure that thou meetest me to-morrow morning here, in this place." The king's son got good and right good treatment this night. Meat of each meat, drink of each drink, warm water to his feet, and a soft bed for his limbs.

On the next day the raven gave him the same sight over seven Bens, and seven Glens, and seven Mountain moors. They saw a bothy far off, but, though far off, they were soon there. He got good treatment this night, as before – plenty of meat and drink, and warm water to his feet, and a soft bed to his limbs – and on the next day it was the same thing.

On the third morning, instead of seeing the raven as at the other times, who should meet him but the handsomest lad he ever saw, with a bundle in his hand. The king's son asked this lad if he had seen a big black raven. Said the lad to him, "Thou wilt never see the raven again, for I am that raven. I was put under spells; it was meeting thee that loosed me, and for that thou art getting this bundle. Now," said the lad, "thou wilt turn back on the self-same steps, and thou wilt lie a night in each house, as thou wert before; but thy lot is not to lose the bundle which I gave thee, till thou art in the place where thou wouldst most wish to dwell."

The king's son turned his back to the lad, and his face to his father's house; and he got lodging from the raven's sisters, just as he got it when going forward. When he was nearing his father's house he was going through a close wood. It seemed to him that the bundle was growing heavy, and he thought be would look what was in it.

When he loosed the bundle, it was not without astonishing himself. In a twinkling he sees the very grandest place he ever saw. A great castle, and an orchard about the castle, in which was every kind of fruit and herb. He stood full of wonder and regret for having loosed the bundle – it was not in his power to put it back again – and he would have wished this pretty place to be in the pretty little green hollow that was opposite his father's house; but, at one glance, he sees a great giant coming towards him.

"Bad's the place where thou hast built thy house, king's son," says the giant. "Yes, but it is not here I would wish it to be, though it happened to be here by mishap," says the king's son. "What's the reward thou wouldst give me for putting it back in the bundle as it was before?" "What's the reward thou wouldst ask?" says the king's son. "If thou wilt give me the first son thou hast when he is seven years of age," says the giant. "Thou wilt get that if I have a son," said the king's son.

In a twinkling the giant put each garden, and orchard, and castle in the bundle as they were before. "Now," says the giant, "take thou thine own road, and I will take my road; but mind thy promise, and though thou shouldst forget, I will remember."

The king's son took to the road, and at the end of a few days he reached the place he was fondest of. He loosed the bundle, and the same place was just as it was before. And when he opened the castle-door he sees the handsomest maiden he ever cast eye upon. "Advance, king's son," said the pretty maid; "everything is in order for thee, if thou, wilt marry me this very night." "It's I am the man that is willing," said the king's son. And on the same night they married.

But at the end of a day and seven years, what great man is seen coming to the castle but the giant. The king's son minded his promise to the giant, and till now he had not told his promise to the queen. "Leave thou (the matter) between me and the giant," says the queen.

"Turn out thy son," says the giant; "mind your promise." "Thou wilt get that," says the king, "when his mother puts him in order for his journey." The queen arrayed the cook's son, and she gave him to the giant by the hand. The giant went away with him; but he had not gone far when he put a rod in the hand of the little laddie. The giant asked him – "If thy father had that rod what would he do with it?" "If my father had that rod he would beat the dogs and the cats, if they would be going near the king's meat," said the little laddie. "Thou'rt the cook's son," said the giant. He catches him by the two small ankles and knocks him – "Sgleog" – against the stone that was beside him. The giant turned back to the castle in rage and madness, and he said that if they did not turn out the king's son to him, the highest stone of the castle would be the lowest. Said the queen to the king, "we'll try it yet; the butler's son is of the same age as our son." She arrayed the butler's son, and she gives him to the giant by the hand. The giant had not gone far when he put the rod in his hand. "If thy father had that rod," says the giant, "what would he do with it?" "He would beat the dogs and the cats when they would be coming near the king's bottles and glasses." "Thou art the son of the butler," says the giant, and dashed his brains out too. The giant returned in very great rage and anger. The earth shook under the sole of his feet, and the castle shook and all that was in it. "Out here thy son," says the giant, "or in a twinkling the stone that is highest in the dwelling will be the lowest." So needs must they had to give the king's son to the giant.

The giant took him to his own house, and he reared him as his own son. On a day of days when the giant was from home, the lad heard the sweetest music he ever heard in a room at the top of the giant's house. At a glance he saw the finest face he had ever seen. She beckoned to him to come a bit nearer to her, and she told him to go this time, but to be sure to be at the same place about that dead midnight.

And as he promised he did. The giant's daughter was at his side in a twinkling, and she said, "Tomorrow thou wilt get the choice of my two sisters to marry; but say thou that thou wilt not take either, but me. My father wants me to marry the son of the king of the Green City, but I don't like him." On the morrow the giant took out his three daughters, and he said, "Now son of the king of Tethertown, thou hast not lost by living with me so long. Thou wilt get to wife one of the two eldest of my daughters, and with her leave to go home with her the day after the wedding." "If thou wilt give me this pretty little one," says the king's son, "I will take thee at thy word."

The giant's wrath kindled, and he said, "Before thou gett'st her thou must do the three things that I ask thee to do." "Say on," says the king's son. The giant took him to the byre. "Now," says the giant, "the dung of a hundred cattle is here, and it has not been cleansed for seven years. I am going from home to-day, and if this byre is not cleaned before night comes, so clean that a golden apple will run from end to end of it, not only thou shalt not get my daughter, but 'tis a drink of thy blood that will quench my thirst this night." He begins cleaning the byre, but it was just as well to keep baling the great ocean. After mid-day, when sweat was blinding him, the giant's young daughter came where he was, and she said to him, "Thou art being punished, king's son." "I am that," says the king's son. "Come over," says she, "and lay down thy weariness." "I will do that," says he, "there is but death awaiting me, at any rate." He sat down near her. He was so tired that he fell asleep beside her. When he awoke, the giant's daughter was not to be seen, but the byre was so well cleaned that a golden apple would run from end to end of it. In comes the giant, and he said, "Thou hast cleaned the byre, king's son?" "I have cleaned it," says he. "Somebody cleaned it," says the giant. "Thou didst not clean it, at all events," said the king's son. "Yes, yes!" says the giant, "since thou wert so active to-day, thou wilt get to this time to-morrow to thatch this byre with birds' down – birds with no two feathers of one colour." The king's son was on foot before the sun; he caught up his bow and his quiver of arrows to kill the birds. He took to the moors, but if he did, the birds were not so easy to take. He was running after them till the sweat was blinding him. About mid-day who should come but the giant's daughter. "Thou art exhausting thyself, king's son," says she. "I am," said he. "There fell but these two blackbirds, and both of one colour." "Come over and lay down thy weariness on this pretty hillock," says the giant's daughter. "It's I am willing," said he. He thought she would aid him this time, too, and he sat down near her, and he was not long there till he fell asleep.

When he awoke, the giant's daughter was gone.

He thought he would go back to the house, and he sees the byre thatched with the feathers. When the giant came home, he said, "Thou hast thatched the byre, king's son?" "I thatched it," says he. "Somebody thatched it," says the giant. "Thou didst not thatch it," says the king's son. "Yes, yes!" says the giant. "Now," says the giant, "there is a fir-tree beside that loch down there, and there is a magpie's nest in its top. The eggs thou wilt find in the nest. I must have them for my first meal. Not one must be burst or broken, and there are five in the nest." Early in the morning the king's son went where the tree was, and that tree was not hard to hit upon. Its match was not in the whole wood. From the foot to the first branch was five hundred feet. The king's son was going all round the tree. She came who was always bringing help to him; "Thou art losing the skin of thy hands and feet." "Ach! I am," says he. "I am no sooner up than down." "This is no time for stopping," says the giant's daughter. She thrust finger after finger into the tree, till she made a ladder for the king's son to go up to the magpie's nest. When he was at the nest, she said, "Make haste now with the eggs, for my father's breath is burning my back." In his hurry she left her little finger in the top of the tree. "Now," says she, "thou wilt go home with the eggs quickly, and thou wilt get me to marry to-night if thou canst know me. I and my two sisters will be arrayed in the same garments, and made like each other, but look at me when my father says, Go to thy wife, king's son; and thou wilt see a hand without a, little finger." He gave the eggs to the giant. "Yes, yes!" says the giant, "be making ready for thy marriage."

Then indeed there was a wedding, and it was a wedding! Giants and gentlemen, and the son of the king of the Green City was in the midst of them. They were married, and the dancing began, and that was a dance? The giant's house was shaking from top to bottom. But bed time came, and the giant said, "It is time for thee to go to rest, son of the king of Tethertown; take thy bride with thee from amidst those."

She put out the hand off which the little finger was, and he caught her by the hand.

"Thou hast aimed well this time too; but there is no knowing but we may meet thee another way," said the giant.

But to rest they went. "Now," says she, "sleep not, or else thou diest. We must fly quick, quick, or for certain my father will kill thee."

Out they went, and on the blue gray filly in the stable they mounted. "Stop a while," says she, "and I will play a trick to the old hero." She jumped in, and cut an apple into nine shares, and she put two shares at the head of the bed, and two shares at the foot of the bed, and two shares at the door of the kitchen, and two shares at the big door, and one outside the house.

The giant awoke and called, "Are you asleep?" "We are not yet," said the apple that was at the head of the bed. At the end of a while he called again. "We are not yet," said the apple that was at the foot of the bed. A while after this he called again. "We are not yet," said the apple at the kitchen door. The giant called again. The apple that was at the big door answered "You are now going far from me," says the giant. "We are not yet," says the apple that was outside the house. "You are flying," says the giant.

The giant jumped on his feet, and to the bed he went, but it was cold – empty.

"My own daughter's tricks are trying me," said the giant. "Here's after them," says he.

In the mouth of day, the giant's daughter said that her father's breath was burning her back. "Put thy hand, quick," said she, "in the ear of the gray filly, and whatever thou findest in it, throw it behind thee." "There is a twig of sloe tree," said he. "Throw it behind thee," said she.

No sooner did he that, than there were twenty miles of black thorn wood, so thick that scarce a weasel could go through it. The giant came headlong, and there he is fleecing his head and neck in the thorns.

"My own daughter's tricks are here as before," said the giant; "but if I had my own big axe and wood knife here, I would not be long making a way through this." He went home for the big axe and the wood knife, and sure he was not long on his journey, and he was the boy behind the big axe. He was not long making a way through the black thorn. "I will leave the axe and the wood knife here till I return," says he.

"If thou leave them," said a Hoodie that was in a tree, "we will steal them." "You will do that same," says the giant, "but I will set them home." He returned and left them at the house. At the heat of day the giant's daughter felt her father's breath burning her back.

"Put thy finger in the filly's ear, and throw behind thee whatever thou findest in it." He got a splinter of gray stone, and in a twinkling there were twenty miles, by breadth and height, of great gray rock behind them. The giant came full pelt, but past the rock he could not go.

"The tricks of my own daughter are the hardest things that ever met me," says the giant; "but if I had my lever and my mighty mattock, I would not be long making my way through this rock also." There was no help for it, but to turn the chase for them; and he was the boy to split the stones. He was not lone, making a road through the rock. "I will leave the tools here, and I will return no more." "If thou leave them," says the hoodie, "we will steal them." "Do that if thou wilt; there is no time too go back." At the time of breaking the watch, the giant's daughter said that she was feeling her father's breath burning her back. "Look in the filly's ear, king's son, or else we are lost." He did so, and it was a bladder of water that was in her ear this time. He threw it behind him and there was a fresh-water loch, twenty miles in length and breadth, behind them.

The giant came on, but with the speed he had on him, he was in the middle of the loch, and he went under, and he rose no more.

On the next day the young companions were come in sight of his father's house. "Now," said she, "my father is drowned, and he won't trouble us any more; but before we go further," says she, "go thou to thy father's house, and tell that thou hast the like of me but this is thy lot, let neither man nor creature kiss thee, for if thou dost thou wilt not remember that thou hast ever seen me." Every one he met was giving him welcome and luck, and he charged his father and mother not to kiss him; but as mishap was to be, an old greyhound was in and she knew him, and jumped up to his mouth, and after that he did not remember the giant's daughter.

She was sitting at the well's side as he left her, but the king's son was not coming. In the mouth of night she climbed up into a tree of oak that was beside the well, and she lay in the fork of the tree all that night. A shoemaker had a house near the well, and about mid-day on the morrow, the shoemaker asked his wife to go for a drink for him out of the well. When the shoemaker's wife reached the well, and when she saw the shadow of her that was in the tree, thinking of it that it was her own shadow – and she never thought till now that she was so handsome – she gave a cast to the dish that was in her hand, and it was broken on the ground, and she took herself to the house without vessel or water.

"Where is the water, wife?" said the shoemaker. "Thou shambling, contemptible old carle, without grace, I have stayed too long thy water and wood thrall." "I am thinking, wife, that thou hast turned crazy. Go thou, daughter, quickly, and fetch a drink for thy father." His daughter went, and in the same way so it happened to her. She never thought till now that she was so loveable, and she took herself home. "Up with the drink," said her father. "Thou hume-spun shoe carle, dost thou think that I am fit to be thy thrall." The poor shoemaker thought that they had taken a turn in their understandings, and he went himself to the well. He saw the shadow of the maiden in the well, and he looked up to the tree, and he sees the finest woman he ever saw. "Thy seat is wavering, but thy face is fair," said the shoemaker. "Come down, for there is need of thee for a short while at my house." The shoemaker understood that this was the shadow that had driven his people mad. The shoemaker took her to his house, and he said that he had but a poor bothy, but that she should get a share of all that was in it. At the end of a day or two came a leash of gentlemen lads to the shoemaker's house for shoes to be made them, for the king had come home, and he was going to marry. The glance the lads gave they saw the giant's daughter, and if they saw her, they never saw one so pretty as she. "'Tis thou hast the pretty daughter here," said the lads to the shoe-maker. "She is pretty, indeed," says the shoemaker, "but she is no daughter of mine." "St Nail!" said one of them, "I would give a hundred pounds to marry her." The two others said the very same. The poor shoemaker said that he had nothing to do with her. "But," said they, "ask her to-night, and send us word to-morrow." When the gentles went away, she asked the shoemaker – "What's that they were saying about me?" The shoemaker told her. "Go thou after them," said she; "I will marry one of them, and let him bring his purse with him." The youth returned, and he gave the shoemaker a hundred pounds for tocher. They went to rest, and when she had laid down, she asked the lad for a drink of water from a tumbler that was on the board on the further side of the chamber. He went; but out of that he could not come, as he held the vessel of water the length of the night. "Thou lad," said she, "why wilt thou not lie down?" but out of that he could not drag till the bright morrow's day was. The shoemaker came to the door of the chamber, and she asked him to take away that lubberly boy. This wooer went and betook himself to his home, but he did not tell the other two how it happened to him. Next came the second chap, and in the same way, – when she had gone to rest – "Look," she said, "if the latch is on the door." The latch laid hold of his hands, and out of that he could not come the length of the night, and out of that he did not come till the morrow's day was bright. He went, under shame and disgrace. No matter, he did not tell the other chap how it had happened, and on the third night he came. As it happened to the two others, so it happened to him. One foot stuck to the floor; he could neither come nor go, but so he was the length of the night. On the morrow, he took his soles out (of that), and he was not seen looking behind him. "Now," said the girl to the shoemaker, "thine is the sporran of gold; I have no need of it. It will better thee, and I am no worse for thy kindness to me." The shoemaker had the shoes ready, and on that very day the king was to be married. The shoemaker was going to the castle with the shoes of the young people, and the girl said to the shoemaker, "I would like to get a sight of the king's son before he marries." "Come with me," says the shoemaker, "I am well acquainted with the servants at the castle, and thou shalt get a sight of the king's son and all the company." And when the gentles saw the pretty woman that was here they took her to the wedding-room, and they filled for her a glass of wine. When she was going to drink what is in it, a flame went up out of the glass, and a golden pigeon and a silver pigeon sprung out of it, They were flying about when three grains of barley fell on the floor. The silver pigeon sprang, and he eats that. Said the golden pigeon to him, "If thou hadst mind when I cleared the byre, thou wouldst not eat that without giving me a share." Again fell three other grains of barley, and the silver pigeon sprang, and he eats that, as before. "If thou hadst mind when I thatched the byre, thou wouldst not eat that without giving me my share," says the golden pigeon. Three other grains fall, and the silver pigeon sprang, and he eats that. "If thou hadst mind when I harried the magpie's nest, thou wouldst not eat that without giving me my share," says the golden pigeon; "I lost my little finger bringing it down, and I want it still." The king's son minded, and he knew who it was he had got. He sprang where she was, and kissed her from hand to mouth. And when the priest came they married a second time. And there I left them.

The Sea-Maiden

THERE WAS ERE NOW A poor old fisher, but on this year he was not getting much fish. On a day of days, and he fishing, there rose a sea-maiden at the side of his boat, and she asked him if he was getting fish. The old man answered, and he said that he was not. "What reward wouldst thou give me for sending plenty of fish to thee?" "Ach!" said the old man, "I have not much to spare." "Wilt thou give me the first son thou hast?" said she. "It is I that would give thee that, if I were to have a son; there was not, and there will not be a son of mine," said he, "I and my wife are grown so old." "Name all thou hast." "I have but an old mare of a horse, an old dog, myself and my wife. There's for thee all the creatures of the great world that are mine." "Here, then, are three grains for thee that thou shalt give thy wife this very night, and three others to the dog, and these three to the mare, and these three likewise thou shalt plant behind thy house, and in their own time thy wife will have three sons, the mare three foals, and the dog three puppies, and there will grow three trees behind thy house, and the trees will be a sign, when one of the sons dies, one of the trees will wither. Now, take thyself home, and remember me when thy son is three years of age, and thou thyself wilt get plenty of fish after this."

Everything happened as the sea-maiden said, and he himself was getting plenty of fish; but when the end of the three years was nearing, the old man was growing sorrowful, heavy hearted, while he failed each day as it came. On the namesake of the day, he went to fish as he used, but he did not take his son with him.

The sea-maiden rose at the side of the boat, and asked, "Didst thou bring thy son with thee hither to me?" "Och! I did not bring him. I forgot that this was the day." "Yes! yes! then," said the sea-maiden; "thou shalt get four other years of him, to try if it be easier for thee to part from him. Here thou hast his like age," and she lifted up a big bouncing baby. "Is thy son as fine as this one?" He went home full of glee and delight, for that he had got four other years of his son, and he kept on fishing and getting plenty of fish, but at the end of the next four years sorrow and woe struck him, and he took not a meal, and he did not a turn, and his wife could not think what was ailing him. This time he did not know what to do, but he set it before him, that he would not take his son with him this time either. He went to fish as at the former times, and the sea-maiden rose at the side of the boat, and she asked him, "Didst thou bring thy son hither to me?" "Och! I forgot him this time too," said the old man. "Go home then," said the sea-maiden, "and at the end of seven years after this, thou art sure to remember me, but then it will not be the easier for thee to part with him, but thou shalt get fish as thou used to do."

The old man went home full of joy; he had got seven other years of his son, and before seven years passed, the old man thought that he himself would be dead, and that he would see the sea-maiden no more. But no matter, the end of those seven years was nearing also, and if it was, the old man was not without care and trouble. He had rest neither day nor night. The eldest son asked his father one day if any one were troubling him? The old man said that some one was, but that belonged neither to him nor to any one else. The lad said he must know what it was. His father told him at last how the matter was between him and the sea-maiden. "Let not that put you in any trouble," said the son; "I will not oppose you." "Thou shalt not; thou shalt not go, my son, though I should not get fish for ever." "If you will not let me go with you, go to the smithy, and let the smith make me a great strong sword, and I will go to the end of fortune." His father went to the smithy, and the smith made a doughty sword for him. His father came home with the sword. The lad grasped it and gave it a shake or two, and it went in a hundred splinters. He asked his father to go to the smithy and get him another sword in which there should be twice as much weight; and so did his father, and so likewise it happened to the next sword – it broke in two halves. Back went the old man to the smithy; and the smith made a great sword, its like he never made before. "There's thy sword for thee," said the smith, "and the fist must be good that plays this blade." The old man gave the sword to his son, he gave it a shake or two. "This will do," said he; "it's high time now to travel on my way." On the next morning he put a saddle on the black horse that the mare had, and he put the world under his head, and his black dog was by his side. When he went on a bit, he fell in with the carcass of a sheep beside the road. At the carrion were a great dog, a falcon and an otter. He came down off the horse, and he divided the carcass amongst the three. Three third shares to the dog, two third shares to the otter, and a third share to the falcon. "For this," said the dog, "if swiftness of foot or sharpness of tooth will give thee aid, mind me, and I will be at thy side." Said the otter, "If the swimming of foot on the ground of a pool will loose thee, mind me, and I will be at thy side." Said the falcon, "if hardship comes on thee, where swiftness of wing or crook of a claw will do good, mind me, and I will be at thy side." On this he went onward till he reached a king's house, and he took service to be a herd, and his wages were to be according to the milk of the cattle. He went away with the cattle, and the grazing was but bare. When lateness came (in the evening), and when he took (them) home they had not much milk, the place was so bare, and his meat and drink was but spare this night.

On the next day he went on further with them; and at last he came to a place exceedingly grassy, in a green glen, of which he never saw the like.

But about the time when he should go behind the cattle, for taking homewards, who is seen coming but a great giant with his sword in his hand. "Hiu! Hau!! Hogaraich!!!" says the giant. "It is long since my teeth were rusted seeking thy flesh. The cattle are mine; they are on my march; and a dead man art thou." "I said, not that," says the herd; "there is no knowing, but that may be easier to say than to do."

To grips they go – himself and the giant. He saw that he was far from his friend, and near his foe. He drew the great clean-sweeping sword, and he neared the giant; and in the play of the battle the black dog leaped on the giant's back. The herd drew back his sword, and the head was off the giant in a twinkling. He leaped on the black horse, and he went to look for the giant's house. He reached a door, and in the haste that the giant made he had left each gate and door open. In went the herd, and that's the place where there was magnificence and money in plenty, and dresses of each kind on the wardrobe with gold and silver, and each thing finer than the other. At the mouth of night he took himself to the king's house, but he took not a thing from the giant's house. And when the cattle were milked this night there was milk. He got good feeding this night, meat and drink without stint, and the king was hugely pleased that he had caught such a herd. He went on for a time in this way, but at last the glen grew bare of grass, and the grazing was not so good.

But he thought he would go a little further forward in on the giant's land; and he sees a great park of grass. He returned for the cattle, and he puts them into the park.

They were but a short time grazing in the park when a great wild giant came full of rage and madness. "Hiu! Haw!! Hoagraich!!!" said the giant. "It is a drink of thy blood that quenches my thirst this night." "There is no knowing," said the herd, "but that's easier to say than to do." And at each other went the men. There was the shaking of blades! At length and at last it seemed as if the giant would get the victory over the herd. Then he called on his dog, and with one spring the black dog caught the giant by the neck, and swiftly the herd struck off his head.

He went home very tired this night, but it's a wonder if the king's cattle had not milk. The whole family was delighted that they had got such a herd.

He followed herding in this way for a time; but one night after he came home, instead of getting "all hail" and "good luck" from the dairymaid, all were at crying and woe.

He asked what cause of woe there was this night. The dairymaid said that a great beast with three heads was in the loch, and she was to get (some) one every year, and the lots had come this year on the king's daughter, "and in the middle of the day (to morrow) she is to meet the Uile Bheist at the upper end of the loch, but there is a great suitor yonder who is going to rescue her."

"What suitor is that?" said the herd. "Oh, he is a great General of arms," said the dairymaid, "and when he kills the beast, he will marry the king's daughter, for the king has said, that he who could save his daughter should get her to marry."

But on the morrow when the time was nearing, the king's daughter and this hero of arms went to give a meeting to the beast, and they reached the black corrie at the upper end of the loch. They were but a short time there when the beast stirred in the midst of the loch; but on the general's seeing this terror of a beast with three heads, he took fright, and he slunk away, and he hid himself. And the king's daughter was under fear and under trembling with no one at all to save her. At a glance, she sees a doughty handsome youth, riding a black horse, and coming where she was. He was marvellously arrayed, and full armed, and his black dog moving after him. "There is gloom on thy face, girl," said the youth. "What dost thou here?" "Oh! that's no matter," said the king's daughter. "It's not long I'll be here at all events." "I said not that," said he. "A worthy fled as likely as thou, and not long since," said she. "He is a worthy who stands the war," said the youth. He lay down beside her, and he said to her, if he should fall asleep, she should rouse him when she should see the beast making for shore. "What is rousing for thee?" said she. "Rousing for me is to put the gold ring on thy finger on my little finger." They were not long there when she saw the beast making for shore. She took a ring off her finger, and put it on the little finger of the lad. He awoke, and to meet the beast he went with his sword and his dog. But there was the spluttering and splashing between himself and the beast. The dog was doing all he might, and the king's daughter was palsied by fear of the noise of the beast. They would now be under, and now above. But at last he cut one of the heads off her. She gave one roar Raivic, and the son of earth, Mactalla of the rocks (echo), called to her screech, and she drove the loch in spindrift from end to end, and in a twinkling she went out of sight. "Good luck and victory that were following thee, lad!" said the king's daughter. "I am safe for one night, but the beast will come again, and for ever, until the other two heads come off her." He caught the beast's head, and he drew a withy through it, and he told her to bring it with her there to-morrow. She went home with the head on her shoulder, and the herd betook himself to the cows, but she had not gone far when this great General saw her, and he said to her that he would kill her, if she would not say that 'twas he took the head off the beast. "Oh!" says she, "'tis I will say it. Who else took the head off the beast but thou!" They reached the king's house, and the head was on the

General's shoulder. But here was rejoicing, that she should come home alive and whole, and this great captain with the beast's head full of blood in his hand. On the morrow they went away, and there was no question at all but that this hero would save the king's daughter.

They reached the same place, and they were not long there when the fearful Uile Bheist stirred in the midst of the loch, and the hero slunk away as he did on yesterday, but it was not long after this when the man of the black horse came, with another dress on. No matter, she knew that it was the very same lad. "It is I am pleased to see thee," said she. "I am in hopes thou wilt handle thy great sword to-day as thou didst yesterday. Come up and take breath." But they were not long there when they saw the beast steaming in the midst of the loch.

The lad lay down at the side of the king's daughter, and he said to her, "If I sleep before the beast comes, rouse me." "What is rousing for thee?" "Rousing for me is to put the ear-ring that is in thine ear in mine." He had not well fallen asleep when the king's daughter cried, "Rouse! Rouse!" but wake he would not; but she took the ear-ring out of her ear, and she put it in the ear of the lad. At once he woke, and to meet the beast he went, but there was Tloopersteich and Tlaperstich, rawceil s'taweeil, spluttering, splashing, raving and roaring on the beast! They kept on thus for a long time, and about the mouth of night, he cut another head off the beast. He put it on the withy, and he leaped on the black horse, and he betook himself to the herding. The king's daughter went home with the heads. The General met her, and took the heads from her, and he said to her, that she must tell that it was he who took the head off the beast this time also. "Who else took the head off the beast but thou?" said she. They reached the king's house with the heads. Then there was joy and gladness. If the king was hopeful the first night, he was now sure that this great hero would save his daughter, and there was no question at all but that the other head would be off the beast on the morrow.

About the same time on the morrow, the two went away. The officer bid himself as he usually did. The king's daughter betook herself to the bank of the loch. The hero of the black horse came, and he lay at her side. She woke the lad, and put another ear-ring in his other ear; and at the beast he went. But if rawceil and toiceil, roaring and raving were on the beast on the days that were passed, this day she was horrible. But no matter, he took the third head off the beast; and if he did, it was not without a struggle. He drew it through the withy, and she went home with the heads. When they reached the king's house, all were full of smiles, and the General was to marry the king's daughter the next day. The wedding was going on, and every one about the castle longing till the priest should come. But when the priest came, she would marry but the one who could take the heads off the withy without cutting the withy. "Who should take the heads off the withy but the man that put the heads on?" said the king.

The General tried them, but he could not loose them; and at last there was no one about the house but had tried to take the heads off the withy, but they could not. The king asked if there were any one else about the house that would try to take the heads off the withy? They said that the herd had not tried them yet. Word went for the herd; and he was not long throwing them hither and thither. "But stop a bit, my lad," said the king's daughter, "the man that took the heads off the beast, he has my ring and my two ear-rings." The herd put his hand in his pocket, and he threw them on the board. "Thou art my man," said the king's daughter. The king was not so pleased when he saw that it was a herd who was to marry his daughter, but he ordered that he should be put in a better dress; but his daughter spoke, and she said that he had a dress as fine as any that ever was in his castle; and thus it happened. The herd put on the giant's golden dress, and they married that same night.

They were now married, and everything going on well. They were one day sauntering by the side of the loch, and there came a beast more wonderfully terrible than the other, and takes him away to the loch without fear, or asking. The king's daughter was now mournful, tearful, blind-sorrowful for her married man; she was always with her eye on the loch. An old smith met her, and she told how it had befallen her married mate. The smith advised her to spread everything that was finer than another in the very same place where the beast took away her man; and so she did. The beast put up her nose, and she said, "Fine is thy jewellery, king's daughter." "Finer than that is the jewel that thou tookest from me," said she. "Give me one sight of my man, and thou shalt get any one thing of all these thou seest." The beast brought him up. "Deliver him to me, and thou shalt get all thou seest," said she. The beast did as she said. She threw him alive and whole on the bank of the loch.

A short time after this, when they were walking at the side of the loch, the same beast took away the king's daughter. Sorrowful was each one that was in the town on this night. Her man was mournful, tearful, wandering down and up about the banks of the loch, by day and night. The old smith met him. The smith told him that there was no way of killing the Uille Bheist but the one way, and this is it – "In the island that is in the midst of the loch is Eillid Chaisfhion – the white footed hind, of the slenderest legs, and the swiftest step, and though she should be caught, there would spring a hoodie out of her, and though the hoodie should be caught, there would spring a trout out of her, but there is an egg in the mouth of the trout, and the soul of the beast is in the egg, and if the egg breaks, the beast is dead."

Now, there was no way of getting to this island, for the beast would sink each boat and raft that would go on the loch. He thought he would try to leap the strait with the black horse, and even so he did. The black horse leaped the strait, and the black dog with one bound after him. He saw the Eillid, and he let the black dog after her, but when the black dog would be on one side of the island, the Eillid would be on the other side. "Oh! good were now the great dog of the carcass of flesh here!" No sooner spoke he the word than the generous dog was at his side; and after the Eillid he took, and the worthies were not long in bringing her to earth. But he no sooner caught her than a hoodie sprang out of her. "'Tis now, were good the falcon grey, of sharpest eye and swiftest wing!" No sooner said he this than the falcon was after the hoodie, and she was not long putting her to earth; and as the hoodie fell on the bank of the loch, out of her jumps the trout. "Oh, that thou wert by me now, oh otter!" No sooner said than the otter was at his side, and out on the loch she leaped, and brings the trout from the midst of the loch; but no sooner was the otter on shore with the trout than the egg came from his mouth. He sprang and he put his foot on it. 'Twas then the beast let out a roar, and she said, "Break not the egg, and thou gettest all thou askest." "Deliver to me my wife?" In the wink of an eye she was by his side. When he got hold of her hand in both his hands he let his foot (down) on the egg and the beast died.

The beast was dead now, and now was the sight to be seen. She was horrible to look upon. The three heads were off her doubtless, but if they were, there were heads under and heads over head on her, and eyes, and five hundred feet. But no matter, they left her there, and they went home, and there was delight and smiling in the king's house that night. And till now he had not told the king how he killed the giants. The king put great honour on him, and he was a great man with the king.

Himself and his wife were walking one day, when he noticed a little castle beside the loch in a wood; he asked his wife who was dwelling in it? She said that no one would be going near that castle, for that no one had yet come back to tell the tale, who had gone there.

"The matter must not be so," said he; "this very night I will see who is dwelling in it." "Go not, go not," said she; "there never went man to this castle that returned." "Be that as it pleases," says he. He went; he betakes himself to the castle. When he reached the door, a little flattering crone met him standing in the door. "All hail and good luck to thee, fisher's son; 'tis I myself am pleased to see thee; great is the honour for this kingdom, thy like to be come into it – thy coming in is fame for this little bothy; go in first; honour to the gentles; go on, and take breath." In he went, but as he was going up, she drew the Slachdan druidhach on him, on the back of his head, and at once – there he fell.

On this night there was woe in the king's castle, and on the morrow there was a wail in the fisher's house. The tree is seen withering, and the fisher's middle son said that his brother was dead, and he made a vow and oath, that he would go, and that he would know where the corpse of his brother was lying. He put saddle on a black horse, and rode after his black dog; (for the three sons of the fisher had a black horse and a black dog), and without going hither or thither he followed on his brother's step till he reached the king's house.

This one was so like his elder brother, that the king's daughter thought it was her own man. He stayed in the castle. They told him how it befell his brother; and to the little castle of the crone, go he must – happen hard or soft as it might. To the castle he went; and just as befell the eldest brother, so in each way it befell the middle son, and with one blow of the Slachdan druidhach, the crone felled him stretched beside his brother.

On seeing the second tree withering, the fisher's youngest son said that now his two brothers were dead, and that he must know what death had come on them. On the black horse he went, and he followed the dog as his brothers did, and he hit the king's house before he stopped. 'Twas the king who was pleased to see him; but to the black castle (for that was its name) they would not let him go. But to the castle he must go; and so he reached the castle. "All hail and good luck to thyself, fisher's son: 'tis I am pleased to see thee; go in and take breath," said she (the crone). "In before me thou crone: I don't like flattery out of doors; go in and let's hear thy speech." In went the crone, and when her back was to him he drew his sword and whips her head off; but the sword flew out of his hand. And swift the crone gripped her head with both hands, and puts it on her neck as it was before. The dog sprung on the crone, and she struck the generous dog with the club of magic; and there he lay. But this went not to make the youth more sluggish. To grips with the crone he goes; he got a hold of the Slachan druidhach, and with one blow on the top of the head, she was on earth in the wink of an eye. He went forward, up a little, and he sees his two brothers lying side by side. He gave a blow to each one with the Slachdan druidhach and on foot they were, and there was the spoil! Gold and silver, and each thing more precious than another, in the crone's castle. They came back to the king's house, and then there was rejoicing! The king was growing old. The eldest son of the fisherman was crowned king, and the pair of brothers stayed a day and a year in the king's house, and then the two went on their journey home, with the gold and silver of the crone, and each other grand thing which the king gave them; and if they have not died since then, they are alive to this very day.

The Draiglin' Hogney

THERE WAS ONCE A MAN who had three sons, and very little money to provide for them. So, when the eldest had grown into a lad, and saw that there was no means of making a livelihood at home, he went to his father and said to him:

"Father, if thou wilt give me a horse to ride on, a hound to hunt with, and a hawk to fly, I will go out into the wide world and seek my fortune."

His father gave him what he asked for; and he set out on his travels. He rode and he rode, over mountain and glen, until, just at nightfall, he came to a thick, dark wood. He entered it, thinking that he might find a path that would lead him through it; but no path was visible, and after wandering up and down for some time, he was obliged to acknowledge to himself that he was completely lost.

There seemed to be nothing for it but to tie his horse to a tree, and make a bed of leaves for himself on the ground; but just as he was about to do so he saw a light glimmering in the distance, and, riding on in the direction in which it was, he soon came to a clearing in the wood, in which stood a magnificent Castle.

The windows were all lit up, but the great door was barred; and, after he had ridden up to it, and knocked, and received no answer, the young man raised his hunting horn to his lips and blew a loud blast in the hope of letting the inmates know that he was without.

Instantly the door flew open of its own accord, and the young man entered, wondering very much what this strange thing would mean. And he wondered still more when he passed from room to room, and found that, although fires were burning brightly everywhere, and there was a plentiful meal laid out on the table in the great hall, there did not seem to be a single person in the whole of the vast building.

However, as he was cold, and tired, and wet, he put his horse in one of the stalls of the enormous stable, and taking his hawk and hound along with him, went into the hall and ate a hearty supper. After which he sat down by the side of the fire, and began to dry his clothes.

By this time it had grown late, and he was just thinking of retiring to one of the bedrooms which he had seen upstairs and going to bed, when a clock which was hanging on the wall struck twelve.

Instantly the door of the huge apartment opened, and a most awful-looking Draiglin' Hogney entered. His hair was matted and his beard was long, and his eyes shone like stars of fire from under his bushy eyebrows, and in his hands he carried a queerly shaped club.

He did not seem at all astonished to see his unbidden guest; but, coming across the hall, he sat down upon the opposite side of the fireplace, and, resting his chin on his hands, gazed fixedly at him.

"Doth thy horse ever kick any?" he said at last, in a harsh, rough voice.

"Ay, doth he," replied the young man; for the only steed that his father had been able to give him was a wild and unbroken colt.

"I have some skill in taming horses," went on the Draiglin' Hogney, "and I will give thee something to tame thine withal. Throw this over him" – and he pulled one of the long, coarse hairs out of his head and gave it to the young man. And there was something so commanding in the Hogney's voice that he did as he was bid, and went out to the stable and threw the hair over the horse.

Then he returned to the hall, and sat down again by the fire. The moment that he was seated the Draiglin' Hogney asked another question.

"Doth thy hound ever bite any?"

"Ay, verily," answered the youth; for his hound was so fierce-tempered that no man, save his master, dare lay a hand on him.

"I can cure the wildest tempered dog in Christendom," replied the Draiglin' Hogney. "Take that, and throw it over him." And he pulled another hair out of his head and gave it to the young man, who lost no time in flinging it over his hound.

There was still a third question to follow. "Doth ever thy hawk peck any?"

The young man laughed. "I have ever to keep a bandage over her eyes, save when she is ready to fly," said he; "else were nothing safe within her reach."

"Things will be safe now," said the Hogney, grimly. "Throw that over her." And for the third time he pulled a hair from his head and handed it to his companion. And as the other hairs had been thrown over the horse and the hound, so this one was thrown over the hawk.

Then, before the young man could draw breath, the fiercesome Draiglin' Hogney had given him such a clout on the side of his head with his queer-shaped club that he fell down in a heap on the floor.

And very soon his hawk and his hound tumbled down still and motionless beside him; and, out in the stable, his horse became stark and stiff, as if turned to stone. For the Draiglin's words had meant more than at first appeared when he said that he could make all unruly animals quiet.

Some time afterwards the second of the three sons came to his father in the old home with the same request that his brother had made. That he should be provided with a horse, a hawk, and a hound, and be allowed to go out to seek his fortune. And his father listened to him, and gave him what he asked, as he had given his brother.

And the young man set out, and in due time came to the wood, and lost himself in it, just as his brother had done; then he saw the light, and came to the Castle, and went in, and had supper, and dried his clothes, just as it all had happened before.

And the Draiglin' Hogney came in, and asked him the three questions, and he gave the same three answers, and received three hairs – one to throw over his horse, one to throw over his hound, and one to throw over his hawk; then the Hogney killed him, just as he had killed his brother.

Time passed, and the youngest son, finding that his two elder brothers never returned, asked his father for a horse, a hawk, and a hound, in order that he might go and look for them. And the poor old man, who was feeling very desolate in his old age, gladly gave them to him.

So he set out on his quest, and at nightfall he came, as the others had done, to the thick wood and the Castle. But, being a wise and cautious youth, he liked not the way in which he found things. He liked not the empty house; he liked not the spread-out feast; and, most of all, he liked not the look of the Draiglin' Hogney when he saw him. And he determined to be very careful what he said or did as long as he was in his company.

So when the Draiglin' Hogney asked him if his horse kicked, he replied that it did, in very few words; and when he got one of the Hogney's hairs to throw over him, he went out to the stable, and pretended to do so, but he brought it back, hidden in his hand, and, when his unchancy companion was not looking, he threw it into the fire. It fizzled up like a tongue of flame with a little hissing sound like that of a serpent.

"What's that fizzling?" asked the Giant suspiciously.

"'Tis but the sap of the green wood," replied the young man carelessly, as he turned to caress his hound.

The answer satisfied the Draiglin' Hogney, and he paid no heed to the sound which the hair that should have been thrown over the hound, or the sound which the hair that should have been thrown over the hawk, made, when the young man threw them into the fire; and they fizzled up in the same way that the first had done.

Then, thinking that he had the stranger in his power, he whisked across the hearthstone to strike him with his club, as he had struck his brothers; but the young man was on the outlook, and when he saw him coming he gave a shrill whistle. And his horse, which loved him dearly, came galloping in from the stable, and his hound sprang up from the hearthstone where he had been sleeping; and his hawk, who was sitting on his shoulder, ruffled up her feathers and screamed harshly; and they all fell on the Draiglin' Hogney at once, and he found out only too well how the horse kicked, and the hound bit, and the hawk pecked; for they kicked him, and bit him, and pecked him, till he was as dead as a door nail.

When the young man saw that he was dead, he took his little club from his hand, and, armed with that, he set out to explore the Castle.

As he expected, he found that there were dark and dreary dungeons under it, and in one of them he found his two brothers, lying cold and stiff side by side. He touched them with the club, and instantly they came to life again, and sprang to their feet as well as ever.

Then he went into another dungeon; and there were the two horses, and the two hawks, and the two hounds, lying as if dead, exactly as their Masters had lain. He touched them with his magic club, and they, too, came to life again.

Then he called to his two brothers, and the three young men searched the other dungeons, and they found great stores of gold and silver hidden in them, enough to make them rich for life.

So they buried the Draiglin' Hogney, and took possession of the Castle; and two of them went home and brought their old father back with them, and they all were as prosperous and happy as they could be; and, for aught that I know, they are living there still.

The Ghosts of Craig-Aulnaic

TWO CELEBRATED GHOSTS EXISTED, once on a time, in the wilds of Craig-Aulnaic, a romantic place in the district of Strathdown, Banffshire. The one was a male and the other a female. The male was called Fhuna Mhoir Ben Baynac, after one of the mountains of Glenavon, where at one time he resided; and the female was called Clashnichd Aulnaic, from her having had her

abode in Craig-Aulnaic. But although the great ghost of Ben Baynac was bound by the common ties of nature and of honour to protect and cherish his weaker companion, Clashnichd Aulnaic, yet he often treated her in the most cruel and unfeeling manner. In the dead of night, when the surrounding hamlets were buried in deep repose, and when nothing else disturbed the solemn stillness of the midnight scene, oft would the shrill shrieks of poor Clashnichd burst upon the slumberer's ears, and awake him to anything but pleasant reflections.

But of all those who were incommoded by the noisy and unseemly quarrels of these two ghosts, James Owre or Gray, the tenant of the farm of Balbig of Delnabo, was the greatest sufferer. From the proximity of his abode to their haunts, it was the misfortune of himself and family to be the nightly audience of Clashnichd's cries and lamentations, which they considered anything but agreeable entertainment.

One day as James Gray was on his rounds looking after his sheep, he happened to fall in with Clashnichd, the ghost of Aulnaic, with whom he entered into a long conversation. In the course of it he took occasion to remonstrate with her on the very disagreeable disturbance she caused himself and family by her wild and unearthly cries – cries which, he said, few mortals could relish in the dreary hours of midnight. Poor Clashnichd, by way of apology for her conduct, gave James Gray a sad account of her usage, detailing at full length the series of cruelties committed upon her by Ben Baynac. From this account, it appeared that her living with the latter was by no means a matter of choice with Clashnichd; on the contrary, it seemed that she had, for a long time, lived apart with much comfort, residing in a snug dwelling, as already mentioned, in the wilds of Craig-Aulnaic; but Ben Baynac having unfortunately taken into his head to pay her a visit, took a fancy, not to herself, but her dwelling, of which, in his own name and authority, he took immediate possession, and soon after he expelled poor Clashnichd, with many stripes, from her natural inheritance. Not satisfied with invading and depriving her of her just rights, he was in the habit of following her into her private haunts, not with the view of offering her any endearments, but for the purpose of inflicting on her person every torment which his brain could invent.

Such a moving relation could not fail to affect the generous heart of James Gray, who determined from that moment to risk life and limb in order to vindicate the rights and avenge the wrongs of poor Clashnichd, the ghost of Craig-Aulnaic. He, therefore, took good care to interrogate his new protégée touching the nature of her oppressor's constitution, whether he was of that killable species of ghost that could be shot with a silver sixpence, or if there was any other weapon that could possibly accomplish his annihilation. Clashnichd informed him that she had occasion to know that Ben Baynac was wholly invulnerable to all the weapons of man, with the exception of a large mole on his left breast, which was no doubt penetrable by silver or steel; but that, from the specimens she had of his personal prowess and strength, it were vain for mere man to attempt to combat him. Confiding, however, in his expertness as an archer – for he was allowed to be the best marksman of the age – James Gray told Clashnichd he did not fear him with all his might, – that he was a man; and desired her, moreover, next time the ghost chose to repeat his incivilities to her, to apply to him, James Gray, for redress.

It was not long ere he had an opportunity of fulfilling his promises. Ben Baynac having one night, in the want of better amusement, entertained himself by inflicting an inhuman castigation on Clashnichd, she lost no time in waiting on James Gray, with a full and particular account of it. She found him smoking his cutty, for it was night when she came to him; but, notwithstanding the inconvenience of the hour, James needed no great persuasion to induce him to proceed directly along with Clashnichd to hold a communing with their friend, Ben Baynac, the great ghost. Clashnichd was stout and sturdy, and understood the knack of travelling much better than our women do. She expressed a wish that, for the sake of expedition, James Gray would suffer her to bear him along, a motion to which the latter agreed; and a few minutes brought them close to the scene of Ben Baynac's residence. As they approached his haunt, he came forth to meet them, with looks and gestures which did not at all indicate a cordial welcome. It was a fine moonlight night, and they could easily observe his actions. Poor Clashnichd was now sorely afraid of the great ghost. Apprehending instant destruction from his fury, she exclaimed to James Gray that they would be both dead people, and that immediately, unless James Gray hit with an arrow the mole which covered Ben Baynac's heart. This was not so difficult a task as James had hitherto apprehended it. The mole was as large as a common bonnet, and yet nowise disproportioned to the natural size of the ghost's body, for he certainly was a great and a mighty ghost. Ben Baynac cried out to James Gray that he would soon make eagle's meat of him; and certain it is, such was his intention, had not the shepherd so effectually stopped him from the execution of it. Raising his bow to his eye when within a few yards of Ben Baynac, he took deliberate aim; the arrow flew – it hit – a yell from Ben Baynac announced the result. A hideous howl re-echoed from the surrounding mountains, responsive to the groans of a thousand ghosts; and Ben Baynac, like the smoke of a shot, vanished into air.

Clashnichd, the ghost of Aulnaic, now found herself emancipated from the most abject state of slavery, and restored to freedom and liberty, through the invincible courage of James Gray. Overpowered with gratitude, she fell at his feet, and vowed to devote the whole of her time and talents towards his service and prosperity. Meanwhile, being anxious to have her remaining goods and furniture removed to her former dwelling, whence she had been so iniquitously expelled by Ben Baynac, the great ghost, she requested of her new master the use of his horses to remove them. James observing on the adjacent hill a flock of deer, and wishing to have a trial of his new servant's sagacity or expertness, told her those were his horses – she was welcome to the use of them; desiring that when she had done with them, she would inclose them in his stable. Clashnichd then proceeded to make use of the horses, and James Gray returned home to enjoy his night's rest.

Scarce had he reached his arm-chair, and reclined his cheek on his hand, to ruminate over the bold adventure of the night, when Clashnichd entered, with her "breath in her throat," and venting the bitterest complaints at the unruliness of his horses, which had broken one-half of her furniture, and caused her more trouble in the stabling of them than their services were worth.

"Oh! they are stabled, then?" inquired James Gray. Clashnichd replied in the affirmative. "Very well," rejoined James, "they shall be tame enough to-morrow."

From this specimen of Clashnichd, the ghost of Craig-Aulnaic's expertness, it will be seen what a valuable acquisition her service proved to James Gray and his young family. They were, however, speedily deprived of her assistance by a most unfortunate accident. From the sequel of the story, from which the foregoing is an extract, it appears that poor Clashnichd was deeply addicted to propensities which at that time rendered her kin so obnoxious to their human neighbours. She was constantly in the habit of visiting her friends much oftener than she was invited, and, in the course of such visits, was never very scrupulous in making free with any eatables which fell within the circle of her observation.

One day, while engaged on a foraging expedition of this description, she happened to enter the Mill of Delnabo, which was inhabited in those days by the miller's family. She found his wife engaged in roasting a large gridiron of fine savoury fish, the agreeable smell proceeding from which perhaps occasioned her visit. With the usual inquiries after the health of the miller and his family, Clashnichd proceeded with the greatest familiarity and good-humour to make herself comfortable at their expense. But the miller's wife, enraged at the loss of her fish, and not relishing such unwelcome familiarity, punished the unfortunate Clashnichd rather too severely for her freedom. It happened that there was at the time a large caldron of boiling water suspended over the fire, and this caldron the enraged wife overturned in Clashnichd's bosom!

Scalded beyond recovery, she fled up the wilds of Craig-Aulnaic, uttering the most melancholy lamentations, nor has she been ever heard of since.

The Fiddler and the Bogle of Bogandoran

LATE ONE NIGHT, as my grand-uncle, Lachlan Dhu Macpherson, who was well known as the best fiddler of his day, was returning home from a ball, at which he had acted as a musician, he had occasion to pass through the once-haunted Bog of Torrans.

Now, it happened at that time that the bog was frequented by a huge bogle or ghost, who was of a most mischievous disposition, and took particular pleasure in abusing every traveller who had occasion to pass through the place betwixt the twilight at night and cock-crowing in the morning. Suspecting much that he would also come in for a share of his abuse, my grand-uncle made up his mind, in the course of his progress, to return the ghost any civilities which he might think meet to offer him. On arriving on the spot, he found his suspicions were too well grounded; for whom did he see but the ghost of Bogandoran apparently ready waiting him, and seeming by his ghastly grin not a little overjoyed at the meeting. Marching up to my grand-uncle, the bogle clapped a huge club into his hand, and furnishing himself with one of the same dimensions, he put a spittle in his hand, and deliberately commenced the combat. My grand-uncle returned the salute with equal spirit, and so ably did both parties ply their batons that for a while the issue of the combat was extremely doubtful. At length, however, the fiddler could easily discover that his opponent's vigour was much in the fagging order. Picking up renewed courage in consequence, he plied the ghost with renewed force, and after a stout resistance, in the course of which both parties were seriously handled, the ghost of Bogandoran thought it prudent to give up the night.

"At the same time, filled no doubt with great indignation at this signal defeat, it seems the ghost resolved to re-engage my grand-uncle on some other occasion, under more favourable circumstances. Not long after, as my grand-uncle was returning home quite unattended from another ball in the Braes of the country, he had just entered the hollow of Auldichoish, well known for its 'eerie' properties, when, lo! who presented himself to his view on the adjacent eminence but his old friend of Bogandoran, advancing as large as the gable of a house, and putting himself in the most threatening and fighting attitudes.

"Looking at the very dangerous nature of the ground where they had met, and feeling no anxiety for a second encounter with a combatant of his weight, in a situation so little desirable, the fiddler would have willingly deferred the settlement of their differences till a more convenient season. He, accordingly, assuming the most submissive aspect in the world, endeavoured to pass by his champion in peace, but in vain. Longing, no doubt, to retrieve the disgrace of his late discomfiture, the bogle instantly seized the fiddler, and attempted with all his might to pull the latter down the precipice, with the diabolical intention, it is supposed, of drowning him in the river Avon below. In this pious design the bogle was happily frustrated by the intervention of some trees which grew on the precipice, and to which my unhappy grand-uncle clung with the zeal of a drowning man. The enraged ghost, finding it impossible to extricate him from those friendly trees, and resolving, at all events, to be revenged upon him, fell upon maltreating the fiddler with his hands and feet in the most inhuman manner.

"Such gross indignities my worthy grand-uncle was not accustomed to, and being incensed beyond all measure at the liberties taken by Bogandoran, he resolved again to try his mettle, whether life or death should be the consequence.Having no other weapon wherewith to defend himself but his biodag, which, considering the nature of his opponent's constitution, he suspected much would be of little avail to him – I say, in the absence of any other weapon, he sheathed the biodag three times in the ghost of Bogandoran's body. And what was the consequence? Why, to the great astonishment of my courageous forefather, the ghost fell down cold dead at his feet, and was never more seen or heard of."

The Bogle

THIS IS A FREAKISH SPIRIT who delights rather to perplex and frighten mankind than either to serve or seriously hurt them. The Esprit Follet of the French, Shakespeare's Puck, or Robin Goodfellow, and Shellycoat, a spirit who resides in the waters, and has given his name to many a rock and stone on the Scottish coast, belong to the class of bogles.

One of Shellycoat's pranks is thus narrated: Two men in a very dark night, approaching the banks of the Ettrick, heard a doleful voice from its waves repeatedly exclaim, "Lost! lost!" They followed the sound, which seemed to be the voice of a drowning person, and, to their astonishment, found that it ascended the river; still they continued to follow the cry of the malicious sprite, and, arriving before dawn at the very sources of the river, the voice was now heard descending the opposite side of the mountain in which they arise. The fatigued and deluded travellers now relinquished the pursuit, and had no sooner done so, than they heard Shellycoat applauding, in loud bursts of laughter, his successful roguery.

The Death Bree

THERE WAS ONCE A WOMAN, who lived in the Camp-del-more of Strathavon, whose cattle were seized with a murrain, or some such fell disease, which ravaged the neighbourhood at the time, carrying off great numbers of them daily. All the forlorn fires and hallowed waters failed of their customary effects; and she was at length told by the wise people, whom she consulted on the occasion, that it was evidently the effect of some infernal agency, the power of which could not be destroyed by any other means than the never-failing specific – the juice of a dead head from the churchyard, a nostrum certainly very difficult to be procured, considering that the head must needs be abstracted from the grave at the hour of midnight. Being, however, a woman of a stout heart and strong faith, native feelings of delicacy towards the sanctuary of the dead had more weight than had fear in restraining her for some time from resorting to this desperate remedy.

At length, seeing that her stock would soon be annihilated by the destructive career of the disease, the wife of Camp-del-more resolved to put the experiment in practice, whatever the result might be. Accordingly, having with considerable difficulty engaged a neighbouring woman as her companion in this hazardous expedition, they set out a little before midnight for the parish churchyard, distant about a mile and a half from her residence, to execute her determination.

On arriving at the churchyard her companion, whose courage was not so notable, appalled by the gloomy prospect before her, refused to enter among the habitations of the dead. She, however, agreed to remain at the gate till her friend's business was accomplished. This circumstance, however, did not stagger the wife's resolution. She, with the greatest coolness and intrepidity, proceeded towards what she supposed an old grave, took down her spade, and commenced her operations. After a good deal of toil she arrived at the object of her labour. Raising the first head, or rather skull, that came in her way, she was about to make it her own property, when a hollow, wild, sepulchral voice exclaimed, "That is my head; let it alone!" Not wishing to dispute the claimant's title to this head, and supposing she could be otherwise provided, she very good-naturedly returned it and took up another. "That is my father's head," bellowed the same voice. Wishing, if possible, to avoid disputes, the wife of Camp-del-more took up another head, when the same voice instantly started a claim to it as his grandfather's head. "Well," replied the wife, nettled at her disappointments, "although it were your grandmother's head, you shan't get it till I am done with it." "What do you say, you limmer?" says the ghost, starting up in his awry habiliments. "What do you say, you limmer?" repeated he in a great rage. "By the great oath, you had better leave my grandfather's head." Upon matters coming this length, the wily wife of Camp-del-more thought it proper to assume a more conciliatory aspect. Telling the claimant the whole particulars of the predicament in which she was placed, she promised faithfully that if his honour would only allow her to carry off his grandfather's skull or head in a peaceable manner, she would restore it again when done with. Here, after some communing, they came to an understanding; and she was allowed to take the head along with her, on condition that she should restore it before cock-crowing, under the heaviest penalties.

On coming out of the churchyard and looking for her companion, she had the mortification to find her "without a mouthful of breath in her body"; for, on hearing the dispute between her friend and the guardian of the grave, and suspecting much that she was likely to share the unpleasant punishments with which he threatened her friend, at the bare recital of them she fell down in a faint, from which it was no easy matter to recover her. This proved no small inconvenience to Camp-del-more's wife, as there were not above two hours to elapse ere she had to return the head according to the terms of her agreement. Taking her friend upon her back, she carried her up a steep acclivity to the nearest adjoining house, where she left her for the night; then repaired home with the utmost speed, made the 'death bree' (broth) from the head ere the appointed time had expired, restored the skull to its guardian, and placed the grave in its former condition. It is needless to add that, as a reward for her exemplary courage, the 'bree' had its desired effect. The cattle speedily recovered, and, so long as she retained any of it, all sorts of diseases were of short duration.

Animals & Fables

nimals have been a storyteller's staple in just about every culture. Even where, as with the sheep who stars in 'The Story of the White Pet', not much appears to be made of the creature's animal nature, the very fact that it is playing a quasi-human part gives a sense of the extraordinary in itself.

Sometimes, as in 'The Tulman', animals act as instruments of enchantment, intermediaries between the fairy and the human realm. Frequently they facilitate what are essentially human actions, like the great goggle-eyed frog who helps the heroine of 'The Well of the World's End'. If kindness to animals is repaid in such stories; cruelty is punished, as in 'The Burgh'. In fables, animals stand in for particular temperaments and talents, as the tale of 'The Fox and the Wolf' pits the former's cunning against the latter's strength.

The Well of the World's End

ONCE UPON A TIME, and a very good time it was, though it wasn't in my time, nor in your time, nor any one else's time, there was a girl whose mother had died, and her father had married again. And her stepmother hated her because she was more beautiful than herself, and she was very cruel to her. She used to make her do all the servant's work, and never let her have any peace. At last, one day, the stepmother thought to get rid of her altogether; so she handed her a sieve and said to her: "Go, fill it at the Well of the World's End and bring it home to me full, or woe betide you." For she thought she would never be able to find the Well of the World's End, and, if she did, how could she bring home a sieve full of water?

Well, the girl started off, and asked every one she met to tell her where was the Well of the World's End. But nobody knew, and she didn't know what to do, when a queer little old woman, all bent double, told her where it was, and how she could get to it.

So she did what the old woman told her, and at last arrived at the Well of the World's End. But when she dipped the sieve in the cold, cold water, it all ran out again. She tried and she tried again, but every time it was the same; and at last she sate down and cried as if her heart would break.

Suddenly she heard a croaking voice, and she looked up and saw a great frog with goggle eyes looking at her and speaking to her.

"What's the matter, dearie?" it said.

"Oh, dear, oh dear," she said, "my stepmother has sent me all this long way to fill this sieve with water from the Well of the World's End, and I can't fill it no how at all."

"Well," said the frog, "if you promise me to do whatever I bid you for a whole night long, I'll tell you how to fill it."

So the girl agreed, and then the frog said:

> *"Stop it with moss and daub it with clay,*
> *And then it will carry the water away;"*

and then it gave a hop, skip and jump, and went flop into the Well of the World's End.

So the girl looked about for some moss, and lined the bottom of the sieve with it, and over that she put some clay, and then she dipped it once again into the Well of the World's End; and this time, the water didn't run out, and she turned to go away.

Just then the frog popped up its head out of the Well of the World's End, and said: "Remember your promise."

"All right," said the girl; for thought she, "what harm can a frog do me?"

So she went back to her stepmother, and brought the sieve full of water from the Well of the World's End. The stepmother was fine and angry, but she said nothing at all.

That very evening they heard something tap tapping at the door low down, and a voice cried out:

> *"Open the door, my hinny, my heart,*
> *Open the door, my own darling;*
> *Mind you the words that you and I spoke,*
> *Down in the meadow, at the World's End Well."*

"Whatever can that be?" cried out the stepmother, and the girl had to tell her all about it, and what she had promised the frog.

"Girls must keep their promises," said the stepmother. "Go and open the door this instant." For she was glad the girl would have to obey a nasty frog.

So the girl went and opened the door, and there was the frog from the Well of the World's End. And it hopped, and it skipped, and it jumped, till it reached the girl, and then it said:

> *"Lift me to your knee, my hinny, my heart;*
> *Lift me to your knee, my own darling;*
> *Remember the words you and I spoke,*
> *Down in the meadow by the World's End Well."*

But the girl didn't like to, till her stepmother said "Lift it up this instant, you hussy! Girls must keep their promises!"

So at last she lifted the frog up on to her lap, and it lay there for a time, till at last it said:

"Give me some supper, my hinny, my heart,
Give me some supper, my darling;
Remember the words you and I spake,
In the meadow, by the Well of the World's End."

Well, she didn't mind doing that, so she got it a bowl of milk and bread, and fed it well. And when the frog had finished, it said:

"Go with me to bed, my hinny, my heart,
Go with me to bed, my own darling;
Mind you the words you spake to me,
Down by the cold well, so weary."

But that the girl wouldn't do, till her stepmother said: "Do what you promised, girl; girls must keep their promises. Do what you're bid, or out you go, you and your froggie."

So the girl took the frog with her to bed, and kept it as far away from her as she could. Well, just as the day was beginning to break what should the frog say but:

"Chop off my head, my hinny, my heart,
Chop off my head, my own darling;
Remember the promise you made to me,
Down by the cold well so weary."

At first the girl wouldn't, for she thought of what the frog had done for her at the Well of the World's End. But when the frog said the words over again, she went and took an axe and chopped off its head, and lo! and behold, there stood before her a handsome young prince, who told her that he had been enchanted by a wicked magician, and he could never be unspelled till some girl would do his bidding for a whole night, and chop off his head at the end of it.

The stepmother was that surprised when she found the young prince instead of the nasty frog, and she wasn't best pleased, you may be sure, when the prince told her that he was going to marry her stepdaughter because she had unspelled him. So they were married and went away to live in the castle of the king, his father, and all the stepmother had to console her was, that it was all through her that her stepdaughter was married to a prince.

The Wedding of Robin Redbreast and Jenny Wren

THERE WAS ONCE AN OLD grey Pussy Baudrons, and she went out for a stroll one Christmas morning to see what she could see. And as she was walking down the burnside she saw a little Robin Redbreast hopping up and down on the branches of a briar bush.

"What a tasty breakfast he would make," thought she to herself. "I must try to catch him."

So, "Good morning, Robin Redbreast," quoth she, sitting down on her tail at the foot of the briar bush and looking up at him. "And where mayest thou be going so early on this cold winter's day?"

"I'm on my road to the King's Palace," answered Robin cheerily, "to sing him a song this merry Yule morning."

"That's a pious errand to be travelling on, and I wish you good success," replied Pussy slyly; "but just hop down a minute before thou goest, and I will show thee what a bonnie white ring I have round my neck. 'Tis few cats that are marked like me."

Then Robin cocked his head on one side, and looked down on Pussy Baudrons with a twinkle in his eye. "Ha, ha! grey Pussy Baudrons," he said.

"Ha, ha! for I saw thee worry the little grey mouse, and I have no wish that thou shouldst worry me."

And with that he spread his wings and flew away. And he flew, and he flew, till he lighted on an old sod dyke; and there he saw a greedy old gled sitting, with all his feathers ruffled up as if he felt cold.

"Good morning, Robin Redbreast," cried the greedy old gled, who had had no food since yesterday, and was therefore very hungry. "And where mayest thou be going to, this cold winter's day?"

"I'm on my road to the King's Palace," answered Robin, "to sing to him a song this merry Yule morning." And he hopped away a yard or two from the gled, for there was a look in his eye that he did not quite like.

"Thou art a friendly little fellow," remarked the gled sweetly, "and I wish thee good luck on thine errand; but ere thou go on, come nearer me, I prith'ee, and I will show thee what a curious feather I have in my wing. 'Tis said that no other gled in the country-side hath one like it."

"Like enough," rejoined Robin, hopping still further away; "but I will take thy word for it, without seeing it. For I saw thee pluck the feathers from the wee lintie, and I have no wish that thou shouldst pluck the feathers from me. So I will bid thee good day, and go on my journey."

The next place on which he rested was a piece of rock that overhung a dark, deep glen, and here he saw a sly old fox looking out of his hole not two yards below him.

"Good morning, Robin Redbreast," said the sly old fox, who had tried to steal a fat duck from a farmyard the night before, and had barely escaped with his life. "And where mayest thou be going so early on this cold winter's day?"

"I'm on my road to the King's Palace, to sing him a song this merry Yule morning," answered Robin, giving the same answer that he had given to the grey Pussy Baudrons and the greedy gled.

"Thou wilt get a right good welcome, for His Majesty is fond of music," said the wily fox. "But ere thou go, just come down and have a look at a black spot which I have on the end of my tail. 'Tis said that there is not a fox 'twixt here and the Border that hath a spot on his tail like mine."

"Very like, very like," replied Robin; "but I chanced to see thee worrying the wee lambie up on the braeside yonder, and I have no wish that thou shouldst try thy teeth on me. So I will e'en go on my way to the King's Palace, and thou canst show the spot on thy tail to the next passer-by."

So the little Robin Redbreast flew away once more, and never rested till he came to a bonnie valley with a little burn running through it, and there he saw a rosy-cheeked boy sitting on a log eating a piece of bread and butter. And he perched on a branch and watched him.

"Good morning, Robin Redbreast; and where mayest thou be going so early on this cold winter's day?" asked the boy eagerly; for he was making a collection of stuffed birds, and he had still to get a Robin Redbreast.

"I'm on my way to the King's Palace to sing him a song this merry Yule morning," answered Robin, hopping down to the ground, and keeping one eye fixed on the bread and butter.

"Come a bit nearer, Robin," said the boy, "and I will give thee some crumbs."

"Na, na, my wee man," chirped the cautious little bird; "for I saw thee catch the goldfinch, and I have no wish to give thee the chance to catch me."

At last he came to the King's Palace and lighted on the window-sill, and there he sat and sang the very sweetest song that he could sing; for he felt so happy because it was the Blessed Yuletide, that he wanted everyone else to be happy too. And the King and the Queen were so delighted with his song, as he peeped in at them at their open window, that they asked each other what they could give him as a reward for his kind thought in coming so far to greet them.

"We can give him a wife," replied the Queen, "who will go home with him and help him to build his nest."

"And who wilt thou give him for a bride?" asked the King. "Methinks 'twould need to be a very tiny lady to match his size."

"Why, Jenny Wren, of course," answered the Queen. "She hath looked somewhat dowie of late, this will be the very thing to brighten her up."

Then the King clapped his hands, and praised his wife for her happy thought, and wondered that the idea had not struck him before.

So Robin Redbreast and Jenny Wren were married, amid great rejoicings, at the King's Palace; and the King and Queen and all the fine Nobles and Court Ladies danced at their wedding. Then they flew away home to Robin's own country-side, and built their nest in the roots of the briar bush, where he had spoken to Pussy Baudrons. And you will be glad to hear that Jenny Wren proved the best little housewife in the world.

The Fox and the Wolf

THERE WAS ONCE A FOX and a Wolf, who set up house together in a cave near the sea-shore. Although you may not think so, they got on very well for a time, for they went out hunting all day, and when they came back at night they were generally too tired to do anything but to eat their supper and go to bed.

They might have lived together always had it not been for the slyness and greediness of the Fox, who tried to over-reach his companion, who was not nearly so clever as he was. ·

And this was how it came about.

It chanced, one dark December night, that there was a dreadful storm at sea, and in the morning the beach was all strewn with wreckage. So as soon as it was daylight the two friends went down to the shore to see if they could find anything to eat.

They had the good fortune to light on a great Keg of Butter, which had been washed overboard from some ship on its way home from Ireland, where, as all the world knows, folk are famous for their butter.

The simple Wolf danced with joy when he saw it. "Marrowbones and trotters! but we will have a good supper this night," cried he, licking his lips. "Let us set to work at once and roll it up to the cave."

But the wily Fox was fond of butter, and he made up his mind that he would have it all to himself. So he put on his wisest look, and shook his head gravely.

"Thou hast no prudence, my friend," he said reproachfully, "else wouldst thou not talk of breaking up a Keg of Butter at this time of year, when the stackyards are full of good grain, which can be had for the eating, and the farmyards are stocked with nice fat ducks and poultry. No, no. It behoveth us to have foresight, and to lay up in store for the spring, when the grain is all threshed, and the stackyards are bare, and the poultry have gone to market. So we will e'en bury the Keg, and dig it up when we have need of it."

Very reluctantly, for he was thinner and hungrier than the Fox, the Wolf agreed to this proposal. So a hole was dug, and the Keg was buried, and the two animals went off hunting as usual.

About a week passed by: then one day the Fox came into the cave, and flung himself down on the ground as if he were very much exhausted. But if anyone had looked at him closely they would have seen a sly twinkle in his eye.

"Oh, dear, oh, dear!" he sighed. "Life is a heavy burden."

"What hath befallen thee?" asked the Wolf, who was ever kind and soft-hearted.

"Some friends of mine, who live over the hills yonder, are wanting me to go to a christening to-night. Just think of the distance that I must travel."

"But needst thou go?" asked the Wolf. "Canst thou not send an excuse?"

"I doubt that no excuse would be accepted," answered the Fox, "for they asked me to stand god-father. Therefore it behoveth me to do my duty, and pay no heed to my own feelings."

So that evening the Fox was absent, and the Wolf was alone in the cave. But it was not to a christening that the sly Fox went; it was to the Keg of Butter that was buried in the sand. About midnight he returned, looking fat and sleek, and well pleased with himself.

The Wolf had been dozing, but he looked up drowsily as his companion entered. "Well, how did they name the bairn?" he asked.

"They gave it a queer name," answered the Fox. "One of the queerest names that I ever heard."

"And what was that?" questioned the Wolf.

"Nothing less than 'Blaisean' (Let-me-taste)," replied the Fox, throwing himself down in his corner. And if the Wolf could have seen him in the darkness he would have noticed that he was laughing to himself.

Some days afterwards the same thing happened. The Fox was asked to another christening; this time at a place some twenty-five miles along the shore. And as he had grumbled before, so he grumbled again; but he declared that it was his duty to go, and he went.

At midnight he came back, smiling to himself and with no appetite for his supper. And when the Wolf asked him the name of the child, he answered that it was a more extraordinary name than the other – 'Be na Inheadnon' (Be in its middle).

The very next week, much to the Wolf's wonder, the Fox was asked to yet another christening. And this time the name of the child was 'Sgriot an Clar' (Scrape the staves). After that the invitations ceased.

Time went on, and the hungry spring came, and the Fox and the Wolf had their larder bare, for food was scarce, and the weather was bleak and cold.

"Let us go and dig up the Keg of Butter," said the Wolf. "Methinks that now is the time we need it."

The Fox agreed – having made up his mind how he would act – and the two set out to the place where the Keg had been hidden. They scraped away the sand, and uncovered it; but, needless to say, they found it empty.

"This is thy work," said the Fox angrily, turning to the poor, innocent Wolf. "Thou hast crept along here while I was at the christenings, and eaten it up by stealth."

"Not I," replied the Wolf. "I have never been near the spot since the day that we buried it together."

"But I tell thee it must have been thou," insisted the Fox, "for no other creature knew it was there except ourselves. And, besides, I can see by the sleekness of thy fur that thou hast fared well of late."

Which last sentence was both unjust and untrue, for the poor Wolf looked as lean and badly nourished as he could possibly be.

So back they both went to the cave, arguing all the way. The Fox declaring that the Wolf must have been the thief, and the Wolf protesting his innocence.

"Art thou ready to swear to it?" said the Fox at last; though why he asked such a question, dear only knows.

"Yes, I am," replied the Wolf firmly; and, standing in the middle of the cave, and holding one paw up solemnly he swore this awful oath:

> *"If it be that I stole the butter; if it be, if it be –*
> *May a fateful, fell disease fall on me, fall on me."*

When he was finished, he put down his paw and, turning to the Fox, looked at him keenly; for all at once it struck him that his fur looked sleek and fine.

"It is thy turn now," he said. "I have sworn, and thou must do so also."

The Fox's face fell at these words, for although he was both untruthful and dishonest now, he had been well brought up in his youth, and he knew that it was a terrible thing to perjure oneself and swear falsely.

So he made one excuse after another, but the Wolf, who was getting more and more suspicious every moment, would not listen to him.

So, as he had not courage to tell the truth, he was forced at last to swear an oath also, and this was what he swore:

"If it be that I stole the butter; if it be, if it be –
Then let some most deadly punishment fall on me, fall on me –
Whirrum wheeckam, whirrum wheeckam,
Whirram whee, whirram whee!"

After he had heard him swear this terrible oath, the Wolf thought that his suspicions must be groundless, and he would have let the matter rest; but the Fox, having an uneasy conscience, could not do so. So he suggested that as it was clear that one of them must have eaten the Keg of Butter, they should both stand near the fire; so that when they became hot, the butter would ooze out of the skin of whichever of them was guilty. And he took care that the Wolf should stand in the hottest place.

But the fire was big and the cave was small; and while the poor lean Wolf showed no sign of discomfort, he himself, being nice and fat and comfortable, soon began to get unpleasantly warm.

As this did not suit him at all, he next proposed that they should go for a walk, "for," said he, "it is now quite plain that neither of us can have taken the butter. It must have been some stranger who hath found out our secret."

But the Wolf had seen the Fox beginning to grow greasy, and he knew now what had happened, and he determined to have his revenge. So he waited until they came to a smithy which stood at the side of the road, where a horse was waiting just outside the door to be shod.

Then, keeping at a safe distance, he said to his companion, "There is writing on that smithy door, which I cannot read, as my eyes are failing; do thou try to read it, for perchance it may be something 'twere good for us to know."

And the silly Fox, who was very vain, and did not like to confess that his eyes were no better than those of his friend, went close up to the door to try and read the writing. And he chanced to touch the horse's fetlock, and, it being a restive beast, lifted its foot and struck out at once, and killed the Fox as dead as a door-nail.

And so, you see, the old saying in the Good Book came true after all: "Be sure your sin will find you out."

The Story of the White Pet

THERE WAS A FARMER BEFORE now who had a White Pet (sheep), and when Christmas was drawing near, he thought that he would kill the White Pet. The White Pet heard that, and he thought he would run away; and that is what he did.

He had not gone far when a bull met him. Said the bull to him, "All hail! White Pet, where art thou going?" "I," said the White Pet, "am going to seek my fortune; they were going to kill me for Christmas, and I thought I had better run away."

"It is better for me," said the bull, "to go with thee, for they were going to do the very same with me."

"I am willing," said the White Pet; "the larger the party the better the fun."

They went forward till they fell in with a dog.

"All hail! White Pet," said the dog. "All hail! thou dog." "Where art thou going?" said the dog.

"I am running away, for I heard that they were threatening to kill me for Christmas."

"They were going to do the very same to me," said the dog, "and I will go with you." "Come, then," said the White Pet.

They went then, till a cat joined them, "All hail! White Pet!" said the cat. "All hail! oh cat."

"Where art thou going?" said the cat. "I am going to seek my fortune," said the White Pet, "because they were going to kill me at Christmas."

"They were talking about killing me too," said the cat, "and I had better go with you."

"Come on then," said the White Pet.

Then they went forward till a cock met them. "All hail! White Pet," said the cock. "All hail to thyself! oh cock," said the White Pet. "Where," said the cock, "art thou going?" "I," said the White Pet, "am going (away), for they were threatening my death at Christmas."

"They were going to kill me at the very same time," said the cock, "and I will go with you."

"Come, then," said the White Pet.

They went forward till they fell in with a goose.

"All hail! White Pet," said the goose. "All hail to thyself! oh goose," said the White Pet. "Where art thou going?" said the goose.

"I," said the White Pet, "am running away because they were going to kill me at Christmas."

"They were going to do that to me too," said the goose, "and I will go with you."

The party went forward till the night was drawing on them, and they saw a little light far away; and though far off, they were not long getting there. When they reached the house, they said to each other that they would look in at the window to see who was in the house, and they saw thieves counting money; and the White Pet said, "Let every one of us call his own call. I will call my own call; and let the bull call his own call; let the dog call his own call; and the cat her own call, and the cock his own call; and the goose his own call." With that they gave out one shout – Gaire!

When the thieves heard the shouting that was without, they thought the mischief was there; and they fled out, and they went to a wood that was near them. When the White Pet and his company saw that the house was empty, they went in and they got the money that the thieves had been counting, and they divided it amongst themselves; and then they thought that they would settle to rest. Said the White Pet, "Where wilt thou sleep to-night, oh bull?" "I will sleep," said the bull, "behind the door where I used" (to be). "Where wilt thou sleep thyself, White Pet?" "I will sleep," said the White Pet, "in the middle of the floor where I used" (to be). "Where wilt thou sleep, oh dog?" said the White Pet. "I will sleep beside the fire where I used" (to be), said the dog. "Where wilt thou sleep, oh cat?" "I will sleep," said the cat, "in the candle press, where I like to be." "Where wilt thou sleep, oh cock?" said the White Pet. "I," said the cock, "will sleep on the rafters where I used" (to be). "Where wilt thou sleep, oh goose?" "I will sleep," said the goose, "on the midden, where I was accustomed to be."

They were not long settled to rest, when one of the thieves returned to look in to see if he could perceive if any one at all was in the house. All things were still, and he went on forward to the candle press for a candle, that he might kindle to make him a light; but when he put his hand in the box the cat thrust her claws into his hand, but he took a candle with him, and he tried to light it. Then the dog got up, and he stuck his tail into a pot of water that was beside the fire; he shook his tail and put out the candle. Then the thief thought that the mischief was in the house, and he fled; but when he was passing the White Pet, he gave him a blow; before he got past the bull, he gave him a kick; and the cock began to crow; and when he went out, the goose began to belabour him with his wings about the shanks.

He went to the wood where his comrades were, as fast as was in his legs. They asked him how it had gone with him. "It went," said he, "but middling; when I went to the candle press, there was a man in it who thrust ten knives into my hand; and when I went to the fireside to light the candle, there was a big black man lying there, who was sprinkling water on it to put it out; and when I tried to go out, there was a big man in the middle of the floor, who gave me a shove; and another man behind the door who pushed me out; and there was a little brat on the loft calling out Cuir-anees-an-shaw-ay-s-foni-mi-hayn-da – Send him up here and I'll do for him; and there was a Gree-as-ich-e, shoemaker, out on the midden, belabouring me about the shanks with his apron."

When the thieves heard that, they did not return to seek their lot of money; and the White Pet and his comrades got it to themselves; and it kept them peaceably as long as they lived.

The Burgh

FOUR WERE WATCHING CATTLE in Baileburgh (Burgh Farm). They were in a fold. The four were Domhnull MacGhilleathain, Domhnull Mac-an-t-Saoir, Calum MacNill, and Domhnull Domhnullach. They saw a dog. Calum MacNill said that they should strike the dog. Said Domhnull MacGhilleathain, "We will not strike. If thou strikest him thou wilt repent it."

Calum MacNill struck the dog, and his hand and his arm lost their power. He felt a great pain in his hand and his arm, and one of the other lads carried his stick home; he could not carry it himself. He was lamenting his hand, and he went where there was an old woman, Nic a Phi, to get knowledge about his hand. She said to him that he would be so till the end of a day and a year; and at the end of a day and year, to go to the knoll and say to it, "If thou dost not let with me the strength of my hand, I or my race will leave neither stick nor stone of thee that we will not drive to pieces."

At the end of a day and year his comrades said, "There is now a day and year since thou hast lost the power of thy hand, come to the knoll till thy hand get its power, as the woman said." He went himself and his comrades. They reached the hill. He drew his stick, and he said to the knoll, "If thou dost not let with me the strength of my hand, I myself or my race will leave neither stick nor stone of thee that we will not drive to pieces." And he got the power of his hand.

The Tulman

HERE WAS A WOMAN in Baile Thangusdail, and she was out seeking a couple of calves; and the night and lateness caught her, and there came rain and tempest, and she was seeking shelter. She went to a knoll with the couple of calves, and she was striking

a tether-peg into it. The knoll opened. She heard a gleegashing as if a pot-hook were clashing beside a pot. She took wonder, and she stopped striking the tether-peg.

A woman put out her head and all above her middle, and she said, "What business hast thou to be troubling this tulman in which I make my dwelling?" "I am taking care of this couple of calves, and I am but weak. Where shall I go with them?" "Thou shalt go with them to that breast down yonder. Thou wilt see a tuft of grass. If thy couple of calves eat that tuft of grass, thou wilt not be a day without a milk cow as long as thou art alive, because thou hast taken my counsel."

As she said, she never was without a milk cow after that, and she was alive fourscore and fifteen years after the night that was there.

Oisean After the Feen

OISEAN WAS AN OLD MAN **after the (time of the) Feen, and he (was) dwelling in the house of his daughter. He was blind, deaf, and limping, and there were nine oaken skewers in his belly, and he ate the tribute that Padraig had over Eirinn. They were then writing the old histories that he was telling them.**

They killed a right big stag; they stripped the shank, and brought him the bone. "Didst thou ever see a shank that was thicker than that in the Feen?" "I saw a bone of the black bird's chick in which it would go round about." – "In that there are but lies." When he heard this, he caught hold of the books with rage, and he set them in the fire. His daughter took them out and quenched them, and she kept them. Oisean asked, with wailing, that the worst lad and dog in the Feen should lay weight on his chest. He felt a weight on his chest. "What's this?" – "I MacRuaghadh" (son of the red, or auburn one). "What is that weight which I feel at my feet?" "There is MacBuidheig" (the son of the little yellow). They stayed as they were till the day came. They arose.

He asked the lad to take him to such a glen. The lad reached the glen with him. He took out a whistle from his pocket, and he played it. "Seest thou anything going past on yonder mountain?" – "I see deer on it." – "What sort dost thou see on it "I see some slender and grey on it." – "Those are the seed of the Lon Luath, swift elk; let them pass." – "What kind seest thou now?" – "I see some gaunt and grizzled." – "Those are the seed of Dearg dasdanach, the red Fierce: let them pass." – "What kind seest thou now?" – "I see some heavy and sleek." – "Let the dog at them Vic Vuiaig!" MacBhuieig went. "Is he dragging down plenty?" – "He is." – "Now, when thou seest that he has a dozen thou shalt check him." When he thought he had them, he played the whistle, and he checked the dog. "Now if the pup is sated with chase, he will come quietly, gently; if not, he will come with his gape open." He was coming with his gape open, and his tongue out of his mouth. "Bad is the thing which thou hast done to cheek the pup unsated with chase." – "When he comes, catch my hand, and try to put it in his gape, or he will have us." He put the hand of Oisean in his gape, and he shook his throat out. "Come, gather the stags to that knoll of rushes." He went, and that is done; and it was nine stags that were there, and that was but enough for Oisean alone; the lad's share was lost. "Put my two hands about the rushy knoll that is here;" he did that, and the great caldron that the Feen used to have was in it. "Now, make ready, and put the stags in the caldron, and set fire under it." The lad did that. When they were here ready to take it, Oisean said to him, "Touch thou them not till I take my fill first." Oisean began upon them, and as he ate each one, he took one of the skewers out of his belly. When Oisean had six eaten, the lad had three taken from him. "Hast thou done this to me?" said Oisean. "I did it," said he I would need a few when thou thyself hadst so many of them." – "Try if thou wilt take me to such a rock." He went down there, and he brought out the chick of a blackbird out of the rock. "Let us come to be going home." The lad caught him under the arm, and they went away. When be thought that they were nearing the house, he said, "Are we very near the house?" "We are," said the lad. "Would the shout of a man reach the house where we are just now?" – "It would reach it." – "Set my front straight on the house." The lad did thus. When he was coming on the house, he caught the lad, and he put his hand in his throat, and he killed him. "Now," said he, "neither thou nor another will tell tales of me." He went home with his hands on the wall, and he left the blackbird's chick within. They were asking him where he had been since the day came; he said he had been where he had often passed pleasant happy days. "How didst thou go there when thou art blind?" – "I got a chance to go there this day at all events. There is a little pet yonder that I brought home, and bring it in." They went out to look, and if they went, there did not go out so many as could bring it home. He himself arose, and he brought it in. He asked for a knife. He caught the shank, he stripped it, and then took the flesh off it. He broke the two ends of the bone. "Get now the shank of the dun deer that you said I never saw the like of in the Feen." They got this for him, and he threw it out through the marrow hole. Now he was made truthful. They began to ask more tales from him, but it beat them ever to make him begin at them any more.

The Widow and Her Daughters

THERE WAS FORMERLY A POOR widow, and she had three daughters, and all she had to feed them was a kailyard. There was a great gray horse who was coming every day to the yard to eat the kail. Said the eldest of the daughters to her mother, "I will go to the yard to-day, and I will take the spinning-wheel with me, and I will keep the horse out of the kail." "Do," said her mother. She went out. The horse came; she took the distaff from the wheel and she struck him. The distaff stuck to the horse, and her hand stuck to the distaff. Away went the horse till, they reached a green hill, and he called out, "Open, open, oh green hill, and let in the king's son; open, open, oh green hill, and let in the widow's daughter." The hill opened, and they went in. He warmed water for her feet, and made a soft bed for her limbs, and she lay down that night.

Early on the morrow, when he rose, he was going to hunt. He gave her the keys of the whole house, and he said to her that she might open every chamber inside but the one. "By all she ever saw not to open that one." That she should have his dinner ready when he should come back, and that if she would be a good woman that he would marry her. When he went away she began to open the chambers. Every one, as she opened it, was getting finer and finer, till she came to the one that was forbidden. It seemed to her, "What might be in it that she might not open it too." She opened it, and it was full of dead gentle women, and she went down to the knee in blood. Then she came out, and she was cleansing her foot; and though she were cleaning it, still she could not take a bit of the blood off it. A tiny cat came where she was, and she said to her, "If she would give a little drop of milk that she would clean her foot as well as it was before. "Thou! ugly beast! be off before thee. Dost thou suppose that I won't clean them better than thou?" "Yes, yes, take thine own away. Thou wilt see what will happen to thee when himself comes home." He came home, and she set the dinner on the board, and they sat down at it. Before they ate a bit he said to her, "Wert thou a good woman to-day was," said she. "Let me see thy foot, and I will tell thee whether thou wert or wert not." She let him see the one that was clean. "Let me see the other one," said he. When he saw the blood, "Oh! ho!" said he. He rose and took the axe and took her head off, and he threw her into the chamber with the other dead people. He laid down that night, and early on the morrow he went to the widow's yard again. Said the second one of the widow's daughters to her mother – "I will go out to-day, and I will keep the gray horse out of the yard." She went out sewing. She struck the thing she was sewing on the horse. The cloth stuck to the horse, and her hand stuck to the cloth. They reached the hill. He called as usual to the hill; the hill opened, and they went in. He warmed water for her feet, and made a soft bed for her limbs, and they lay down that night. Early in the morning he was going to hunt, and he said to her that she should open every chamber inside but one, and "by all she ever saw" not to open that one. She opened every chamber till she came to the little one, and because she thought "What might be in that one more than the rest that she might not open it?" She opened it, and it was full of dead gentlewomen, and her own sister amongst them. She went down to the knee in blood. She came out, and as she was cleaning herself, and the little cat came round about, and she said to her, "If thou wilt give me a tiny drop of milk I will clean thy foot is well as it ever was." "Thou! ugly beast! begone. Dost thou think that

I will not clean it myself better than thou?" "Thou wilt see," said the cat, "what will happen to thee when himself comes home." When he came she set down the dinner, and they sat at it. Said he – "Wert thou a good woman to-day?" "I was," said she. "Let me see thy foot, and I will tell thee whether thou wert or wert not." She let him see the foot that was clean. "Let me see the other one," said he. She let him see it. "Oh! ho!" said he, and he took the axe and took her head off. He lay down that night. Early on the morrow, said the youngest one to her mother, as she wove a stocking – "I will go out with my stocking to-day, and I will watch the gray horse. I will see what happened to my two sisters, and I will return to tell you." "Do," said her mother, "and see thou dost not stay away. She went out, and the horse came. She struck the stocking on the horse. The stocking stuck to the horse, and the hand stuck to the stocking. They went away, and they reached the green hill. He called out as usual, and they got in. He warmed water for her feet, and made a soft bed for her limbs, and they lay down that night. On the morrow he was going to hunt, and he said to her – "If she would behave herself as a good woman till he returned, that they would be married in a few days." He gave her the keys, and he said to her that she might open every chamber that was within but that little one, "but see that she should not open that one." She opened every one, and when she came to this one, because she thought "what might be in it that she might not open it more than the rest?" she opened it, and she saw her two sisters there dead, and she went down to the two knees in blood. She came out, and she was cleaning her feet, and she could not take a bit of the blood off them. The tiny cat came where she was, and she said to her – "Give me a tiny drop of milk, and I will clean thy feet as well as they were before." "I will give it thou creature; I will give thee thy desire of milk if thou will clean my feet." The cat licked her feet as well as they were before. Then the king came home, and they set down his dinner, and they sat at it. Before they ate a bit, he said to her, "Wert thou a good woman to-day?" "I was middlin," said she; "I have no boasting to make of myself." "Let me see thy feet," said he. She let him see her feet. "Thou wert a good woman," said he; "and if thou holdest on thus till the end of a few days, thyself and I will be married." On the morrow he went away to hunt. When he went away the little cat came where she was. "Now, I will tell thee in what way thou wilt be quickest married to him," said the cat. "There are," said she, "a lot of old chests within. Thou shalt take out three of them; thou shalt clean them. Thou shalt say to him next night, that he must leave these three chests, one about of them, in thy mother's house, as they are of no use here; that there are plenty here without them; thou shalt say to him that he must not open any of them on the road, or else, if he opens, that thou wilt leave him; that thou wilt go up into a tree top, and that thou wilt be looking, and that if he opens any of them that thou wilt see. Then when he goes hunting, thou shalt open the chamber, thou shalt bring out thy two sisters; thou shalt draw on them the magic club, and they will be as lively and whole as they were before; thou shalt clean them then, and thou shalt put one in each chest of them, and thou shalt go thyself into the third one. Thou shalt put of silver and of gold, as much in the chests as will keep thy mother and thy sisters right for their lives. When he leaves the chests in thy mother's house, and when he returns he will fly in a wild rage: he will then go to thy mother's house in this fury, and he will break in the door; be thou behind the door, and take off his head with the bar; and then he will be a king's son, as precious as he was before, and he will marry thee. Say to thy sisters, if he attempts the chests to open them by the way, to call out, 'I see thee, I see thee,' and that he wilt think that thou wilt be calling out in the tree." When he came home he went away with the chests, one after one, till he left them in her mother's house. When he came to a glen, where he thought she in the tree could not see him, he began to let the chest down to see what was in it; she that was in the chest called out, "I see thee, I see thee!"

"Good luck be on thy pretty little head," said he, "if thou canst not see a long way!"

This was the way with him each journey, till he left the chests altogether in her mother's house.

When he returned home on the last journey, and saw that she was not before him, he flew in a wild rage; he went back to the widow's house, and when he reached the door he drove it in before him. She was standing behind the door, and she took his head off with the bar. Then he grew a king's son, as precious as ever came; there he was within and they were in great gladness, She and himself married, and they left with her mother and sisters, of gold and silver, as much as left them well for life.

The Sharp Grey Sheep

THERE WAS A KING AND a queen, and they had a daughter, and the queen found death, and the king married another. And the last queen was bad to the daughter of the first queen, and she used to beat her and put her out of the door. She sent her to herd the sheep, and was not giving her what should suffice her. And there was a sharp (horned) grey sheep in the flock that was coming with meat to her.

The queen was taking wonder that she was keeping alive and that she was not getting meat enough from herself, and she told it to the henwife. The henwife thought that she would send her own daughter to watch how she was getting meat, and Ni Mhaol Charach, the henwife's daughter, went to herd the sheep with the queen's daughter. The sheep would not come to her so long as Ni Mhaol Charach was there, and Ni Mhaol Charach was staying all the day with her. The queen's daughter was longing for her meat, and she said – "Set thy head on my knee and I will dress thy hair." And Ni Mhaol Charach set her head on the knee of the queen's daughter, and she slept.

The sheep came with meat to the queen's daughter, but the eye that was in the back of the head of the bald black-skinned girl, the henwife's daughter, was open, and she saw all that went on, and when she awoke she went home and told it to her mother, and the henwife told it to the queen, and when the queen understood how the girl was getting meat, nothing at all would serve her but that the sheep should be killed.

The sheep came to the queen's daughter and said to her –

"They are going to kill me, but steal thou my skin and gather my bones and roll them in my skin, and I will come alive again, and I will come to thee again."

The sheep was killed, and the queen's daughter stole her skin, and she gathered her bones and her hoofs and she rolled them in the skin; but she forgot the little hoofs. The sheep came alive again, but she was lame. She came to the king's daughter with a halting step, and she said, "Thou didst as I desired thee, but thou hast forgotten the little hoofs."

And she was keeping her in meat after that.

There was a young prince who was hunting and coming often past her, and he saw how pretty she was, and he asked, "Who's she?" And they told him, and he took love for her, and he was often coming the way; but the bald black-skinned girl, the henwife's daughter, took notice of him, and she told it to her mother, and the henwife told it to the queen.

The queen was wishful to get knowledge what man it was, and the henwife sought till she found out who he (was), and she told the queen. When the queen heard who it was she was wishful to send her own daughter in his way, and she brought in the first queen's daughter, and she sent her own daughter to herd in her place, and she was making the daughter of the first queen do the cooking and every service about the house.

The first queen's daughter was out a turn, and the prince met her, and he gave her a pair of golden shoes. And he was wishful to see her at the sermon, but her muime would not let her go there.

But when the rest would go she would make ready, and she would go after them, and she would sit where he might see her, but she would rise and go before the people would scatter, and she would be at the house and everything in order before her muime would come. But the third time she was there the prince was wishful to go with her, and he sat near to the door, and when she went he was keeping an eye on her, and he rose and went after her. She was running home, and she lost one of her shoes in the mud; and he got the shoe, and because he could not see her he said that the one who had the foot that would fit the shoe was the wife that would be his.

The queen was wishful that the shoe would fit her own daughter, and she put the daughter of the first queen in hiding, so that she should not be seen till she should try if the shoe should fit her own daughter.

When the prince came to try the shoe on her, her foot was too big, but she was very anxious that the shoe should fit her, and she spoke to the henwife about it. The henwife cut the points of her toes off that the shoe might fit her, and the shoe went on her when the points of the toes were cut.

When the wedding-day came the daughter of the first queen was set in hiding in a nook that was behind the fire.

When the people were all gathered together, a bird came to the window, and he cried –

"The blood's in the shoe, and the pretty foot's in the nook at the back of the fire."

One of them said, "What is that creature saying?"

And the queen said – "It's no matter what that creature is saying; it is but a nasty, beaky, lying creature." The bird came again to the window; and the third time he came, the prince said – "We will go and see what he is saying."

And he rose and he went out, and the bird cried – "The blood's in the shoe, and the pretty foot's in the nook that is at the back of the fire."

He returned in, and he ordered the nook at the back of the fire to be searched. And they searched it, and they found the first queen's daughter there, and the golden shoe on the one foot. They cleaned the blood out of the other shoe, and they tried it on her, and the shoe fitted her, and its like was on the other foot. The prince left the daughter of the last queen, and he married the daughter of the first queen, and he took her from them with him, and she was rich and lucky after that.

The Fox and the Little Bonnach

THE FOX WAS ONCE GOING over a loch, and there met him a little bonnach, and the fox asked him where he was going. The little bonnach told him he was going to such a place.

"And whence camest thou?" said the fox.

"I came from Geeogan, and I came from Cooaigean, and I came from the slab of the bonnach stone, and I came from the eye of the quern, and I will come from thee if I may," quoth the little bonnach.

"Well, I myself will take thee over on my back," said the fox.

"Thou'lt eat me, thou'lt eat me," quoth the little bonnach.

"Come then on the tip of my tail," said the fox.

"Oh! I will not; thou wilt eat me," said the little bonnach.

"Come into my ear," said the fox.

"I will not go; thou wilt eat me," said the little bonnach.

"Come into my mouth," said the fox.

"Thou wilt eat me that time at all events," said the little bonnach.

"Oh, I will not eat thee," said the fox. "At the time when I am swimming I cannot eat anything at all."

He went into his mouth.

"Oh! ho!" said the fox, "I may do my own pleasure to thee now. It is long since it was heard that a hard morsel is good in the mouth of the stomach."

The fox ate the little bonnach. Then he went to the house of a gentleman, and he went to a loch, and he caught hold of a duck that was in it, and he ate that.

He went up to a hill side, and he began to stroke his sides on the hill.

"Oh king! how finely the bullet would spank upon my belly just now."

Who was listening but a hunter.

"It will be tried upon thee directly," said the hunter.

"Bad luck to the place that is here," quoth the fox, "in which a creature dares not say a word in fun that is not taken in earnest."

The hunter put a bullet in his gun, and he fired at him and killed him.

How the Cock Took a Turn Out of the Fox

THE RUSSET DOG came to a house, and he caught hold of a cock. He went away with the cock, and the people of the town-land went away after him.

"Are they not silly!" quoth the cock, "going after thee, and that they cannot catch thee at any rate." The cock was for that he should open his mouth that he might spring out.

When the fox saw that the cock was so willing to go along with himself, he was so pleased.

"Oh! musician, wilt thou not say, 'It is my own cock that is here', and they will turn back," said the cock.

The fox said, "Shê-mo-haolach-hay-n-a-han;" and when the fox opened his mouth the cock sprung away.

Historical Legend

Among the most important function of myth is in explaining where a particular country and its culture comes from. 'The Origin of Loch Ness' explains how this famous feature was formed, in the most fanciful – but at the same time the most literal and matter-of-fact – of terms.

More subtly, though, myths may offer an account of a nation's history that seems satisfying to it emotionally – however sceptical scholarly historians may be. 'Young Glengarry, the Black Raven' makes of a real historical figure an emblem of youth and daring – and loyalty. As for the figure formerly known as 'Bonnie Prince Charlie', historians have not been forgiving. Charles Edward Stuart's bid to win the British throne in 1745 was criminally incompetent in both conception and execution. As we see in 'Allan Donn and Annie Campbell' and 'Prince Charlie and Mary Macleod', however, he became a focus for stories of romantic patriotism.

The Inheritance

THERE WAS ONCE A FARMER, and he was well off. He had three sons. When he was on the bed of death he called them to him, and he said, "My sons, I am going to leave you: let there be no disputing when I am gone. In a certain drawer, in a dresser in the inner chamber, you will find a sum of gold; divide it fairly and honestly amongst you, work the farm, and live together as you have done with me;" and shortly after the old man went away. The sons buried him; and when all was over, they went to the drawer, and when they drew it out there was nothing in it.

They stood for a while without speaking a word. Then the youngest spoke, and he said – "There is no knowing if there ever was any money at all;" the second said – "There was money surely, wherever it is now;" and the eldest said – "Our father never told a lie, There was money certainly, though I cannot understand the matter." "Come," said the eldest, "let us go to such an old man; he was our father's friend; he knew him well; he was at school with him; and no man knew so much of his affairs. Let us go to consult him."

So the brothers went to the house of the old man, and they told him all that had happened. "Stay with me," said the old man, "and I will think over this matter. I cannot understand it; but, as you know, your father and I were very great with each other. When he had children I had sponsorship, and when I had children he had gostji. I know that your father never told a lie." And he kept them there, and he gave them meat and drink for ten days.

Then he sent for the three young lads, and he made them sit down beside him, and he said –

"There was once a young lad, and he was poor; and he took love for the daughter of a rich neighbour, and she took love for him; but because he was so poor there could be no wedding. So at last they pledged themselves to each other, and the young man went away, and stayed in his own house. After a time there came another suitor, and because he was well off, the girl's father made her promise to marry him, and after a time they were married.

But when the bridegroom came to her, he found her weeping and bewailing; and he said, 'What ails thee?' The bride would say nothing for a long time; but at last she told him all about it, and how she was pledged to another man. 'Dress thyself,' said the man, 'and follow me.' So she dressed herself in the wedding clothes, and he took the horse, and put her behind him, and rode to the house of the other man, and when he got there, he struck in the door, and he called out, 'Is there man within?' and when the other answered, he left the bride there within the door, and he said nothing, but he returned home. Then the man got up, and got a light, and who was there but the bride in her wedding dress.

"'What brought thee here?' said he. 'Such a man,' said the bride. 'I was married to him to-day, and when I told him of the promise we had made, he brought me here himself and left me.'

"'Sit thou there,' said the man; 'art thou not married?' So he took the horse, and he rode to the priest, and he brought him to the house, and before the priest he loosed the woman from the pledge she had given, and he gave her a line of writing that she was free, and he set her on the horse, and said, 'Now return to thy husband.'

"So the bride rode away in the darkness in her wedding dress. She had not gone far when she came to a thick wood where three robbers stopped and seized her. 'Aha!' said one, 'we have waited long, and we have got nothing, but now we have got the bride herself.' 'Oh,' said she, 'let me go: let me go to my husband; the man that I was pledged to has let me go. Here are ten pounds in gold – take them, and let me go on my journey.' And so she begged and prayed for a long time, and told what had happened to her. At last one of the robbers, who was of a better nature than the rest, said, 'Come, as the others have done this, I will take you home myself.' 'Take thou the money,' said she. 'I will not take a penny,' said the robber; but the other two said, 'Give us the money,' and they took the ten pounds. The woman rode home, and the robber left her at her husband's door, and she went in, and showed him the line – the writing that the other had given her before the priest, and they were well pleased."

"Now," said the old man, "which of all these do you think did best?" So the eldest son said, "I think the man that sent the woman to him to whom she was pledged, was the honest, generous man: he did well." The second said,

"Yes, but the man to whom she was pledged did still better, when he sent her to her husband." "Then," said the youngest, "I don't know myself; but perhaps the wisest of all were the robbers who got the money." Then the old man rose up, and he said, "Thou hast thy father's gold and silver. I have kept you here for ten days; I have watched you well. I know your father never told a lie, and thou hast stolen the money." And so the youngest son had to confess the fact, and the money was got and divided.

Castle Urguhart and the Fugitive Lovers

GLEN-URQUHART, WHERE CASTLE URQUHART is situated, is one of the most beautiful of our Highland valleys, distant from Inverness some fourteen miles, and expands first from the waters of Loch-Ness into a semi-circular plain, divided into fields by hedgerows, and having its hill-sides beautifully diversified by woods and cultivated grounds. The valley then runs upwards some ten miles to Corriemonie, through a tract of haugh-land beautifully cultivated, and leading to a rocky pass or gorge half-way upwards or thereabouts, which, on turning, an inland valley, as it were, is attained, almost circular, and containing Loch-Meiglie, a beautiful small sheet of water, the edges of which are studded with houses, green lawns, and cultivated grounds.

Over a heathy ridge beyond these, two or three miles, we reach the flat of Corriemonie, adorned by some very large ash and beech trees, where the land is highly cultivated, at an elevation of eight or nine hundred feet above, and twenty-five miles distant from, the sea. At the base of Mealfourvonie, a small circular lake, of a few acres in extent, exists, which was once thought to be unfathomable, and to have a subterranean communication with Loch-Ness. From it flows the Aultsigh Burn, a streamlet which, tumbling down a rocky channel, at the base of one of the grandest frontlets of rock in the Highlands, nearly fifteen hundred feet high, empties itself into Loch-Ness within three miles of Glenmoriston. Besides the magnificent and rocky scenery to be seen in the course of this burn, it displays, at its mouth, an unusually beautiful waterfall, and another about two miles further up, shaded with foliage of the richest colour. A tributary of the Coiltie, called the Dhivach, amid beautiful and dense groves of birch, displays a waterfall as high and picturesque as that of Foyers; and near the source of the Enneric River, which flows from Corriemonie into the still waters of Loch-Meiglie, another small, though highly picturesque cascade, called the Fall of Moral, is to be seen. Near it is a cave large enough to receive sixteen or twenty persons. Several of the principal gentlemen of the district concealed themselves here from the Hanoverian troops during the troubles of the '45.

On the southern promontory of Urquhart Bay are the ruins of the Castle, rising over the dark waters of the Loch, which, off this point, is 125 fathoms in depth. The castle has the appearance of having been a strong and extensive building. The mouldings of the corbel table which remain are as sharp as on the day they were first carved, and indicate a date about the beginning of the 14th century. The antiquary will notice a peculiar arrangement in the windows, for pouring molten lead on the heads of the assailants. It overhangs the lake, and is built on a detached rock separated from the adjoining hill, at the base of which it lies, by a moat of about twenty-five feet deep and sixteen feet broad. The rock is crowned by the remains of a high wall or curtain, surrounding the building, the principal part of which, a strong square keep of three storeys, is still standing, surmounted by four square hanging turrets. This outward wall encloses a spacious yard, and is in some places terraced. In the angles were platforms for the convenience of the defending soldiery. The entrance was by a spacious gateway between two guard rooms, projected beyond the general line of the walls, and was guarded by more than one massive portal and huge portcullis to make security doubly sure. These entrance towers were much in the style of architecture peculiar to the Castles of Edward I of England, and in front of them lay the drawbridge across the outer moat. The whole works were extensive and strong, and the masonry was better finished than is common in the generality of Scottish strongholds.

The first siege Urquhart Castle is known to have sustained was in the year 1303, when it was taken by the officers of Edward I who were sent forward by him, to subdue the country, from Kildrummie, near Nairn, beyond which he did not advance in person, and of all the strongholds in the North, it was that which longest resisted his arms.

Alexander de Bois, the brave governor, and his garrison, were put to the sword. Sir Robert Lauder of Quarrelwood, in Morayshire, governor of the Castle in A.D. 1332, maintained it against the Baliol faction. His daughter, marrying the Earl of Strathglass, the offspring of their union, Sir Robert Chisholm of that Ilk, became Laird of Quarrelwood in right of his grandfather. After this period it is known to have been a Royal fort or garrison; but it is very likely it was so also at the commencement of the 14th century, and existed as such in the reigns of the Alexanders and other Scottish sovereigns, and formed one of a chain of fortresses erected for national defence, and for insuring internal peace. In 1359 the barony and the Castle of Urquhart were disponed by David II to William, Earl of Sutherland, and his son John. In 1509 it fell into the hands of the chief of the Clan Grant, and in that family's possession it has continued to this day.

How it came into the possession of John Grant, the 10th Laird, surnamed the 'Bard,' is not known; but it was not won by the broadsword, from Huntly, the Lieutenant-General of the King. It has been the boast of the chiefs of the Clan Grant that no dark deeds of rapine and blood have been transmitted to posterity by any of their race. Their history is unique among Highland clans, in that, down to the period of the disarming after Culloden, the broadswords of the Grants were as spotless as a lady's bodkin. True it is, there were some dark deeds enacted between the Grants of Carron and Ballindalloch, and at the battles of Cromdale and Culloden the Grants of Glenmoriston were present; but far otherwise was the boast of the Grants of Strathspey – a gifted ancestry seemed to transmit hereditary virtues, and each successive scion of the house seemed to emulate the peaceful habits of his predecessor. That this amiable life did not conceal craven hearts is abundantly evident from the history of our country. There is a continual record of gallant deeds and noble bearing in their records down to the present time, and there are few families whose names, like the Napiers and the Grants, are more conspicuous in our military annals. But their rise into a powerful clan was due to the more peaceful gifts, of 'fortunate alliances' and 'royal bounties.'

It is much to be regretted that so little has been transmitted to posterity of the history of this splendid ruin of Castle Urquhart.

The probability is that it is connected with many a dark event over which the turbulence of the intervening period and the obscurity of its situation have cast a shade of oblivion.

The most prominent part of the present mass, the fine square tower at the north-eastern extremity of the building, is supposed to have been the keep, and is still pretty entire. From this point, the view is superb. It commands Loch-Ness from one end to the other, and is an object on which the traveller fixes an admiring gaze as the steamer paddles her merry way along the mountain-shadowed water. On a calm day the dashing echo of the Fall of Foyers bursts fitfully across the Loch, and when the meridian sun lights up the green earth after a midsummer shower, a glimpse of the distant cataract may be occasionally caught, slipping like a gloriously spangled avalanche to the dark depths below. The story in which the castle was the principal scene of action is quite characteristic of the times referred to. A gentleman of rank, who had been out with the Prince and had been wounded at Culloden, found himself on the evening of that disastrous day on the banks of the River Farigaig, opposite Urquhart Castle. He had been helped so far by two faithful retainers, one of whom, a fox-hunter, was a native of the vale of Urquhart. This man, perceiving the gentleman was unable to proceed further, and seeing a boat moored to the shore, proposed that they should cross to the old Castle, in a vault of which, known only to a few of the country people, they might remain secure from all pursuit. The hint was readily complied with, and in less than a couple of hours they found themselves entombed in the ruins of Urquhart Castle, where sleep shortly over-powered them, and the sun was high in the heavens next day ere any of them awoke. The gentleman's wound having been partially dressed, the fox-hunter's comrade yawningly observed "that a bit of something to eat would be a Godsend." "By my troth it would," said the fox-hunter, "and if my little Mary knew aught of poor Eoghainn Brocair's (Ewan the fox-hunter) plight, she would endeavour to relieve him though Sassenach bullets were flying about her ears." "By heaven! our lurking-place is discovered!" whispered the gentleman, "do you not observe a shadow hovering about the entrance." "'Tis the shadow of a friend," replied the Brocair; and in an instant a long-bodied, short-legged Highland terrier sprung into the vault. "Craicean, a dhuine bhochd," said the overjoyed fox-hunter, hugging the faithful animal to his bosom, "this is the kindest visit you ever paid me." As soon as the shades of evening had darkened their retreat, Eoghainn untied his garter, and binding it round the dog's neck, caressed him, and pointing up the Glen, bade him go and bring the Brocair some food. The poor terrier looked wistfully in his face, and with a shake of his tail, quietly took his departure. In about four hours 'Craicean' reappeared, and endeavoured by every imaginable sign to make Eoghainn follow him outside. With this the Brocair complied, but in a few seconds he re-entered, accompanied by another person. Eoghainn having covered the only entrance to the cave with their plaids, struck a light and introduced to his astonished friends his betrothed, young Mary Maclauchlan. The poor girl had understood by the garter which bound the terrier's neck, and which she herself had woven, that her Eoghainn was in the neighbourhood, and hastened to his relief with all the ready provisions she could procure; and not least, in the estimation of at least two of the fugitives, the feeling maiden had brought them a sip of unblemished whisky. In this manner they had been supplied with aliment for some time, when one night their fair visitor failed to come as usual. This, though it created no immediate alarm, somewhat astonished them; but when the second night came and neither Mary nor her shaggy companion appeared, Eoghainn's uneasiness on Mary's account overcame every other feeling, and, in spite of all remonstrance, he ventured forth to ascertain the cause of her delay. The night was dark and squally, and Eoghainn was proceeding up his native glen like one who felt that the very sound of his tread might betray him to death. With a beating heart he had walked upwards of two miles, when his ears were saluted with the distant report of a musket. Springing aside, he concealed himself in a thicket which overhung the river. Here he remained but a very short time when he was joined by the Craicean dragging after him a cord several yards in length. This circumstance brought the cold sweat from the brow of the Brocair. He knew that their enemies were in pursuit of them, that the cord had been affixed to the dog's neck in order that he might lead to their place of concealment; and alas! Eoghainn feared much that his betrothed was at the mercy of his pursuers. What was to be done? The moment was big with fate, but he was determined to meet it like a man. Cutting the cord and whispering to the terrier, "cul mo chois" (back of my heel) he again ventured to the road and moved warily onward. On arriving at an old wicker-wrought barn, he saw a light streaming from it, when creeping towards it, he observed a party of the enemy surrounding poor Mary Maclauchlan, who was, at the moment, undergoing a close examination by their officer. "Come girl," said he "though that blind rascal has let your dog, who would certainly have introduced us to the rebels, escape, you will surely consult your own safety by guiding me to the spot; nay, I know you will, here is my purse in token of my future friendship, and in order to conceal your share in the transaction you and I shall walk together to a place where you may point me out the lurking place of these fellows, and leave the rest to me; and do you," continued he, turning to his party, "remain all ready until you hear a whistle, when instantly make for the spot." The Brocair crouched, as many a time he did, but never before did his heart beat at such a rate. As the officer and his passive guide took the road to the old Castle, Eoghainn followed close in their wake, and, when they had proceeded about a mile from the barn, they came upon the old hill road when Mary made a dead halt, as if quite at a loss how to act. "Proceed, girl," thundered the officer, "I care not one farthing for my own life, and if you do not instantly conduct me to the spot where the bloody rebels are concealed, this weapon," drawing his sword, "shall within two minutes penetrate your cunning heart." The poor girl trembled and staggered as the officer pointed the sword at her bosom, when the voice of Eoghainn fell on his ear like the knell of death, "Turn your weapon this way, brave sir," said the Brocair, "Turn it this way," and in a moment the officer and his shivered sword lay at his feet. "Oh, for heaven's sake," screamed the fainting girl, "meddle not with his life." "No, no, Mary; I shall not dirty my hands in his blood. I have only given him the weight of my oak sapling, so that he may sleep soundly till we are safe from the fangs of his bloodhounds." That very night the fugitives left Urquhart Castle and got safe to the forests of Badenoch, where they skulked about with Lochiel and his few followers until the gentleman escaped to France, when Eoghainn Brocair and his companion ventured once more, as they themselves expressed it, 'to the communion of Christians.' The offspring of the Brocair and Mary Maclauchlan are still in Lochaber.

Young Glengarry, the Black Raven

ONCE UPON A TIME old Glengarry was very unpopular with all the northern chiefs, in consequence of his many raids and creachs among the surrounding tribes, but although he was now advanced in years and unable to lead his clan in person, none of the neighbouring chiefs could muster courage to beard him in his den single-handed. There was never much love lost between him and the chief of the Mackenzies, and about this time some special offence was given to the latter by the Macdonells, which the chief of Eilean Donan swore would have to be revenged; and the insult must be wiped out at whatever cost. His clan was at that time very much subdivided, and he felt himself quite unable to cope with Glengarry in arms. Mackenzie, however, far excelled his enemy in ready invention, and possessed a degree of subtlety which usually more than made up for his enemy's superior physical power.

'Kintail' managed to impress his neighbouring chiefs with the belief that Glengarry proposed, and was making arrangements, to take them all by surprise and annihilate them by one fell swoop, and that in these circumstances it was imperative, for their mutual safety, to make arrangements forthwith by which the danger would be obviated and the hateful author of such a diabolical scheme extinguished root and branch. By this means he managed to produce the most bitter prejudice against Glengarry and his clan; but all of them being convinced of the folly and futility of meeting the 'Black Raven,' as he was called, man to man and clan to clan, Mackenzie invited them to meet him at a great council in Eilean Donan Castle, the following week, to discuss the best means of protecting their mutual interests, and to enter into a solemn league, and swear on the 'raven's cross' to exterminate the hated Glengarry and his race, and to raze, burn, and plunder everything belonging to them.

Old Glengarry, whom the ravages of war had already reduced to one son of several, and he only a youth of immature years, heard of the confederacy formed against him with great and serious concern. He well knew the impossibility of holding out against the combined influence and power of the Western Chiefs. His whole affections were concentrated on his only surviving son, and on realizing the common danger, he bedewed him with tears, and strongly urged upon him the dire necessity of fleeing from the land of his fathers to some foreign land until the danger had passed away. He, at the same time, called his clan together, absolved them from their allegiance, and implored them also to save themselves by flight; and to their honour be it said, one and all spurned the idea of leaving their chief in his old age alone to his fate, exclaiming – "that death itself was preferable to shame and dishonour." To the surprise of all, however, the son, dressed in his best garb, and armed to the teeth, after taking a formal and affectionate farewell of his father, took to the hills amidst the contemptuous sneers of his brave retainers. But he was no sooner out of sight than he directed his course to Lochduich, determined to attend the great council at Eilean Donan Castle, at which his father's fate was to be sealed. He arrived in the district on the appointed day, and carefully habilitating himself in a fine Mackenzie tartan plaid, with which he had provided himself, he made for the stronghold and passed the outer gate with the usual salutation – "Who is welcome here?" and passed by unheeded, the guard replying in the most unsuspicious manner – "Any, any but a Macdonell." On being admitted to the great hall he carefully scanned the brilliant assembly. The Mackenzie plaid had put the company completely off their guard; for in those days no one would ever dream of wearing the tartan of any but that of his own leader. The chiefs had already, as they entered the great hall, drawn their dirks and stuck them in the tables before them as an earnest of their unswerving resolution to rid the world of their hated enemy. The brave and intrepid stranger coolly walked up to the head of the table, where the Chief of Kintail presided over the great council, threw off his disguise, seized Mackenzie by the throat, drew out his glittering dagger, held it against his enemy's heart, and exclaimed with a voice and a determination which struck terror into every breast – "Mackenzie, if you or any of your assembled guests make the slightest movement, as I live, by the great Creator of the universe, I will instantly pierce you to the heart." Mackenzie well knew by the appearance of the youth, and the commanding tone of his voice, that the threat would be instantly executed if any movement was made, and he tremulously exclaimed – "My friends, for the love of God, stir not, lest I perish at the hands of my inveterate foe at my own table." The appeal was hardly necessary, for all were terror-stricken and confused, sitting with open mouths, gazing vacantly, at each other. "Now," said the young hero, "lift up your hands to heaven and swear by the Long, am Bradan, agus an Lamh Dhearg (the ship, the salmon, and the bloody hand), that you will never again molest my father or any of his clan." "I do now swear as you request" answered the confused chief. "Swear now," continued the dauntless youth, "you, and all ye round this table, that I will depart from here and be permitted to go home unmolested by you or any of your retainers." All, with uplifted hands, repeated the oath. Young Glengarry released his hold on Mackenzie's throat sheathed his dirk and prepared to take his departure, but was, curious to relate, prevailed upon to remain at the feast and spend the night with the sworn enemies of his race and kindred, and the following morning they parted the best of friends. And thus, by the daring of a stripling, was Glengarry saved the fearful doom that awaited him. The youth ultimately became famous as one of the most courageous warriors of his race. He fought many a single combat with powerful combatants, and invariably came off victorious. He invaded and laid waste Glenmoriston, Urquhart, and Caithness. His life had been one scene of varied havoc, victory, ruin, and bloodshed. He entered into a fierce encounter with one of the Munros of Fowlis, but ultimately met the same fate at the hands of the 'grim tyrant' as the greatest coward in the land, and his body lies buried in the churchyard of Tuiteam-tarbhach.

A Legend of Invershin

LONG AGES AGO THERE STOOD in the vicinity of Invershin a strong massive castle, built and inhabited by a foreign knight – a stern, haughty man – of whose antecedents nothing could be learned with certainty, although there were plenty of rumours concerning him; the most generally received one being that he had fled from his own country on account of treason, or some other crime. Be that as it may, he had plenty of wealth, built a splendid castle, and kept a great number of retainers. He was extremely fond of fishing, and

spent the greater part of his time in the pursuit of the gentle craft. He invented a peculiar kind of cruive, so ingeniously constructed that the salmon on entering it set in motion some springs to which bells were attached: thus they literally tolled their own funeral knell. He was accompanied in his exile by his daughter Bona, and his niece Oykel, both alike beautiful in face and figure, but very dissimilar in disposition. Bona was a fair, gentle being, who seemed formed to love and be loved. Oykel was a dark beauty, handsome, proud, and vindictive.

Among their numerous household there was one who, without being a relative, seemed on terms of intimacy and equality. He was called Prince Shin of Norway, and was supposed to have retired to this northern part of the kingdom for the same reason as his host. He was young, handsome, and brave, and, as a matter of course, the two young ladies fell violently in love with him. For a while he wavered between the two, but at last he fixed his affections upon the gentle Bona, and sought her hand in marriage. The old knight gave his consent, and the future looked bright and full of happiness for the young lovers.

The proud Oykel was deeply mortified at the prince for choosing her cousin in preference to herself, and the daily sight of their mutual attachment drove her into a perfect frenzy of jealousy and wounded pride, until at length nothing would satisfy her but the death of her rival. She accordingly bribed one of her uncle's unscrupulous retainers to murder her cousin Bona, vainly hoping that in time the prince would transfer his love to herself. The ruffian carried out his cruel order, and concealed the body in a disused dungeon of the castle.

Great was the consternation and dismay caused by the sudden and mysterious disappearance of the lovely Bona; hill and dale, mountain and strath, corrie and burn, were searched in vain; river and loch were dragged to no purpose. Prince Shin was inconsolable; he exerted himself to the utmost in the fruitless search, then, wearied in mind and body, he wandered listless and sad through the flowery fields of Inveran until he reached the birchen groves of Achany, the quiet solitude of which suited better his desolate state. Here, with no prying eyes to see his misery, nor babbling tongues to repeat his sighs and exclamations, he gave himself up for a while to the luxury of grief. Then arose in the breast of the father the agonizing suspicion of foul play; but upon whom could his suspicions fall? Who could have the slightest reason or incentive to injure the kind and gentle Bona?

He pondered and mused in gloomy solitude until the terrible idea grew in his mind that it must have been her lover and affianced husband who had thus so cruelly betrayed her trustful love. "Yes," he muttered, "it must be Prince Shin who has committed this diabolical crime; he has tired of her, and took this way to release himself from his solemn contract with her and me, but the villain shall not escape; his punishment shall be as sudden and as great as his crime."

Having thus settled his conviction of the Prince's guilt, he caused him to be seized during the night, and thrown into the same dungeon in which, unknown to him, lay the body of his beloved daughter.

The accusation and his seizure was so sudden and unexpected, that for a time Shin lay in his dungeon totally overwhelmed with grief and indignation – grief at the loss of his bride, and indignation at the suspicion and treatment of himself. He was at length aroused and startled by hearing a faint moan somewhere near him, as if from some one in great pain. He strained his eyes to pierce the gloomy darkness that surrounded him; at last, guided by the sound being repeated, he discovered at the other end of the dungeon a recumbent figure, so still and motionless, that it might have been lifeless, but for the occasional faint, unconscious moan. "Alas!" exclaimed he, "this is another victim of treachery and cruelty, who is even worse off than I, but who can it be? I have missed no one from the castle, except my adored and lamented Bona." While thus speaking, he knelt down to examine the figure more closely, and as he began to get used to the gloom, he could see a little better, when to his inexpressible horror, dismay, and astonishment, he discovered it to be no other than his lost bride, whose young life was fast ebbing away through a frightful stab in her snow-white bosom.

Nearly frantic with grief, he strove with trembling hand to staunch the blood and bind up the wound, at the same time calling her by every endearing name that love could suggest. Again and again he kissed her cold lips, and pressed her tenderly to his heart, trying in vain to infuse life and warmth to the inanimate form of her he loved so well. He was interrupted in his melancholy task by the heavy door of the dungeon creaking on its rusty hinges, as it slowly opened to admit a man-at-arms, whom Shin recognised as one of the foreign retainers of the old knight.

"Ah! Randolph, is it thou they have sent to murder me? Well, do thy work quickly, death has lost its terrors for me, now that it has seized on my Bona; but yet I would that another hand than thine should strike the fatal blow, for I remember, tho' perhaps thou forgettest, the day when stricken down in the battle-field thou wert a dead man, had not I interposed my shield, and saved thy life at the risk of my own." So saying, he looked the man calmly but sadly in the face.

Randolph had, on first entering, seemed thunder-struck at seeing the prince, and looked, during the delivery of his speech, more like a victim than an executioner; he changed colour, trembled, and finally, throwing himself at the feet of the prince, faltered out with broken voice, "Oh! my lord; indeed, indeed, you do me wrong. I knew not that you were here; never would I raise an arm to injure you, my benefactor, my preserver? No, I came to – to – –." Then glancing from the prince to the lady Bona, he hid his face in his hands and groaned out, "I knew not you loved her, or I would rather have died than – –."

A sudden light broke in on the mind of Shin, he sprang like a tiger at the trembling man, and seizing him by the throat, thundered out, "Accursed villain, is it thou who hast done this foul deed? thy life shall be the forfeit." Then changing his mind, he loosened his deadly grasp, and flinging the man from him as though he were a dog, muttered between his close-set-teeth, "I will not soil my hands with the blood of such a dastard, he is only the base tool of another." Then raising his voice, he continued, "Tell me, thou double-dyed traitor, who set thee on to do this most horrible deed? and for what reason? See that thou tellest me the truth, villain, or by the bones of my father, I will dash thy brains out on the stones beneath our feet."

The trembling Randolph then explained how he, being absent from the castle on a foraging expedition, knew nothing of the betrothal of Prince Shin and the lady Bona, that on his return he was sent for by Oykel, who, in a private interview, told him she was engaged to the prince, and that Bona, through jealousy, was trying all she could to set the old knight against Shin, and had even laid a plot to poison both her and the prince, and that he (Randolph), believing this specious story, and being greatly attached to the prince, was easily prevailed upon by Oykel to murder her cousin; that he had temporarily hidden her body in the dungeon, and was now come to remove it, and was astonished and horrified to find she was still alive. He then went on to say, that he thought he saw a way to undo some of the mischief he had been the means of doing, and that was to assist Shin to escape, and to carry the lady Bona to a place of safety, until it was seen whether she would recover, and what turn affairs might take at the castle. The prince gladly availed himself of his assistance. They made their escape, and remained in concealment for some time until Bona had somewhat recovered her strength.

In the meantime Oykel, driven to distraction at the disappearance of Shin, seeing the utter fruitlessness of her crime, stung by remorse, and rendered reckless by the pangs of unrequited love, threw herself into the river, which has ever since been called by her name, and which, it is said, is still haunted by her restless, weary spirit. Bona is commemorated in Bonar.

Prince Shin and Bona now came from their concealment, and being fully reconciled to the old knight, were married with great pomp, and shortly afterwards sailed away to Norway, where they lived long and died happy.

Allan Donn and Annie Campbell

DONALD CAMPBELL OF SCALPAY, HARRIS – whose name is on record in connection with Prince Charles, when a refugee in the Western Isles after his defeat at Culloden – had a very beautiful daughter, who was so modest, pleasant, and affectionate, that she had few equals in the Isles. The charming Annie was for some considerable time, previous to the year 1768, loved by Allan Morrison, son of Roderick Morrison, of Stornoway, a ship captain. Being a gallant, and withal a comely young man, his affection was reciprocated by the fair Annie.

Captain Allan – he was seldom called Morrison – traded with his vessel principally between Stornoway and the Isle of Man, but he frequently went to Spain. Like many other lovers, Captain Allan, when he returned from abroad, presented the object of his affections with small presents of silk and linen – rare articles in the Highlands in those days. The more Allan saw of his Annie, the more he loved her, and he ardently longed for the day when they should be united in wedlock. This day was at length fixed; but before the happy event could take place, a voyage to the Isle of Man and back had to be accomplished. It was arranged, however, that the preliminary ceremony – the 'contract' – should be gone through prior to setting out on the voyage, on the evening before setting sail. For this purpose, one afternoon in the spring of 1768, Captain Allan left Stornoway for Scalpay with his vessel. Besides having a select number of relatives on board, who were to be present at the ceremony, he was accompanied by another ship, commanded by his brother, Captain Roderick. It was a fine day, with a nice breeze of fair wind, when they set sail. They did not proceed far, however, when the wind, which veered round to the south, rose suddenly to a perfect hurricane. To make matters worse, a blinding sleet shortly afterwards set in. Nobly, but in vain, did both the ships strive to bear up against the furious onsets of the rolling Minch; but notwithstanding their brave efforts to reach Scalpay before nightfall, they had barely got as far as the Shiant Isles when it was pitch dark, and thus their already dangerous situation became more perilous still. That each vessel might know the position of the other, a red light, in addition to the usual white one, was exhibited on the masts of both, and the brothers, being determined to arrive at their destination that night, if possible, continued to battle against the mighty billows, which now dashed themselves with fearful force against the creaking planks of the vessels, and anon broke over them with a deafening noise. This did not continue long when it became apparent that they could not possibly hold out much longer together. This was at least part of Captain Roderick's surmises, when he suddenly heard loud cries proceeding from his brother's ship. Being slightly in advance of Captain Allan at the time, and supposing that the shouts were intended as a sign for him to keep up his courage, he paid very little attention to the matter, for under the circumstances there was no possibility of rendering the least aid, should such be required. Above the sound of the raging tempest, the shouts from Allan's ship continued to be distinctly heard for a few seconds, when lo! all of a sudden, the screaming ceased, and the lights on the mast suddenly disappeared. It was then, and only then, that Captain Roderick understood the real meaning of the shouts which came from his brother's crew, whose ship had been sinking, and had now evidently gone to the bottom. Although there was but little hope of his being able much longer to keep his own ship afloat, Captain Roderick, like a brave sailor and an affectionate brother, directly made for the spot where the lights of his brother's ship were last observed, but nothing, alas! was seen or heard of the ship or crew. The deep wail which now rose from Captain Roderick's crew was truly heart-rending. From that day till now nothing has been seen of Captain Allan's crew or his ship.

Soon after the foundering of the gallant ship the gale moderated so much that Captain Roderick was able to reach the north harbour of Scalpay early next morning. Being expected there the previous night, none of the Campbells – who were, as might be supposed, greatly concerned for Captain Allan's safety, knowing, as they did, that his non-arrival arose from the furious tempest – went to bed that night. They were, therefore, by early dawn on the top of the hill which flanked their house, which is still standing, and from which they secured a view of the Minch in all directions. From this position they early descried Captain Roderick's ship making for the island. As the brave vessel passed up through the narrow Sound of Scalpay, the Campbells, and chief among them the fair Annie, some relatives and friends, stood on the north-east point of the island, and, thinking it was Captain Allan's ship, welcomed her with waving handkerchiefs. But their gay signs of joy were but of short duration, for presently a small flag was observed half-mast-high, and the next moment a sharp scream burst from the lovely Annie, exclaiming that Allan Donn was gone! Captain Roderick's ship soon cast anchor; in a few minutes he landed, and conveyed the sad tidings of his brother's and relatives' untimely end, as above described.

We will not attempt to describe the effect which this melancholy intelligence had upon the fair Annie, whose grief at that moment knew no bounds – her heart broke for him whom she would never see again. Refusing to be comforted, she might be seen at early dawn, mid-day, and twilight, wandering sorrowfully on the shore, looking for her "dear Allan's body," and crying "Allain Duinn Shiubhlainn leat." She continued thus while she lived, which was only a few days, her heart having, it is said, literally burst. It is even asserted that her pure white breast wasted to that extent that an aperture was formed opposite her heart. She composed a song or lament for her devoted lover each day afterwards while she lived.

The song composed by Annie Campbell on the day she received the tidings of her beloved's death, is entitled, 'Allain Duinn, Shiubhlainn leat.' It has a peculiarly touching air, and is still sung by many people on the Island of Harris, and it is now published in Part II of Mr Sinclair's 'Oranaiche.'

It was an oft expressed wish of the broken-hearted maiden that her body should be buried in the sea, that she might share her 'dear Allan's grave.' But whether her friends promised compliance with her request is not said. It is worthy of note, however, that his name was the last word she uttered. Surrounded by a crowded chamber of weeping friends, her gentle spirit took its flight to that brighter region which lies beyond the grave; and, though grief had wasted her body to a mere shadow, the same pleasant features which graced her in life continued to adorn her even when embraced in the cold arms of death. Her demise excited universal regret in the whole Outer Hebrides.

The respect and admiration in which Annie Campbell was held by her acquaintances in life were fully demonstrated at her death, for during the week in which her body lay in state at Scalpay, scores of people who could not, on account of the throng, obtain admission to the house of mourning, although kept open day and night, might be seen, with sad countenances and sorrowful hearts, standing around it from morn to eve, and eve to morn, and the respectful silence which prevailed among them was such that 'the fall of a pin might be heard.' Some people may be disposed to say that to devote a whole week to the ceremony called the 'leekwake,' was a needless waste of time. But, considering the great preparations which had to be made for the deceased lady's funeral, it must be confessed that it was short enough. Fifteen gallons of whisky, two or three large creelfuls of beef, mutton, and fowl, and a corresponding supply of newly-baked oaten cake, and cheese, were generally required at the interment of a common person in the Highlands in the olden times; and although they had neither pastry nor confections from Edinburgh, nor brandy from Cognac, at Annie's funeral, the expenditure was, nevertheless, most profuse. There was gin from Schiedam, wine from Oporto, and whisky from Berneray, in unlimited quantities; and as to the supply of oat and barley meal cakes, cheese, beef, mutton, and fowl, it was simply enormous.

Rodel, the place of interment, was only twelve miles from the island of Scalpay, but, on account of the large number of people which was to take part in the proceedings at Cille Chliaran (Rodel churchyard), which is supposed to have been built in the tenth century, and was dedicated to St Clement, three large galleys, or boats, were required for the funeral procession. One of the boats, which was manned by a select crew, was intended for the coffin and chief mourners; another was for the deceased's kinsfolk and friends, and the third for carrying the provisions. The day fixed for the funeral arrived – it was a Saturday in the year 1768 – a day which will be remembered in Harris while a Highlander breathes on its soil. On the morning of that day, the three boats left Scalpay for Rodel. In the foremost boat, Am Bata Caol Cannach, was the coffin, and the chief mourners were Kenneth Campbell, deceased's brother; Campbell of Marrig, Campbell of Strond, Macleod of Hushinish, Macleod of Luskintyre, and two or three other leading Harris-men. It also contained several casks of rum, gin, &c. The morning was so calm and pleasant, that the surface of the Minch seemed like a huge sheet of glass, so that the sails, which seamen depend so much upon, were useless; but, stripped to the shirts, the stalwart oarsmen pulled their respective galleys through the briny water with great speed. The little procession had hardly passed Rudha Reibinish when a smart head-wind began to blow. The horizon was soon afterwards darkened by a sheet of black clouds that betokened the approaching storm, which almost immediately set in. It soon blew a perfect hurricane, against which oars could make little headway. At the outset of the rising wind, the Bata Caol Cannach set sail, was thus carried far out to sea, and was in mid-channel when the tempest was at its height. The sails were torn to shreds, and the snow, which began to fall thick and fast, hid the land from view. They were now in a most critical position, for it was impossible for any boat to live long in such an awful sea, and the boat was half full of water. They gave up all hope of surviving many moments longer, and each began to pray earnestly for his soul's salvation, when to their still greater horror, the form of a female – Annie's phantom – was observed quite near them, following in the wake of their boat. This extraordinary circumstance was at once laid down as one of the direst omens. Nor need we wonder much if it did, when we consider the peculiar circumstances under which the figure appeared, and the superstitious beliefs which then, and to a certain extent still, prevail in the Highlands. Each time the phantom, which seemed to scowl angrily upon them, appeared, the Bata Caol Cannach shipped fearful seas. Life being sweet, the poor fellows used every means in their power to keep their vessel afloat. They used the wine and gin ankers, out of which they knocked the ends, spilling the liquor among the salt water, for bailing the boat. The phantom still followed, and was coming closer and closer to the boat's stern, when they recalled to mind Annie's oft expressed desire to be buried in the sea, that she might share Allan's grave; and they at once concluded that her spirit followed them, first in the storm, and now in visible shape, to enforce compliance with her last request. Some of them, therefore, advised that the coffin should be immediately committed to the deep; but to this proposal Kenneth Campbell, the deceased's brother, would not consent. He was sitting in the stern of the boat, and his late sister's spirit drew so near to him that she could put her hand on his shoulder. He chanced to have a bunch of keys in his pocket, to which some fabulous charm was attached, and he threw them to the phantom to appease her, but without effect. By this time some of the crew lay helplessly in the bottom of the boat, when one of the most courageous proposed that, to lighten the craft, the 'knocked up' men should be thrown overboard. "Not one," replied an elderly man, "of the living shall be put out, till the dead is put out first." He had hardly finished speaking, when a huge sea rolled over the boat, which almost swamped her, and the coffin, which was then floating in the boat, striking Kenneth Campbell on the chest, had almost pitched him overboard. He, thereupon, immediately ordered it to be thrown out, an order which, we need hardly say, was directly obeyed; but another tremendous sea again threw it into the water-logged boat. They managed, however, with great difficulty to unship it again, and knocking one of the ends out of it with their oars, all that remained of the fair Annie sank in a twinkling to the bottom of the sea, and the angry spirit immediately disappeared.

Meanwhile, the other two boats, which had never raised their sails at all, went ashore at Manish. Having landed, the men proceeded at once by land to Rodel, where they communicated the manner of their parting with the Bata Caol Cannach, as above described. All agreed that she had foundered, "for it was impossible," they said, "for any open, or other boat, to live in the Minch that day." This was a terrible circumstance – a calamity which plunged the whole country into an overwhelming grief. The deaths of Annie Campbell and Allan Donn were wholly absorbed by this extraordinary affair – an affair which seemed, to all appearance, to be nothing less than a judgment from God; for the flower of all the Harris gentlemen shared in one hour the same watery grave. The sorrow caused by this sad occurrence was so universal that a dry eye could not be found that evening from one end of Harris to the other; and this general grief continued for days and nights together, for all sympathised with the bereaved.

But to return to the Bata Caol Cannach, which we left water-logged, and about to sink in the middle of the Minch. It was a remarkable coincidence, that as soon as the cold clay of the fair maiden sank in the sea, the furious storm immediately abated, and the raging billows ceased their wild commotion. The Bata Caol Cannach was then bailed as quickly as possible, and one of the men – Malcolm Macleod – happening to have his plaid along with him, it was hoisted before the wind instead of a sail. The boat's stern was turned to the wind which drove it forward at a considerable rate, but, being pitch dark, none of them knew whither they were going. A new danger now began to alarm them – the danger of the boat being dashed to pieces on some shore. This fresh evil had only presented itself when the Bata Caol Cannach's keel struck the ground. The gratitude to an all-ruling Providence that filled their hearts at that moment none but those similarly situated can tell. They immediately leaped ashore, leaving the boat in the spot where it struck; and after wandering about for some time, stumbled upon a house, where they were kindly received and cared for. On entering this house, they discovered that one of their number was amissing, and, hungry and exhausted though they were, they immediately went to search for him, and found him lying insensible in the bows of the boat. He was at once carried to the house which they had just left, and with much care and attention he soon recovered. The place where the Bata Caol Cannach went ashore, and where the men were so hospitably entertained, was Snizort, in the Isle of Skye. It was some time before the Harris-men had thoroughly recovered from the hardships they underwent; but, as soon as they were able to undertake the journey, they returned home.

Kenneth Campbell, Annie's brother, was afterwards also drowned. He commanded a vessel, and being met by a French pirate, his ship, after being robbed, was sent to the bottom, every soul on board perishing. There are many other anecdotes connected with the men who composed the crew of the Bata Caol Cannach on the occasion referred to, but I must conclude, merely mentioning that the body of the unfortunate Allan Donn was found at the Shiant Isles shortly after the death of his sorrowing lover Annie, and was interred with befitting solemnities in the family sepulchre in Lewis. As an extraordinary coincidence, the body of the fair Annie Campbell was soon after Di-Sathairn an Fhuadaich also found at the Shiant Isle, and in the very spot where the body of her lover had been recovered. Whether it was placed in the same grave as Allan tradition does not record.

Malcolm Macleod, grandson of Malcolm Macleod, whose plaid was used as a sail in the Bata Caol Cannach, an elder in the Free Church at Tarbert, Harris, who only died about two years ago, repeatedly told me the above story. The Bata Caol Cannach was so called on account of having been purchased by the Campbells from a man in the island of Canna.

Coinnach Oer

COINNACH OER, WHICH MEANS dun Kenneth, was a celebrated
man in his generation. He has been called the Isaiah of the
North. The prophecies of this man are very frequently alluded
to and quoted in various parts of the Highlands; although little is
known of the man himself, except in Ross-shire. He was a small
farmer in Strathpeffer, near Dingwall, and for many years of his life
neither exhibited any talents, nor claimed any intelligence above
his fellows. The manner in which he obtained the prophetic gift
was told by himself in the following manner:

As he was one day at work in the hill casting (digging) peats, he heard a voice which seemed to call to him out of the air. It commanded him to dig under a little green knoll which was near, and to gather up the small white stones which he would discover beneath the turf. The voice informed him, at the same time, that while he kept these stones in his possession, he should be endued with the power of supernatural foreknowledge.

Kenneth, though greatly alarmed at this aerial conversation, followed the directions of his invisible instructor, and turning up the turf on the hillock, in a little time discovered the talismans. From that day forward, the mind of Kenneth was illuminated by gleams of unearthly light; and he made many predictions, of which the credulity of the people, and the coincidence of accident, often supplied confirmation; and he certainly became the most notable of the Highland prophets. The most remarkable and well known of his vaticinations is the following: "Whenever a M'Lean with long hands, a Fraser with a black spot on his face, a M'Gregor with a black knee, and a club-footed M'Leod of Raga, shall have existed; whenever there shall have been successively three M'Donalds of the name of John, and three M'Kinnons of the same Christian name, oppressors will appear in the country, and the people will change their own land for a strange one." All these personages have appeared since; and it is the common opinion of the peasantry, that the consummation of the prophecy was fulfilled, when the exaction of the exorbitant rents reduced the Highlanders to poverty, and the introduction of the sheep banished the people to America.

Whatever might have been the gift of Kenneth Oer, he does not appear to have used it with an extraordinary degree of discretion; and the last time he exercised it, he was very near paying dear for his divination.

On this occasion he happened to be at some high festival of the M'Kenzies at Castle Braan. One of the guests was so exhilarated by the scene of gaiety, that he could not forbear an eulogium on the gallantry of the feast, and the nobleness of the guests. Kenneth, it appears, had no regard for the M'Kenzies, and was so provoked by this sally in their praise, that he not only broke out into a severe satire against their whole race, but gave vent to the prophetic denunciation of wrath and confusion upon their posterity. The guests being informed (or having overheard a part) of this rhapsody, instantly rose up with one accord to punish the contumely of the prophet. Kenneth, though he foretold the fate of others, did not in any manner look into that of himself; for this reason, being doubtful of debating the propriety of his prediction upon such unequal terms, he fled with the greatest precipitation. The M'Kenzies followed with infinite zeal; and more than one ball had whistled over the head of the seer before he reached Loch Ousie. The consequences of this prediction so disgusted Kenneth with any further exercise of his prophetic calling, that, in the anguish of his flight, he solemnly renounced all communication with its power; and, as he ran along the margin of Loch Ousie, he took out the wonderful pebbles, and cast them in a fury into the water. Whether his evil genius had now forsaken him, or his condition was better than that of his pursuers, is unknown, but certain it is, Kenneth, after the sacrifice of the pebbles, outstripped his enraged enemies, and never, so far as I have heard, made any attempt at prophecy from the hour of his escape.

Kenneth Oer had a son, who was called Ian Dubh Mac Coinnach (Black John, the son of Kenneth), and lived in the village of Miltoun, near Dingwall. His chief occupation was brewing whisky; and he was killed in a fray at Miltoun, early in the present century. His exit would not have formed the catastrophe of an epic poem, and appears to have been one of those events of which his father had no intelligence, for it happened in the following manner:

Having fallen into a dispute with a man with whom he had previously been on friendly terms, they proceeded to blows; in the scuffle, the boy, the son of Ian's adversary, observing the two combatants locked in a close and firm gripe of eager contention, and being doubtful of the event, ran into the house and brought out the iron pot-crook, with which he saluted the head of the unfortunate Ian so severely, that he not only relinquished his combat, but departed this life on the ensuing morning.

The Dwarfie Stone

FAR UP IN A GREEN valley in the Island of Hoy stands an immense boulder. It is hollow inside, and the natives of these northern islands call it the Dwarfie Stone, because long centuries ago, so the legend has it, Snorro the Dwarf lived there.

Nobody knew where Snorro came from, or how long he had dwelt in the dark chamber inside the Dwarfie Stone. All that they knew about him was that he was a little man, with a queer, twisted, deformed body and a face of marvellous beauty, which never seemed to look any older, but was always smiling and young.

Men said that this was because Snorro's father had been a Fairy, and not a denizen of earth, who had bequeathed to his son the gift of perpetual youth, but nobody knew whether this were true or not, for the Dwarf had inhabited the Dwarfie Stone long before the oldest man or woman in Hoy had been born.

One thing was certain, however: he had inherited from his mother, whom all men agreed had been mortal, the dangerous qualities of vanity and ambition. And the longer he lived the more vain and ambitious did he become, until at last he always carried a mirror of polished steel round his neck, into which he constantly looked in order to see the reflection of his handsome face.

And he would not attend to the country people who came to seek his help, unless they bowed themselves humbly before him and spoke to him as if he were a King.

I say that the country people sought his help, for he spent his time, or appeared to spend it, in collecting herbs and simples on the hillsides, which he carried home with him to his dark abode, and distilled medicines and potions from them, which he sold to his neighbours at wondrous high prices.

He was also the possessor of a wonderful leathern-covered book, clasped with clasps of brass, over which he would pore for hours together, and out of which would tell the simple Islanders their fortunes, if they would.

For they feared the book almost as much as they feared Snorro himself, for it was whispered that it had once belonged to Odin, and they crossed themselves for protection as they named the mighty Enchanter.

But all the time they never guessed the real reason why Snorro chose to live in the Dwarfie Stone.

I will tell you why he did so. Not very far from the Stone there was a curious hill, shaped exactly like a wart. It was known as the Wart Hill of Hoy, and men said that somewhere in the side of it was hidden a wonderful carbuncle, which, when it was found, would bestow on its finder marvellous magic gifts – Health, Wealth, and Happiness. Everything, in fact, that a human being could desire.

And the curious thing about this carbuncle was, that it was said that it could be seen at certain times, if only the people who were looking for it were at the right spot at the right moment.

Now Snorro had made up his mind that he would find this wonderful stone, so, while he pretended to spend all his time in reading his great book or distilling medicines from his herbs, he was really keeping a keen look-out during his wanderings, noting every tuft of grass or piece of rock under which it might be hidden. And at night, when everyone else was asleep, he would creep out, with pickaxe and spade, to turn over the rocks or dig over the turf, in the hope of finding the long-sought-for treasure underneath them.

He was always accompanied on these occasions by an enormous grey-headed Raven, who lived in the cave along with him, and who was his bosom friend and companion. The Islanders feared this bird of ill omen as much, perhaps, as they feared its Master; for, although they went to consult Snorro in all their difficulties and perplexities, and bought medicines and love-potions from him, they always looked upon him with a certain dread, feeling that there was something weird and uncanny about him.

Now, at the time we are speaking of, Orkney was governed by two Earls, who were half-brothers. Paul, the elder, was a tall, handsome man, with dark hair, and eyes like sloes. All the country people loved him, for he was so skilled in knightly exercises, and had such a sweet and loving nature, that no one could help being fond of him. Old people's eyes would brighten at the sight of him, and the little children would run out to greet him as he rode by their mothers' doors.

And this was the more remarkable because, with all his winning manner, he had such a lack of conversation that men called him Paul the Silent, or Paul the Taciturn.

Harold, on the other hand, was as different from his brother as night is from day. He was fair-haired and blue-eyed, and he had gained for himself the name of Harold the Orator, because he was always free of speech and ready with his tongue.

But for all this he was not a favourite. For he was haughty, and jealous, and quick-tempered, and the old folks' eyes did not brighten at the sight of him, and the babes, instead of toddling out to greet him, hid their faces in their mothers' skirts when they saw him coming.

Harold could not help knowing that the people liked his silent brother best, and the knowledge made him jealous of him, so a coldness sprang up between them.

Now it chanced, one summer, that Earl Harold went on a visit to the King of Scotland, accompanied by his mother, the Countess Helga, and her sister, the Countess Fraukirk.

And while he was at Court he met a charming young Irish lady, the Lady Morna, who had come from Ireland to Scotland to attend upon the Scottish Queen. She was so sweet, and good, and gentle that Earl Harold's heart was won, and he made up his mind that she, and only she, should be his bride.

But although he had paid her much attention, Lady Morna had sometimes caught glimpses of his jealous temper; she had seen an evil expression in his eyes, and had heard him speak sharply to his servants, and she had no wish to marry him. So, to his great amazement, she refused the honour which he offered her, and told him that she would prefer to remain as she was.

Earl Harold ground his teeth in silent rage, but he saw that it was no use pressing his suit at that moment. So what he could not obtain by his own merits he determined to obtain by guile.

Accordingly he begged his mother to persuade the Lady Morna to go back with them on a visit, hoping that when she was alone with him in Orkney, he would be able to overcome her prejudice against him, and induce her to become his wife. And all the while he never remembered his brother Paul; or, if he did, he never thought it possible that he could be his rival.

But that was just the very thing that happened. The Lady Morna, thinking no evil, accepted the Countess Helga's invitation, and no sooner had the party arrived back in Orkney than Paul, charmed with the grace and beauty of the fair Irish Maiden, fell head over ears in love with her. And the Lady Morna, from the very first hour that she saw him, returned his love.

Of course this state of things could not long go on hidden, and when Harold realised what had happened his anger and jealousy knew no bounds. Seizing a dagger, he rushed up to the turret where his brother was sitting in his private apartments, and threatened to stab him to the heart if he did not promise to give up all thoughts of winning the lovely stranger.

But Paul met him with pleasant words.

"Calm thyself, Brother," he said. "It is true that I love the lady, but that is no proof that I shall win her. Is it likely that she will choose me, whom all men name Paul the Silent, when she hath the chance of marrying you, whose tongue moves so swiftly that to you is given the proud title of Harold the Orator?"

At these words Harold's vanity was flattered, and he thought that, after all, his step-brother was right, and that he had a very small chance, with his meagre gift of speech, of being successful in his suit. So he threw down his dagger, and, shaking hands with him, begged him to pardon his unkind thoughts, and went down the winding stair again in high good-humour with himself and all the world.

By this time it was coming near to the Feast of Yule, and at that Festival it was the custom for the Earl and his Court to leave Kirkwall for some weeks, and go to the great Palace of Orphir, nine miles distant. And in order to see that everything was ready, Earl Paul took his departure some days before the others.

The evening before he left he chanced to find the Lady Morna sitting alone in one of the deep windows of the great hall. She had been weeping, for she was full of sadness at the thought of his departure; and at the sight of her distress the kind-hearted young Earl could no longer contain himself, but, folding her in his arms, he whispered to her how much he loved her, and begged her to promise to be his wife.

She agreed willingly. Hiding her rosy face on his shoulder, she confessed that she had loved him from the very first day that she had seen him; and ever since that moment she had determined that, if she could not wed him, she would wed no other man.

For a little time they sat together, rejoicing in their new-found happiness. Then Earl Paul sprang to his feet.

"Let us go and tell the good news to my mother and my brother," he said. "Harold may be disappointed at first, for I know, Sweetheart, he would fain have had thee for his own. But his good heart will soon overcome all that, and he will rejoice with us also."

But the Lady Morna shook her head. She knew, better than her lover, what Earl Harold's feeling would be; and she would fain put off the evil hour.

"Let us hold our peace till after Yule," she pleaded. "It will be a joy to keep our secret to ourselves for a little space; there will be time enough then to let all the world know."

Rather reluctantly, Earl Paul agreed; and next day he set off for the Palace at Orphir, leaving his lady-love behind him.

Little he guessed the danger he was in! For, all unknown to him, his step-aunt, Countess Fraukirk, had chanced to be in the hall, the evening before, hidden behind a curtain, and she had overheard every word that Morna and he had spoken, and her heart was filled with black rage.

For she was a hard, ambitious woman, and she had always hated the young Earl, who was no blood-relation to her, and who stood in the way of his brother, her own nephew; for, if Paul were only dead, Harold would be the sole Earl of Orkney.

And now that he had stolen the heart of the Lady Morna, whom her own nephew loved, her hate and anger knew no bounds. She had hastened off to her sister's chamber as soon as the lovers had parted; and there the two women had remained talking together till the chilly dawn broke in the sky.

Next day a boat went speeding over the narrow channel of water that separates Pomona (on the mainland) from Hoy. In it sat a woman, but who she was, or what she was like, no one could say, for she was covered from head to foot with a black cloak, and her face was hidden behind a thick, dark veil.

Snorro the Dwarf knew her, even before she laid aside her trappings, for Countess Fraukirk was no stranger to him. In the course of her long life she had often had occasion to seek his aid to help her in her evil deeds, and she had always paid him well for his services in yellow gold. He therefore welcomed her gladly; but when he had heard the nature of her errand his smiling face grew grave again, and he shook his head.

"I have served thee well, Lady, in the past," he said, "but methinks that this thing goeth beyond my courage. For to compass an Earl's death is a weighty matter, especially when he is so well beloved as is the Earl Paul.

"Thou knowest why I have taken up my abode in this lonely spot – how I hope some day to light upon the magic carbuncle. Thou knowest also how the people fear me, and hate me too, forsooth. And if the young Earl died, and suspicion fell on me, I must needs fly the Island, for my life would not be worth a grain of sand. Then my chance of success would be gone. Nay! I cannot do it, Lady; I cannot do it."

But the wily Countess offered him much gold, and bribed him higher and higher, first with wealth, then with success, and lastly she promised to obtain for him a high post at the Court of the King of Scotland; and at that his ambition stirred within him, his determination gave way, and he consented to do what she asked.

"I will summon my magic loom," he said, "and weave a piece of cloth of finest texture and of marvellous beauty; and before I weave it I will so poison the thread with a magic potion that, when it is fashioned into a garment, whoever puts it on will die ere he hath worn it many minutes."

"Thou art a clever knave," answered the Countess, a cruel smile lighting up her evil face, "and thou shalt be rewarded. Let me have a couple of yards of this wonderful web, and I will make a bonnie waistcoat for my fine young Earl and give it to him as a Yuletide gift. Then I reckon that he will not see the year out."

"That will he not," said Dwarf Snorro, with a malicious grin; and the two parted, after arranging that the piece of cloth should be delivered at the Palace of Orphir on the day before Christmas Eve.

Now, when the Countess Fraukirk had been away upon her wicked errand, strange things were happening at the Castle at Kirkwall. For Harold, encouraged by his brother's absence, offered his heart and hand once more to the Lady Morna. Once more she refused him, and in order to make sure that the scene should not be repeated, she told him that she had plighted her troth to his brother. When he heard that this was so, rage and fury were like to devour him. Mad with anger, he rushed from her presence, flung himself upon his horse, and rode away in the direction of the sea shore.

While he was galloping wildly along, his eyes fell on the snow-clad hills of Hoy rising up across the strip of sea that divided the one island from the other. And his thoughts flew at once to Snorro the Dwarf, who he had had occasion, as well as his step-aunt, to visit in bygone days.

"I have it," he cried. "Stupid fool that I was not to think of it at once. I will go to Snorro, and buy from him a love-potion, which will make my Lady Morna hate my precious brother and turn her thoughts kindly towards me."

So he made haste to hire a boat, and soon he was speeding over the tossing waters on his way to the Island of Hoy. When he arrived there he hurried up the lonely valley to where the Dwarfie Stone stood, and he had no difficulty in finding its uncanny occupant, for Snorro was standing at the hole that served as a door, his raven on his shoulder, gazing placidly at the setting sun.

A curious smile crossed his face when, hearing the sound of approaching footsteps, he turned round and his eyes fell on the young noble.

"What bringeth thee here, Sir Earl?" he asked gaily, for he scented more gold.

"I come for a love-potion," said Harold; and without more ado he told the whole story to the Wizard. "I will pay thee for it," he added, "if thou wilt give it to me quickly."

Snorro looked at him from head to foot. "Blind must the maiden be, Sir Orator," he said, "who needeth a love-potion to make her fancy so gallant a Knight."

Earl Harold laughed angrily. "It is easier to catch a sunbeam than a woman's roving fancy," he replied. "I have no time for jesting. For, hearken, old man, there is a proverb that saith, 'Time and tide wait for no man,' so I need not expect the tide to wait for me. The potion I must have, and that instantly."

Snorro saw that he was in earnest, so without a word he entered his dwelling, and in a few minutes returned with a small phial in his hand, which was full of a rosy liquid.

"Pour the contents of this into the Lady Morna's wine-cup," he said, "and I warrant thee that before four-and-twenty hours have passed she will love thee better than thou lovest her now."

Then he waved his hand, as if to dismiss his visitor, and disappeared into his dwelling-place.

Earl Harold made all speed back to the Castle; but it was not until one or two days had elapsed that he found a chance to pour the love-potion into the Lady Morna's wine-cup. But at last, one night at supper, he found an opportunity of doing so, and, waving away the little page-boy, he handed it to her himself.

She raised it to her lips, but she only made a pretence at drinking, for she had seen the hated Earl fingering the cup, and she feared some deed of treachery. When he had gone back to his seat she managed to pour the whole of the wine on the floor, and smiled to herself at the look of satisfaction that came over Harold's face as she put down the empty cup.

His satisfaction increased, for from that moment she felt so afraid of him that she treated him with great kindness, hoping that by doing so she would keep in his good graces until the Court moved to Orphir, and her own true love could protect her.

Harold, on his side, was delighted with her graciousness, for he felt certain that the charm was beginning to work, and that his hopes would soon be fulfilled.

A week later the Court removed to the Royal Palace at Orphir, where Earl Paul had everything in readiness for the reception of his guests.

Of course he was overjoyed to meet Lady Morna again, and she was overjoyed to meet him, for she felt that she was now safe from the unwelcome attentions of Earl Harold.

But to Earl Harold the sight of their joy was as gall and bitterness, and he could scarcely contain himself, although he still trusted in the efficacy of Snorro the Dwarf's love-potion.

As for Countess Fraukirk and Countess Helga, they looked forward eagerly to the time when the magic web would arrive, out of which they hoped to fashion a fatal gift for Earl Paul.

At last, the day before Christmas Eve, the two wicked women were sitting in the Countess Helga's chamber talking of the time when Earl Harold would rule alone in Orkney, when a tap came to the window, and on looking round they saw Dwarf Snorro's grey-headed Raven perched on the sill, a sealed packet in its beak.

They opened the casement, and with a hoarse croak the creature let the packet drop on to the floor; then it flapped its great wings and rose slowly into the air again its head turned in the direction of Hoy.

With fingers that trembled with excitement they broke the seals and undid the packet. It contained a piece of the most beautiful material that anyone could possibly imagine, woven in all the colours of the rainbow, and sparkling with gold and jewels.

"'Twill make a bonnie waistcoat," exclaimed Countess Fraukirk, with an unholy laugh. "The Silent Earl will be a braw man when he gets it on."

Then, without more ado, they set to work to cut out and sew the garment. All that night they worked, and all next day, till, late in the afternoon, when they were putting in the last stitches, hurried footsteps were heard ascending the winding staircase, and Earl Harold burst open the door.

His cheeks were red with passion, and his eyes were bright, for he could not but notice that, now that she was safe at Orphir under her true love's protection, the Lady Morna's manner had grown cold and distant again, and he was beginning to lose faith in Snorro's charm.

Angry and disappointed, he had sought his mother's room to pour out his story of vexation to her.

He stopped short, however, when he saw the wonderful waistcoat lying on the table, all gold and silver and shining colours. It was like a fairy garment, and its beauty took his breath away.

"For whom hast thou purchased that?" he asked, hoping to hear that it was intended for him.

"'Tis a Christmas gift for thy brother Paul," answered his mother, and she would have gone on to tell him how deadly a thing it was, had he given her time to speak. But her words fanned his fury into madness, for it seemed to him that this hated brother of his was claiming everything.

"Everything is for Paul! I am sick of his very name," he cried. "By my troth, he shall not have this!" and he snatched the vest from the table.

It was in vain that his mother and his aunt threw themselves at his feet, begging him to lay it down, and warning him that there was not a thread in it which was not poisoned. He paid no heed to their words, but rushed from the room, and, drawing it on, ran downstairs with a reckless laugh, to show the Lady Morna how fine he was.

Alas! alas! Scarce had he gained the hall than he fell to the ground in great pain.

Everyone crowded round him, and the two Countesses, terrified now by what they had done, tried in vain to tear the magic vest from his body. But he felt that it was too late, the deadly poison had done its work, and, waving them aside, he turned to his brother, who, in great distress, had knelt down and taken him tenderly in his arms.

"I wronged thee, Paul," he gasped. "For thou hast ever been true and kind. Forgive me in thy thoughts, and," he added, gathering up his strength for one last effort, and pointing to the two wretched women who had wrought all this misery, "beware of those two women, for they seek to take thy life." Then his head sank back on his brother's shoulder, and, with one long sigh, he died.

When he learned what had happened, and understood where the waistcoat came from, and for what purpose it had been intended, the anger of the Silent Earl knew no bounds. He swore a great oath that he would be avenged, not only on Snorro the Dwarf, but also on his wicked step-mother and her cruel sister.

His vengeance was baulked, however, for in the panic and confusion that followed Harold's death, the two Countesses slipped out of the Palace and fled to the coast, and took boat in haste to Scotland, where they had great possessions, and where they were much looked up to, and where no one would believe a word against them.

But retribution fell on them in the end, as it always does fall, sooner or later, on everyone who is wicked, or selfish, or cruel; for the Norsemen invaded the land, and their Castle was set on fire, and they perished miserably in the flames.

When Earl Paul found that they had escaped, he set out in hot haste for the Island of Hoy, for he was determined that the Dwarf, at least, should not escape. But when he came to the Dwarfie Stone he found it silent and deserted, all trace of its uncanny occupants having disappeared.

No one knew what had become of them; a few people were inclined to think that the Dwarf and his Raven had accompanied the Countess Fraukirk and the Countess Helga on their flight, but the greater part of the Islanders held to the belief, which I think was the true one, that the Powers of the Air spirited Snorro away, and shut him up in some unknown place as a punishment for his wickedness, and that his Raven accompanied him.

At any rate, he was never seen again by any living person, and wherever he went, he lost all chance of finding the magic carbuncle.

As for the Silent Earl and his Irish Sweetheart, they were married as soon as Earl Harold's funeral was over; and for hundreds of years afterwards, when the inhabitants of the Orkney Isles wanted to express great happiness, they said, "As happy as Earl Paul and the Countess Morna."

Saint Columba

SOON AFTER SAINT COLUMBA ESTABLISHED his residence in Iona, tradition says that he paid a visit to a great seminary of Druids, then in the vicinity, at a place called Camusnan Ceul, or Bay of Cells, in the district of Ardnamurchan. Several remains of Druidical circles are still to be seen there, and on that bay and the neighbourhood many places are still named after their rites and ceremonies; such as Ardintibert, the Mount of Sacrifice, and others. The fame of the Saint had been for some time well known to the people, and his intention of instructing them in the doctrines of Christianity was announced to them. The ancient priesthood made every exertion to dissuade the inhabitants from hearing the powerful eloquence of Columba, and in this they were seconded by the principal man then in that country, whose name was Donald, a son of Connal.

The Saint had no sooner made his appearance, however, than he was surrounded by a vast multitude, anxious to hear so celebrated a preacher; and after the sermon was ended, many persons expressed a desire to be baptized, in spite of the remonstrances of the Druids. Columba had made choice of an eminence centrally situated for performing worship; but there was no water near the spot, and the son of Connal threatened with punishment any who should dare to procure it for his purpose. The Saint stood with his back leaning on a rock; after a short prayer, he struck the rock with his foot, and a stream of water issued forth in great abundance. The miracle had a powerful effect on the minds of his hearers, and many became converts to the new religion. This fountain is still distinguished by the name of Columba, and is considered of superior efficacy in the cure of diseases. When the Catholic form of worship prevailed in that country it was greatly resorted to, and old persons yet remember to have seen offerings left at the fountain in gratitude for benefits received from the benignant influence of the Saint's blessing on the water. At length it is said that a daughter of Donald, the son of Connal, expressed a wish to be baptized, and the father restrained her by violence. He also, with the aid of the Druids, forced Columba to take refuge in his boat, and the holy man departed for Iona, after warning the inhospitable Caledonian to prepare for another world, as his life would soon terminate.

The Saint was at sea during the whole night, which was stormy; and when approaching the shores of his own sacred island the following morning, a vast number of ravens were observed flying over the boat, chasing another of extraordinary large size. The croaking of the ravens awoke the Saint, who had been sleeping; and he instantly exclaimed that the son of Connal had just expired, which was afterwards ascertained to be true.

A very large Christian establishment appears to have been afterwards formed in the Bay of Cells; and the remains of a chapel, dedicated to Saint Kiaran, are still to be seen there. It is the favourite place of interment among the Catholics of this day. Indeed, Columba and many of his successors seem to have adopted the policy of engrafting their institutions on those which had formerly existed in the country. Of this there are innumerable instances, at least we observe the ruins of both still visible in many places; even in Iona we find the burying-ground of the Druids known at the present day. This practice may have had advantages at the time, but it must have been ultimately productive of many corruptions; and, in a great measure, accounts for many superstitious and absurd customs which prevailed among that people to a very recent period, and which are not yet entirely extinct. In a very ancient family in that country two round balls of coarse glass have been carefully preserved from time immemorial, and to these have been ascribed many virtues – amongst others, the cure of any extraordinary disease among cattle. The balls were immersed in cold water for three days and nights, and the water was afterwards sprinkled over all the cattle; this was expected to cure those affected, and to prevent the disease in the rest. From the names and appearance of these balls, there is no doubt that they had been symbols used by the Archdruids.

Within a short distance of the Bay of Cells there is a cave very remarkable in its appearance, and still more so from the purposes to which it has been appropriated. Saint Columba, on one of his many voyages among the Hebrides, was benighted on this rocky coast, and the mariners were alarmed for their own safety. The Saint assured them that neither he nor his crew would ever be drowned. They unexpectedly discovered a light at no great distance, and to that they directed their course. Còlumba's boat consisted of a frame of osiers, which was covered with hides of leather, and it was received into a very narrow creek close to this cave. After returning thanks for their escape, the Saint and his people had great difficulty in climbing up to the cave, which is elevated considerably above sea. They at length got sight of the fire which had first attracted their attention. Several persons sat around it, and their appearance was not much calculated to please the holy man. Their aspects were fierce, and they had on the fire some flesh roasting over the coals. The Saint gave them his benediction; and he was invited to sit down among them and to share their hurried repast, with which he gladly complied. They were freebooters, who lived by plunder and robbery, and this Columba soon discovered. He advised them to forsake that course, and to be converted to his doctrines, to which they all assented, and in the morning they accompanied the Saint on his voyage homeward. This circumstance created a high veneration for the cave among the disciples and successors of Columba, and that veneration still continues, in some degree. In one side of it there was a cleft of the rock, where lay the water with which the freebooters had been baptized; and this was afterwards formed by art into a basin, which is supplied with water by drops from the roof of the cave. It is alleged never to be empty or to overflow, and the most salubrious qualities are ascribed to it. To obtain the benefit of it, however, the votaries must undergo a very severe ordeal. They must be in the cave before daylight; they stand on the spot where the Saint first landed his boat, and nine waves must dash over their heads; they must afterwards pass through nine openings in the walls of the cave; and, lastly, they must swallow nine mouthfuls out of the holy basin. After invoking the aid of the Saint, the votaries within three weeks are either relieved by death or by recovery. Offerings are left in a certain place appropriated for that purpose; and these are sometimes of considerable value, nor are they ever abstracted.

Strangers are always informed that a young man, who had wantonly taken away some of these not many years since, broke his leg before he got home, and this affords the property of the Saint ample protection.

The Origin of Loch Ness

WHERE LOCH NESS NOW IS, there was long ago a fine glen. A woman went one day to the well to fetch water, and she found the spring flowing so fast that she got frightened, and left her pitcher and ran for her life; she never stopped till she got to the top of a high hill; and when there, she turned about and saw the glen filled with water. Not a house or a field was to be seen! "Aha!" said she, "Tha Loch ann a nis." (Ha Loch an a neesh). There is a lake in it now; and so the lake was called Loch Ness (neesh).

Prince Charlie and Mary MacLeod

THE FATE OF THE CHEVALIER and his devoted Highlanders forms one of the most romantic and darkest themes in the history of Scotland, so rich in historical narrative, song, and tradition –

> *Still freshly streaming*
> *When pride and pomp have passed away,*
> *To mossy tomb and turret grey,*
> *Like friendship clinging.*

In the contemplation of their misfortunes, their faults and failings are forgotten, and now that the unfortunate Chevalier's name and memory have become 'such stuff as dreams are made of,' every heart throbs in sympathy with the pathetic lyric 'Oh! wae's me for Prince Charlie.'

In the present day, when it is not accounted disloyal to speak kindly of the Prince, or of those who espoused his cause – one cannot help indulging in admiration of the courage and cheerfulness with which he bore trials, dangers, and 'hairbreadth 'scapes by flood and field,' nor wonder at the devotedness of the poorer Highlanders; their affection to his person; the care with which they watched over him in his wanderings; and, above all, the incorruptible fidelity which scorned to betray him, though tempted by what, in their poverty, must have seemed inconceivable wealth.

The history of the rising, and particularly of what followed after Culloden, relating to Prince Charlie, although generally minute, gives but little idea of the wonderful dangers he incurred, and the escapes he made. One should, in order to form a moderately correct idea of his hardships, have listened to those who had been out with him, as they, in the late evening of their days, talked of the past, and of the "lad they looed sae dearly," or heard their descendants, who were proud of their forbears, having been out in the '45, when –

> *The story was told, as a legend old,*
> *And by withered dame and sire,*
> *When they sat secure from the winter's cold,*
> *All around the evening fire.*

His capabilities of enduring cold, hunger, and fatigue prove that his constitution was of a very high order, and not what might have been expected from the descendant of a hundred kings brought up in the enervating atmosphere of courts. The magnanimity was surprising with which he bore up under his adverse lot, and the very trying privations to which he was subjected. The buoyancy of spirit with which he encountered the toils that hemmed him round, seemed to gather fresh energy from each recurring escape while wandering about, a hunted fugitive.

His appearance when concealed in the cave of Achnacarry as described by Dr Cameron, who was for a time a companion of his wanderings, is not suggestive of much comfort, but rather of contentedly making the most of circumstances. "He was then," says Dr Cameron, "bare footed; he had an old black kilt and coat on, a plaid, philabeg, and waistcoat, a dirty shirt, and a long red beard, a gun in his hand, a pistol and dirk by his side. He was very cheerful and in good health, and, in my opinion, fatter than when he was at Inverness." His courage and patience during his wandering drew forth even the admiration of his enemies, while his friends regretted that one capable of so much was so wanting in decision of character when it was urgently required by his own affairs, and the fortunes and lives of those who had perilled all for his sake. His friends, rich and poor, "for a' that had come and gane," were staunch in his favour to the very death; while his enemies, hounded on by a scared and vindictive Government, and earnestly anxious to enrich themselves by obtaining the reward offered for his capture, left no means untried to secure his person.

Among the many who signalized themselves in these attempts was one Ferguson, who, in command of a small squadron, cruised round the coast in search of the Prince and his fugitive friends, but in reality sparing none on whom it was possible or not dangerous to vent those feelings of oppression and worse, which the cruel Cumberland had made a fashion as regards Highlanders and the Highlands, and a sure recommendation to the notice of Government.

Soon after Culloden, Ferguson appeared off the coast and dropped anchor in Loch-Cunnard. A party landed there and proceeded up the strath as far as the residence of Mackenzie of Langwell, who was married to a near relation of Earl George of Cromartie. Mackenzie got out of the way, but the lady was obliged to attend some of her children who were confined by small-pox. The house was ransacked, a trunk containing valuable papers, and among these a wadset of Langwell and Inchvennie from the Earl of Cromartie, was burnt before her eyes, and about fifty head of black cattle were mangled by their swords and driven away to their ships.

Similar depredations were committed in the neighbourhood, without discrimination of friends or enemies. So familiarized were the west Highlanders and Islanders with Captain Ferguson, his cutter and crew, that they were in the habit of jeering him and them by calling after them – "Tha sinn eolach air a h-uile car a tha na t'eaman" – (We are acquainted with every turn in your tail) – a source of great irritation to the annoyed commander, who knew well the fugitives were hiding on the West Coast of Inverness-shire, and consequently resolved to adopt every species of decoy to entrap the Prince and his companions. To deceive the inhabitants of this wild and extensive coast, Ferguson pretended to give over the search and leave for Ireland. The Highlanders, wondering what would be the next move, were not deceived, nor did they relax their watchful precautions. The dwellers at Samalaman, the most western point of Moidart, had been especially harassed, as it was suspected they were in the confidence of Prince Charles. The suspicion was correct, and therefore, although they went about their usual employments they kept many an anxious look towards the ocean – many a lonely watch and walk was taken for the protection of the hunted wanderers.

To those who are not oppressed by anxiety the look-out from this headland is of surpassing beauty. Few scenes are equal to that presented in a midnight walk by moonlight along the sea beach, the glossy sea sending from its surface a long stream of dancing and dazzling light, no sound to be heard save the small ripple of the idle wavelets or the scream of a sea bird watching the fry that swarms along the shores! In the short nights of summer the melancholy song of the throstle has scarcely ceased on the hillside when the merry carol of the lark commences, and the snipe and the plover sound their shrill pipe. Again, how glorious is the scene which presents itself from the summits of the hills when the great ocean is seen glowing with the last splendour of the setting sun, and the lofty hills of the farther isles rear their giant heads amid the purple blaze on the extreme verge of the horizon.

Nothing of all this, for they were sights and scenes of continual recurrence, did Mary Macleod feel. Mary was a bold, spirited, handsome girl, who, in company with her father and two brothers forming the boat's crew, knew well all ocean's moods, and often braved the storms so common on that coast, and so fatal to many toilers of the deep.

On the morning of the fifth day after the departure of Captain Ferguson, Mary arose as usual to prepare the food for the family, and in going outside for a basket of peat fuel was surprised to observe a strange looking little vessel at anchor in a dark creek in the opposite island of Shona which partly occupies the mouth of Loch-Moidart. Time was when a circumstance, so apparently trivial, would have created no wonder nor left in the mind any cause for suspicion; but now Mary carefully scanned the low long dark hull of the craft, and her tanned and patched sails, which ill agreed with the trimness about her, and which at once spoke against her being a fishing craft or smuggler. "Cuilean an t-seann mhadaidh" (cub of the old fox) sighed the girl as she returned to the house to communicate the circumstance to the rest of the family, each of whom on reconnoitring the vessel confirmed her opinion. "Well then," said Mary, "let us advise the neighbours to betake themselves to their daily employment without seeming to suspect the new comer, and above all let us warn the deer of the mountain that the bloodhounds have appeared."

As the Moidart men were about to go to sea they were visited by a couple of miserable looking men from the suspected craft. One of them who spoke in Irish made them understand that they had lately left the coast of France laden with tobacco and spirits, some of which they would gladly exchange for dried fish and other provisions of which they were much in want, having been pursued for the last three days by an armed cutter, from which they had escaped with difficulty, and from which they intended to conceal themselves for some days longer in their present secluded anchorage. The fishermen, pretending to commiserate their condition, replied that they had no provisions to spare, and left only more convinced that Mary's suspicions were well founded. Matters remained in this state for a few days, the craft lying quietly at anchor, and her six hands, being, it was said, the full complement of her crew, sneaking about in all directions, in pairs, on pretence of searching for provisions. At last, after an unusually fine day the sun sank suddenly behind a mountain mass of clouds which for some time before had been collecting into dense columns, whose tall and fantastic shapes threw an obscurity far over the western horizon.

The coming storm was so apparent that the fishermen of Samalaman secured their boats upon the beach just as some heavy drops, bursting from the region of the storm clouds, showed that the elemental war had begun.

The Atlantic rolled its enormous billows upon the coast, dashing them with inconceivable fury upon the headlands, and scouring the sands and creeks, which, from the number of shoals and sunken rocks in them, exhibited the magnificent spectacle of breakers white with foam extending for miles. The blast howled among the grim and desolate rocks. Still greater masses of black clouds advanced from the west, pouring forth torrents of rain and hail. A sudden flash illuminated the gloom, and was followed by the crash and roar of thunder which gradually became fainter until the dash of the waves upon the shore prevailed over it.

Far as the eye could reach the ocean boiled and heaved in one wide extended field of foam, the spray from the summits of the waves sweeping along its surface like drifting snow.

Seaward no sign of life was to be seen, save when a gull, labouring hard to bear itself against the breeze, hovered overhead, or shot across the gloom like a meteor. Long ranges of giant waves rushed in succession to the shore, chasing each other like monsters at play. The thunder of their shock echoed among the crevices and caves, the spray mounted along the face of the cliffs in columns, the rocks shook as if in terror, and the baffled wave returned to meet its advancing successor.

By-and-bye there came a pause like the sudden closing of a blast furnace, or as if the storm had retired within itself; but now and then, in fitful bursts, proclaiming that its power was but partially smothered. During the conflict of the elements Mary Macleod seemed to suffer the most acute agonies of mind; and no sooner did it abate than, wrapping herself in her plaid, she sallied out and proceeded towards the sea shore. There, straining her eyes over the dark and fearful deep, she thought she saw, by a broad flash of lightning, a small speck on the wild waters, pitching as if in dark uncertainty, about the mouth of Loch-Moidart. With the speed of frenzy away flew the maiden to the nearest cottage, and grasping a burning peat and a lapful of dried brushwood, she, with equal speed, retraced her steps to the shore. In an instant the beacon threw its crackling flame far over the loch, and in an instant more the small black craft at Shona had cut from her moorings and stood out to the entrance of the bay. Now rose the struggle in Mary's mind. There stood the maid of Moidart in the shade of the lurid beacon, listening to the fitful blast, like the angel of pity. Something was passing on in the troubled bosom of that dark loch over which she often looked, that drew forth all the energies of her soul; but what that something was, was as hidden to her as futurity. She was startled from this state of intense feeling by a momentary flash on the water, instantaneously followed by a crash among the rocks at her side, and then came booming on her ear a sound as if the island of Shona had burst from its centre. "A Dhia nan dùl bi maile ris" (God of the elements be with him) ejaculated Mary as she bent her trembling knees on the wet sand, and then, like a spring from life to death, a boat rushed ashore, grounding on the shingle at her feet. A band of armed men immediately sprung on land, one of whom, gently clasping the girl, pressed her to his heart. "Failte 'Phrions" faltered Mary, giving a momentary scope to the woman in her bosom, but instantly recollecting herself, she whispered, "Guide him some of you to the hut of Marsaly Buie in the copse of Cul-a-chnaud, and I shall meet you there when the sun of the morning shall show me the fate of the pursuer." By this time the intrepid girl was joined by the villagers, who extinguished all traces of the late fire, and carried the stranger's boat where none but a friend could find it. The storm had again broken from its restless slumber, and the rain and sickly sun of the following day showed the pretended smuggler scattered on the beach. She appeared to have been well armed, and the easily recognised body of Captain Ferguson's first mate was one of the twelve who were washed ashore.

The Rout of Moy

THE RIVER FINDHORN, WHICH RISES in the Monadh-liath Mountains, flows through the glen of Strathdearn. Its scenery passes from Alpine to Lowland, exhibits almost every variety of the picturesque, strikes the eye with force or delight all the way from the source to the sea, and is not excelled in aggregate richness by the scenery of any river or stream north of the Tay.

The river is remarkable for the rapidity with which it rises and falls, and for its swift torrent, which, when in flood, often takes a straight course at the cost of much injury to life and property. In 1829 Sir Thomas Dick Lauder, with powerful dramatic effect, told the story of the floods which then ravaged Morayshire along the courses of the rivers descending from the Monadh-liath and Cairngorm Mountains, notably the Findhorn and Spey, both of which rose to an unexampled height, in some parts of their course to fifty feet above their natural level.

The valley of Strathdearn will amply repay a visit. The Findhorn begins at the very head of the valley, and first issues forth through a remarkable rent in the rock called Clach Sgoilte, or the cloven stone. As it passes onwards it is joined by various small streams, proceeding from minor glens called shealings, into which the Highlanders were in the habit of driving their cattle to feed on abundance of the richest natural grass, sheltered from the scorching heat of the summer sun. There are, indeed, many lovely spots along the course of the river, and by the little rills among the hills, unknown now, save to the shepherd and the gamekeeper, servants of the sportsman who rents the district. There are the natural wood trees, 'the oak and the ash, and the bonnie elm tree,' the alder and the birch, the lady of the wood, and then the rivulets which drop from pool to pool, and anon hiding themselves among sandstone ledges deeply bedded in dark sedge and broad, bright burdoch leaves, and tall angelica, and tufts of king and crown and lady fern. Up the glens there are bits of boggy moor, all fragrant with the gold-tipped gale, and the turf is enamelled with the hectic marsh violet and the pink pimpernel, and the pale yellow-leaf stars of the butterwort, and the blue bells and green threads of the ivy-leaved campanula. And then to stop a few minutes and look around on the earth, like one great emerald, set round with heathery amethyst roofed with sapphire, in the distance the blue sea and blue mountains, and covering all the bright blue sky overhead; and under foot the wayside fringed with the purple vetch, the golden bed-straw, and the fragrant meadow-queen, while at intervals the wild rasp bushes, adorned with their crimson berries, offer a tempting refreshment to the passing bird, and the bare footed boy and girl ramblers. The time of the wild rose is past, but the hips and haws will soon put on their red, red coats, the coral beads are even now in cluster on the rowan tree, while the bramble trails over every ditch with its delicious load of juicy, purpling fruit. 'Eheu fugaces labuntur anni!' Well does the schoolboy love the rough skinned bramble, and often in the sunny days of boyhood do his fingers and lips know the stains of its luscious blobs:

> "The bramble berries were our food,
> The water was our wine,
> And the linnet in the self same bush,
> Came after us to dine.
> And grow it in the woods sae green,
> Or grow it on the brae,
> We like to meet the bramble bush,
> Where'er our footsteps gae."

As the ramble proceeds, the surrounding country becomes highly picturesque. Now we have a crag robed in lichen cropping upwards, and crowned with heather and tangled foliage; now we have a little runlet jinking among the seggans, and singing a sweet undersong as it steals down its tiny glen; and now a landscape all yellow with 'golden shields flung down from the sun,' in the foreground, and the glorious hills backing all behind. Verily, Strathdearn is a lovely glen.

About a mile from the church of Moy there is a singular hollow, called 'Ciste craig an eoin,' (the Chest of the craig of the bird), surrounded by high rocks, and accessible only through one narrow entrance. Situated close to the Pass called 'Starsach nan Gael' – the Doorstep of the Highlanders – it was used as a place of concealment for their wives and children by the Highlanders during their absence on predatory excursions into the low country. This is the scene of one of those romantic achievements which so marked the rebellion of '45.

Previous to the battle of Culloden, Prince Charlie was for some days at Moyhall, the guest of Colonel Ann, as Lady Mackintosh was called. The Chief himself, with a prudence to be commended, took the Royalist side, leaving what in this case was hardly the weaker vessel to espouse the cause of the Prince, for whom the distant clans were arming. Mackintosh himself was absent in Ross-shire, in the King's service, but his wife, who was a daughter of Farquharson of Invercauld, entertained the Prince, and was so enthusiastic in his cause that she afterwards raised a regiment of 400 of her husband's clan and followers to support him.

With these she joined Lord Strathallan, who had been left by Prince Charles at Perth, to collect troops and military stores, and these Mackintoshes afterwards fought at Culloden. Her ladyship was no favourer of half measures. At times she rode at the head of her regiment, with a man's hat on her head and pistols at her saddle-bow – hence her soubriquet of Colonel Ann.

That Prince Charles was at Moyhall, the guest of Lady Mackintosh, was well known to the Earl of Loudon, whose detachment of Royalist troops then occupied Inverness, about twelve miles distant. At breakfast his lordship, discussing his information with his officers, suddenly formed the decision to move on Moyhall in order to surprise the young Chevalier, gain the offered reward, and save the country from further bloodshed. A Highland lassie who waited at table in the 'Horns' overheard their plans, and at once, bare-footed and bare-headed, ran on to Moyhall to tell of the danger.

The tidings produced consternation and confusion, for there were no troops to defend the House of Moy, nor meet the coming foe. But Colonel Ann and the council of war she assembled were equal to the occasion. Donald Fraser, the Chief's blacksmith, afterwards known as 'Caiptin nan Cuignear,' the Captain of the Five, at once left his forge, and taking along with him five men whom she named, hurried off with sword and musket to repel the 1500 invading troops.

It was in the dusk of the evening when they reached the narrow pass of Craig an Eoin, two miles from the Hall, and there they waited the approach of the foe. There was a quantity of turf divots and peats set up to dry in small hillocks or stacks, and Donald and his men, in order the better to watch the motions of the troops, placed themselves a few hundred yards asunder among these heaps, concealed by the shadows of the hills rising on either side.

They were hardly in ambush when they became aware of the approach of the soldiers. It was the dusk of the evening. Now was the time for action. Fraser waited until the army was within 100 yards, when, starting up, the command was passed from Donald, and then from man to man, in a loud voice, along a distance of nearly a quarter of a mile – 'The Mackintoshes, the Macgillivrays, the Macbeans to form instantly the centre; the Macdonalds on the right, and the Frasers on the left.' All this in the hearing of the commander-in-chief of the Royal army, accompanied by the firing of the muskets of the concealed party. Macrimmon, the piper in the advanced guard of the Macleods, fell, and this, coupled with the fear that masses of Highlanders were ready to surround them, and cut them to pieces, caused the troops to flee back precipitately to Inverness, where Lord Loudon, not considering himself safe, continued his route to Sutherlandshire, a distance of seventy miles, where he took up his quarters.

Fraser returned quietly with the dirk of the fallen piper, and was locally promoted to the rank of captain. He fought afterwards bravely at Culloden, and his sword is still kept, with many another piece of rusty armour, at Tomatin House.

Thus ended what has been humorously called the Rout of Moy.